NOTHING LIKE THE MOVIES

Also by
Lynn Painter

Better Than the Movies
The Do-Over
Betting on You

NOTHING LIKE THE MOVIES

LYNN PAINTER

SIMON & SCHUSTER BFYR

NEW YORK AMSTERDAM/ANTWERP LONDON
TORONTO SYDNEY/MELBOURNE NEW DELHI

SIMON & SCHUSTER BFYR
An imprint of Simon & Schuster Children's Publishing Division
1230 Avenue of the Americas, New York, New York 10020

Cover design by Sarah Creech based on series design by Heather Palisi

Also available in a SIMON & SCHUSTER BFYR hardcover edition
Interior design by Tom Daly
The text for this book was set in EB Garamond.
Manufactured in the United States of America
First SIMON & SCHUSTER BFYR paperback edition September 2025
4 6 8 10 9 7 5 3
CIP data for this book is available from the Library of Congress.
ISBN 9781665947138 (hc)
ISBN 9781665947145 (pbk)
ISBN 9781665947152 (ebook)

For my silly little WesLiz love lovers:
this book only happened because of you, and I'm forever grateful

SHE'S.
NOT.
YOU.

NEW YEAR'S EVE

"If my fifteen-year-old self could see me now,
he would punch me in the dick."
—*Set It Up*

Wes

"This place is *packed*."

"Dude, I told you," Adam said, loading a piece of gum into his mouth and smirking as we walked into the party. Loud music was booming from a speaker somewhere, and everyone appeared to be talking *over* the sound.

I followed him and Noah up the stairs and into the living room, where it looked like everyone I knew from high school was in attendance. *Shit.* People were *everywhere*, sitting on couches and standing around, and I instantly regretted my decision to go out.

"Bennett!" Alex ran over from the other side of the room and wrapped her arms around me, pulling me down into a hug.

"Happy New Year, Benedetti," I said, swallowing hard as I hugged her back.

"How *are* you?" she asked, and I hated the way she smiled

when she pulled away. It was one of those pitying smiles, like she was asking how I was handling the fact that my life had turned to shit.

"Good," I said, torn between being happy that my friends were back from college—*holy balls I have a social life again*—and kind of hating being social. Because as nice as everyone was, I could tell they all felt sorry for me. Sorry about my dad, sorry about the fact I'd dropped out of college, sorry about the fact I was no longer playing baseball.

I was one hell of a sorry guy.

Since Noah and Adam got back, I'd said *absolutely not* every time they invited me out. But for some reason, New Year's Eve made me cave. The fact that it was a holiday had softened me, apparently, which I was now regretting.

Because nothing felt the same.

The last time I was with these people, we all had big plans for our futures.

And . . . well, *they* still did.

I, on the other hand, had pivoted.

When my dad died (two weeks after I moved in at UCLA), I came home for the funeral and never left, deciding to bail on school and everything that the future held for me. *As if I had a choice.* Now that it'd been a few months since his heart attack, I was firmly settled into full-time employment at the grocery store with a side-hustle as an Uber driver. Life was fucking *great*.

"Come on—Michael's playing Money Bet in the kitchen," Noah said, pointing. "It's too loud over here."

Money Bet, the new favorite party game, was basically just dares with money attached. Some guys I worked with at the store made it up, and when I mentioned it to Adam and Noah, they went nuts with it.

I followed them into the kitchen, stopping to grab a drink before sitting down at the table.

"It's about time, Bennett," Michael said from his spot at the other end of the table, drawling just enough to let me know he was already buzzed. "You've been a hermit all break."

I gritted my teeth when I heard the first few notes of that old song from *Fearless* playing in the other room. It just *figured* that the party would have *that* song playing in the background. It was 100 percent on-brand for my life lately.

"I've been busy," I said, picking up my cup and downing the entire thing. I wasn't *trying* to get drunk, but I wasn't trying *not* to either. We'd pregamed a little at Noah's with his brother, so I had a nice start.

"Money bet five says Bennett can't make it from here," Noah said, pushing an empty can in front of me and gesturing toward the kitchen sink.

"Accept," I said, then hurled the can in the direction of the sink, watching it bounce off the counter and clatter to the ground.

"You suck," he replied, and I pulled a five-dollar bill out of my pocket and set it in front of him.

"Still better than you."

"Joss just got here," Noah said, looking down at a text, "with my chicken sandwich, hell yes."

I said, "Money bet chicken sandwich says y—"

I trailed off when I saw her.

She. Was. There.

Holy *shit*.

Libby was standing in the living room.

I'd managed to avoid her for the entire two weeks she'd been home on break, but now we were at the same party.

On New Year's Eve.

Are you kidding me, Universe? I'd vetoed three different parties that night, parties where I thought she might show up, but I'd assumed this one would be safe.

I'm not sure if things got quiet or loud, blurry or hyperfocused, but I know the universe changed as I looked at Liz, everything melting into impressionistic streaks of fuzzy background colors. She was talking to Joss, smiling, and the emptiness I felt at the sight of her, a gnawing ache, made it hard for me to breathe.

I hadn't seen her, in person, since the day of my dad's funeral. We'd done the long-distance thing for a few weeks after that, but then I ended it.

I had no choice.

I can't breathe without you, but I have to . . .

My fingers itched to touch her, to go to her, to grab her hand and pull her into the kitchen with me so we could laugh about Money Bet and convince someone to do something ridiculous.

But she wasn't mine to touch anymore.

It felt like a thousand memories of her—smiling at me, laughing with me, tangled up in my arms in my dorm room—swirled together and crashed into my lungs like a ninety-mile-an-hour fastball.

She was wearing a slouchy sweater, black and soft and oversize, with the front tucked into her plaid skirt. She looked nice, all dark tights and cute boots, but my eyes focused like lasers on the sun-kissed shoulder the sweater had exposed and the inky edge of her tattoo that was peeking out from underneath.

Calling to me.

Because I knew that tattoo better than I knew my own, probably because I'd never simply looked at hers. No, I'd explored hers, traced hers, kissed hers, studied that inked-on latitude like her body was my map and those coordinates were my true north.

You're the only thing I know like the back of my hand...

God*damn*it.

"Money bet three says you can't guess the card," I said to Adam, grabbing the deck from the middle of the kitchen table and trying to distract myself. I was pretty sure I couldn't handle the memories that were sure to kick my ass if I continued looking at Liz.

And almost worse than the memories were the questions that never seemed to go away when I thought about her.

Does she still go to the beach to read? Has she been to our In-N-Out since I left? What songs has she added to her freshman year playlist?

And I didn't even let myself consider whether or not she was seeing someone.

I was better off not knowing.

I'd deleted my social media accounts after deciding not to go back to school, partially because I knew I'd spend the rest of my life creeping on her and partially because what the hell would I post that mattered? While my friends were sharing pics from frat parties and studying for finals, it'd be wicked cool for me to post a slice of my life as well, right?

Worked a double shift at the grocery store today and taught myself how to fix the blower motor on the furnace. Runs like a dream now. #blessed

"Accept. And it's a queen," he said, smiling like an ass.

I turned over the jack. "So, so wrong, son."

"We want to play." Joss walked into the kitchen and sat in the empty chair between Adam and Noah, dropping a fast-food bag onto the table as Adam tossed three dollars at me.

"I love you and this sandwich," Noah said, tearing into the bag. "So much."

I felt like my entire body was on alert, buzzing, knowing Liz wouldn't be far behind Joss. I kept my eyes on the cards as Adam said, "All right, Jo—money bet five says you can't say the Pledge of Allegiance backward."

There was laughter and heckling when she started, but I couldn't hear over the roaring in my ears as I felt Liz take the empty seat on the other side of Adam. Red hair and Chanel No. 5 became my atmosphere, the mix that I breathed into my lungs and that seeped in through my pores. I refused to look at her—*I can't fucking do it*—but my face burned as I felt her eyes on me.

Shit, shit, shit. I started shuffling the cards as Joss kept going.

"Nice beard, Bennett," she said quietly, her voice diving into my bloodstream and pumping to every part of my body.

I inhaled through my nose and had to look.

I mean, I couldn't ignore her.

I raised my eyes from the cards, and then everything inside me stilled as she smiled at me.

Because it was the same.

Her smile was the same knee-weakening smile that she'd given me the first time she said she loved me, in the parking lot of the animal shelter in Ogallala, Nebraska. Red lips, twinkling green eyes, pink cheeks—

Holy shit, she doesn't hate me.

I swallowed and didn't know what to do as a million questions ran through my head.

Why didn't she hate me? She was crying the last time we spoke, for the love of God.

She was supposed to hate me.

What the hell am I supposed to do now?

I didn't realize we were just staring at each other until Noah said, "For Christ's sake, kids, get a room. Money bet twenty says Liz and Wes won't kiss."

Silence hit the kitchen with an open hand, the awkward slap echoing as no one quite knew how to react. Before I could process that and find a way to make his words disappear, Liz raised her chin and said, "Accept."

If I were standing, I'm pretty sure I would've stumbled backward from the force of that tiny little six-letter word, crashing into my chest like an uppercut. I heard nothing but my own heartbeat, pounding like a bass drum in my skull, as I looked at her Retrograde Red mouth, smiling and daring me to kiss her.

I clenched my teeth as my mind ran wild, because I'd never wanted anything more than I wanted to kiss her at that moment. I wanted to pull her onto my lap and lose myself in her kiss, in the warmth I hadn't felt since the day she'd waved to me from the security line before flying back to LA.

But if I did, I knew we'd get back together. No way was I strong enough to let her go again, even when it was the best thing for her.

And it *was* the best thing.

So I swallowed, pushed back my chair, and stood as I looked down into her emerald gaze.

"That's a hard pass for me," I said, a little shocked by how unfeeling my voice sounded when every cell in my body was drowning in feelings.

I left the kitchen, not interested in the bullshit that Noah yelled as I walked away—"Why are you such a dick?"—or the verbal takedown Joss was sure to deliver the next time she saw me.

Fuck them all, I thought as I headed out the back door, needing to get the hell away from there.

But I knew, as I sat alone on the deck at midnight, staring at the orange tip of a Swisher while everyone inside the house yelled, "Happy New Year," that I'd never forgive myself for what my words had done to her face.

CHAPTER ONE

A YEAR AND A HALF LATER

"I hate you so much that it makes me sick."
—*10 Things I Hate About You*

Wes

I shut off my alarm—six a.m.—and sat up in the dark.

AJ, my roommate, muttered, "Sadistic assbag," and rolled over in his bed while I climbed out of mine and got dressed. We'd been sent to the same Canadian summer baseball league and stayed with the same host family, so even though it was only the first day of fall classes, it felt like we'd lived together for years. I knew he'd sleep in until five minutes before we had to leave for lifting, but I wanted to be wide awake and ready to go hard when we hit Acosta in a couple of hours.

I put in my AirPods and cranked "Trouble's Coming" as I took off down the hill, making my way past dorms whose names I'd yet to learn. I'd run every morning since move-in, and there was just something about campus in the early hours, before it came alive, that I loved. Seeing the sun rise, listening to the birds (between songs), running past the green trees on the hill that somehow felt *different* from the green trees back home; I was smitten with California.

I was smitten with UCLA, to be precise.

And honestly—my smittenhood probably had more to do with the fact that it was where my second chance was happening than the location itself. Yes, it was a gorgeous setting, but it was the setting where my dreams were taking place.

That was the sappy shit that I felt in my bones as I slowed to let a scooter zip past me. Because I was obsessed with the possibilities of this place. The baseball potential (both college and fingers-crossed MLB), the educational potential, the *other* potential; this spot on the map, Westwood, was like the starting point of my everything.

I kind of wanted to break into song as I jogged around a dude with a hose who was washing out a trash can; I was that big of a sap.

Instead, I gave him a chin-nod and kept running.

Good morning, my dude.

AJ might've thought I was out of my mind for running so early every day, but he was just a baby, an eighteen-year-old who'd barely had time to shed the title of prom king before reporting to school.

I, on the other hand, was a twenty-year-old freshman with a lot to prove.

Because two years ago, I'd had everything.

Then I lost it all.

So now that I had a second chance to grab on to that everything, you could bet your ass I wasn't casually reaching.

No, sir, I was greedily grabbing with both hands and never letting go.

I was carpe diem–ing the crap out of my life, throwing myself into every single moment because I knew firsthand how fleeting those moments could be. I mean, if I was being honest, I was absurdly giddy about my first day of school. Like, I didn't want to spew bullshit like *today's the first day of the rest of my life* (that was tragically close to *live, laugh, love*, right?), but it kind of felt like it was.

And I was so ready.

I ran my three-mile loop, showered, then grabbed a breakfast burrito with AJ at Ackerman before we took scooters over to Acosta.

I fucking loved the scooters.

Since I hadn't brought a car to college and didn't own a bike, the Bird scooters that could be found all over campus were the stuff of my dreams.

Wes + scooters = HEA

God, I really am an overexcited kindergartener on my first day of school, aren't I?

I was still nerding out when I got to my first class—lifting had done nothing to hack my buzz.

"Welcome to Civil Engineering and Infrastructure."

I entered the lecture hall the second the professor started speaking, which meant that all hundredish students in the enormous classroom turned their eyes away from him to witness my entrance.

Way to go, dipshit.

I'd completely underestimated the amount of time it took to get from Acosta to Boetler Hall, so my decision to grab a protein smoothie with AJ after lifting had been a total mistake.

But I'd been so stoked after being the top baseball lifter of the day—*hell yes*—that it'd seemed like a brilliant idea (at the time). Why not hang out for a few extra minutes, doing nothing but reveling in the fact that so far, on Day One, I'd yet to screw up?

I quickly took an empty seat in the front, unzipping my backpack and pulling out a notebook (I was *not* a laptop guy when it came to note-taking). It was an intro course, the introductory course for civil and environmental engineering majors, so the last thing I needed was to miss any important information.

"Instead of going over the syllabus with you, such a cliché thing to do on the first day, I'm going to trust that you are capable of reading it. You look like a smart bunch." Professor Tchodre, a tall man with a serious mustache, stood at the table in the front of the hall and said, "So let's get started, shall we?"

I pressed on the eraser of my mechanical pencil, opened the notebook, and got ready to take notes.

"In this class, we will be looking at the role of civil engineers in infrastructure development and preservation."

I started writing as he launched into the material, still blown away by the fact that I was taking an engineering course on the first day of my first quarter. I'd assumed gen eds would fill my freshman year, bogging me down with pointless classes like world music and anthropology, so it felt amazing that I was enrolled in this, as well as chem and calc.

I'd *missed* math and science in the two years I'd been out of school, as crazy as it sounded.

I blamed Mrs. Okun, my tenth-grade physics teacher.

She talked me into attending an engineering camp in Missouri the summer after my sophomore year (during the two weeks between summer and fall ball), and I really hadn't known what to expect. I'd really only gone because it was a two-week getaway from boring Nebraska, right?

I never would've imagined how much I'd love being around other people who liked math and science in the same way that I did. Before camp, I'd been a good student with no clue what I wanted to do with my life, aside from being a major league pitcher, of course.

But the minute I had arrived, it felt like I'd found my spot. I understood the way everything worked in that place, with those people; it all made sense. That camp lit something inside me and made me feel like I was meant to follow the engineering path, even though baseball was my higher priority.

So the fact that I was finally here, in a lecture hall, on my way to making it happen?

It felt huge.

I basically wrote down Tchodre's every word until class ended, knowing I wouldn't need the majority of the info but not really caring. I took college for granted the first time, the idea that *of course* I could go if I wanted to, but after seeing those options disappear, I had an entirely different outlook now.

I was cherishing every fucking piece of it.

Bring on the notes, the study sessions, and the term papers—I wanted it all.

After that I went to chem, followed by lunch and a quick nap. I needed rest before practice, a little quiet time to get my head right, because as great as it was that I'd killed it at lifting, that didn't mean dick if I couldn't throw.

"You sure you don't wanna hoop?" AJ yelled from the living room as he and some of the guys got ready to go shoot for an hour at the Hitch courts.

I loved pickup games, but I needed to save every bit of my energy for the first practice of my collegiate career.

"Nah, I'm good," I yelled back, setting a timer on my phone and closing my eyes.

But sleep was elusive.

Because now that I'd made it here and had *officially* begun my educational and athletic career at UCLA, the time had finally come.

It was time to get Liz Buxbaum back.

CHAPTER TWO

"Before you came into my life I was capable of making all kinds of decisions. Now I can't. I'm addicted. I have to know what you think. What do you think?"

—*Two Weeks Notice*

Liz

Oh my God—is that . . . ?

It was seven o'clock and the sun was barely up, so most of Westwood was still asleep.

But not me.

I was out for a run.

And so was *that* guy, Mr. I'm-Trying-to-Break-a-Land-Speed-Record with the long legs. He was way in front of me, an extraordinarily tall dude who was probably a freshman basketball player, and I narrowed my eyes.

No, I definitely do not know that giant.

"Ever Since New York" played in my AirPods, an underrated Harry song and also, in my opinion, a total slice of autumn. Even though it was warm in LA, my head was already Stars Hollow–vibing because the fall quarter had officially arrived.

Which meant my playlists were buried in musical piles of freshly raked leaves.

Yes, it's a little too early for a PSL playlist, but I don't care.

Because the first day of classes felt magical. It was almost like you could *smell* the crisp, unmarred freshness of a new term. It seemed like anything in the world was possible.

Especially this year.

After two years of applying for meaningless industry jobs that did nothing to further my future career except teach me the easiest way to transport coffee from store to office, I had an internship.

And not just *any* internship.

It was with Lilith Grossman.

I realized, when I waved to the groundskeeper who was hosing down the sidewalk, that I was smiling like a weirdo, but I couldn't help it.

Because I actually landed a gig for my junior year that had the potential to pay huge dividends in my future.

And it started today.

Last year, one of my roommates (Clark) worked for the athletic department's video production team. I didn't know anything about most sports, but he told me they had a part-time paid opening, so I thought, *What the hell*?

I applied because I needed money.

It wasn't an internship; it was just a part-time student job.

A job that I fell in love with.

I was just a grunt who took photos and videos of athletes—at practice, during games, during lifting; that was my job. I basically just did whatever they needed me to do, hauling equipment to all varieties of athletic events.

At first I sucked at all of it.

And then I sucked less.

Because it scratched my creative itch. Just like music had the power to transform a moment in film, I realized that the way I captured an athlete with my camera had the power to create a story. Even though I was just a lackey in the department, I personally got a lot out of it.

So when the announcement came that Lilith Grossman, award-winning documentary producer, was going to be making a sports documentary at UCLA and needed an intern, I applied in a heartbeat.

Mostly because she worked for HEFT Entertainment.

Not only was she an accomplished video producer in the sports world, but she was a producer who had countless projects with my dream company. HEFT Entertainment consisted of HEFT Motion Pictures and HEFT Television, as well as HEFT Music. Both sides of the company were huge and worked with the biggest names in music and film.

If they were winning an Oscar or a Grammy, they were probably with HEFT.

So obviously, as someone who wanted to be a music supervisor for film and television, getting an internship there was huge. A lot of my heroes had gotten their starts there, and now I was going to be one of them.

I still couldn't believe it.

Technically the internship started today, but Lilith and I had been working together for a few weeks now. She'd reached out to see if I'd be interested in helping her get things set up on campus. She'd have an office at Morgan (the J.D. Morgan Center was where the staff and admin for all athletic teams had their offices) for the duration of the project, and since I had stayed in LA over the summer when most of my friends had not, I jumped at the chance.

And it had been the *best* decision.

I hadn't known what to expect from a successful producer—I'd kind of assumed she'd be an asshole, to be honest—but she was the opposite. She was this incredibly successful woman who seemed to want to share—*with me!*—everything that she knew.

She took me to lunch at a sushi place at the Grove, and she asked me about my goals. And when I told her, she pulled a pen out of her handbag and started mapping—on a napkin—how best she thought I could achieve them.

And her insight was everything.

Because *my* plan had been to get my BA in Music Industry with a Music Supervision concentration, and then . . . pray for a job somewhere in music supervision.

But Lilith turned me on to the idea of getting a job in music licensing as a first step.

In licensing, you'll work with music, but you'll also work with film and TV. You'll be earning a salary—very important, that whole money thing—while creating these valuable relationships that will ultimately be the key to getting the job you really *want.*

Then she went on to list a handful of my idols who'd apparently gotten *their* starts in licensing.

And it made so much sense.

Music supervisors worked with licensing on a daily basis, so how better to get my foot in the door? Now, in addition to the courses required for my degree, I was loading up on everything licensing-related and tacking on a licensing certification.

It truly felt like a road map to my dreams.

I'm smiling again, I realized as I stopped at the corner to wait on the light.

I was smiling like a damn fool, jogging in place, but it was impossible not to.

Because this year was about to be *everything*.

Honestly, I was still beaming like a middle schooler in love when I walked into my first class.

"Are you kidding me right now, Buxbaum?"

I grinned even bigger as I headed for the front of Horace's classroom. "What?"

"What?" Horace Hanks, music professor and my all-time favorite teacher, gestured in my direction. "It's the first day of class and you don't even bring a notebook? A backpack? A pencil? I'm insulted by your lack of school supplies."

"Come on, Hor," I said, sitting down at the same desk I'd frequented for all four of his classes I'd previously taken. "You and I both know that you don't just teach—you perform. I've learned that the best way to capture your . . . um, brilliance is to record your class and just rewatch before exams."

"I don't hate the sound of that," he said, scratching his bald head. "But my feelings are still bruised by the disrespect."

"My apologies," I said, pulling out my phone to make sure it was silenced.

Horace lost his mind when a phone went off.

I hit record when class (Psychology and Music Management) began, and the man did not disappoint. He'd always reminded me of that drama teacher on *Victorious* (which was probably why I liked him so much), teaching in a wildly unorthodox manner that was equal parts hilarious and embarrassing.

One time he'd sung an entire lecture. In falsetto.

His methods were bonkers, but somehow they worked. I always learned so much from him.

My next class was in the same building (though less entertaining and more boring), and after that, I headed to Morgan for my first official internship meeting. I was nervous, even though Lilith had been super nice the times we'd met, because she was so amazing that I didn't want her to see how amazing I *wasn't*.

I approached her office, where I could see her working at her computer, and I knocked on the open door. "Knock, knock."

She looked up and smiled. "Come in and sit, Liz."

God, the woman was cool. She had a blond bob, with razor-sharp ends so crisp, it looked like she'd just left the salon. She was wearing a navy blazer over a white button-down shirt with the collar flipped up, ripped jeans, and a pair of tall red pumps. She had that pulled-together LA look about her, like she was ready to do a photo shoot for *Vogue* called *Business-Casual Chic*.

I took a seat in one of her guest chairs and said, "So how's it going?"

It was impossible for me not to small talk when I was nervous.

"Great, actually," she said, giving me a warm smile. "I had a meeting this morning with the AD, and we have a lot of exciting ideas for this project."

"That's fantastic," I said, so excited to be part of this. "Any you can share?"

"Well, I'll share everything with you because we're a team, but I want to wait until they give me the stamp of approval. I don't want to get your hopes up for what I think is a brilliant plan if it doesn't happen."

"That's fair."

"So here's your first internship assignment," she said, crossing her arms and leaning back in her chair. "First of all, email me your class schedule—and your work schedule—so I know when you're available for networking, but include which courses you're taking and who your instructors are."

"Okay," I said coolly, like I wasn't freaking out that she was talking about networking.

"Your coursework is priority because you need that degree, but I really think we need to make the most out of this internship from a career standpoint, don't you?"

I couldn't be cool when she said things like that. I mean, Lilith Grossman, saying that to *me*? Yeah, I couldn't hold back the thousand-watt nerd-grin as I nodded. Because Lilith had all the connections I could ever dream about.

My voice was a little too excited when I nodded and agreed. "Absolutely I do."

"If you're willing to devote the time, I say we lean hard into creating some foundational business relationships."

"I'm definitely willing," I said, regretting the tiny squeal in my voice.

"Perfect. And the second part of your assignment," she said, glancing at her watch before abruptly standing and pushing her chair behind her with the backs of her knees, "is to watch a season of *HBO Hard Knocks*—any season, really."

I nodded. "Okay."

She grabbed a set of keys from the corner of the desk and put her phone in her jacket pocket. "I have to head out, but send me the info and watch a season of the show. I'll be in touch in the next couple days, hopefully with all the initial project information."

"Sounds great."

I very nearly skipped to Epicuria at Ackerman for food after that, buzzing in anticipation of everything that was about to happen in my life. It felt like the sun was shining brighter that day, the birds were chirping louder, and I wanted to do cartwheels across campus after I ordered food and took it back to the production office.

It felt like I was on the precipice of everything finally happening, and it was impossible not to hum along to the "You Could Start a Cult" (my favorite song at the moment) that was playing in my headphones.

When I got to my cubicle, upstairs and on the other side of the building from Lilith's office, I wolfed down a salad at my desk and edited some of the footage I'd taken of the football players on move-in day for a Reel I was making. I was still doing the grunt-work job for the athletic department, so that tiny cube kind of felt like home.

"Hey," Clark said, dropping his stuff onto his desk. "I thought you were going to do the baseball team lift this morning."

"I traded with Cody because I had an early class," I said, not looking up from my computer. "So now I'm doing their practice this afternoon."

"A lot of new freshmen," he said, and I heard the tone of his laptop turning on. "Am I old if I say they all look like little babies?"

"They do, though," I agreed, thinking back to my freshman year. It was all a blur now, thank God, a fuzzy haze of stress and sad songs on repeat. "It's bizarre that we were that wide-eyed and adorable just two short years ago."

"You can spot 'em a mile away, too," he agreed, his keyboard clicking. "It's even in the way they walk to class. Something about their steps screams *this is my first time*. It's like they clench their nervous asses and it gives them a weird gait."

"Do you know if there's any more ranch in the fridge?" I asked, taking a drink of water to wash down my very dry lettuce.

"It's all expired."

"Dammit."

"We need to go grocery shopping for the work fridge, because I also noticed there's no ketchup or horseradish."

I minimized my file to find another image. "Who needs horse-radish at work?"

"Who doesn't?" Clark sounded dead serious. "Horseradish is good on everything."

"Says you."

We worked like that, side by side, for a couple of hours, barely speaking. It was always that way with us. Clark was like my platonic soulmate. I was as comfortable with him as I was with myself, and sometimes it felt like we were just extensions of each other.

Well, except for the horseradish adoration. That was all him.

Finally, at three o'clock, he towered over my cube and said, "Should we head over to Jackie?"

Jackie Robinson Stadium was where the baseball team did their thing. I nodded and saved my work. "So what do they want exactly?"

"Just some general baseball preseason content," he said, shrugging before raising his hands to adjust his hair. "Lifting, practicing—a couple Reels showing this year's team."

"Cool," I said, closing my laptop and sliding it into its bag. "That should be easy."

"Yup. No big deal at all."

We headed toward his truck, nearly getting mowed down by a couple of bros on scooters while we walked toward the parking lot. I smiled in spite of the near-miss, though, because nothing said school was back in session like nearly getting run over by an e-scooter.

CHAPTER THREE

"The moment I saw you downstairs, I knew . . ."
—*My Favorite Wife*

Wes

"You think you can get tickets?" AJ murmured, stretching his elbow over his head. He was wearing those stupid sunglasses that he'd bought for five bucks in Canada, but I wasn't judging, because the sun was shining directly into my shadeless eyes.

For once, I was jealous of his god-awful style.

"Probably," Mick answered, leaning into a hip stretch. "But I need to know how many to ask for."

"You're in, right, Bennett?"

The team was warming up, running through stretches, but AJ was doing double duty, trying to get us tickets to an "epic" party that was happening Friday night. Since I didn't know anyone at UCLA yet, aside from the guys on the field beside me, I figured I'd just follow along and see what transpired.

"Sure," I replied as I stretched my hamstring. Partying wasn't a priority for me, but I wasn't opposed to being social either.

After the hitters split off for base running and we (the pitchers) started working the bands, I heard my name.

"Bennett, you're up."

I glanced toward the bullpen, and Ross was looking over at me. He was the pitching coach, but none of us actually called him Coach.

He was just Ross.

I jogged over, ready to throw, even as my stomach had reservations. *Fucking breathe and calm down,* I told myself. I'd played baseball for basically my entire life, so I needed to chill with the nervous butterflies.

It was only practice.

Riiiiiiight. To me, it felt like a hell of a lot more than that. After not being able to practice for two entire seasons, it felt huge that I was there, that these opportunities suddenly existed for me again after they'd all disappeared.

I saw Woody (bullpen catcher) getting ready, but when I reached Ross, he leaned his back against the fence and casually said, "So tell me about your first day."

I wasn't sure what he was looking for when he said it like we were just two random dudes chatting. I glanced toward Woody before replying, "Um, well—"

"Come *on,*" Ross said, shaking his head with a half smile on his face. The guy had always reminded me of young Kevin Costner (circa *Bull Durham*) because he was not your typical coach. He never yelled and he wasn't intense.

He didn't even seem like an athlete, to be honest.

He was just . . . cool, like he was simply a decent human who knew a lot about baseball. He said, "Don't come up with a bullshit answer for the coach. You and I both know this first day of school is more than that to you, and I'm curious how it's gone so far. What do you think of your classes?"

Ross was the one I called when I quit the team two years ago, and he was the one I called when I wanted to come back.

He was also the one who said *thanks, but no thanks* the first ten times I begged.

Two seasons off is just too much, kid.

"They're great," I said, meaning it. "I mean, definitely not easy, but at least they seem interesting."

"Good," he said, turning his head to spit. "Everything else going okay for you? I'm sure it's a little weird, after everything."

Talk about understatements. "Yeah, it's very weird, but in a good way."

"Had Fat Sal's yet?"

"Not yet."

"Well, don't," he replied, giving me a smirk. "That stuff'll clog your arteries and give you a jiggly ass. Stick to Bruin meal-plan shit."

"I am." I'd heard a lot about Fat Sal's, but I was too hyperfocused on performance right now to put a lot of garbage in my body. I said, "Everything here is too expensive, anyway."

"Right? Fucking LA, man." He gave his head a shake, straightened, and said, "You ready to throw a few?"

I followed him and threw bullpens, which felt amazing. There was nothing in the world like throwing a fastball (when it hit exactly where it was supposed to), and all those ridiculous butterflies disappeared the second my first pitch smacked into Woody's glove.

I was on a roll—*hell yes*—until I noticed there was a giant blond dude filming me.

What the hell?

"Ignore him," Ross said, apparently reading my face. "They've got crews filming all the time for social media; you'll get used to it."

"Ah," I said, feeling a twinge of apprehension in my gut. I was working my ass off to be chill and not focus on the fact that how well I performed in preseason could basically determine my entire baseball future, so the last thing I needed was to have strangers with cameras adding pressure.

"It's just Clark," Woody yelled, grinning in the direction of the giant. "Nobody cares what that asshole thinks."

"Oh, your mom cares," the guy (Clark, apparently) replied with a laugh, though he didn't lower the camera to stop filming me. "And she told me to tell you 'hi.'"

"Tell her 'hi' back," Woody said, pulling his face mask back down, "and ask her if she can get me tickets to your party."

"She's pretty exhausted, but I will," Clark said, which even made me laugh. "Now shut the hell up so this guy can throw."

"Thanks," I said, taking a deep breath.

"No problem." Clark moved over and lowered himself to his knees. "Trust me, it takes a village to shut down a Woody."

CHAPTER FOUR

"Never let the fear of striking out keep
you from playing the game."
—*A Cinderella Story*

Liz

"Buxxie!"

I turned and Jimmy Rockford was waving me over to the dugout with his enormous arms. He was a senior catcher coming off of a torn ACL, and the guy was built like a gorilla.

A ginger gorilla with a braided beard. He was a lot to look at, but that was part of his charm.

"Yeah?" I asked, pausing my playlist as I pointed toward the field, where it looked like the outfielders were getting in their fly ball reps. "I need to get shots so I can't chat right now."

"Any extra tickets for Friday? My brother wants to come."

As if. His twin brother, Johnny, played rugby with Clark and was a walking stereotype. He was huge and rough and wild, and when he drank, he was prone to fighting and general destruction.

I liked Johnny, but I wasn't about to invite him to a party at our adorable new off-campus apartment.

"Sorry," I said as I walked in the other direction, grateful my roommates and I had all agreed upon a strict adherence to the party rule. The three of them were wildly social—I was less so, and it just made sense to use tickets to ensure our parties didn't get too big. "I'm all out. Check with Clark, though!"

Clark was over by the bullpen, getting footage of the pitchers. I could see the back of his head (not tough when he was six foot seven with a blond man-bun), so I unzipped my camera bag while I approached and pulled out everything I'd need.

"Right on time," he said to me as he filmed someone throwing, somehow knowing I was there without looking up.

"Heads up, Johnny Rockford is looking for a ticket."

Clark muttered, "I already told that fucker no."

"Ten bucks says he shows up anyway." I set down my bag, adjusted the camera settings, then raised it to take shots of the guy Clark was filming.

Clark and I had gotten good at being invisible, and since most of the athletes were used to being filmed, no one even noticed us there. I looked through the lens at the tall pitcher as he let loose with a fastball, and wow—that was some impressive speed.

At a glance he didn't look familiar, so he was probably a freshman.

Although technically I was behind him and couldn't see his face at all, so I guess I meant that his *backside* didn't look familiar.

No, his backside just looked like a very nice baseball backside.

God bless the woman who designed baseball pants.

And yes—it had to be a woman.

"Crap—do you have a spare battery?" I asked, irritated that I forgot to charge the camera while I'd been in the office. The little icon in the corner was blinking, which meant I was down to only a couple of minutes.

"My bag," he said, still taking video. "In the back of the truck."

"Okay," I said, annoyed I'd overlooked the obvious. *Charge the freaking battery, dumbass.* "I guess I'm going back to the truck, then."

"If you see they've started BP, would you mind getting some shots?" Clark finally lowered his camera and looked at me. "I have a feeling that's going to be better content than bands and bullpens."

"Sure." I ran back to the truck, and after changing the battery, I spent the next hour getting shots of batting practice. It was fun to see a lot of the players from last year—Mick and Wade were my favorites—and to watch the new guys. UCLA had the number-one recruiting class in the country, which didn't necessarily guarantee a good season, but it made their preseason feel like more than just training.

It felt like a prologue.

I zoomed in on Wade as he did tee drills, snapping shot after shot of the seriousness on his never-serious face.

God, it's great to be back. I never would've imagined I could fall in love with sports, but so help me God, this job had made it happen.

Because in addition to learning the ropes by doing things like labeling footage and holding the film crew's stuff, the craziest thing had come out of my low-level production job. I'd discovered that in addition to music, I loved the process of taking flat footage of athletes in their habitat and tweaking it into a compelling story about the human experience.

"Wanna go to Ministry of Coffee when you're done?"

I lowered the camera and Clark was standing there, his equipment all packed up. He said, "I'm bringing coffee for, like, half of my night class tonight, so I could use the extra hands."

Typical Clark. He knew half the class and it was only the first day. "You're finished already?"

I glanced down at my watch and *wow*—we'd already been there for two hours.

"Yeah, but I can wait if you're not," he said, running a hand over his hair. "I've got, like, ten people I promised tickets to since we got here, so I can text them while I wait."

"I know you're overselling the party, by the way," I said accusingly, reaching down to grab my bag. "But I think I've got enough hitting shots. Let's go get coffee and figure out how screwed we are."

"Sounds good to me." He pulled out his sunglasses and slid them up the bridge of his nose. "But the world's not going to end if our party goes a little big, you know."

"Says you." I rolled my eyes and started walking with him toward the parking lot. "You're not the one who can't sleep when there are still sixty people in the living room at three in the morning."

"It definitely wasn't sixty," he said, throwing his arm over my shoulder. "And if you would've just drunk a little more, sleeping wouldn't have been a problem."

I had to laugh at that, because Clark was fazed by nothing.

Ever.

A bomb could go off in his bedroom and he'd say something trite like, "Well, I guess the universe thought it was time for me to redecorate."

"Just tell me you didn't promise Woody a ticket," I said, knowing without a doubt that he probably had. Every person I knew loved the bullpen catcher from Alabama, Mr. Southern Charm, but I did not. He wasn't a bad guy, but I went on a date with him last year. It was my one and only college date before I realized I no longer believed in romance when he (A) told me he hated cats, (B) called me "Red" like that was a universally accepted pet name for a redhead, and (C) kissed my neck while we were standing in line at the movie theater concession stand.

And ever since that ill-fated date, *every time* I saw him, I had the pleasure of answering his twenty questions about why I never let him take me out again.

"I gave some to a couple of the freshman pitchers," Clark said defensively, "so I *had* to give one to Woody. I mean, he was right there—I had no choice."

I shook my head at my pathetically soft friend. "Well, if I murder him, I'm making you bury the body and get rid of the evidence."

"Deal," he said. "I'll even spring for the shovel."

CHAPTER FIVE

"No matter what happens in the next five minutes, I want you to know that when I opened this door, I was so happy to see you that my heart leapt. It leapt in my chest."
—*For Love of the Game*

Wes

The first week flew by.

The baseball part of it, aka Hell Week, was pretty intense. Practice, lifting, position-specific practice, conditioning; I spent more time suffering with my teammates than I did with my course-work.

Which sent me scootering to the library every night in an attempt to stay ahead of my studies. Powell was the main library on campus, the one that made sense for me to use as my studying home base, but I liked to go a little farther and study at the music library.

Because it was quieter.

Okay, that was total bullshit.

I studied at the quiet music library in hopes of running into a certain music student who might also be studying there. A music student with green eyes, copper hair, and tattooed daisies on her hip.

A music student I dreamed about nearly every night.

Whose voice I could still hear, whose perfume I could still smell.

I had yet to see her, but I sensed she was close. I had a few ideas on how to accidentally run into her, i.e., spend an entire day studying in the lobby of Schoenberg, where all her music classes were likely held; ask my teammate Eli's girlfriend, who worked in the registrar's office, to screenshot Liz's schedule; call Mr. Buxbaum and beg for intel; call Helena and beg for intel; etc. But I needed my life to slow down in order for me to make it happen.

So, on Friday night, as I walked back to my dorm after a chaotic first week and zero Liz sightings at the library, I was really looking forward to going out. Not to get shit-faced, but just to let loose with the guys and have an entire evening where I wasn't thinking about school or baseball.

Or her.

I punched my code into the keypad and pushed open the door.

"It's about fucking time," Wade (first baseman and one of my suitemates) said, looking like a douche as he stood in the middle of the shared living room wearing tight jeans, a white T-shirt, a black blazer—what the hell—and a goddamn fedora on his big head. "I am ready to go."

He was with Mickey (catcher/other suitemate) and AJ, who *weren't* dressed like Bruno Mars, *thank God*, and they all appeared to be waiting on me.

"Where—to a costume party?" I asked, dropping my backpack onto the coffee table.

"Don't be jealous of my style, Bennett," Wade said, dusting the front of his jacket like he was big shit.

"Oh, I am definitely not that."

"Just get yourself together because we already called an Uber and it's on the way," AJ said. "If I'm not dancing soon, I'm gonna lose it."

My favorite thing about AJ was the fact that he didn't give a damn what anyone thought about him. And not in an asshole way, but in a true-to-himself way. My boy loved dancing (like all-out, covered in sweat because he's dancing so hard), he loved K-dramas, and he would argue to the death the merits of seltzer being better than beer.

"How long?" I asked, really wanting a shower after speeding back to Hitch under the warm California sun.

AJ looked at his phone. "It says my driver, Larissa, is twelve minutes away."

"I can shower in three." I went into the bedroom to grab clean clothes and yelled, "I'm good in jeans and a T-shirt, right?"

"No, you scrub," Wade replied at the exact second AJ and Mickey yelled in unison, "Yes!"

I ducked into the shower and was ready just in time to slide into Larissa's ride with everyone else. AJ started chatting up Larissa because she was exactly his type—dark-haired bombshell with book quotes tattooed on her arm—but she was having none of his bullshit. She dropped us at an apartment complex that was swanky as hell, and I was in shock as we got into the elevator.

"Wow." I looked at the illuminated numbers on the elevator

display as the doors closed behind us. "College students live here?"

I couldn't even fathom a guess as to how much the rent would be in a place like this. It wasn't a building for twentysomethings. It was a building for wealthy adults.

And trust-fund babies.

I mean, the *doorman* was collecting party tickets, for God's sake.

What the hell are we doing here? I pressed the 2 button.

"Clark said his roommate's parents are loaded," Wade said, "and that they bought the condo just so their kid can rent it from them every month."

"Damn," I said. Clark—the giant at practice with the video camera—seemed down-to-earth and very chill, so I was surprised he lived with someone so wealthy. "Must be nice."

"Right? Why don't I have friends like that?" AJ said, finger-combing his hair as he stared at his reflection in the elevator wall.

When the doors opened, we could immediately hear the music coming from down the hall. I wasn't sure how anyone was able to pull off that noise level without the neighbors calling the cops. Maybe the units in the building were insulated so well that they couldn't hear it?

Doubtful.

We followed the sound to 2C. The door was closed, but it was so loud on the other side that knocking would be ridiculous. AJ turned the knob, pushed, and just like that—the party was upon us.

We stepped inside and holy *balls*—I was impressed.

Holy, *holy* balls.

Was this what parties were like in LA, or was this unusual?

From our spot in the foyer, we could see a living room packed full of people. Some were dancing, some were talking, but the sound system was what had me losing my mind. This party sounded like we were in a club. Like, yes, the music was loud, but the sound was incredible.

Also—"Heaven Angel" was a banger I hadn't heard in way too long.

I could see a huge kitchen off to the right of the living room, where there appeared to be even more people drinking. It was controlled chaos, though, in spite of how huge it was. Unlike the high school parties back home, where couches sometimes caught fire and fights were known to break out, everyone was actually behaving.

How is this possible?

"See why I said we had to get tickets?" Wade said, grinning. "Insane, right?"

"Unreal," I shouted, laughing because it *was* insane. *Are we on a reality show?*

"I love you, man," AJ yelled to Wade, his eyes all over the room like he was a toddler who'd woken up in the middle of Santa's workshop. I followed his starstruck gaze and noticed that there were a lot of girls there.

A lot, yet I didn't care because I didn't see the only one who mattered.

"Let's go get some beers," Mickey yelled, pointing somewhere where I assumed there were beers.

I didn't know where we were going, but I was all in.

CHAPTER SIX

"I don't know very much about him,
except that I love him."
—*It Happened One Night*

Liz

"Come get your shot, Bux!"

"No, thanks," I said—yelled, rather, giving a wave to Campbell from my spot in the corner as the party started getting crowded. "I'm good!"

"You're not good until we say you're good!" She picked up the four shot glasses from the kitchen island in front of her, held them over her head, and made her way toward me with my other two roommates following behind her.

It was a tradition, on house-party nights, for the four of us to share a shot together before things got crazy.

My roommates were as follows: Campbell, a sophomore soccer player who was stunningly beautiful and could also drink anyone—*man, woman, or frat boy*—under the table; Clark, a senior who was as good at rugby as he was at knitting, and Leonardo, a charming

Italian biology major whose parents were loaded, hence the luxury *right-across-from-campus* apartment we were renting from them for next to nothing.

So basically it was me—someone who only socialized when forced—and three engaging humans who lived to entertain. I'd never been into partying—too loud, too crowded, too boozy—but after I told them that, my amazing roommates created a role that managed to turn me into a party fiend.

I was the DJ. At every party we ever had.

Leo built a raised workstation in the corner of the living room, so I could see everything from my platform, but I was out of the way so people didn't really notice me unless they were trying.

I spent the days before a party curating the perfect party playlist, timing out the songs to match the tone of a party's chronology: chill music when people were mingling at the beginning, a mix of everything people liked to sing along and dance to when they started getting rowdy, and then I brought out all the bangers (Clark's word choice, not mine) for when things were roaring.

There was nothing quite like the rush of seeing it work, of seeing everyone shout-singing to my musical selections. I was obsessed with it, obsessed to the point that I'd become quite the little party planner just to witness it all go down, over and over again.

Last year we had one big(ish) party each quarter, all with themes: the *Oh, Shit—We're Back Bash* (tonight was version 2.0), the *Christmas Slay*, the *Anti–Valentine's Day Party*, and the *School's Out for the Summer, so Everyone Kiss Extravaganza*.

Leo, being Leo, invited all our neighbors (most of whom were grown-ass successful adults) and also gave them his phone number so they could reach him if the party got too loud. I thought he was insane the first time, but they loved him for it and we had trouble-free parties.

Before my made-up role of DJ came to pass, whenever I was forced to go to a party, I'd just stand beside whomever I came with and wait for fun to happen, which, spoiler—it didn't. As someone not looking for romance, not a big drinker, and not incredibly fond of conversation with strangers, "fun" wasn't synonymous with a college party for me.

But not anymore. Because now I was able to enjoy my favorite parts without dreading the rest. I got to do the whole cute outfit/good makeup thing, which was the best part of going to a party (that night I'd found the perfect black-and-white dotted dress to go with my red Chucks). I was able to be excited for an event and have fun with my friends, yet I got to watch from afar while being invisible and doing music.

And it helped that my roommates were stingy with their invites. Campbell's tickets usually went to soccer players and their significant others, Leo mostly invited scientists and a smattering of beautiful girls, Clark's went to baseball friends and rugby players (who were hard-core but surprisingly sweet), and mine usually went to random athletes (that I knew) who asked me for tickets while I was working.

Bottom line—there weren't many strangers at our parties, which made them feel safe.

"Here," Campbell said, handing me a shot of vodka as Clark and Leo grabbed theirs.

"What's the toast tonight, kiddos?" Clark said, his loud voice hard to hear over the noise as he held up his shot. His hair was in a high ponytail, which looked both ridiculous and amazing on him, somehow.

"Work hard, play hard, stay hard," Leo said, raising his glass to Clark's, ruining the obnoxiousness of the toast by giggling his adorable high-pitched laugh.

"To working hard," Campbell said, rolling her eyes and joining the toast.

"To all the hardness," I yelled as we clinked and tossed back our shots. I glanced toward the door as it opened and more people came in, then said, "Now leave me alone. DJ Lizzie needs to work."

Wade Brooks walked in as my roommates dispersed, wearing that stupid fedora that I'd told him no less than ten times made him look like a douche. I'd given him my last few tickets—he and his friends were always fun—and I was glad I did when I saw Mick follow him in. I met them last year, and they loved to party, but the baseball guys never got handsy or turned creepy when drunk, which I very much appreciated.

Bonus points for being better than a large portion of the general male population.

I took a drink of my Captain Morgan and Coke as a couple more guys came in behind them, a short blond and a tall—

Oh my God.

Oh my God!

I gasped, coughing on my drink as my hand clutched my chest. I squinted and stared, unable to believe my eyes as I tried to get a better look. Everything in my body—my breath, my heart, the movement of the blood in my veins—came to a complete and total stop. I was paralyzed, entirely frozen, as I watched him laugh at something the blond guy said.

Dear God, it was Wes.

Wes Bennett was in my apartment.

I was instantly lightheaded as I tried to process his presence, the power of *Wes-in-the-flesh* overwhelming after two years of watered-down, diluted memories.

I think I'm going to faint.

This was impossible. How was he there? Why was he there? Was he visiting someone?

This can't be happening. My stomach felt like a huge knot, a huge knot that was surrounded by a plague of wing-flapping moths, as I watched Wes Bennett enter my living room.

Dear God, Wes is in my house.

I took a deep breath and tried my hardest to remain calm, to not feel like I was about to pass out or throw up, but my heart was beating too fast. He was grinning and talking to Wade and the blond—*his smile is exactly the same*—and I felt like I couldn't catch my breath.

I might be having a heart attack.

I'd forgotten how tall he was—*maybe I hadn't*—but he looked even bigger now. His shoulders had expanded and his chest looked wide under his Cubs T-shirt, like he was the professional version of the recreational boy I'd once known.

His face looked harder, like he'd lost all the excess and was whittled down into only sharp angles and dark eyes, and the neck I'd always been distracted by looked somehow more intriguing.

Could a neck be muscular?

God, how is he still so beautiful?

He threw his head back and laughed, and even though I couldn't hear it over the noise, I knew exactly what it sounded like.

A laugh I'd recognize anywhere.

God, I hated him for looking that good.

He wasn't *allowed* to look that good.

They headed toward the kitchen, probably looking for beer, and I tried to take a deep breath and get a grip.

But it was impossible when, unbidden, so freaking unwelcome, the memory of the last time I'd spoken to him came at me.

New Year's Day, two years ago.

I showed up at his house with questions, positive the rumor couldn't be true.

And then he'd looked me in the eye and told me that it was.

Why is he here now, after all this time?

Does he even know this is my house?

I lifted my glass and gulped down the last of my drink, very aware of the way my hands were shaking. I wanted to run and hide, yet at the very same time I felt like screaming his name just to see his reaction.

I needed to get a grip.

I needed to calm down.

I needed air.

CHAPTER SEVEN

"I wanted it to be you. I wanted it to be you so badly."
—*You've Got Mail*

Wes

"I think she went outside."

I followed Wade out the patio door and onto the huge balcony as he tried finding Campbell Someone. Apparently she lived here and he was slightly obsessed with her, so since I had nothing better to do, I accompanied him on his search.

It might prove amusing, watching Brooks drool all over himself.

"Is that her?" I asked, nodding my head in the direction of a tall blonde in a very short dress. There really *were* a lot of girls at the party; no wonder he'd been foaming at the mouth to get here.

"No," Wade said, "but maybe Liz knows. Come on."

I barely had time to register the name "Liz" when I saw her.

Oh. My. God.

There she is.

Libby, holy shit.

She was standing there by herself on the balcony, looking like everything I'd ever wanted. The sights and sounds of the party—of the world—disappeared as my eyes drank her in, desperate and needy after being deprived of the sight of her for way too long.

God, was it weird that I felt a little choked up? My throat was tight as I tried taking a deep breath, but it felt impossible.

Because there she was.

Finally.

She's here. Liz is within reach, holy shit.

And how was it possible that she'd gotten prettier? It felt like years—and also minutes—since I'd last touched her, and I clenched all ten of my fingers, a little dizzy from the power of my want.

She was wearing a black dress that looked amazing on her, but it didn't matter. The dress was unnecessary, like her clothes weren't important anymore, which was a weird thing to think, but they didn't matter.

Clothes were merely a distraction.

Because her skin—*face, arms, perfect legs*—had a glow now, like she been in residence with the warm rays of the California sun twenty-four hours a day, seven days a week. *Which makes sense since she hasn't been home in two years.* With her long, loose braid and slick, nude lips, Libby was a summer siren whose magic had nothing to do with what she was wearing.

She fucking glowed, I swear to God, and the words Blake Rose was singing through the speakers as Wade and I approached made the hairs on the back of my neck stand up.

Me and you

We're supposed to be together—

"Hey, Buxxie, where's your roomie?" Wade asked, walking right up to her and pulling on her braid.

"What?" Liz blinked and looked confused as she gave him a vague smile, like he'd pulled her back from a million miles away.

And then she saw me.

Her smile disappeared, her cheeks flushed, and she swallowed, looking as shocked as I felt. I swear to God I heard her gasp, but that might've been me. Because after haunting my dreams for almost two years, Libby was suddenly standing right in front of me, looking up at me with those long-lashed green eyes.

Looking like everything I'd ever needed.

Am I fucking trembling? I could smell the Chanel No. 5 on her skin, and I wanted to hyperventilate on it because *holy shit* I was finally close enough to breathe her in.

"Hey, Buxbaum," I managed, which was ludicrous. There was so much history between us, a million "I love you"s and a thousand stolen kisses, yet the two words I managed to piece together in her presence were the same words I might use to say hi to any random stranger who shared her last name.

You brilliant, charming idiot.

"Wes. Oh my God." Her voice was scratchy, but I wanted to drop to my knees and beg her to say it ten more times. *Slow down and say it again, Lib.* She blinked fast and gave me a polite "How *are* you?"

Cool was impossible. I felt the ridiculousness of my smile as it became my entire personality. I was a clown, grinning from head to toe, but I couldn't reel it in because it was finally happening. I'd daydreamed (on a daily basis) about running into Liz since the moment I committed to UCLA, and there was just no way for me to disguise my absolute joy in this moment. "Better now."

Her eyes moved all over my face, like she had a million questions she was trying to work through. "Yeah, um—"

"Focus, Liz," Wade interrupted, snapping his fingers, oblivious to the reunion happening in front of him. "Where is Campbell?"

She shook her head like he was ridiculous. "Hiding from you, probably."

"Now, see," he teased, grinning. "That's just mean."

She was flustered, a wrinkle between her brows as she blinked fast, but she teased him back. "And necessary. You go too hard."

"I tell Campbell that she's beautiful," he said, "and she acts like I've insulted her. Make it make sense."

"You tell her she's beautiful when you *remember she exists*," Liz corrected, giving him a smirk that I felt in my knees. "You only think of her when we have a party, and then you follow her around like a puppy for the entire night."

"Because I'm smitten," he said, grinning like she'd given him a compliment. "And lovestruck."

"That's not actually a thing," she said, rolling her eyes, and jealousy hit me hard in the gut. I wanted to tease her and to have her tease me back—that was *our* thing. I think I missed that more than I missed kissing her.

Okay, that's a lie, but being Liz's friend was everything.

Wade gave his head a shake. "You're the most unromantic female I've ever met, Bux."

"Thank you," she said offhandedly, barely noticing his comment, but I felt lost, like I was in class and missed something in the assignment.

Because Liz Buxbaum, unromantic?

"Not a compliment," Wade said, laughing.

"And you're not smitten, you're just intrigued because you aren't used to being rejected." She smiled like he was a mischievous child, absolutely manhandling the wildly overconfident first baseman. "Trust me, Wade, if she treated you like the baseball god that so many foolish people think you are, you'd be over her in a hot min—"

"Ooh, there she is," he interrupted, and then he just sprinted away from us, running across the balcony and back inside.

"Well," I said as Liz and I watched him disappear into the apartment. "There he goes."

The vibe changed in an instant. Liz crossed her arms and chewed on the inside of her cheek, looking like she wanted to be anywhere but here. Her cheeks were flushed, but my face was on fire as her eyes moved to a spot just past my shoulder.

Like she didn't want to look at me.

I cleared my throat and said, "So. Liz. Hi."

Hi—it was absurd. Maybe better than *hey, Buxbaum*, but still one casual syllable, like we were lab partners who'd seen each other earlier that day and not two people who'd seen each other—

"Hi, Wes." She put her hands in her pockets, and the smile she'd had for Wade was long gone. Her face was all tension as she said, "I, um, I had no idea you were in LA. Are you here visiting someone, or . . . ?"

She trailed off, and it was obvious she hadn't even considered the idea that I might be a student.

"I'm back, actually," I said, wondering how that week together in LA when we were incoming freshman could feel like two lifetimes ago. "I'm restarting the whole freshman-year-at-UCLA thing."

If she were drinking, she would've done a spit-take. Her eyes widened and her perfectly arched brows went all the way up. "You're a student? *Here?*"

I nodded. "And I'm back on the team."

Her eyebrows went down and crinkled together, and she sounded like she couldn't believe it when she said, "You're playing baseball again?"

Yeah, I can hardly believe it myself. After my dad died, I couldn't even look at a baseball, so *of course* this didn't make sense to her. She'd been there—well, on the other end of the phone—when I freaked out at the thought of ever pitching again. "I am."

"Oh. Um, that's really great." She nodded but her eyebrows remained scrunched together. "So you are a student athlete here, at UCLA. This year. Right now."

It would've been funny, the difficulty she was having wrapping her mind around it, but the fact that she looked the opposite of happy took any humor out of the situation. Her face left no question that she didn't want to have this conversation—or any conversation—with *me*.

I remembered the last thing she'd said to me, New Year's Day two years ago—*God, I hate you*—as I confirmed, "That's correct."

"Well, that's really fantastic," she said loudly, smiling politely, looking over my shoulder like she was searching for an escape. "How's Sarah? And your mom?"

"Good," I replied, hating that she was turning to *we're strangers* small talk. I knew what kind of shampoo she used, I knew the color-coding of her book annotations, and I knew the exact spot on her neck where a kiss would wreak havoc on her ability to breathe, goddamnit.

It was wrong to pretend we used to sort of know each other and that this moment between us wasn't huge.

"And Otis?"

"You're seriously asking about my dog?" I leaned my head a little closer to hers, needing to mess with her and coax the Libby out of her. "I think that's as far on the small-talk scale as you can go, Buxbaum."

"You're probably right," she said, her green eyes flashing in irritation. "I guess that means we've reached the end of our conversation."

"That's not what I meant," I said, reaching out to take my turn tugging on her braid. "I was referring to your very boring questions. Maybe try spicing things up a little, like asking how my—"

"But I don't care," she snapped, smacking my hand. "About how your anything is."

"Ouch." I couldn't help it; I was grinning again. God, I'd missed this so much. I stepped a little closer and said, "No need to get snarky, Lib."

"And don't call me that," she said, her teeth gritted.

"My bad," I said, putting up my hands. It felt good to get under her skin, so I said, "Maybe we should go somewhere and catch up."

"Lizard!" A huge dude with a ponytail who looked a lot like a bleach-blond Aquaman appeared beside Liz, and it took me a half second to realize it was Clark, the guy who'd been filming at practice.

And who lived there. He said, "Are you ever coming back?"

He was standing close to her, close enough that they were clearly friends.

Or . . . more?

No.

Probably no.

Please no.

Who the hell was this guy to her?

"I just needed some fresh air," Liz said, pasting a huge smile on her face as she looked at the dude.

But it was so fake.

Wasn't it? She wasn't *really* that happy to see the giant, was she?

"This is Wes Bennett, my old next-door neighbor," Liz said, waving a hand in my direction like I didn't matter. Like I'd just been some kid in her neighborhood, not the guy who had a tattoo on his arm that perfectly matched the one on her shoulder.

Shit. Had she gotten it removed?

She wouldn't have, would she? I mean, that sort of thing was expensive, wasn't it?

It was insane, that I was focusing on that of all things, but it'd break my whole fucking heart if that tattoo was no longer there.

"We were childhood buddies," she explained, her mouth smiling at me while her eyes did the opposite.

I tilted my head. "Is that what we were?"

I hadn't thought it was possible, but her cheeks got even redder as she met my gaze and bit out, "Yup."

Damn, but I need to kiss her.

"And this," she said to me as she pointed to the guy, "is Clark."

Just *Clark*? No explanatory title, like "my friend" or "a jackass" or "my bodyguard"? Who was Clark to her?

"Nice to officially meet you, man," he said, reaching out and shaking my hand. "Impressive throwing today."

"Thanks," I said, unsure how to behave when this question mark of a person was being annoyingly nice.

"There's a lot of buzz around the whole number-one-recruiting-class-in-the-country thing," he said. "And I myself am hard-core ready to fanboy all over that exhibition game in a couple weeks, so consider yourself warned."

Exhibition game. I swallowed around what felt like a razor when he uttered those two words, and I lied, "Yeah, really looking forward to it."

"I watched film from summer league, and your fastball is money."

"Thanks." I looked back at Liz, and she was watching us with her eyes narrowed, either in irritation or confusion. Maybe both.

So I said to her, "So did you want to get out of here?"

"Oh, I don't think Clark would like that," she said, going big on that frozen grin again.

Now *my* eyes narrowed, because she had that conniving Little Liz look on her face.

"Why not?" I asked, at the exact second Clark looked at her and asked, "Why not?"

Liz blinked fast and said to me, while wrapping her arms around the dude's stupid enormous bicep, "Because my boyfriend gets very jealous."

CHAPTER EIGHT

"I like this boy. . . . And he likes someone else. . . ."
"Well, obviously this boy is a complete moron."
—*Clueless*

Liz

I glanced up at Clark, and he wasn't hiding it.

He had zero idea what I was doing.

"You get very jealous," I said to Clark in a cheesy singsong voice, trying to transmit my thoughts with my eyes as I breezily said, "Even though you think you don't."

His eyebrows screwed together and he looked confused.

Dammit.

"Oh, you guys are together?" Wes asked—*at least someone got it*—and he didn't look like he cared at all. He asked it the way someone would ask *Do you like the cheese dip?*, and something about that stung.

Even though *I* was the one who didn't care anymore.

I was the one who was over it.

Dammit.

"Yes," I said, nodding a little too enthusiastically. "We are."

"We are?" Clark asked, still confused, and then it was almost comical (if it wasn't so horrifying) when his eyes got huge, and he said, "Yes, we are. Dating. We are dating and I am her boyfriend."

Oh, for God's sake. I cleared my throat and said around a ridiculous smile, "It's new, so, uh . . ."

"New?" Wes tilted his head and looked at me like I'd just sprouted antlers.

Oh my God, how can this be happening?!

I looked at Wes's stupid face, his beautiful, awful, terrible face, and just couldn't believe he was actually there.

That he was there, and I was doing *that*.

"Because we've been friends for so long," I said in an oddly high-pitched voice that reminded me of Ross Geller when he said *I'm fine* in response to Rachel and Joey kissing. "You know how that can be, right?"

So much for pretending you remember nothing, you idiot.

That made something change in his face, and my eyes were pulled to that hard jaw as it clenched and unclenched before he said, "I do."

Good.

"I still can't believe it," Clark said, raising a hand and pinching my cheek while grinning at me so stupidly that I would've laughed if—again—the situation wasn't so horrifying. "One day we were buddies, and the next she was all 'Clarkie, I have feelings,' and I was like 'holy crap, Lizard, I have feelings too,' and now we're together. It's, like, really surreal."

"*So* surreal," I agreed, giving a little laugh while wanting to kick Clark's obnoxious ass. "A whirlwind, really."

"It *is* like a whirlwind," Clark said way too loudly, smiling and pinching my cheek again, followed by two little pats.

I removed his huge hand from my face—*the jackass*—and said, "Yeah, so that's the sitch."

The sitch? *What are you, in middle school, you moron?*

"Wow." Wes looked from my face to Clark's, and then he gave me a half smile. Said in that teasing tone of his, "Well, you look great together. I mean, the whole she-only-reaches-his-armpit thing never misses. You guys are adorable."

"Yeah," I said, nodding emphatically like a lunatic while wanting to throat punch him.

You guys are adorable? What the hell was *that* supposed to mean?

"Thanks," Clark agreed, obliviously nodding along.

"Well," Wes said, looking entirely unfazed by the situation. He scratched his eyebrow and said, "Listen, my friends are probably wondering where I disappeared to, so I should go find them—"

"Yeah," I interrupted, nodding once more. "Good seeing you again."

"Oh, you too, Lib," he said, giving me a wink before turning and walking away. *A wink, oh my God.* I watched him cross the balcony and duck inside, looking like just another college dude at a party, and I had no idea why I felt so pissed.

For some reason, I wanted to drag him back outside and force him to, like, watch me kiss Clark with obnoxious tongue or something, anything to make him upset.

He wasn't allowed to be unaffected by me, because that was supposed to be my role.

DAMMIT.

"What the hell was that?" Clark stepped in front of me so I had to look at him. "Have you lost your mind?"

"Yes," I groaned, rolling my eyes and shaking my head. "Obviously I've completely lost it."

"Please explain yourself. And here," he said, holding out his cup. "Drink this. You look like you need it."

"I do. What is it—who cares," I mumbled, taking his cup and slamming the contents.

Noooooo not whiskey my throat is on fire.

"Jesus, Liz," Clark said, half laughing as I handed back the cup and tried not to gag. "That's fifty-dollar bourbon."

"It's awful," I gasped, my eyes literally watering. "Oh my God."

He walked over to the other side of the balcony, grabbed a bottle of water out of one of the coolers, then brought it over. "So now. What is the story with you and Wes Bennett—other than the fact that you were 'childhood buddies,' and why the hell did you tell him I'm your boyfriend?"

I grabbed his arm and pulled him toward the railing, wanting to make sure no one could overhear us. I uncapped the water and took a long drink before I explained, "It's complicated, but basically we dated in high school and I haven't seen him since things ended. And let's just say it was a little . . . *messy.*"

"A little, my ass. It looked like a lottle," Clark said.

"It's ancient history and I'm totally over it." That was accurate. Succinct and emotionless, without a tinge of the rage that'd sparked in my center when he'd said *Is that what we were?*

Yes, I definitely still hated him.

The lyrics from "Congrats" whispered through my psyche—

You broke my fucking heart

You tore my world apart

"But he wanted to go somewhere and catch up," I said, shaking my head and gritting my teeth as I spiraled. "And I just couldn't. I mean, why would he even suggest that? How could he think I'd want to—"

"It's okay," he interrupted, giving me a sympathetic smile. "Exes are weird like that, and I totally get it."

"You do?" I said, surprised because I didn't even get it myself. I'd spent years in Wes Bennett detox, and I was a healed woman. His presence—*holy shit how can he be a student here now?!*—should've been an annoyance at most.

So why had seeing him felt akin to getting an electric shock?

And not in a good way at all.

Clark took out his ponytail and finger-combed his curly blond hair. "Here's the thing, though. Fake-boyfriending me is a terrible idea."

"Why?" My eyes kept roaming behind him, looking to see if Wes had come back out. "If he thinks I have a boyfriend who is seven feet tall and freakishly strong, he'll know I'm over him *and* he'll probably steer clear."

But even as I said it, I knew that if Wes wanted to mess with me, nothing would stop him.

But surely he didn't want that.

"But do you really want everyone to think we're dating? Think about it. We live together *and* work together. If this gets out, people are going to think it's juicy as hell," he said, and he wasn't wrong.

But as I sifted through the pros and cons, there wasn't really anything that seemed awful about this idea. I didn't date—*at all*—so people thinking I was Clark's girlfriend wasn't going to mess up anything on that front.

In fact, it'd be nice for everyone to think that a massive rugby player was my boyfriend. For once I wouldn't have to come up with excuses as to why I had zero interest in dating anyone, ever.

Although.

"God, I'm so selfish," I said, realizing the sacrifice it would be for Clark. "This would totally screw up your love life if people thought you had a girlfriend, wouldn't it?"

"I'm not worried about *that*," he said, shrugging. "I mean, I'm assuming we will fake-break up in the near future, once you know how to handle yourself around him."

"Yeah, for sure we will," I said, wondering if I'd ever know how to do that.

Because I never would've guessed that at this point in my life, almost two years later, I'd feel so shaken by his presence. I would've expected a polite reunion, with a few lingering unkind thoughts about him that would disappear the moment he walked away.

That was how it was supposed to go.

Whyyyyyyyy aren't I numb by now?

"Okay, so maybe this," Clark said, getting that patented Clark grin on his face that meant he was all in. "Let's go with what we just said to Bennett, that this is brand-new. Like, we just discovered we have feelings, and we're just starting to explore it. That way when people act like he's wrong, like, *no, they're just friends*, it makes sense why no one knows."

"See, this is why I want to date you," I teased, feeling a little better. "You think of all the details."

"Right? I'm awesome," he said around a smile, pinching my cheek again. "This is going to be kind of fun."

"I will stab you," I said as I smacked his hand, laughing in spite of everything, "if you don't keep your enormous pie-plate hands off my face. Got it?"

"Oh, Lizard," he said, giving in to a loud laugh. "You're adorable when you huff. Let me text our roommates so they know the plan, and then let's go get you another drink, girlfriend of mine."

We went back into the party after he sent Campbell and Leo the message, and I was glad I had a buzz when he grabbed my hand and led me into the kitchen. Because there was Wes, sitting on the stool where I ate my yogurt every morning, grinning and playing cards with his friends.

Who were actually my friends.

Who'd actually been my friends first.

And he was in my kitchen, what the hell?!

I felt like I needed a time-out to get my head right because it was all too much.

"Is Buxxie actually going to hang with us?" Wade teased, his hair a mess since he'd finally shed the stupid hat. He had a handful of cards in his fists and a few cans of beer in front of him as he grinned and said, "I thought you only did music at your parties."

"I begged," Clark said, pulling me closer and wrapping his arm around my shoulders, "and Lizzie was nice enough to choose me over music. At least for a solid five minutes."

"Lizzie?" Mickey, who was at the other end of the table, said. "What the hell is this 'Lizzie' shit? Are we allowed to call you that now? Because I recall it being expressly forbidden."

I really wanted the attention to land on anyone else, because I could feel Wes watching this stupid interaction. *Wes, the only person to ever seriously call me Lizzie.* I pushed my lips into a smile and said, "Well—"

"Only *I* can call her that," Clark interrupted, his voice loudly obnoxious.

Oh God. I couldn't bring myself to look at Wes's face.

Wade's eyes narrowed. "Did I miss something? Are you guys a thing now?"

I sucked at lying, so I just shrugged and smiled. "Maybe."

"Oh my God, little Buxxie's blushing," Mickey said, and I knew blushing had to be an understatement because it felt like my skin was on fire. "This is adorable."

"Shut it," I said, rolling my eyes. "I'm going back to the music."

"Oh, come on, baby," Clark teased. "Don't go yet."

That made Mick laugh, and I wriggled out from under Clark's arm as the moment passed and the card game moved on. I turned to escape to the living room, to get away from the kitchen and lose myself in the music, but not before making eye contact with Wes.

Whose dark eyes were intensely on me, like he was searching for something.

That face was impossible to read as I held his gaze like a deer in the headlights, unsure what was passing between us. I swallowed and tucked my hair behind my ears—*get it together, Buxbaum*—and it felt like my knees might literally give out as I exited the kitchen as quickly as possible.

What. The. Hell. Universe?

CHAPTER NINE

"I mean, I know it's been awkward as ass,
but there's no need to leave."
—*Bridget Jones's Diary*

Wes

I was done.

Everyone was still partying, but I needed to get the hell out of there. After the Clark bombshell, I'd sat in the kitchen for a solid hour, pretending to be into the card game while my brain kept exploding over and over again.

Liz had a boyfriend.

I'd always known it was a possibility, but I guess I hadn't truly accepted that possibility because I felt *floored* by the revelation. And before I had a moment to get a grip on the shittiness of that little morsel, Wade informed me that Clark was her roommate.

Her *roomfuckingmate.*

She *lived* with her new boyfriend.

I felt sick. My gut was literally churning and it was very possible I was going to vomit, so I needed to get out of there fast. I'd looked for Liz after she left the kitchen—*God only knows why*—but she seemed to have disappeared completely.

I made my way through the packed living room, bouncing off the jumping people who all seemed to be singing along to "DJ Got Us Fallin' in Love," until I reached AJ's side. I tapped him on the arm and shouted, "I'm going to walk back."

"What?" He stopped dancing and leaned closer to hear me, looking at me like I was nuts. "You're going to walk back? *Now?*"

"Yeah," I snapped, absolutely uninterested in talking about it.

"Why? Do you even know how to get back from here?" He took a drink of his beer before saying, "Why the hell would you want to miss this?"

"I just do." I was going to lose it if I stayed another minute, so I said, "I'll see you back home."

"Wait," he yelled as I walked away, but I needed to leave. I pushed through the people, not even bothering with "excuse me" as I elbowed through the crowd, and I'd made it to the front door when he grabbed my arm. "Bennett!"

I turned around and it was almost comical how sweaty he was and how confused he looked. Thankfully the foyer was quieter than the rest of the apartment, so I didn't have to yell anymore.

"Dude, I have to go," I said, shaking my head.

"You okay, though? Wandering through the streets of LA in the dark seems like a bad idea." He sounded like a worried parent when he said, "I don't know how much you've had, but I'll wait for an Uber with you if you want."

God, he's such a good dude. I didn't know what to say or how to explain my behavior, so I said, "I'm totally sober; I just can't be here anymore."

"Well, maybe we can—"

"Remember my ex?"

He stopped talking and didn't get it for a second, muttering, "No, I don't think so," under his breath before saying, "Wait—the redhead from high school?"

I'd gotten hammered one night during summer league and spilled a *lot* to AJ, probably more than I'd ever shared with any other human. We'd never really discussed it after that night, but I somehow knew he remembered all of it.

He was just that guy.

"Yeah." I nodded and said, "Well, apparently this is her apartment."

"What do you mean this is—oh my God!" His eyes got huge, and he said, *"Liz?"*

"Shhhhhh," I said, looking behind him to make sure no one was listening. "Shut up, will you?"

"Are you telling me," he whisper-yelled, "that Buxxie is your ex?"

"Yes," I bit out, "and calm your ass down."

"But Bennett," he said, looking at me like I'd just delivered the world's most shocking news. "I don't understand. You didn't know—"

"I knew she was a student at UCLA, but I didn't know she lived in this apartment, and I sure as hell didn't know she has a boyfriend."

"Duuuude." AJ tilted his head and looked at me like I was a pathetic puppy. "No way did it go down like this."

"Unbelievable, right?" I still felt queasy about the whole thing, mostly because I couldn't stop hearing Clark call her "baby."

Gross. It was gross, right?

"Baby" was an offensive pet name, in my opinion.

Fuck.

"Go," AJ said, pointing at the door. "Because your face is getting redder by the minute. Get out of here, clear your head, and text me when you get home so I know you made it safe."

"Thanks, man," I said, pulling open the door and exiting the noisy apartment. I wasn't looking forward to discussing this with AJ later—that guy loved talking about feelings—but at least I knew I could trust him to keep it to himself.

I left the building and just started walking, grateful for the fresh air and quiet, but it didn't take long for me to get good and lost.

UCLA was a huge school, and during daylight hours, I had the area pretty much figured out. But when it was dark, forget about it. My sense of direction went to shit. I gave my car to my sister because I had a whole team to mooch rides off, but figuring out where you were on foot was somehow more challenging than when you were behind the wheel.

I texted AJ: **I think I'm walking in circles in the neighborhood by the party. Is there a trick to getting out?**

I looked at my display and realized I'd been walking for forty minutes.

I was starting to think my GPS was dicking me around.

Of course, the entire time I'd been walking I was picturing Liz and Clark, so the haze of jealous rage might've impaired my nighttime navigational skills.

Yeah, I was insanely jealous.

Jealous to the nth degree.

So jealous it was choking me.

Which pissed me off because it was stupid, right?

But even though my brain knew it was logical for her to date someone else, my body wanted to wipe the floor with Clark for being the one whose arm she wrapped her hands around.

Honestly, I should've been happy for her because the dude seemed nice. *Really, really nice, actually.* But somehow I just knew he wasn't right for her. I might not be The One (even though I was pretty sure I was), but there was no way Ponytail was, either.

She said "new."

That they were "new."

So, how new?

Were we talking days, weeks—what constituted new?

Had they kissed yet?

"No," I muttered to myself as I walked, the thought of that making my stomach churn. I mean, it'd been years—*of course* she'd kissed someone else by now. I knew that, but seeing her face again and smelling her perfume and hearing the sound of her voice made everything feel so close.

My phone buzzed in my hand. **AJ: Airdrop your location**

I did, and then my phone buzzed again. I expected it to be AJ, but it was my sister.

Which also wasn't a surprise. Sarah was in all my business, all the time.

Sarah: How's the epic party? Are you hard-core kegging?

I texted: **Walking home, actually.**

Sarah: So early?

I replied: **Liz was there.**

Almost immediately, she was FaceTiming me.

Dammit. I didn't feel like talking about it, but I also knew she wouldn't go away.

"I knew I shouldn't have told you," I said as I answered, fully aware that I would never not tell her. Sarah had gone from annoying little sister to the only person in the world I could count on after my dad died and my mom had her issues, so we kind of told each other everything.

Spoiler: You get really close with your siblings when you have to learn survival together.

"Oh my God," she said, like I hadn't spoken. "Did you talk to her?"

Sarah had on her glasses, which meant she was ready for bed. The kid hated glasses and had always waited until right before bed before taking out her contacts.

"I did," I said, not wanting to rewind that polite small-talk nightmare.

"Oh my God, Wes, I was right!" Sarah, the romantic, had wanted me to track down Liz the second I got to LA. "This is fate, I just know—"

"She was with her boyfriend."

"She has a *boyfriend*?" My sister, not one to be deterred, immediately launched into a fact-finding mission. "And he was there? Is it serious?"

"I had the privilege of meeting him and talking to them—*together*—as a couple."

"Noooo—*quel* nightmare," she sighed in horror, her eyes wide. "What was he like?"

I hated him. I hated him so much. Because, "He seemed like a really great guy."

"Oh my God, the *worst*," she said, groaning and shaking her head. "What about the time? Do you know how long they've been talking?"

"That's the weird part," I said, leaning back and stretching out my legs. "Liz said it's new, that they've just started dating, and then they both said they're still getting used to it. The guy was like, 'Oh, yeah, that's right—I'm your boyfriend.'"

"What?" Sarah must've flipped on a light because it was brighter now. "They are *still getting used to it*?"

"I know," I said, still a little confused by that. "Like how?"

"Obviously it isn't serious, then. What else?"

"What else what?"

"What else happened with Liz, you moron? What did you two say to each other?"

"It was all very polite," I said, my gut in a knot as I replayed the very cordial reunion. "Like we were total strangers."

"Gross," she said, almost in a whine.

"I know." I sighed and tried pushing back the disappointment. "But even if she was single, Sar, it probably wouldn't matter because she still hates me."

"She said that?"

"No, but it was obvious." It was all over her face when she looked at me. "Trust me."

She leaned closer to the camera and pointed her finger at me. "Wesley, you need to tell her the truth."

"I mean, how can I when she isn't single?" I'd love for her to know the truth, but there wasn't a good way to just spit out those words. "It doesn't exactly come up in the conversations we aren't having."

"I don't know, but you just have to say it. Spit out the words." She shrugged and said, "Even if it's awkwardly blurted-out in the middle of the quad, just get the truth out there."

"I don't think UCLA has a *quad*."

"Wesley."

"Sarah Beth." I looked up at the full moon and stood. "I honestly don't think that would change anything."

"But it could change everything, you idiot!" She was all fired up now, making me actually regret telling her because I was too exhausted to deal with her attitude.

"I'll think about it," I said, dropping to sit on the curb.

"Why wait? Why think? Go back to the party and shout it, Wesley!"

"I have to go."

"Dammit, Wes, you need to strike now, while it's new—don't you see that? If you drag your feet, it might become . . . *not* new with the boyfriend, and then it *definitely* won't matter."

"I'll call you tomorrow, kid," I said. "I'm hanging up now."

"But—"

I disconnected the call. I knew she had the best of intentions, but I didn't want to talk about this. Not with her or anyone.

No, I'd much rather stew and lose my mind over this all by myself.

And she was wrong, by the way.

Because I knew Liz. Giving her the hard press with shouted confessions, after not speaking for almost two years, would only push her away. It was why I hadn't tracked her down on move-in day.

I was being patient.

If we were ever going to have a second chance, I needed to convince her to become my friend first. To let me in again.

Which seemed a hell of a lot more difficult now that she had a boyfriend.

As if on cue, my daily watch alarm went off.

It was 12:13 a.m.

Seriously, Universe, you're hilarious.

Fuck *me*.

Liz had teasingly set the alarm for me the summer we were together, so that every night I would be forced to stop and recognize the anniversary of the moment we'd kissed under the streetlight on prom night.

Silly little love lover.

I wasn't sure why I'd never deleted the alarm, to be honest.

"Bennett, you little bitch," I heard as a car slowed beside me. I narrowed my eyes and saw Wade, Mickey, AJ, and a girl I didn't know, all crammed into a silver Honda that had a silver-haired man behind the wheel. Mickey rolled down the front passenger window and said, "Get in."

"I can't believe you're done at the party already," I said, putting my phone in my pocket.

"Campbell said she was hungry," AJ said from where he appeared to be squeezed against the door in the back seat, "so Brooks called an Uber so we can go get some food."

The girl—Campbell, presumably—gave me a wave and a smile.

"Get your sweet ass in the car," Wade said, sticking his head out the back window, "'cause we're goin' to Fat Sal's."

I wasn't sure if they were going back to the party after Fat Sal's or not, but at least I could call myself an Uber from there if that was the plan. I squeezed into the back seat, wedged between Wade and the door as I slammed it, and the driver stomped on the gas.

"What kind of a dumbass walks home when they don't know where they're going?" Mickey asked, giving me a drunk grin. "You had our little AJ all worried about you."

"I'd worry about *you*, too, if you went wandering around LA in the dark by yourself," AJ said, which made Wade laugh.

"Of course you would," he said, reaching out a hand to pat AJ's knee. "Mama Bear."

"Why did you walk?" Campbell asked, leaning forward to talk to me around the Wade that was between us. "Couldn't get an Uber?"

I got tripped up for a second, because this girl was Liz's roommate, right? I doubted she knew anything about me—yet—because Liz hadn't even known I was here until a few hours ago, but I had a weird feeling that I should try to make a good impression.

"Something like that," I said, acting like it was a whim instead of me having a full-on meltdown over her roommate's current relationship status. "I'm Wes, by the way."

"Campbell," she said, smiling. "And you used to date Liz, right?"

"What the *what*?" Wade shouted, even though he was right next to me. His mouth hung wide open for a second before he said, "You went out with Buxxie?"

Dammit. The last thing I wanted was to discuss Liz and my history with Wade.

Or anyone, for that matter.

Well, except for Liz.

"She was my next-door neighbor back home," I said, trying to downplay it.

"The girl next door?" he said, laughing. "Whooo, Bennett, I gotta know more."

"It was a long time ago," I said, dismissing him because I was dying to hear what Liz had said to her roommate about me. I turned back to Campbell and said, "So, yes, I did."

"That's what Clark said," she replied, "but no worries—he's super chill about it."

"Oh," I said like a dumbass, but I had trouble pulling words together because, like . . . did that mean Liz hadn't said *anything* about me? Was her boyfriend the one talking about me? "That's good."

And why was Clark so chill? Shouldn't he be the slightest bit jealous of our history?

And why am I being so neurotic?

"Yeah," she agreed. "And Wade told me all I could ever need to know about *you*."

"Oh?" I said, glancing at Brooks's stupid smirk, wondering what the hell he could've said.

"He said you're a pitcher from 'NebraskaIdaHoma.'"

"All those states in the middle of the country just run together," Wade said defensively, shrugging. "I can't be expected to keep track of which one our little lefty comes from."

"Brooks is a shining endorsement of the Texas school system, don't you think?" AJ said to Campbell.

"Well, they say everything is bigger in Texas," she said, "so—"

"That's right, honey," Wade interrupted, looking drunk as hell while he beamed at her.

"—I think it's safe to say ignorance is not excluded from that expression."

Campbell grinned at Wade, her head cocked like she was waiting for his comeback, and it made sense that she was friends with Liz. They both had a sweetness about them that was surrounded by a layer of smart wit, like they were capable of being kind while also destroying you if you dared to deserve it.

Wade's voice was all confidence when he said, "Honey, I will fucking label an entire United States map for you—with every state capital starred—if that will make you like me."

"Can you do it while you're drunk?" she asked, sounding like she was trying not to laugh. "On a Fat Sal's napkin?"

"Tonight?" he asked, looking marginally less cocky as the car came to a stop across the street from the restaurant.

"Sure," she said, and she kept talking as we all got out of the Uber. "I will make a US map while we wait in the food line, and then you can show off your geographical knowledge while we eat."

"This is a fantastic plan," I said as we got in line.

"Okay—you guys order," Mick said to AJ and me, handing me

a wad of cash, "and we'll grab that open table and get started."

"Yeah," Campbell agreed, holding out her card. "I'd like the stromboli fries, please."

"Get me the Fat Bruin," Mick said. "What do you want, Brooks?"

"Fat Texas and fries," Wade said, still wielding that drunk-ass smile. "And quit being so excited to see me fail."

"Can't quell this thrill," Mick said, shaking his head. "It's what I live for."

As soon as the three of them went over to the one empty table (Fat Sal's was crazy busy on Friday nights), AJ said, "So how're you doing?"

"I'm fine," I said, glancing back at the patio to make sure Campbell was way out of earshot. "It's fine."

"Good." He stepped forward when the line moved. "I just can't believe it's Buxxie, though. *Buxxie* is your ex? That's wild."

"How well do you know her?" I asked, genuinely curious. Now that I was marginally calmer—only because I was distracted—I wanted to hear all about what he knew of California Liz.

"I don't know her at all," he said, "but I know *of* her from Wade and Mick."

They were both sophomores.

"Yeah?" I said, impressed by how casual I sounded when I really wanted to pull out a notebook and write down every detail he had pertaining to Liz Buxbaum.

"Yeah. Apparently Liz works for the video production department, so she's always around, filming and taking photos of practices and workouts. Her team is the one that generates the content that the athletic department puts on social media."

"No way."

Liz works in the athletic department?

I had not expected that.

"Yeah. I guess that's how everyone knows her."

"Everyone knows her?"

"Sounds like." The line moved and he stepped forward again. "And I asked a few guys about Clark, but apparently this thing with him and Liz is brand-new, because no one seems to think they're anything more than friends."

"I see." I felt a little better hearing that, because my chances were a hell of a lot greater if they'd just started dating than if they'd been together for a while.

"So what's your plan?" AJ asked.

That brought my full attention to him, to his face as he gave me a weird look. I'd never once mentioned to him—even when drunk—my intention to ultimately win her back, so I was a little surprised by the comment. "What do you mean?"

"I mean that you're wearing the same asshole expression you get on your face when you're trying to sit a batter. You look . . . intentional, Bennett."

The people in front of us moved out of line, and I stepped up to the counter to order.

Yeah, I was definitely *intentional*.

Regarding Lizzie, I had all the intentions in the world.

CHAPTER TEN

"I love that you get a little crinkle above your nose when you're looking at me like I'm nuts. I love that after I spend the day with you, I can still smell your perfume on my clothes. And I love that you are the last person I want to talk to before I go to sleep at night."

—*When Harry Met Sally*

Liz

"Any questions?"

I shoved my laptop into my backpack as Elaine Lowell, my Forensic Musicology instructor, waited for questions—questions that would not be coming. I'd taken one of her classes before, and she was absolutely brilliant yet utterly terrifying.

The building could be on fire and no one would dare ask that woman where the extinguishers were.

She'd just assigned a huge amount of reading—reading that was sure to put me to sleep. It was important information that I'd definitely be using in the real world, but there was only so much a person could read about music copyrights before their eyelids got droopy.

I'd probably go to the music library later to read the text, because my roommates were far too noisy to make the comprehension of boring material possible.

"Okay, then, you're free to go."

I followed the rush to exit and was almost to the door when I heard her say, "Liz? Can you hang back for a sec?"

"Sure." *Oh shit, oh shit, oh shit.* I swallowed and walked over to the lecture podium, where she was packing up her things, wondering what this could possibly be about. "What's up?"

She smiled—a warm smile—and I was taken aback, because I'd never seen her smile before. She was a high-powered entertainment attorney with that whole I-don't-have-time-for-anything vibe, so I just assumed she didn't know how.

That she'd never cared enough to learn.

"I just wanted to let you know that I'm always available for questions and extra discussion. Lilith Grossman is a good friend of mine, and she reached out to let me know her intern is in my class."

Oh. I'd emailed my schedule to Lilith like she'd asked, but I hadn't expected her to look at it and actually interact with it.

Or reach out to an industry professional to make a connection.

"Thank you," I said, nodding and smiling—basically gushing. "I really appreciate that. I'm positive I'll take you up on the offer."

"You definitely should," she said, still smiling. "I'm happy to help anytime."

I left the classroom totally energized, and as I exited Schoenberg and put in my AirPods, a burst of gratitude popped through me. The fact that I was even there, in LA, taking music classes in such a gorgeous place—it was more than enough.

But now I was making connections in my dream career? Before I was even a senior?

It was huge.

I assigned "Unwritten" to this moment (I was always looking for a reason to steal it back from *The Hills*, anyway), cranking it as I headed down Bruin Walk toward Morgan for my meeting with Lilith. I was visualizing a movie scene in my head as I walked through the busy crowd of students going to class, the music playing as the protagonist crossed the picturesque campus with a cheesy smile on her face.

Reaching for something in the distance

So close you can almost taste it—

"On your left!"

"Gah!" I squeaked and jumped out of the way as a scooter buzzed past me, so close to running me down that I could literally feel the breeze when it passed.

Jackass.

I wasn't surprised to see it was an athlete at the helm. I wasn't sure why, but they were the ones I always saw using scooters. I watched the guy zip in and out of foot traffic like a NASCAR driver, fast and unfazed, and I gritted my teeth when I saw the height of the dude and his Bruins Baseball backpack.

Are you freaking kidding me?

I couldn't be positive, but that idiot looked a lot like Wes Bennett from behind.

As if hearing me, the guy suddenly whipped the scooter around and came back in the opposite direction, riding toward me.

Whyyyyyy, Universe?

It was definitely Wes, and he was wearing his smart-ass grin as he scootered toward me.

"I cannot believe the slowpoke I almost flattened is Lizzie Buxbaum," he said, turning yet again so now he was riding alongside me.

"Believe it," I said, and I just kept walking, hoping he'd go away.

"I'm really sorry for the near-miss."

I glanced over at him. He didn't look sorry as he watched me, slow-riding on that scooter while wearing the bratty half smile that brought back a thousand memories I didn't want to remember.

No, he looked amused as his mouth slid into an even bigger grin. "This is when you say, 'That's okay, Wes.'"

"No, this is when I say, 'Can you go scooter somewhere else, Wes?'"

His eyes were dancing when he said, "I *do* have to get to class, so I'm going to let that slide."

"Oh, joy," I muttered, walking a little faster.

"But Lib?" he said, his voice scratching the part of my brain that used to listen to Bazzi on repeat.

"Don't call me that," I snapped, nearly speed-walking even though I knew there was no escaping him.

He sighed dramatically and said, "It was really great seeing you."

And then he zipped away.

It felt like my teeth were going to shatter because I was gritting them so hard as he disappeared from my line of sight.

Why is this happening to me?

I'd spent all of Saturday spiraling, freaking out about the fact that he was here. Every time I was able to calm down and convince myself it was no big deal—it's been years and we're both different people now—I'd picture his face when he smirkily said, *Is that what we were?* and the rage was immediately back.

Asshole.

Because it wasn't fair that he was here. This was *my* place, dammit.

I had a life that I liked at school, a life that came *after* the ruins of us. A life built *because* my first attempt had crashed and burned. So somehow, the idea of Wes in close proximity to it felt precarious, like his smart-ass *it was really great seeing you* presence could ruin all the little wonderfuls that I'd carefully created.

And God—my job (and now my internship) was all about UCLA athletics. It was important to me, and I was terrified he was going to mess it up or make me love it less. And in addition to that, how was I supposed to avoid him when the primary task of my vocation was to capture athletes on film, and he was an athlete?!

Gaaaaaaaaah.

Somehow he'd just landed in the center of my million-miles-away-from-Omaha world and it wasn't fair.

Clark brushed the whole thing off and thought I was totally overreacting.

"First of all, he thinks you have a boyfriend, so I'm sure he'll stay away from you because I'm ridiculously intimidating. Second, it's not even baseball season yet, so we won't do jack with the team until spring. And if there *are* baseball assignments, I'll just focus on the pitchers, and you can do the rest. Problem solved."

I took a deep breath and told myself Clark was right.

This was a huge school, so the odds were in my favor that run-ins like the one we'd just had would be few and far between. And Clark's plan for Wes-avoidance was totally doable.

It was going to be fine.

This was no big deal, a minor irritation at most, and it was totally feasible that I could absolutely avoid any further interactions with Wes Bennett.

"I'd like to imbed you with the baseball team."

My coffee immediately went down the wrong tube, and I started coughing, hacking as Lilith patiently waited for me to recover. *Imbed you with the baseball team.* Dear God, this couldn't be good. As soon as I was able to speak, I gasped, "What?"

She crossed her arms and said, "I'm sure you heard that *Baseball America* has determined UCLA has the number-one recruiting class in the nation, right?"

"Yes."

"Well, your tiny little social media post of the team's preseason practice on Friday got more likes than the football content. And they had a *game* on Saturday."

She looked pleased, which made me beyond pleased.

I was also surprised that Lilith was paying attention to the athletic department's social media posts, to be honest.

The woman was on top of everything.

"People are excited about the baseball team," she said. "Boosters are excited. Everyone wants to see more of this promising bunch of players."

I rubbed the spot between my eyebrows that was getting a headache.

"What, um, what does 'imbed' mean in this instance, exactly?" I asked, trying my hardest to sound like I didn't have stakes in her answer.

"Did you watch *Hard Knocks* yet?"

"Yes." Yesterday I'd binge-watched the latest season, and it was a fantastic docuseries that covered the day-to-day of an NFL team during their season. "I loved it."

"Well, good, because that's what we want to do with the baseball team. *We* want to brand this team and this content. We haven't finalized the verbiage, but I'm leaning toward *Bruins Baseball: Building a Championship Team*."

"Oh," I said, nodding and trying to focus while my mind ran wild.

"We want followers to be inundated with day-in-the-life-of-a-Bruins-baseball-player content, as well as short player interviews to introduce this year's team. I'd like for you to think of yourself as an honorary Bruin teammate and basically go to class, then baseball, then sleep. Rinse and repeat. I'd love to see three or four Reels a week until fall ball ends."

What?? Noooooooo.

Was she seriously telling me she wanted me to dedicate my every waking hour to the baseball team? The baseball team that *he* was a member of?

And I would have to interview him?

I would absolutely open with the song "Disaster" in this scene if my life was a movie.

This could be a disaster

There's so many factors . . .

"What do you think, Liz?" she asked, looking excited.

"It sounds amazing," I lied, my stomach filling with dread. "Um, so is this for the production department, or is this—"

"No, this is all you." She gave me an eyebrow raise and said, "This is your next internship assignment."

Oh God, oh God, oh God.

"It's a pretty big time commitment, though," she said, standing and coming around to perch on the edge of her desk. "I've confirmed that the general schedule for the team is workouts at six thirty a.m. every day, followed by morning classes, then position coach practices for players after lunch—those are only three times a week, thank God. After that, there's actual practice every day, conditioning three times a week, and then study hall to make sure the players aren't falling behind. The life of a student athlete is not for the meek."

My head was spinning. How in the world was I going to do all that by myself and keep up with my studies?

And my job?

It seemed impossible, but I also wasn't about to say no.

Not to Lilith.

Because the thing of it was, she'd already become more than a professional mentor to me; she was my hero. I didn't know exactly how old she was, but she was young for what a powerhouse she was at HEFT, as well as the work she did with the NFL. I'd seen hundreds of pictures of her getting sideline shots at important games like the Super Bowl, and she was such an inspiration that I'd rather do almost anything than disappoint her.

"Even though this is your internship 'assignment,' it's work that the AD wants done so you'll be able to loop it through your job and have access to your usual resources. He okayed pulling someone to be your dedicated counterpart, so if you have a coworker you prefer teaming up with and they're interested, let me know who that is and I'll pass on the word."

So I can still work with Clark. That was a relief, even though I was still completely overwhelmed by what she was proposing.

"Let me ask him, but I'm pretty sure Clark Waters would totally be interested, and he's great."

"Wonderful," she said, picking up her phone to type in Clark's name. "The details are still being ironed out, Liz, but it's very likely this little assignment could actually end up in the documentary."

"What?" That made all other thoughts cease, because until now, the only thing I thought I'd be contributing to a legitimate film documentary was my assistance. "Really?"

She nodded and looked up from her phone. "Obviously my hands are the ones that will be all over the film—I'm terribly territorial and don't like to share, to be honest. But if this preseason content hits the way I think it will, it'll be great to have these clips in the first act. Especially the intros."

"Yeah, um, about the intros," I said, clearing my throat, unsure exactly what to say. "I feel like there's something I need to make you aware of."

"Oh?" Lilith narrowed her eyes and asked, "What is it?"

"Well, it seems that one of the players and I have, uh . . . a complicated history, I guess you could say." My cheeks were warm as I explained. "I haven't seen him in years, and until Friday, I had no idea he was even at UCLA, much less on the baseball team. But I just feel like I should put it out there, before we get started, that I used to have a relationship with Wes Bennett."

She tilted her head. "The new ace?"

Was that how he was being referred to—the new ace?

"Yes."

"I see." She crossed her arms. "Should I be concerned by the word 'complicated'? Are there issues I should be aware of?"

"No, no," I corrected, shaking my head. "Nothing like that—it was totally a normal high school dating relationship. I just thought you should know, in case you thought it was a conflict of interest or something."

"I don't have any issues with it," she said slowly, giving me serious eye contact. "As long as you can work with him professionally. Can you?"

"Of course I can," I exclaimed, nodding wildly. "It's ancient history, truly."

"Good," she said, straightening and walking back around the desk. "So do you think you can juggle your coursework and *Hard Knocks*? How do you feel about this assignment?"

I definitely can't juggle it all.

Maybe I can, though . . . ?

I have no idea!

My anxiety-riddled brain was running wild, but when I looked at Lilith, at this inspiring woman who was all over everything, I realized that I could be too.

I mean, of *course* I could.

Because I wasn't Little Liz anymore.

I loved where I was in life. I loved my friends, loved my school, and I was obsessed with my internship. I could handle my studies, and I *would* handle this challenge.

Because if Wes Bennett hadn't showed up a few days ago, I would be screaming over this opportunity and celebrating my unbelievable good luck.

So I couldn't let someone from my past, someone I hadn't seen in years, ruin it for me.

"I can absolutely handle it, and I can't wait." I smiled, meaning it, and said, "I think it's time to get imbedded."

CHAPTER ELEVEN

"People do fall in love. People do belong to each other, because that's the only chance anybody's got for real happiness."
—*Breakfast at Tiffany's*

Wes

"Easy."

Woody popped up from his squat behind the plate and threw back the ten balls that'd been in the dirt beside him as Ross said, "Don't give up accuracy for speed."

What the hell was that, Wesley?

I caught each ball and dropped them by my feet, wiping my forehead with the back of my arm. "Okay."

"You got this, Bennett." Woody dropped back down and held out his glove. "Let's go."

"Let's go." I flipped the ball, running my index finger along the seam before taking a deep breath to clear my head.

Because even though my dad was dead—it'd been two years since he'd had the heart attack in his La-Z-Boy in front of the

Cubs/Mets game on TV—every time I pitched, he was right there with me.

I heard his voice with every bullpen I threw.

Occasionally I heard him when I was doing well, but mostly he spoke to me when I was struggling. Which really messed with my ability to power through because even though his voice was saying things like *throw 'em the gas* and basically growling about how crappy I was pitching, it made me miss him.

So much.

Which was nuts, right? How did it make me miss him when it reminded me of what a psycho he'd been about baseball?

"Wes?" Ross looked at me with raised eyebrows.

Fuck.

"On it," I said before winding up and letting loose with another fastball.

"Better," he said as Woody dropped the ball he'd caught and held out his glove to catch another.

Better, but you need to throw harder, kid. Throw 'em the gas and quit being soft.

"Shut up," I said under my breath as I threw hard, relishing the loud smack of the ball hitting Woody's glove.

"Okay," Ross said, taking off his baseball cap and putting it on again.

I grabbed another ball, refusing to let his voice into my head. I threw a curve this time, watching it drop over the plate. It was perfect, *hell yes*, and then I heard it.

Liz's voice, laughing.

Was I seriously hearing her voice now too?

"Another one just like that," Woody said, tossing the ball to his right.

I grabbed another ball, inhaled through my nose, and let loose with a killer fastball, *hell yes.*

"Let's gooo," Eli yelled from behind me, which meant the shortstops were here for their practice. I was about to throw another one when I heard him say, "Did you guys get that curve on camera?"

I turned my head and—*holy damn*—there was Liz.

And her boyfriend.

Clark and his man-bun were filming my pitching again, which bugged the piss out of me as I stared into his video camera and wondered if he could see the annoyance in my eyes. I knew I was going to have to get used to random people with cameras popping up to film for social media, but something about him being there felt intrusive.

Irritating as hell.

You have my girl—isn't that enough?

Liz was standing on a step stool near Eli, wearing shorts, a Bruins basketball T-shirt, and a pair of blue high-top Converse with little smiley faces all over them. Her hair was pulled up in a ponytail, her eyes were covered with Ray-Bans, and she was looking down, messing with something on the long-lensed camera in her hands.

Hands with perfectly trimmed blue-and-yellow fingernails.

God, she's beautiful.

I hadn't seen her since my accidental (sort of but not really) buzz-by on the scooter last week. AJ said she'd been around, filming at his BP and infielders practice, but I'd somehow managed to miss her until now.

"Nice balk, Bennett," Ross barked, and I forced my attention back to pitching as he muttered, "Pay attention."

Dammit.

I was good at shutting everything out so I finished strong, but I didn't like the way it felt. I used to love when Liz went to my high school games because for someone who didn't enjoy sports, she got into it. She wore my alternate jersey to every game (with a flowery little skirt, of course) and yelled things like *you got this, Bennett*, even though she didn't know dick about baseball.

And she had the most incredible feedback. *I love the way you look like you want to kill the batter when you release the ball. Did you know you spin the ball before every pitch? I made a list of walk-up songs you should use in college.*

I could still remember the list, because it was all songs she didn't personally enjoy but that she felt "worked" for the situation. I took my responsibility very seriously and chose number five, which made her happy because it was her favorite as well (even though she said she'd never forgive Kanye for what he'd done).

"DNA."—Kendrick Lamar

"Trophies"—Young Money

"Step into a World"—KRS-One

"Welcome to the Jungle"—Guns N' Roses

"Power"—Kanye West

But now I felt unsettled by her presence. Because what did she even see now when she watched me?

The asshole she hated?

Some random freshman pitcher who was struggling with consistency?

Her annoying childhood next-door neighbor?

She wasn't by the bullpen anymore when I grabbed my stuff; she and her giant had moved over to film the shortstops from the third base line. *Which is good,* I reminded myself as my eyes sought out that shimmery red ponytail. *I don't need the distraction.*

Because watching them work together, now that I knew they were dating and living together, was just too much. No amount of mental toughness could keep me focused when that was happening in my line of sight.

I was all about getting closer to her, but I wanted nothing to do with close proximity to *them*.

A couple of hours later, I found myself dealing with it again. "For the love of God, why are *they* here?" I asked, sitting down next to Mickey and unzipping my backpack, watching as Liz squatted in front of the table where Wade and AJ were studying, her camera in front of her face.

Her boyfriend was on the other side of the room, recording Eli and Luke as they studied—invading my space with their presence.

"Dude." Mick looked at me like I was a dick. "You don't like Buxxie and Clark?"

Mick had gotten so hammered at Liz's party that he seemed to have missed or forgotten the news that Liz and I used to date, and I wasn't about to enlighten him.

It was only a matter of time, with Wade's big mouth, so I'd just let it unfold organically.

Later.

"No, I mean, they're fine," I said, wanting to laugh at the detached way I'd said the word "fine," as if I was talking about the lighting in the study room or something I had absolutely no opinion on. "But it seems weird they'd be making TikToks about a team study hall. Like, who wants that shit on their feed?"

"Oh, it's *way* bigger than that," he whispered, a smug grin landing on his face. "They're doing a whole big content thing about us. Liz and Clark are baseball dedicated now."

"What?"

"The athletic department," he said quietly, but I could tell he was excited, "wants to do a preseason series about the baseball team. So those two are going to follow us around, like, all the time until fall ball ends."

"Talk about a distraction," I said, taking out my laptop and calmly speaking as if it was no big deal, even though my brain was running in a hundred different directions, jumping up and down and shouting.

Because Liz being around all the time was huge, like a golden opportunity to make some headway with her.

But not with her boyfriend beside her, for God's sake.

I mean, wasn't it enough that I'd given her up and walked away? Now I was supposed to spend time with her every day and watch her work closely with Clark?

"Not gonna lie, I won't mind having Liz around all the time."

Yeah, that doesn't help either. I swallowed and didn't look up as I opened my computer and gave Mick a noncommittal "Yeah?"

There was a smile in his voice when he said, "I don't know what she was like as a little kid when you knew her, but she's cool as hell now."

What was she like? For some reason, my mind immediately ran to that night on the beach two summers ago, the night that was now permanently hardwired in my brain the same way breathing and talking were.

I could still feel that night in my bones, I swear to God.

It was two days after we arrived in LA, and we'd been so geeked-out about living in California that we grabbed a blanket, found a beach where we could make a fire, and spent hours there that night, doing nothing but being together on the sand.

I could still see the glow of the fire reflected in her eyes, and I could almost hear the waves and the soft music coming from her Bluetooth speaker.

I remember thinking I had you—

"She was cool," I said. *And she definitely wasn't always a little kid when I knew her.*

"Isn't that right, Truck Nuts?" Mickey yelled around a laugh.

"What's that?" Wade yelled back from the other side of the room.

"I was telling Bennett here that Liz is my hero."

Wonderful. I was positive Liz was looking our way—and her *Clark* surely was too—but I was keeping my head down and pretending I had no idea what was going on outside my laptop.

Wade said, "Just because our girl gave me a garbage nickname doesn't mean she's a hero."

"Says you," I heard Liz mumble as she kept filming.

"Yeah, says you," Mickey said, grinning. He leaned closer to me and said quietly, "He tried hitting on her last year, and she said he was the human embodiment of plastic truck nuts. Obnoxious and try-hard is what she called him."

"He didn't get mad?" I asked, my voice almost a whisper, trying to imagine Liz saying something so ballsy. It seemed way too bold for her.

"How could he when it was *her* saying it?"

"What do you mean? Because she's usually so sweet?" I asked, my lips barely moving because I didn't want her to think I was talking about her.

"No," he said, squinting like that was ridiculous. "It was pretty on-brand for her, honestly, which was why he couldn't be mad. She's like one of the guys—it'd be like *you* saying it to him."

Like one of the guys? I could tell he didn't mean it in a sexist "not like other girls" way, but like he legitimately considered her just some dude he knew.

But Liz was not capable of being "one of the guys."

Was she?

"You're telling me that a girl who looks like *that*," I said, even quieter than before, "is thought of as one of the guys."

He shrugged. "She doesn't date, doesn't take any crap, is hilarious, and she's great at what she does."

"She's dating Clark, remember?"

"I still can't believe that." He screwed his face together like he didn't get it. "So I guess she didn't date until *now*."

I did glance over then, and Clark was standing next to her, saying something that was making her smile the smile that I hadn't seen in so long.

Her undiluted happy smile.

God, that smile.

I stared, frozen, just memorizing the curve of her mouth. I felt more than jealousy as she gifted him that grin—I felt hungry. Desperate. Like he was getting a lavish buffet of something I was starving for. Like he was rolling around in piles of money while I begged for pennies.

Like he'd won the lottery and was making me watch him claim the prize.

Her eyes shifted. Found mine.

Shit.

I winked—*what the hell are you doing, you tool?*—and attempted to go back to studying.

"Waters," Mickey said, his voice freaking *loud*. "How'd you get Buxxie to go out with you?"

Every head in the study hall turned in their direction.

"Are you kidding me?" I heard Eli say from the other side of the room. "Bux and the giant?"

Liz blinked fast, those green eyes looking guilty as her cheeks got instantly pink.

Clark, on the other hand, smiled proudly and put his arm around Liz. "Yes, we're talking, but kindly mind your own business, okay?"

I hate him. I don't care that he's nice. *I fucking hate him.*

Also, why did he have to hang all over her like that with his giant ape arms? Give the girl some breathing room.

She couldn't like it.

I mean, who would want the weight of that ridiculous arm on their shoulders?

"How long has this been going on?" Eli asked, undeterred. "Buxxie?"

"It's new," Liz said, shrugging. "Now shut up so I can take pictures of you geniuses studying, okay?"

I used my fingerprint to unlock my Mac and clicked into email, trying to get control over the way my gut felt when that Neanderthal started laughing like everything was hilarious. I needed to be studying, not creepily watching Liz as she smiled at someone.

Focus, you jackass.

I was looking for the email from my speech professor about our group project, but the first message I saw was from someone named Lilith Grossman, and the subject was "interview." I had no idea who that was, but when I opened it, I found out quick.

Anger filled my chest as I read the message.

From: Lilith Grossman <lgrossman@heftent.com>

Date: September 29 at 4:53 PM

Subject: Interview

To: <wbennett@athletics.ucla.net>

Hi Wes,

As you know, the production department will be

creating a content series for the baseball program. I believe the coaching staff notified the team of my staff's all-access pass to all things baseball, and this will also include player interviews for a "meet the team" segment, which we will begin scheduling in the next week.

I wanted to reach out to you personally because, as I'm sure you're aware, the fans are very excited to have you at UCLA. Not only are you an amazing athlete with a promising career, but your story is one that makes people root for you.

Please let your coaches know your availability. We're excited to chat with you, and I can't wait to dive into this and create a really beautiful story about life, loss, and carrying on.

Best,

Lil

Lilith Grossman

Creative Content Producer

I felt like I'd been punched in the chest as I read it again.

Life, loss, and carrying on?

Was this Lilith person serious?

She wanted me to *dive into* my *really beautiful story*? I wanted to rage as I stared at my computer screen. I could accept the privacy invasion for something that the entire team was being subjected to, but if she thought I was going to include my dad's death in my intro to bump up her ratings, she had another thing coming.

The nerve of this stranger.

"Screw that," I said under my breath.

"Huh?" Mickey said, not looking up from whatever he was working on.

I gritted my teeth and tried to calm down, to not be pissed, but I was just so tired. Everyone wanted to romanticize my story, to act like it was this charming story arc that went something like: boy has everything and loses it, boy works hard, boy gets it all back. The end.

But the reality was more like: boy does something that causes his family to lose everything, boy destroys girl in the process, boy goes home because he has no other choice, boy hits rock bottom, boy works his ass off, boy gets back, but now can he stay back?

That question was the stuff of my nightmares. *What if I get injured? What if my arm goes out and I lose my scholarship before I finish school?* D1 sports were cutthroat; I'd learned that firsthand. If I tanked and a better pitcher was available, they wouldn't think twice about telling me not to return next year. The coaches pretended we were all one big happy family, but I'd lose my spot so damn fast if I didn't perform.

"Nothing." I clicked into to the search window and typed in my professor's name. The athletic department might require the team to let Liz and her boyfriend film everything, but there was no way in hell they were going to force me to talk about everything that happened with my father.

CHAPTER TWELVE

"Not that you're not attractive. It's just that maybe you're not that attractive to me."
—*Holidate*

Liz

The federal statute of limitations for music copyright infringement is three years, but there is a circuit split on whether "discovery" is taken into consideration (when the plaintiff becomes aware or reasonably should have become aware of the infringement).

I was trying to read my notes about *Arnstein v. Porter* at one of the tables in the library, but my eyes didn't want to stay open. It was dark outside, raining, and the building was pretty empty, which was exactly what I needed for concentration but didn't exactly help my tiredness. We'd been "imbedded" for a full week now (Clark was all in on being my partner), and tonight he was covering baseball's study hall by himself so I could get some actual studying done.

Ironically, the study halls that forced the players to keep up with their coursework were taking up every minute of my study time, making me fall behind already. I had a test in the morning over text I'd yet to read, which was never good.

I grabbed my Red Bull, because it was eight thirty but felt like two a.m., and I was taking a drink when I saw him.

Wes.

Immediately, "Everywhere" by Niall Horan cued up in my brain, because it was the only song I could possibly assign to this moment.

Feels like every time I turn a corner
You're standing right there

Because *kill me now*, Wes was studying at a table over by the windows. *What the hell is he doing here?* I liked studying in the music library, as opposed to Powell, because it was small and quiet and lacking in people who might distract me.

But why would *he* be there? He wasn't a music student, and I was pretty sure he was a south campus guy (if he was still going for engineering). In addition to that, I knew he was a freshman, so how had he even stumbled upon this spot?

He had on glasses—he only wore those when his eyes got tired—and his blue baseball cap was on backward, making him look . . . *gaaaaah* so annoying.

Because what were the odds? And how long had he been there?! I wanted to scream because it was ridiculous. How was it that he'd been entirely absent from my life for almost two years, and now all of a sudden he was popping up every time I went anywhere?

And shouldn't he be at the baseball study hall right now?

He was looking in my general area, but hopefully he hadn't noticed me.

Because I still didn't know how to act around him. Clark was a champ and had been doing most of the filming that was Wes-centered, so I hadn't had any one-on-one interactions with him since the day he tried running me down with his scooter.

Thank God.

But Lilith wanted me to help her with the intros next week, so I needed to begin the process of reaching out to the players to schedule our meetings. Players that included—sigh—that guy over there in the glasses.

When I wasn't near him, I was able to think very adulty about the whole thing. Last night I lay in bed thinking things like, *it's been two years*, *that was a long time ago*, and *he doesn't matter to me anymore*. We were in the past, and he was simply someone I used to know.

But for some reason, the second he appeared in a room, those thoughts left my head. They disappeared, and all I was left with was the confusing way it felt like I still hated him.

I didn't care anymore, so why did his face make me want to hurt him?

It could have something to do with the cocky expression he's always wearing. I mean, yes, it'd been years, and we were both over the mess of us, but shouldn't he at least look like he felt the tiniest bit guilty when we ran into each other?

I went back to staring at my book, hoping he'd disappear while I read the text.

But I read one paragraph before I heard, "I know you saw me."

I glanced over and yes—he was talking to me. It would've been yelling anywhere else, talking to someone from a few tables over, but in the nearly empty library, he wasn't even raising his voice.

"How come you aren't at the study hall?" I asked, my eyes going back to the book.

Don't look at his face. His glasses were like Medusa's snakes, capable of turning my already stone heart into something squishy.

Or something.

Shit.

"I needed a break from all the togetherness." I heard him clear his throat before he asked, "How come *you* aren't?"

It's none of your business was what I felt like screaming, but I politely said, "I needed to study. Clark's there."

"Ah, yes, of course," he said, his voice thick with sarcasm as I heard him close his book. "Your boyfriend *Clark*."

I rolled my eyes and kept reading, not wanting to do this. Or anything. I just wanted him to disappear.

"You said it's new, right?" he asked. "You and Clark are *new*?"

I sighed and kept my eyes on the page. "Yes."

"How new? Are we talking a couple days, a couple weeks . . . ?" His voice trailed off as if he expected me to jump in and answer.

And I was not prepared to do that.

Partially because he didn't deserve to know anything about my life—*the dick*—and partially because I had no freaking idea how long my fake boyfriend and I were supposed to have been fake-dating.

Gah.

"I'm not doing this," I said, raising my eyes and glancing his way. "I need to study."

God, those glasses.

"Yeah," he said, slow-nodding as he put his book in his backpack and zipped it up. "So you should maybe just answer quickly. How new?"

"No," I snapped. How did he think he had any right to ask any question about my life? "My love life is none of your business."

"Oh, *love life*?" he asked, narrowing his eyes as his mouth got that old familiar teasing smirk. He slung his backpack over his shoulder and said, "You consider him *love life* material?"

I closed my book and shoved it into my bag. Stood, because I needed to get out of there. "I'm going to go study. Have a great night."

I grabbed my backpack and took one step before he ran over and grabbed my arm. "Wait, Liz. I'm sorry."

I couldn't take a deep breath as he looked down at me, so close, as his fingers burned their impressions into the skin he was touching. He smelled the same—*how does he smell the same*—and my heart started racing.

Dark eyes slid over my face, making me feel weak—*weak too weak oh God*—before he said in a deep, quiet voice, "It's none of my business, and I didn't mean to be an asshole."

I breathed in through my nose, hating the way my heart raced as I smelled the Altoids on his breath. "Okay."

"You ready, Lizard?"

I gasped, jerked out of the moment by Clark, who had somehow appeared out of thin air.

"Y-yes," I said, hating the way my voice wavered as Wes dropped his hand, and I stepped away from him and closer to Clark.

"Ross was pissed you skipped study hall, bro," Clark said,

grinning at Wes like they were besties as water literally dripped from his long hair. "He was all 'where the hell is Bennett?'"

"I texted him—we're good," Wes said, a crease forming between his eyebrows.

"That's great news, because now that we're on your jock twenty-four seven, I don't want you to get suspended and ruin the fun." Ever since I'd told him that it was fine for him to like Wes—that it wouldn't bother me in the least if he fanboyed over my ex (as long as he kept up our charade), because I was totally over him—Clark was an absolute goof. His baseball obsession made him behave like an adolescent superfan. "Are you going to In-N-Out?"

"What?" Wes asked, looking from Clark to me as if he was confused. I imagine it seemed a little bonkers that my "boyfriend" was a Wes stan and not the least bit jealous of our past.

But then our eyes met and held for a second, and I wondered if Wes was remembering how we once called the In-N-Out closest to campus *our* In-N-Out.

Doubtful, I thought, turning my gaze toward Clark.

"Some of the guys are going to get food," he explained, "so I was going to grab Liz and head that way, since I drove here. You can catch a ride with us."

Noooooooo. No! I said, "I kind of wanted to go home now, so . . . maybe . . ."

"You want me to drop you off?" Clark asked, totally missing my attempt for us to ditch Wes.

"Yeah, if you're too tired, you should absolutely go home," Wes said, nodding and looking like he definitely didn't want me to go.

He seemed downright smug when he said, "It's just burgers and fries, Buxbaum. You won't miss *any* exciting moments."

You'd like that, wouldn't you?

"Actually, I *am* a little hungry," I said, not at all interested in going but very definitely interested in not letting Wes Bennett dictate what I was doing. I lifted my chin and said, "I guess we could go for a little bit."

"Awesome," Clark said, beaming, oblivious to the way Wes smirked at me like he knew what I was thinking, and the way I glared back at him like I was trying to make him spontaneously combust with the heat of my hatred. "Let's go, kids."

As he turned and headed for the door without waiting for me, obviously forgetting I was his fake girlfriend, I made the mistake of glancing at Wes.

Who was looking at me with a *wow, nice boyfriend* half smile on his face that made me want to elbow him.

"I can't believe you're getting the truck so I don't have to walk through the rain, hon," I said in a sweet voice, trying to imply that my boyfriend did thoughtful things like this for me all the time. "Thank you."

I swear to God I heard Wes mockingly mutter "hon" just before Clark stopped and turned around. He was the worst actor, because I watched confusion cross his face—*ugh*—before a bell went off in his brain and he nodded. "Of course, *baby girl*."

Baby girl. Ewwwww. Such a gross pet name, one I was positive Wes would be laughing at if I were to look at him.

Don't look at him.

I inhaled through my nose and calmly said, "I love the way you're so thoughtful. I'll just wait at the door while you go get the truck."

"Yeah, me too," Wes said.

That made my head whip toward him in shock. *"What?"*

He shrugged and looked positively pleased with himself. "I forgot my umbrella."

"You're good, Bennett. No need for more than one person to get drenched," Clark said, pushing open the door. "I'll be right back, guys."

I clutched the shoulder strap of my backpack and stared straight ahead, looking out at the rain while wishing the guy to my right would disappear. *This is unbelievable.* What were the odds he wouldn't talk? Was there a shot that he'd just stand there and look at his phone like a normal human whose presence wasn't welcome?

"So does he know about us?"

Yeah, I didn't think so. I sighed and tilted my head, trying to crack my very tense neck. I didn't want to look at him, so I kept my eyes on the door when I said, "What?"

"The big guy from your 'love life' out there," he said with mockery in his voice. "Does he know about our past?"

I *did* look at him then, and I don't know what I expected, but it wasn't sincerity.

Yet there he stood, in those damn glasses and his blue Bruins Baseball cap, looking at me like he was genuinely curious as to whether or not Clark knew about our relationship.

"*Of course* he does," I said breezily, not really knowing what I was going for when I added, "I tell him everything. He absolutely knows that we dated for a few months in high school."

His face lost its softness, his mouth flattening into a serious line as his jaw flexed. "Is that seriously how you think of it?"

For a second, it all came back. I stared at his face and felt faint as everything that had ever happened between us rushed at me. Ketchup hearts and raindrop kisses, Gracie Abrams and tear-soaked goodbyes.

Noah Kahan on repeat for months.

My breath was stuck in my chest as the past hit me like a wave.

"I *don't* think of it," I said, shrugging and doing an incredible job of sounding absolutely unaffected.

Because I wasn't affected. *Dammit.* I said, "It's ancient history."

His jaw flexed again, but his demeanor changed. Like he had an idea, God help me. His eyes got a teasing glint and he said, "So it's totally water under the bridge now?"

I saw the truck pulling up and said, "Why wouldn't it be? It's been years."

"Well, that is excellent news," I heard him say as I pushed open the door.

I took a step outside, ready to be drenched by the rain, but the second I exited the building, Wes's backpack was over my head. I looked to my right, and he was holding it over my hair with one hand, his eyes in front of him like he wasn't even thinking about it.

He was keeping me dry on autopilot.

"Don't overthink it, Buxbaum," he said, still not looking at me while reading my mind. "I'd do it for anyone."

I ignored that—and my stupid fluttery stomach—as I pulled

open the passenger door of Clark's old Dodge truck.

But as soon as I looked inside, I sighed yet again.

Because his truck had a bench seat, which meant I'd be squished in the middle of a Wes-and-Clark front-seat sandwich. I'd ridden in his vehicle many times, but I'd never paid attention to the logistics of the decades-old Dodge.

Until now.

"Need a boost?" I heard from behind me.

"No, thank you," I said through gritted teeth as I climbed into the truck.

I scooched as close as I could get to Clark without getting between him and the stick shift on the floor, but it wasn't enough. When Wes's big body slid in beside me and he closed the door, his thigh was touching mine.

His outer left was touching my outer right, his soft Nike sweatpants touching my black leggings.

I could feel the heat of his leg through the fabric, I swear to God.

I looked down and reached for the lap belt, very aware of how close my fingers were to his waist. Not only that, but his lowered head while he buckled his seat belt had our faces way too close together—*Altoids*—and his hands very nearly touching my waist as he clicked his buckle into place.

I almost headbutted him in my jerking attempt to back away from him.

He gave me a little smile, and I knew I looked like a skittish animal, like one of those cats overreacting to the presence of a damn cucumber.

I could see in those dark eyes that he was fully aware of my internal chaos.

"Cool truck," he said, his deep voice startling me (I *was* a freaking cat, dear Lord) in the quiet truck cab.

"Thanks, man," Clark said, putting the truck in gear and letting out the parking brake. "It w—"

"Speaking of *cool*," Wes interrupted, and I looked away from him to stare at the back-and-forth of the windshield wipers. I couldn't look at him anymore. "I think it's really *cool* that you're *cool* about Liz and me. About our history."

My mouth fell open for a split second, because I couldn't believe he was bringing this up to the guy he thought was my new boyfriend, but I quickly shut it before he knew his assholery had gotten to me. I couldn't stop myself from muttering, "You just said 'cool' three times in one sentence."

"Cool," he muttered back, so quiet that I wasn't even sure he'd said it.

"Why wouldn't I be?" Clark asked, shrugging and leaning forward to turn up the defroster. The windshield was completely fogged over. "I mean, if Liz says it's ancient history, then I'm totally cool. Jesus Christ, it's gonna be a minute—this bitch is impossible to see through."

Wes turned his body a little, so he was facing us just the tiniest degree, and he said, "It's *cool*."

Stop saying "cool"!

"I'm in no hurry," Wes went on to say, "so I'm cool with waiting it out."

The raindrops were loud on the truck roof, and I felt completely and utterly trapped between Nike sweatpants, my lies, and the past.

I reached out and cranked up the volume on the radio, so loud that conversation was impossible, and I swear to God, I heard Wes laugh.

But I couldn't be sure.

Things didn't get any better when we got to the restaurant.

Because as Clark stood beside the big table, filming the guys over there (mostly seniors) and laughing at their antics, I was attempting to take quality stills and keep it together in spite of the fact that the conversation at the smaller table turned toward me.

The smaller table that consisted of Wade, AJ, Mickey, Eli, and Wes.

"How bad was the hangover after your party, Bux?" Mick asked, his mouth full of food. "You were pretty sloshed when we left."

"Shut up, I'm working," I said, pasting a smile onto my face as I kept taking photos.

The last thing I needed was for Wes to think that my drunkenness had anything to do with his appearance in my house.

"Wait—Buxbaum was hammied?" he asked, a smile in his voice. "The Little Liz I used to know was not a drinker."

"Obviously I'm no longer 'Little' Liz," I snapped, keeping my eyes on AJ through the lens as I took photos of him shoving French fries into his mouth and grinning like a child.

"Obviously," Wade agreed, which made me flip him off.

"And no one says 'hammied' here, Bennett," I added grumpily, sounding like a pouty child.

But something about the stupid word everyone in our high school used to use for partying irritated me. I'd been gone for years—hadn't even returned for breaks—so the last thing I wanted was to be reminded of those silly little Omaha details.

Gaaah why does he always make me revert to Little Liz?

"I'm gonna start, though," AJ said. "I like it. I am gonna get fucking *hammied* next weekend."

"I was *hammied* as shit last Friday," Wade declared, grinning proudly.

Mick was laughing when he opened his big mouth and shared, "I don't know if I'd say she was *hammied*, but she was screaming along to every word of 'Sabotage.' It was very impressive."

"Not doing this," I said, lowering to my knees to get a shot from below the table, thankful the camera was in front of my hot face.

Because "Sabotage." There was no way Wes was missing that reference, dammit.

I loved that song my senior year and used to crank it in Wes's car all the time. We used to sing-yell along to every word with all the windows down.

So yes, I'd been absolutely *hammied* at my party while I'd screamed the lyrics in an attempt to exorcise old demons.

"I want to hear more about 'Little' Liz," Eli said, taking off the lid to his cup before raising it to his mouth. "What was Buxxie like in high school?"

I held my breath and waited, wanting to disappear. I wished the floor would open up and swallow me whole as I waited for Wes Bennett to mess with what I had here, to poke his finger into the relationships and reputation I'd built for myself in California.

"Liz was always," he said, pausing like he was searching for the right words. Since he was sitting beside Mick, I was able to see his face through my camera without him seeing me watching.

And suddenly my heart was in my throat because he wasn't wearing the I-live-to-mess-with-you expression anymore. His mouth was relaxed in a soft smile when he grabbed a fry and said, "Her own person. She was that girl who didn't follow the crowd unless they were going to the same place she was already planning to go. She did her own thing."

Wade looked directly at me—through the camera—and teased, "But she had braces and glasses, right? I bet Bux rocked a retainer in her yearbook photo."

I coughed out a little laugh. "I only wore my retainer at night, asshole."

That made everyone laugh, but suddenly Wes's eyes were on mine. We were both smiling, remembering the night on our road trip when he'd discovered I slept in a retainer, and my throat felt impossibly tight.

"If she was that cool," Eli said, "then why'd she date *you*, Bennett?"

It felt like he was talking directly to me when he shrugged and said, "I have no idea."

"Looks like they're done," AJ said, breaking the moment, and I was a little shaky as I turned my camera to get shots of the guys at the other table as they stood and started cleaning up their stuff.

Dinner was apparently over.

Thank God.

But hours later, when I was finally miles away from Wes and in my comfy pajama pants, I was still frazzled. I'd been parked on the couch with my laptop since getting home from In-N-Out, working on a Reel, and I was pretty sure I was finally done.

I hit play, watching it one final time.

Frank Ocean was the perfect backdrop for the BRUINS BASEBALL WEEK TWO piece (I would never not be moved by "Pink + White"), and I knew it was good as I saved the file.

Lilith was going to love it.

But how was it fair that I'd just spent hours—*hours*—mining film that had a good amount of Wes Bennett content in it? Talk about torture. It was obscene that anyone should have to spend hundreds of minutes staring at photos—and videos—of their ex-boyfriend looking hot, right?

It was as if the cosmos hated me and was like, *Y'know what'd be funny? Let's make her watch him working out and wearing a baseball uniform. Oh—and let's be sure she has to stare at shots of him wearing his glasses and studying too; that shit will kill her.*

I sent the file to Lilith and cc'd Clark, and then I shut down and went to bed.

But sleep was elusive.

Because what the hell, Universe?

It just wasn't fair.

CHAPTER THIRTEEN

"How do you know when it's
the right person?"
—*The Summer I Turned Pretty*

Wes

"Settle your ass down, Bennett."

Woody threw back the ball and pulled down his face mask. Dropped to a squat and waited for me to get my head out of my ass.

I took a deep breath, trying to find calm.

"I'm good," I said, desperate to convince him, knowing the coaching staff valued his feedback on all things pitching. I was throwing shit, and I needed to get it together.

I took off my cap and wiped my forehead because it was hotter than hell.

And then I gritted my teeth because Clark was in my peripheral vision, filming my epic meltdown.

As if sucking didn't suck enough, Liz's boyfriend was here to capture the suckitude.

Stupendous.

Because my pitches were all over the place.

No matter what drills we were doing.

The game was next week, and I needed to get all of this *shit* together.

I tried reminding myself it was only an exhibition game, but the reminder didn't help.

It was only an exhibition game, just a casual fall-ball situation where everybody played, but for me, it was the most stressful game I'd ever prepared for. It was the game that haunted me, the game that was going to set the tone for whether I was actually able to get past the nonsense in my head.

And I wanted to get the start so badly, even though it didn't matter.

I flipped the ball and ran my finger along the seam.

Heard my father's voice, loud and clear in my head.

"Dammit," I muttered, then threw the damn ball.

Another wild pitch that Woody had to chase.

"Did you grab my bag?" I heard Liz say from the direction of the dugout, presumably to Clark. "Or is it in the truck?"

I ground my teeth together, wondering if Ross had read my message yet. It was just too much, having the two of them everywhere. After witnessing them hugging as I headed into the locker room to change yesterday, I might've fired off an email questioning whether it was a good idea for the team to constantly be distracted by cameras.

Was I fully aware of the fact that if it was anyone else, I probably wouldn't care that much?

Absolutely.

But this was how it was, and it was bugging the crap out of me.

It irritated me as I threw the next pitch—finally controlled—and I was crazy annoyed while I nailed the pitches that followed.

By the time I was finished, I was ready to rage about their constant distracting presence.

But I was also relieved that I'd stopped tanking.

That my game was back for now.

That I'd fucking *killed* after the initial hiccups, praise Jesus.

"Way to work through it," Ross said as he walked by, not slowing long enough for me to mention my latest email. "The last set was a lot better."

"Thanks," I said, loading my stuff in my bag, so relieved that I'd finished strong.

But as I walked out of the bullpen area, there they were again. Liz and Clark were standing side by side, talking quietly next to the fence *right beside me*, so there was no way to avoid them.

"Hey. Wes." Liz squinted in the bright sun, clearing her throat, and when I didn't slow, she started walking beside me, her boyfriend following at a distance while looking down at his phone. "I'm starting to schedule the meet-the-team intros, and I was wondering when you're available."

I kind of wanted to laugh at that, because from the sound of it, she'd been scheduling them for almost a week. Everyone on the team who I talked to on a regular basis was all set up for their intros already.

I'd been starting to wonder if she was planning on skipping me entirely.

I'd been hoping.

Because even though Lilith assured me via email that they wouldn't ask me about my dad, I was nervous.

"By 'available' you mean . . . ?" I said, unable to stop myself. It was ridiculous how much I'd missed messing with her.

"You know *exactly* what I mean," she snapped, her eyes narrowed in irritation as she looked straight ahead, like she refused to dignify me with a glance. "It won't take more than thirty minutes."

"I'm available now," I said, the smell of her perfume making me drunk on the idea of having thirty minutes alone with her.

"Oh." There was a crinkle between her eyebrows as she blinked fast in surprise and stopped. "Well, I don't think Clark can because he has class."

Perfect.

I hadn't known that Clark was going to be a part of it, and now he wouldn't have to be.

"It's probably the only time I can squeeze you in this week," I lied, "because I'm buried in homework."

That part wasn't a lie. I wasn't sure if it was UCLA, college in general, or just my chosen field of study, but every one of my classes had gone from zero to a hundred on homework mere days into the quarter.

I was swamped.

"No, that'll work, Liz," Clark said, pulling his keys out of his pocket. "We only need one-shot filming for these casual intros, so you can just use your phone."

"I thought we were going to do two," she said, looking up at him with a *help me* look on her face that should've amused me, but it didn't.

It made me feel like shit.

I never would've thought she'd want to be rescued from *me*.

"That was for the interviews, not for the meet-the-team intros." He put on a pair of sunglasses and said, "One'll be perfect. Go nail this down, and I'll see you at home."

See you at home.

That haunted me. I obsessed over it, the logistics of their situation, and my jaw hurt from the clench as I watched him walk away.

They lived together.

In the same apartment.

They were there together, every fucking night—

LA-LA-LA-LA-LA NO.

"Okay," Liz said, squinting up at me as the warm sun wrapped around us. I'd missed her size, the perfect angular distance between her eyes and mine when I looked down at her. She said, "Well, I guess we're doing this now. Let's go to the mound."

"The mound?" I'd pictured us going to a conference room or something.

"I want to center the 'UCLA Baseball' on the backstop behind you," she said, and I could tell her mind was all work now as her eyes narrowed on a spot in the distance. "And the lighting's great. Are you good with sitting on the ground for the interview?"

"Sure," I said, getting tripped up by the closeness of her face under mine. Of long lashes and shiny lips in point-blank range. As if reading my thoughts, her gaze came back to me.

A moment—maybe two—hovered between us.

God, she's so pretty.

At the start of practice, I saw her filming the infield drills and thought no one had ever looked so good in leggings and a Bruins hoodie. Like, the way the blue ribbon in her hair perfectly matched the UCLA on the football hoodie was ridiculous. Seriously. What the hell was she even doing, looking that gorgeous at a practice?

And what happened to the dresses and flowers?

I wasn't complaining, *God no*, but Liz definitely had a different vibe now.

I didn't think I'd even seen her in a pastel yet.

She swallowed—*is she nervous?*—and tucked her hair behind her ears before saying, "So let's go."

She turned and started marching away from me, toward the field, and I was happy as hell to follow, clicking behind her in my cleats. Liz obviously knew her way around Jackie and didn't slow until she was on the field, standing behind the pitcher's mound.

"I'd like to have you sitting on the mound, facing the outfield, just relaxed," she said, staring toward home plate with her eyes narrowed. "Like . . ."

I dropped to the ground, leaning back on my palms with my ankles crossed in front of me, happy to follow her directions.

Her eyebrows squished together as she looked down at me and—*holy shit yes*—her mouth quirked. It quirked for the slightest of seconds, like she wanted to laugh as I rested at her feet with my legs stretched out in front of me.

"That." She tilted her head and looked toward the stands. "That might be perfect."

"Why, thank you," I said, giving her a cheesy grin.

She shook her head and rolled her eyes, but still looked slightly amused.

It feels like I've won something.

"So I'm asking everyone the same questions," she said as she lowered to her knees and unzipped her bag. She pulled out a notebook first, opening it to a page where her perfect cursive was looped all over the place, and then she got out an extendable tripod and started messing with the height. "Very basic stuff like where you're from, what position you play, et cetera. I'm recording the entire thing and making cuts later, so just let me know if there's something you want deleted. And if you wouldn't mind, please answer as if we don't know each other."

"So I should call you *Miz* Buxbaum and ask for your number?"

"Hilarious," she said, her eyes on the tripod. "I just mean that I'd like you to answer as if I don't know your story."

"You *don't* know my story," I said, then wondered why I even said that. "Not all of it, at least."

She didn't look up from her equipment, but her hands stilled for a second when I said that. They immediately went back to work, and all she said was, "True."

I'd always been obsessed with the way the sun played with her hair, and that hadn't changed. Direct sunlight made it shimmer, I swear to God, and every strand looked like copper as she knelt in the infield grass.

She put her phone on the tripod, raised it slightly, then dropped her hands at her sides. "Okay, I think we're ready."

She pressed record, then picked up the notebook.

"So tell me your name, your position, and where you're from."

I can handle that one. "My name is Wes Bennett, and I'm a left-handed pitcher from Omaha, Nebraska."

"Perfect," she said quietly, her eyes on her notebook. "What made you want to be a Bruin?"

"Now or the first time?" I asked.

She looked up from the page, surprised. "Is the answer different this time?"

The truth was that when I was in high school, UCLA was my number-two choice until the night Liz told me she was going there. That changed everything, and after that, no other schools even stood a chance.

"Yes," I said, not sure exactly how to expound upon that. "I've been a Bruins fan my entire life, but the first time I stepped foot on campus, I fell hard for Westwood. So hard that when I decided to go back to school after dropping out, there was no question that UCLA was the only option. I'd rather not play than play anywhere else."

"Good," she said, but there was a wrinkle between her brows, like something about that answer bothered her. I must've read it wrong, though, because she moved on with a very vanilla question. "What's your major and why?"

"I'm majoring in civil engineering with a minor in environmental engineering," I said, realizing I sounded ridiculously boring. "I can't remember why, to be honest, because it's just what I've always wanted to do."

"Math nerd," she said under her breath, a tiny smile on her mouth as her eyes stayed on the page, and I felt that smile in the center of my chest because *holy God, Liz was teasing me*.

About something from our past.

She'd always thought it was funny that I liked math. *How can someone so unserious be good at math?* She sucked at math, and it'd somehow pissed her off that I didn't.

"Stop being so jealous, Libby," I teased back, but instantly regretted it because her smile disappeared the minute I used her old nickname.

Dammit.

"Okay—next question," she said, clearing her throat. "Which of your teammates would you call if you needed a ride at three in the morning?"

"Powers," I said without pause.

"Which of your teammates would you call if you needed help planning a bank heist?"

"Mick for sure," I said around a laugh.

"Which of your teammates would you set up with your little sister?"

"That's not on the list."

"Answer the question."

"None of them," I said in disgust. "Sarah's too young to date college guys."

"She is *in* college," Liz said with a snort, her smile back.

"A freshman," I said defensively. "She's not even eighteen yet."

"AJ Powers is an eighteen-year-old freshman, dumbass," she said, and I knew she was forgetting about the interview entirely. "They are basically the same age."

"Why are you trying to marry my baby sister off to a baseball player?" I asked.

"Why are you trying to pretend your sister's a baby?" she replied, laughing a little.

"I think the better question, for the record, would've been, 'Which of your teammates would you murder for dating your sister?'"

"And the answer to that question would be . . . ?" she asked.

"Brooks."

"Weapon of choice?" she asked.

"Baseball bat."

"I thought college pitchers didn't take BP," she said, and the breeze blew a few strands of hair across her cheek. "You really think you could still connect?"

"I know I could."

"So cocky about your murderous abilities," she murmured, looking back at the notebook. "Okay, so tell me your three favorite things about UCLA so far."

Liz Buxbaum, Liz Buxbaum, and Liz Buxbaum.

"The food, the scooters, and the libraries."

"The *libraries*?" I could see I'd shocked her with that one.

"There's just something about studying in these libraries that feels so innately . . . collegiate, right?" I really was a little in love with them. "Like, you walk into Powell, and it feels like every movie you've ever seen about college. The dark wood, the desk lamps, the intricate carvings on the arched ceilings—how can you not be inspired to read and learn in a place like that?"

Liz was staring at me, her eyes all over my face like she was trying to make sense of something. She probably thought I was being a smart-ass, but I meant every word. After assuming college was no longer an option for me, it was still mind-boggling to be able to walk into Powell and spend hours at a table with only my studies to worry about.

"And what's surprised you most—so far—about UCLA?" she asked.

"Just the fact that I get to be here at all."

She had that crinkle between her eyebrows again, the one that told me she didn't like my answer, but it was the honest-to-God truth.

I woke up every day shocked as hell that it wasn't a dream, the dream I'd dreamed so many nights during the almost two years I'd been away.

I really was back, holy shit.

"I think that's it," Liz said, interrupting my thoughts. She stopped recording and pulled her phone off the tripod. "Thanks a lot for squeezing me in, Wes."

Night or day, Lib. "No problem."

• • •

I basically sprinted to class after that, very late. My professor gave me the stink eye as I slid in the door, sweaty and out of breath, interrupting her lecture because the only available seat was in the center of the lecture hall.

I was mortified as I squeezed through everyone—"excuse me, excuse me, sorry"—plopped down, and unzipped my backpack.

I was mortified, but not actually sorry.

Because somehow, it felt like I'd made progress with Liz that day. She still wasn't happy I was there, but it felt like the ice between us had melted just the tiniest bit. It made the idea of *something* between us seem possible.

I felt hopeful.

But then I didn't see her at all the rest of the week.

I heard she was doing interviews, but they were always when I wasn't around. And Clark was by himself every time my bullpens and workouts were filmed, with no sign of Liz anywhere.

She'd disappeared again, and along with her, my good stuff on the mound had also gone missing.

I was trying my hardest and digging my deepest, but I was painfully inconsistent. One second, I was throwing nasty pitches that had Woody grinning, and the next he was chasing wild shit and my breaking balls weren't breaking at all.

And the exhibition game was just around the corner.

It was a pointless goal, to be nabbed to start in a game that counted for nothing, but for me, that game counted for everything.

And it'd been my primary focus since recommitting to the team.

I needed it to exorcise some ghosts.

I was well aware of the fact that since I was a freshman, I probably wouldn't start in many *actual* games this season, if any.

But Ross thought this one was a possibility.

You throw enough filth to get the start, but you've gotta get rid of the shit, kid.

I finally got desperate, and on Saturday morning I called him.

"Ross here," he answered.

"Hey, it's Bennett," I said, feeling a little weird about calling him even though he always said he was available twenty-four seven. "Do you have any time for extra workouts this weekend?"

"Goddamnit," he said, sounding like he was still in bed. "I've been waiting for you to get your head out of your ass and make this call, but did you have to do it when I'm hungover?"

"Uh," I said, smiling even though he sounded legit pissed. "Yes . . . ?"

"Fuck off," he said, "and meet me in an hour."

CHAPTER FOURTEEN

"I think the three of us make
a wonderful pair."
—*Seems Like Old Times*

Liz

"Good morning, sunshine."

I walked into the kitchen and rolled my eyes as Leo grinned at me from where he was sitting on the counter in SpongeBob pajama pants and a hoodie, eating a bowl of cereal. The weekend had gone by way too fast, and I wasn't quite ready for Monday to be here yet.

I'd spent the weekend editing the player intros and making some Reels, so I was in desperate need of another day to catch up on my studies.

"How long have you been up?" I asked.

I liked getting up early to run before class every day, but Leo liked getting up at four a.m. every day because of no reason. He simply liked *tacking extra time onto my morning*, he said, which made sense on paper but not when it came time to crawl out from under comfy blankets.

"Since, like, four fifteen," he said, shrugging. "Slept in today."

"Uh-huh." I pressed the power button on the Keurig and walked over to the fridge, opening the door to grab my yogurt. "Did you get my rent?"

I usually Venmoed my rent payment to him, but since my grandma gave me a wad of have-fun-at-college money when I visited her last month, I stuck the cash under his door this time.

"Yeah," he said offhandedly, and it still blew my mind that it didn't matter to him.

At all.

Leo, who was the sweetest, most thoughtful human, didn't really think about money because he'd never had to. It was bizarre, the thought of growing up that way. I'd never been poor, but I'd also been very aware throughout my childhood that there were a million things we couldn't afford.

Honestly, I still woke up every morning and squealed a little that I was somehow living in a really nice apartment for the same amount I'd been paying for the dorms.

But for Leo, it was the norm.

"I was thinking we should get a cat," he said, looking dead serious.

I grabbed the tiny jar of Oui and shut the fridge. "Isn't this a pet-free building?"

"Come on, we all see the dog walkers on the elevators and know it's just for show," he said. "I want a fat tabby."

"Aren't your raccoons enough?" I grabbed a spoon and climbed onto one of the stools.

"Watching them through a window is far different than snuggling them," he said.

"True," I said, shrugging. "And I'm game. I miss my cat."

"You should send for him," Leo said, his face breaking into an excited grin. "Fitzpervert can be besties with Bridget."

"You're going to name your cat 'Bridget'?"

"I will if Mr. Fitzpervert is coming to live with us."

"No cats," Campbell said, stumbling into the kitchen. Her long curls were sticking up everywhere, and she was wearing a cropped shirt that said FUCKET and a pair of boxers. "They pee on your stuff, and the apartment will smell like litter."

"You grinch," Leo growled. "Butt out."

"I hate cats," she said, walking toward the Keurig. "I think I might be allergic."

"Liar." I pulled the lid off my yogurt.

"Speaking of liars," she said, turning to point her finger at me. "I thought you said that you and Wes Bennett just 'casually dated' for a couple months in high school."

"Yeah, so . . . ?" I stuck my spoon into my yogurt. "What about it?"

"AJ Powers is my lab partner, and he assumed that I knew that you and his roommate were 'madly in love' your freshman year at UCLA."

"What?" I didn't even know what to say—what to think—as she looked at me like I was a sneaky liar. How did he know that—had Wes said something? "What did he say?"

"We were talking about the party and how fun it was at Fat

Sal's afterward when I totally faced Wade with a map of the United States," she said, opening the coffee maker and putting a pod inside. "And when I mentioned you, he goes, 'It's wild that they were madly in love their freshman year and now they're like strangers.'"

My breath got stopped up in my chest. "Why does he think we were 'madly in love'?"

"Holy crap," Leo said, hopping off the counter and coming closer. "Was Miss Anti-Romance madly in love?"

"Shhhhhh, what else did he say?" I asked, even as my logical brain screamed *it doesn't matter!*

Had Wes told his roommate that we'd been madly in love?

Had he said it recently?

Because I was still a little . . . unsettled by his interview, by how quickly we'd fallen back into what felt like us. The second I let my guard down and stopped focusing on how much I hated him, there he was, lying back in the grass and making me laugh.

Totally unacceptable. Had I learned *nothing* from everything that happened?

"Well, I didn't want him to know that he knew more than me," Campbell said, turning around and shrugging. "So I just kind of said 'yeah, wild' and we moved on. But I want the whole story."

"Yeah, me too," Leo agreed, nodding. "Tell us the story."

"We all deserve to know," I heard from behind me. Apparently Clark was up too, because he said, "Especially me, your boyfriend."

"Gaaaah, I don't want to talk about it," I squealed, no longer hungry for yogurt. Or anything. "The short story is that we dated in high school, went away to college together, but then he almost immediately moved back home because his dad died, and then we broke up. The end."

"That isn't a short story," Clark said, breezing past me on his way to the fridge for his daily morning Red Bull. "That's a lame-ass run-on sentence. You're going to allow us each three questions, or Leo will evict you."

"What in God's name are you wearing?" I asked offhandedly, because it looked like Clark was wearing an old lady's purple housecoat.

"An old lady's purple housecoat," he replied. "It's vintage Kmart that I thrifted and am in love with, so please refrain from disparaging my garment."

"Why are you in love with it?" Campbell asked. "And I don't mean that disparagingly—I'm just curious."

"I appreciate the clarification, and I love it because it feels like I'm just walking around in my underpants, yet I'm covered enough that I can drink coffee on the balcony."

"Can I try it?" Leo asked, looking intrigued by that description.

"It'll be huge on you," Campbell answered. "You're like a foot shorter than him."

"Yeah, hands off my housecoat." Clark opened the refrigerator, grabbed a Red Bull, and shut the door. "Now, my three questions."

"Leo's not going to evict me," I said, rolling my eyes, absolutely unwilling to discuss Wes with them.

"Just answer the damn questions." Campbell crossed her arms and said, "Number one."

"I'm first," Clark interrupted, nudging her over with his hip. "Number one. Why did you break up?"

"Yeah, why?" Campbell repeated, nudging back.

I don't want to focus on this when I have an entire day in front of me, dammit. I shrugged and said, "I thought we were good, and then one day he just said he didn't want to do the long-distance thing anymore."

"So he broke up with you?" Leo asked, squeezing in front of them both. His blue eyes were huge as he said it, like it was impossible to believe.

"Yes." I swallowed and wasn't going to think about it as anything more than a general "we broke up" story.

"What an idiot," Campbell said at the same second Clark said, "What a dick."

But then Leo ruined my ability to disconnect with his next question.

"Oh my God," he said, looking disgusted. "Since you were long distance, please tell me he didn't do it over the phone like a total ass-weasel."

"He did," I said, inhaling through my nose, trying to remain in the present, but the comment sent me right back to the past.

Because yes—he definitely did it over the phone.

October
Two Years Ago

Wes: Are you home right now?

I was sitting at the desk in my dorm room when he texted,

reading *The Awakening* for American Lit. I got that instant rush of happy dopamine when I saw his name on my phone—WESSY MCBENNETTFACE—just like I did every single day since he'd moved home, and I set down the book and stood.

Talking to Wes was best when I was comfy.

I ran over to my bed, plopped onto my stomach, and texted: **I am home and am eagerly awaiting the sight of your face! 3-2-1 . . .**

In the weeks since he left, we'd fallen into a routine. I went to class all day and he went to work, and as soon as he got home, we basically FaceTimed with each other all night until one of us—or both—fell asleep on the call.

I missed him so much, and nothing was the same with him gone, but the fact that I could still see him all the time, and talk to him, made it work.

But instead of hearing the familiar "incoming FaceTime" sound, my phone actually started ringing. *He was calling me?* I answered on speaker with, "Did you forget how to FaceTime?"

"No." I heard him clear his throat, and then he said, "I just thought it might be better to call you today."

"But whyyyy?" I teased, rolling onto my back and looking up at the ceiling. "I miss out on seeing your dumb face if we talk on the phone the way our ancestors used to. What are we, boomers now?"

"We need to talk, Liz, and—"

"Don't you know that you can't use the expression 'we need to talk' in daily conversation?" I teased.

He sounded stressed, which wasn't unusual since his dad died, but I was good at teasing him into relaxing. Lately he seemed distant when I called, but I wasn't taking it personally because life kind of sucked for his family at the moment. I joked, "Movies have made those words a no-no. Maybe say . . . 'guess what' instead, or perhaps 'let's have some wonderful discourse, Lizzie.' Anything is better than 'we need to talk.'"

He sighed, and it hurt my heart that he was having a rough day.

But then he snapped, "But we *do* need to talk."

I sat up, immediately knowing this was different. He sounded nothing like himself, not like the Wes he was with me. He sounded . . . detached.

Clinical.

Like a stranger.

Stop overthinking, I told myself, staring down at the flowers on my yellow sundress. *Things are just tough for him right now.*

But I knew in the back of my mind that he hadn't even sounded like this on the day he'd gotten the call about his dad. He'd been devastated and sad, but he hadn't sounded *cold*.

"Okay, so let's talk," I said calmly. There was no reason for me to feel the rising panic that had my heart racing. "What's up?"

I heard him take a deep breath, and then he said, "This long-distance thing just isn't working for me."

"What?" I had no idea what he meant by that. "What do you mean?"

"I can't do this anymore, with you on the other side of the country and me back here," he said, blurting it out like he'd practiced it a thousand times. Like he'd been thinking about this a lot. "It just feels like we're delaying the inevitable."

"What are you saying? What's inevitable? Do you want me to move back?" My hands were shaking as I tried keeping up with words that didn't make sense. Last night, we'd fallen asleep together on the phone while watching a *Friends* marathon, and just the other day he'd randomly texted at three in the morning to tell me how much he loved me.

So he definitely wasn't, like, breaking up with me.

So what was he doing?

"Or are you talking about returning to school?" I asked. "I don't know if—"

"I think we should take a break," he interrupted, sounding frustrated.

"You do?" I felt all the blood rush from my face, and I could hear my heart beating in my ears as his words kept echoing in my head. *I think we should take a break.*

"It just doesn't work, living separate lives. I think it's better if we both just do our own thing and move on."

"Move on?" I felt like I couldn't breathe. "Are you breaking up with me, Wes?"

Even though it was obvious, I was somehow still utterly shocked when he said, "Yes."

I gasped.

"Oh," I managed, incapable of anything more. My throat was tight as I blinked back tears, as I tried figuring out how this was happening.

Wes is breaking up with me.

"Please know that it isn't you, Lib," he said, his voice cracking.

"You're amazing and perfect, but it's just not meant to be for us anymore."

I wanted to say something, to scream *You're wrong! What are you doing?!*, but I couldn't speak. There were a thousand sobs inside me, filling my throat and making it too tight for words. I couldn't see the flowers on my dress anymore, the tears blurring out everything but the California sun that was shining through the window, garishly mocking the moment with its brightness.

"I'm sorry, Lib," he said quietly. "I'm so sorry."

Through the haze of my shock and heartbreak, I saw a reason that made sense.

A reason that didn't make it hurt any less, but I loved him, so I'd have to accept it.

I wiped at my cheeks and tried sounding like I was fine. "I know everything's a mess right now, so it's fine if you want to take a break from us while you're dealing with all of it. I'll still be here as your friend, and we can revisit the rest later."

"No, Liz." He made a noise, like an unhappy laugh or a groan, and then he said, *"No."*

"No?"

"No, don't you get it?" He sounded upset now. "I need a clean break. From *us*."

I felt like I'd been slapped when he said that, like a part of me was being ripped away. "You don't even want to be friends?"

"I think it's best if we call it done and just walk away."

"Oh my God," I whispered. I could forgive him for anything

after what he'd just gone through, but I didn't know how he could do this. How he could want this.

He was the center of my world; *we* were my center.

How could he be fine with not being in my life anymore?

God. *He didn't want me in his life anymore.*

"Is this why you didn't FaceTime?" I said, hating that he could hear I was crying but somehow unable to stop myself from asking. "Because you knew it'd be awkward as hell when I started crying?"

He didn't say anything. I waited, but he didn't say a word.

"Wes."

"I have to go now," he said, his voice thick and quiet. "I just . . . can't . . ."

And then I watched through tear-blurred eyes as the call was dropped and his name disappeared from my phone's display.

"Hello?" Campbell snapped her fingers in front of my face. "Where'd you go, Elizabeth?"

I blinked and felt like I'd just gone back in time. Literally. I gave my head a shake and said, "Ugh—to the bad place."

"So what happened after that?" Leo asked. "He broke up with you, and then . . . ?"

"Then I bawled my eyes out for a few months and moved on," I said, as if it'd been that easy. "End of story."

"What about *him*, though?" Clark asked. "He's back at UCLA—how did that happen?"

"I genuinely have no idea," I admitted, really curious about that part of it. "I've stayed in LA every summer to work, and my dad comes to California for holidays, so Omaha is like a former life, in a way. The only person I keep in touch with is my friend Joss, but she pronounced him 'dead to her' when he dumped me, so she's never mentioned him. I literally know nothing about his life after we broke up."

"I think we should table the questions for now," Clark said, pushing Campbell out of the way as he stepped forward to lean his arms on the counter in front of me. "I don't like your face right now. You okay, kid?"

"Of course. I'm good," I said, grateful for my friends as Clark smiled at me with fatherly concern in his eyes. I was also grateful that I meant it—I *was* good. It'd been years, Wes and I were different people, and I was fine now.

But I kept thinking about it on my run, the way I hadn't been fine for a long time after the breakup. I cried a million tears into the Emerson Baseball sweatshirt that I didn't give back, mourning a loss I couldn't understand.

It'd been impossible to accept, going from *madly in love* to *utterly alone* overnight.

God, I'd foolishly overthought so many things from that phone call.

He sounded sad. Did his voice crack at the end, just before he hung up? What if this has everything to do with his dad's death and he still actually loves me?

Maybe I should call him.

I'd deluded myself into believing so many things about that conversation until I went home for Christmas break. Then I learned—on New Year's Day—the real reason why he'd dumped me.

It had nothing to do with his father, or him somehow still loving me, and everything to do with a beautiful girl named Ashley.

I'd been a foolish, silly-hearted little love lover back then.

But now I am not.

My brain hit reset when I showered, thank God, and I spent the rest of the day focused on my classes. I had two tests—aced one and struggled with the other—before lunch, and then a guest speaker in my last lecture gave me a hand cramp from all the copious note-taking.

By the time Clark pulled up so we could go to Jackie, I was exhausted.

My phone buzzed.

Lilith: Can you post another Reel today?

I got into the truck and replied: **After practice?**

She texted back: **That's perfect. It's been a couple days, and with the exhibition game around the corner, we need to be pushing out a lot more.**

I shot off a quick **of course**, thrilled that she trusted me to post content without running it past her first. I was excited about that as we drove toward the field, and when "Supermassive Black Hole" came up on Clark's playlist, I knew exactly what I was going to do.

I loved Muse—especially the *Resistance* album—but it was impossible for me not to picture the *Twilight* baseball scene when that song was playing.

Which cracked my brain wide open when we got to Jackie and the team was already on the field, practicing.

I swapped equipment with Clark because I needed a lot of hitting and running footage, which would be perfect to set with the song and do a spin-off take of the iconic (in my opinion) vampire baseball scene.

So he was taking stills, and I was on video.

And honestly, it was clicking so well, and I was so into it, that I didn't even notice Wes.

I dove in the second we got there, thrumming with the buzz of freshly sparked creativity. I focused first on hitting drills, getting as many long-ball shots as I could from every batter. After that, I switched to base running, really zooming in to capture the snap of the ball as it landed in the glove.

It wasn't until I decided to get pitching shots, really wanting the long extensions that accompanied the release of the ball, that I actually noticed Wes.

Of course, he was on the mound, so he didn't even know I was there.

He'd always been hyperfocused when it came to baseball. His entire demeanor changed when he jogged out of the bullpen, the easygoing attitude replaced with an intensity that burned white-hot in the darkness of his brown eyes. Like a match had been tossed directly into the fuel of his passion.

That jarring contradiction, the crackling electrical undercurrent juxtaposed over his quick-to-laugh carelessness, was a powerful thing to behold.

He was that way—zero-to-one-hundred intensity—with a

couple other things as well, but I sure as hell wasn't going to let my mind wander in that direction.

Ahem.

Focus, Liz.

Film, Liz.

And film I did.

The more I filmed, the more I noticed the tiny details.

Like the way he still flipped the ball and trailed the seam with two fingers before every throw. And the way he still squeezed the ball and took a big, deep breath before every pitch.

Something about those things felt romantic, the ritual and habit of his hands on the ball. It was almost as if his fingertips and those stitches were a comfortable old couple, intimately familiar with every inch of each other after a lifetime of shared touches.

I need to get some up-close shots of his hands on the ball.

I kept filming.

And God—he was an artist with the ball.

He *was*.

The way his face went blank and intense, all at once, just before he let loose with a throw that was violent in its speed, slapping into the glove with brute force, yet incredibly nuanced in its pinpoint accuracy.

His long, lean arm, fully extended on release.

The kick of his leg as he fired the ball.

The rushing exhale of his breath when he let it fly.

I was on my knees, on my stomach, on my tiptoes, and on the

stepladder; he was giving me every shot I wanted and making me greedy for better angles. Circling like a planet in orbit as I needed more, more, more. Even after he finished pitching, I filmed him playing catch with Mick and Wade, my camera now fully obsessed with his left hand and its relationship with the baseball.

"Think we got enough?"

"Huh?" I lowered the video camera and was shocked to see Clark—or anyone, for that matter—beside me in the dugout. I'd been so sucked into the balletlike mechanics of that ball and its journey from Wes's hand to the sweet spot of the bat, that everything else in the world had ceased to exist.

"You are in the zone, Bux," he said, shaking his head. "You usually only give me that stupid stare when you're doing music."

"I, uh," I said, for some reason out of breath and still not quite there, "I was getting amazing vampire baseball footage."

Because he was Clark, he knew exactly what that meant, and he squealed. "Yes! Supermassive Cullen family, fucking yes. This Reel is going to be amazing, bro."

He was right—it would be. And as I listened to him go on about it, I got even more excited. Because I'd been able to forget—emotionally—about my history with Wes when he'd been pitching. The flashback from earlier that day was gone, nowhere to be found as I did my job.

I, Liz Buxbaum, could focus on Wes Bennett, the ace pitcher, and concentrate on the creative part of my job without falling apart.

He was just another random athlete at the university.

This wasn't going to be a big deal at all.

CHAPTER FIFTEEN

"Oh my God, look at your face.
You love her."
—*Prom Pact*

Wes

I stepped under the showerhead, turning my face up and letting the hot water pour over me. I was one of the last guys there because I'd stayed late to talk to Ross after practice, so it was quiet in the locker room.

My muscles were sore, I was tired, yet I couldn't remember the last time I felt this alive.

Because *praise Jesus*, after working my ass off over the weekend, I was back. I'd just spent an entire practice being Steady Freaking Eddie, as consistent as I'd ever been in my entire life. Pitching actually felt *fun* again today, mostly because my dad's voice hadn't whispered a single syllable as I threw strike after strike.

I hadn't wanted practice to end.

Especially when Liz was there the entire time, filming me.

Sure, Clark was around, but that dude was taking random pictures of everyone.

Liz, on the other hand, had been primarily focused on me.

I knew she was just doing her job, but anytime she was in my world, I was happier.

I got dressed and was almost ready to take off when I saw it.

The starting lineup.

The starting lineup for Saturday's exhibition game was taped up by the door.

My good mood was immediately wiped out by stress as I slowly walked over. Half the guys probably hadn't even looked at it because it wasn't a real game; who cared who was starting? The coaches were going to rotate everyone in and out, so it legitimately didn't matter.

To anyone but me.

I inhaled through my nose and stepped closer, my eyes tracking down the list, looking for the pitcher.

"You up for it?" I heard from behind me.

"What?" I turned around, and Ross was leaning against the wall, looking down at his phone.

"We've got you down for the start," he said, his eyes still on the phone. "And I just want to make sure you're ready."

"Seriously?" Normally I'd try to be cool, but it was Ross. I was beaming like a goddamn toddler as I couldn't stop myself from yelling, "You're not messing with me, right?"

"Christ, Bennett, you're embarrassing yourself," he said, but the smile on his face was almost as big as mine. "It's just an exhibition game—settle down."

"I can't," I said, wondering why my throat was scratchy.

"I know." He gave me a nod, like he was acknowledging the *everything* that the exhibition game meant to me personally, and said, "Just don't do something stupid like busting an ankle or throwing out your arm before Saturday."

"I won't," I said around a laugh, a little too close to happy tears for my comfort.

I pretty much sprinted out of there (after ripping the paper off the wall and putting it in my bag because I knew my mom would want it), filled with a wild energy that gave me the urge to turn cartwheels all the way back to campus, I swear to God.

The second I was outside, I FaceTimed Sarah.

"What?" she answered, and it looked like she was walking to class. Or from it. She was definitely walking somewhere on campus as she said, "Why are you bothering me when I'm late to class?"

"Because I thought I should give you a heads-up that I'm starting Saturday, just in case you want to ditch Stanford to road-trip it down here and catch an exhibition game."

"Oh my God!" Sarah screamed, her face swallowed by that little-brat smile of hers. She stopped walking and said, "You're starting, holy shit!"

"Right?" I said, still in shock.

"Did you tell Mom yet?" she asked, still squealing. "I doubt she can come, but she'll want to know! Oh my God!"

"No, you're the first person I called," I said, wondering if I'd ever be able to stop smiling.

"As it should be, Wesley," she laughed, raising a knuckle to wipe the corner of her eye. "Gaaaah, I'm so happy for you!"

Sarah was one of the only people who actually understood why it was so important to me, which made it important to her, too.

It felt big for the Bennetts, after everything.

It was a chance for a redo.

"Thanks," I said, swallowing hard. "I'll let you get to class, and I have some happy skipping to do that cannot be done properly—or safely—while holding a phone."

"Yeah, you go. Safety first. Later," she said, laughing as she disconnected the call.

I was on cloud nine for the rest of the week, feeling like I'd passed some sort of test by getting the start. My mother bawled like a baby on FaceTime, which made me get a little choked up. It also made me remember the time I'd avoided FaceTiming Liz because I didn't want her to see *me* cry, but no way in hell was I looking back at the past right now.

Not when there was so much to look forward to.

That forward-only vision was the main reason I gave a big old "hell no" to Lilith Grossman when she emailed again, asking if she could do a follow-up interview to the one Liz had already done.

She said she'd love to really delve into the amazing way I'd "overcome adversity."

No fucking thank you.

I'd been a team player and answered Liz's questions like a

good boy, but I was hard-passing on anything more.

Especially when Liz wasn't involved.

I pitched lights-out at all the practices leading up to the game, and by the time Friday night rolled around, I had a hard time sleeping because I was so excited.

It was finally here.

But the instant I woke up Saturday morning, I could feel that the stress was back. Every ounce of excitement I'd had was now replaced with fear. *What if I fail?* I laughed with the guys when we grabbed breakfast at B-Plate, trying a fake-it-till-you-make-it attitude as they acted like it was just a regular day, but my stomach was in a thousand tiny knots as I forced down a Bruin scramble and some oatmeal.

And as we rode to the field in Mick's car, I contributed to their inane conversation while trying to shut down my inner monologue that went something like *don't screw up don't screw up don't screw up*.

I needed to get a grip, but it was like my brain was fixated on all the ways this could go south. Getting the start had put one of my ghosts in the grave, but what if I screwed up? What if all I'd accomplished with the start was to showcase how hard I could choke in a game?

What if I proved to the coaching staff that they'd been wrong to give me this second chance?

"Why so quiet, Bennett?" Brooks asked as we did stretches on the field. He was relaxed and grinning, his knee planted in the grass, and I was jealous of his energy. "I don't think I've heard you say dick today."

"Dick," I muttered with a forced grin, working into shoulder rotations while attempting some deep breathing.

I looked out at the stands and inhaled slowly through my nose. It was a warm California afternoon, with barely a breeze, and a record number of fans had turned out for the exhibition game. The packed-out vibe at Jackie was electric, with music booming through the speakers as the snap of balls hitting gloves was like bonus percussion to the party vibe.

It was fall-ball perfection.

I let out my breath through my mouth, glancing toward where my sister was sitting with her feet propped up on the seat in front of her, a blue *B* painted on her cheek.

God, she's a cheeseball, I thought, and seeing her obnoxiousness somehow helped.

This is what I've been working toward, and I need to enjoy it.

I told myself that as I finished stretches, but as soon as I grabbed my glove and started warming up, my dad's voice was all I could hear.

What was that, Wesley? Squirrely shit, I heard as I threw high and inside, just as clearly as if he'd been on his feet in the stands the way he'd been at all my high school games.

Stop it.

I wiped my forehead as Mickey threw back the ball.

It's only warm-ups. *Chill.*

But when I threw a wild pitch that Mick had to chase, I started freaking out a little.

Because I was going to blow it.

No wonder you didn't want me to come to the game last time, I heard my dad yell from the stands. *Quit messing around and throw 'em the gas.*

Dear God. He'd said those words to me—*quit messing around and throw 'em the gas*—no fewer than three million times over the course of my life. It'd been annoying as shit when he was alive, but now it was like nails on a chalkboard, mixed with a bloodcurdling scream.

I was obviously losing my mind when I couldn't stop hearing my dad's voice, right?

I took a deep breath, trying my hardest to concentrate on clearing my mind. I closed my eyes and tried to find calm.

But I could only picture his face.

Which kind of made it hard to breathe.

I threw another pitch.

Mickey should punch you in the face for making him chase that trash. I looked out at the stands, at the spot behind home where he'd always stood, but no one was there.

Of course not.

Because he's dead, you psycho.

I was going to blow it, goddamnit.

CHAPTER SIXTEEN

"I love you. I knew it the minute I met you.
I'm sorry it took so long for me to catch up."
—*Silver Linings Playbook*

Liz

"Why does he look like that?"

"Like what?" Clark was on my left, filming, and I was crouched over by the visitors' dugout with my camera.

"Like he isn't pitching," I said, my zoom fully engaged on Wes's face. "He always looks like he's going to murder someone when he's throwing, but today he looks like he needs a nap."

Clark made a noise like he found that funny. "I don't know what that means."

I watched as Wes threw another ball that Mickey had to chase, and I could sense in the dugout across from me that the coaches who appeared to be standing around doing nothing were actually watching closely.

I looked through the camera and could almost *see* the doubt about the new freshman lefty. It had that vibe, like they were watching something fall apart and didn't quite know what to do.

Shit.

Regardless of my feelings for him, I didn't want him to fail.

"It means he needs to find whatever always pissed him off on the mound," I said, feeling panicked as Wes looked nothing like the way he'd looked every time I'd ever seen him pitch. "Or something."

I wasn't sure why, but I felt anxious. Like, anxious to the point where I wanted to talk to him, to find something I could say to remind him to chill the hell out and just do what he knew how to do.

Just pitch, Wes.

I didn't know him anymore and had no idea what was going on in his head, but it was obvious that his issue was there. He still had the talent and mechanics, but he was clearly sabotaging himself.

Which, honestly, wasn't surprising.

Right after his dad died, when his coaches wanted to know when he'd be coming back to school, Wes kind of lost it. I vividly remember the panic in his eyes as he told me (on a FaceTime call) that he didn't think he could even look at a baseball now that his dad was gone, much less throw one.

The idea of it made him physically ill.

So that had to be what this was, not the actual pitching itself.

He had to know that, right?

I mean, of course he did.

But what if he didn't in this moment? I set down the camera, reached into my bag, and ripped a page out of my notebook.

"Can you do me a huge favor?" I asked Clark, digging out a pen. I knew my words probably wouldn't help, because he had an entire coaching staff with all the baseball wisdom in the world to share with him.

But I was compelled to do *something* to try to help him.

Just in case.

I scrawled out a sentence, then folded the paper in half.

"What do you need?" Clark lowered his camera and looked over at me.

"I need you to run this over to the dugout and give it to Wes Bennett when he comes off the field."

It was insane, both that I thought my words about baseball could help and also that I was trying to help the jackass who'd broken my heart, but I couldn't stop myself.

This wasn't about us, after all; it was about, like, UCLA sports.

"I was going to move over there for the first pitch, so sure," he said, his eyes narrowed. "But are you sure you want your boyfriend to be the one passing notes to your ex?"

"It's not a love note," I said, suddenly nervous as hell about what I was about to do. It was a terrible idea, reaching out to Wes Bennett, but I somehow felt like I needed to. "So I think it'll be fine."

"Then I'm on it," he said, taking the paper from my fingers before walking away.

When the team started coming off the field, I pretended to be taking shots while I watched Wes through the camera lens. He dropped his glove onto the bench and grabbed a bottle of water, his face full of tension.

Where the hell is Clark?

I kept watching, the voyeur with the camera, as Wes squirted water into his mouth, his throat moving around a swallow that was wildly distracting. *Why is that distracting?* My heart was racing—*oh God*—when Clark appeared beside him. I couldn't read his lips, but as Clark spoke to Wes, I had regrets.

Maybe I shouldn't have sent him into the dugout.

Wes lowered the bottle and looked at Clark through narrowed eyes, like he didn't quite understand, but Clark just kept talking.

And then he held out the paper—*oh Gawwwwwwwwd*—the paper that I had sent over.

Oh my God.

I felt shaky as I watched Wes's big fingers unfold the note.

What was I thinking??

His dark eyes spent a few moments on the paper, and I felt like a fool.

Like a ridiculous, childish moron who thought her inane words about baseball could somehow help a D1 college pitcher throw himself out of a funk.

My face was on fire because I was mortified by my impulsivity.

Wes looked up from the paper and said, "Thanks, man"—with a nod—before Clark turned and walked away.

But as soon as Clark was gone, I watched Wes's mouth slide into a slow, wide smirk.

That smirk, dear God.

And then he was looking at me.

Even though the camera was between us, as well as the home-plate portion of the infield, his eye contact was intensely direct as he mouthed the words "thank you."

To me.

I quickly turned my back to him, unwilling to acknowledge what'd just transpired. My face was scorchingly hot as I started taking shots of the outfield, of the fans in the stands, of anything that wasn't Wes Bennett.

I was the world's biggest loser because it was such a Little Liz move, sending a missive via courier to the pitcher in the dugout. The little weirdy loved that stuff, and I was mad at myself for accidentally doing something she would've approved of.

But as soon as the game started, I stopped caring.

The stadium had a first-game-of-the-season electricity about it, where it seemed like every attendee was watching with bated breath in anticipation of what was about to come. It was sunny and warm, without a cloud in the sky, and the whole package was a creator's dream: the perfect setting with the perfect action.

I was almost overwhelmed by the wealth of images in front of me, my hands in a frenzy to capture as much as I could. My camera and I were all over the place, but I froze when "Power" started playing over the speakers.

I turned just in time to see Wes take the mound.

He was all powerful legs and wide chest as he walked out, big and imposing in the pin-striped uniform. He moved like he was going to get an easy three or kick the crap out of any batter who dared to make contact, and holy, holy shit, he was a sight to behold.

Underneath the Bruin-blue baseball cap, his face was a mask of rigid concentration.

I was holding my camera, but too stunned by his walkout to do anything but stare.

Wes Fucking Bennett, ladies and gentlemen.

I had zero interest in him, but objectively speaking, he looked like baseball perfection.

I moved to a better vantage point so I could get shots of his warm-up throws, which were relaxed and accurate. *So far, so good,* I thought, but I was nervous when the first batter from the other team came out.

Again—I had no skin in Wes's game, but as a fan of all things Bruins, I wanted the team to do well during their first official outing.

I watched Wes take a breath and trace the seam of the ball, and then he kicked up that front leg, and it was on. He threw a fastball down the middle, then another one, then finished off the first batter with a curveball that was ridiculous.

The fans cheered, and I was able to breathe a sigh of relief as Wes readjusted his cap while the next batter came out.

And as I snapped photos of the next two hitters that he made light work of, I realized that my concern for him was actually a great sign. It was proof, indisputable evidence, that I was light-years away from being the girl he'd once destroyed.

Our history was so far in my past that I was genuinely able to cheer for his success.

CHAPTER SEVENTEEN

"You're in love with me. Why?"
"Beats the shit out of me."
—*The Ugly Truth*

Wes

"That felt so damn good."

"Agreed," I said to Mickey as we ran toward the dugout, and I felt like I was floating. I would've liked to be cool and not smile as the relaxed crowd cheered for us, but that was impossible.

Because I'd just pitched a no-hitter.

Granted, it was a one-inning no-hitter in an exhibition game, which didn't mean dick, but it felt like twelve innings in the World Series to me. Swear to God, I felt lighter now than I'd felt since moving to LA, now that I'd pitched through the bullshit.

"Fucking fire, Bennett," Ross said without looking at me as I stepped down into the dugout, and those three words meant a lot.

I wasn't some little kid who needed a father figure now that I no longer had one, but there was something about Ross's opinions—and respect—that mattered a hell of a lot to me.

"Thanks," I said, throwing down my glove and reaching for a water.

I felt like I could do anything.

Because not only had I shut down the voices and pitched my game, but Liz tried to help me.

Liz. Tried. To. Help. Me.

Me.

I kind of didn't know what to do with that, especially when her boyfriend had been the one to bring me the note, but I'd take it.

Because something about knowing she cared that I was struggling felt important. Not for her and me in regard to our past or future, but for me. I'd struggled alone through a lot since my dad died, and it felt good to know she was still there.

She might be further away, and she might not love me anymore, but she was still fucking there.

And that made me feel closer to *whole* than I'd felt in years.

After that inning, the rest of the game was like a party.

I stood in the dugout, leaning on the rail with guys on both sides of me, and for the first time since committing (the second time around), it felt like I belonged. Like I was supposed to be there. I realized at the bottom of the ninth, as we beat on the fence when the closer came in, that I finally didn't feel like the guy who found a way in but still wasn't sure if it was going to stick or not.

No, it was *my* team, and I wasn't going anywhere.

After the game, I grabbed a quick dinner with Sarah before she went to meet up with friends she had in LA. It was laid-back, the perfect ending to the day, and it wouldn't be my sister if she didn't butt her nose in and say, "I saw Liz by the dugout, by the way."

"Yeah?" I said, rolling my eyes as I finished the last of my steamed rice. I loved the Boiling Crab—we'd come here with my parents on my first college visit—and I basically wanted to lick my plate clean every time. "Congratulations on having eyes."

"Thanks," she said, grinning as she lifted her last crab leg. "But what are you waiting for with her, Wes? Why don't you—"

"Shhhhh," I interrupted, flicking her crab leg so it fell onto her plate. "Save the bossiness for tomorrow. Don't ruin my moment."

"Dammit, Wes," she said around a laugh as she retrieved the leg.

The truth was that I doubted anything could hack the raging buzz I had from the one-two punch of good baseball and Liz Buxbaum. I was on top of the world, and even though I knew she'd be excited about it, I couldn't bring myself to tell Sarah about the note.

Because what if she found a way to explain it away?

That note was on a piece of paper that came from Liz's notebook (she *loved* notebooks and usually had no less than six going at once), was folded by Liz's fingers (the same ones that had danced magic over piano keys while I begged for more), and was handed off by Liz's grip (that I could still feel on my shoulders) to be sent to me.

To *me*.

I didn't want it to make sense, to be honest, because it felt like a beginning.

"Fine. But I think you're a moron for not saying anything when she's right there," she said. She took a bite before adding, "You are a fool for pressing your nose against the glass when there's still a chance you can have that donut."

"You did *not* just call her a donut."

"Just because there's another customer inside the bakery with your donut in his cart doesn't mean you can't still grab it. Pastries are fair game until they hit the conveyor belt."

"I . . ." I stopped and dropped my fork, shaking my head. It was hard not to laugh all the time when dealing with Sarah because she was so . . . *Sarah*. "I'm not sure if I should be concerned about your intensity for baked goods, horrified you're wielding such terrible analogies, or focused on straightening you out."

"All of the above, probably," she said, shrugging. "Also, I have regrets because I think 'donut' could be a euphemism for something nasty, but I'm not sure."

"You're an idiot," I laughed, reaching for one of her fries.

After she dropped me off, I decided not to go out with the guys. I wanted to savor the waning hours of the memorable day, so instead of hitting a party, I hit the steps outside my dorm. I leaned back on my elbows and looked up at the dark sky, soaking in the warmth of the Westwood night as the quiet sounds of Saturday-night-on-the-hill played around me.

I pulled out my phone and scrolled through my contacts until I got to her.

Libby.

I'd deleted all previous messages after the breakup, mostly because I knew I'd never stop rereading them like a favorite book. I could see myself as an eighty-five-year-old man, no longer communicating in any language other than recycled Buxbaum if I didn't make it disappear.

I looked at her name and paused, wondering if I should do it.

"What the hell," I muttered to myself, then thumbed out a message.

Is this still your number, Buxbaum?

I don't know what I expected, but it wasn't immediate conversation bubbles.

"Holy shit." I sat up straight, staring at the bright phone in the darkness, but the bubbles disappeared almost immediately.

Is it her? It has to be her, right?

People didn't actually get new phone numbers, did they?

I sat there with my phone in my hand for a long time, waiting, but she never responded.

Not that I'd expected her to, but after the note, it suddenly felt like anything was possible.

Which explained why, on Monday, the smell of her perfume had me searching for her in the hallway as I walked out of chem. Thousands of people in the world probably wore that scent, but the second it found my nose, my eyes were on the hunt for red hair.

And that old song found my head.

You got anesthesia in your Chanel No. 5 . . .

I squeezed around the girl in front of me, who was slow-exiting CS50 while looking down at her phone, and as soon as I cleared her—

Holy *shit*.

There she was.

Liz.

I almost didn't believe it.

She was actually there.

She was standing by the wall on the other side of the doors, watching on tiptoes as the people poured out of the lecture hall.

Like she was looking for someone.

I had to force myself not to grin as I went straight for her. "Can I help you find someone, Buxbaum?"

She hadn't seen me coming, so she looked at me in surprise. "Oh. Um, hey, Wes."

"I can't believe you're stalking me already," I said, reaching out a hand to mess with her hair. "And we *just* reconnected."

"Haha," she said, but she didn't roll her eyes. And she didn't smack my hand. No, Liz tucked her hair behind her ears and said, "I actually was waiting for you."

Oh, what's this?

Something shot through my body—*happiness, maybe*—as I committed to memory the way Liz Buxbaum looked on the day she'd shown up at my building to wait for me.

Long curls, pink lips, white cardigan, white jeans.

"Do you have five minutes?" she asked, leaning in a little like she didn't want anyone to hear her. "I just need to run something by you really quickly."

Did I have five minutes? For Liz? My entire life, the answer to that had been something along the lines of *hell fucking yes*. Electricity still shot through every cell in my body when she spoke to me, and I was positive that was never going to change.

For better or for worse.

"It's work-related," she added breathlessly, as if to make sure I didn't think it was personal.

It was idiotic that something similar to disappointment settled in my belly. *What did you expect, that she was going to tell you she missed you?*

I mean, of course it was work-related.

"I have to get to my next class," I said, injecting boredom into my tone so she didn't see how pathetic I was, how off I'd been about what her appearance here could mean. "Is it something your big man can help you with?"

"No," she said, her eyes flashing with irritation before she plastered on another made-up smile and said in a weirdly peppy voice, "But it's five minutes, Wes. Surely you can spare five tiny minutes."

"My next class is at Kaplan," I said, curious to know what she was up to, "if you want to walk with me."

"Okay," she said, nodding and adjusting her backpack, but I could tell that her mind was going a million miles an hour. We didn't talk as we walked through the crowded hallway, but once we stepped outside, she cleared her throat and repeated, "Okay."

I glanced over at her (well, down and over because she seemed shorter all of a sudden) as we walked on top of the red bricks of the courtyard, and something about the moment slapped me with a homesickness so strong, I nearly stumbled.

How was the strength of my want still so overpowering?

I mean, the setting was messing with me for sure. The tall trees lining the sidewalk, the stone buildings, the immaculate fall vibes as students walked to class in the warm afternoon sun; this was everything we'd experienced the first time around.

Those Polaroid days of our first week at UCLA.

I'd piggybacked her down this very path when her shoes gave her blisters, and she joked that we were like Jess and Rory at Yale, if Jess had wanted to go to Yale and Yale was hot and had leaves that only turned marginally yellow.

She'd assigned "In Between" to what she called our "WesLiz montage."

Knock it off.

"Thank you for letting me talk to you," she said politely, looking like she was about to launch into a prepared presentation. "I promise to stay under five minutes."

"See that you do," I said, looking away from her and at the space in front of us as we walked, the damn lyrics ribboning around the campus trees.

He hates it when she's crying, he hates when she's away
Even at their worst, they know they'll still be okay...

"Of course," she said, going even harder on the manners. "So here's the thing. I know Lilith has reached out to you about doing another interview, and I totally understand why you declined."

"You do," I said calmly, more as a statement than a question as I struggled to digest what she'd just said. Was she seriously here to try to talk me into doing Lilith's interview? *That* was what brought her to my side of campus? To convince me I should tell my story of "overcoming adversity" so the athletic department could get more clicks?

"I mean, I totally get wanting to keep your personal life private," she said. "But she really just wants to talk about how you came to be at UCLA—and on the baseball team—again. That's not really so private, is it?"

I kept walking, knowing she was probably right, but still feeling apprehensive as hell.

Because not only did I *not* want to revisit that time in my life, but there was also a lot of stuff that went down in my family that I really didn't want to share with the public.

In the past, when faced with awkward silence, Liz tended to ramble.

Apparently my lack of response triggered that reaction in her, because she launched into a babbling sales pitch, going on and on about how nice it would be for me to be able to share what'd happened with the world.

When we got to Kaplan and stopped walking, she finished with, "It's an incredible story, the way it all transpired, and I think it'd be really cool for you to share it."

"What's incredible about it, exactly?" I asked.

"What?" She looked surprised by that question, her eyebrows crinkling.

"I'm just wondering what you know about my 'inspirational story,'" I said as I realized I had no idea what she knew about my return. "And why you think it's inspiring at all."

She pressed her lips together and looked at me, her eyebrows scrunched as the breeze lifted the tips of her copper hair. *God, I love those freckles.* She sighed, pushed at her hair, and admitted, "To be honest, I don't know anything. But if Lilith thinks it's a good story, then it's a good story."

So she'd never been curious enough about me to look. *Noted.*

"Who the hell is Lilith, anyway?" I asked, unable to hide the irritation. "I don't think I've even met her, yet she always seems to be in my inbox."

"She's my boss. I'm her intern."

"Oh, well that clears it up." I could tell by the way Liz raised her chin that she didn't feel like elaborating, so I said, "Well, I appreciate you crossing campus to do her dirty work, but please tell her 'no, thank you.'"

"'No, thank you,'" she repeated slowly, obviously surprised I didn't cave. She cleared her throat and said, "So, no, then? You won't consider it at all?"

"Nope," I said, allowing myself to stare into her eyes for a second under the guise of polite eye contact.

My happy place.

"Why not?" she asked, her eyebrows going down. "I promise that we'll give you total control during the interview, and this will give you the chance to make your story what you want it to be."

I shrugged, knowing my story would always be the story I didn't want it to be because it centered on my dad's death. "I just don't."

"What can I say to convince you?" she asked, sounding—and looking—a little desperate. "We'll let you review footage, we'll cut anything you want us to cut, we'll reshoot—"

"I'm not doing it," I interrupted, hoping she'd just accept it and move on.

"Why won't you at least *consider* it?" she asked, her pitch rising in frustration. "It's one tiny interview, Wes."

"That I would like to pass on," I repeated. "But thank you."

"Gaaah," she said, then continued through clenched teeth, "why are you so stubborn about this?"

"Why are you so hell-bent on making sure it happens?" I asked, and as soon as I said it, I realized that was it. The thing that I was missing. "I seriously doubt that you care to hear my making-it-back-to-LA story, so what's the deal?"

She blinked fast. "I just think your experience—"

"Bullshit," I interrupted.

She blinked faster. "Don't you want to tell—"

"No," I bit out, running a hand over my head. "What's in this for you, Liz? Why are you trying so hard to talk me into it?"

"Because I don't want to let Lilith down, okay?" she said, her voice rising as she squinted into the sun. "I don't expect you to care, but Lilith is, like, a really big deal in the industry. She has a million connections that could mean everything for my career someday. So if I have a chance to do her a favor, I *am* going to be hell-bent on making it happen."

Her cheeks were red, her eyes hot, and my chest was burning as I watched her crackle.

"Please just consider starting the interview," she said, reaching out her hand and setting it on my arm. Squeezing just the smallest amount, the physical manifestation of her need to convince me. Did she even realize she was touching me? "If it's too intrusive, you can stop, but at least try."

I still didn't want to do it, but I couldn't deny Liz what she wanted.

I was a weak, weak man.

I looked into the eyes that I saw every night when I closed my own and said, "Okay, I'll do it."

CHAPTER EIGHTEEN

"As you wish."
—*The Princess Bride*

Liz

"What?" I wasn't sure I'd heard him right. "You seriously will?"

I couldn't believe it.

When Lilith asked me that morning if I'd be willing to talk to Wes for her, to put in a good word and convince my *old friend* to consent to the interview that he'd refused (multiple times, apparently), I knew it was a terrible idea.

Wes would either mess with me for funsies or just straight-up refuse.

Either way, I wouldn't get the win for Lilith.

But here he stood, his dark eyes serious as he watched me, almost like no one else was there. Like he couldn't see the people going around us and into Kaplan, and his only thought was on me and our conversation.

He said, "Yes. But under one condition."

I inhaled through my nose, trying to snort some patience because here it was. Knowing Wes, this condition was going to make my life hell. I looked up at him and said, "What's the condition?"

He said, "I'll do the interview, but only if *you* ask the questions."

"But that's Lilith's job," I said, ignoring whatever wildness was going on in my stomach as Wes spoke to me with the kind of intense eye contact that would've dropped a weaker version of Liz. I let go of his arm—when had I even grabbed it?—and said, "I can't do that."

"Then I can't do the interview," he said, shrugging as if he didn't care before turning and walking away from me.

"I seriously can't tell my award-winning filmmaker of a boss that I'm doing the interview for her documentary—come on," I yelled at his back, trying to convince him. "And why would you want that? She's way better than I'll ever be."

"But I trust you," he said, turning around and walking backward. "I don't want to discuss this with anyone, ever, but if I have to, I'd choose you over anyone else."

I trust you.

It hurt, how hard that sentence smacked me, because he shouldn't. He didn't deserve to trust me.

I'd choose you over anyone else.

And he hadn't chosen me, not in the past.

Not when it mattered.

For some reason, his calm words that should've felt . . . nice to hear maybe, I guess, knocked me a little off my foundation, making me wobbly.

It's all in the past, I reminded myself.

Now we were just two people who used to know each other.

I took a deep breath and said, "I can ask her, I suppose."

"Yeah," he said, nodding. "You should do that."

"Okay. Um." I was rattled when I said, "When are you available to do it?"

He stopped at the bottom of the stairs and crossed his arms, watching me with an unreadable expression on his face. "I'll have to check and get back to you. Do you still have the same number?"

Oh God.

We both knew what he was asking. Wes was asking if I'd gotten the text he'd sent the other night.

"Yes," I said, my voice barely audible.

Because the emotions that'd run through me when I'd seen his name on my phone had been almost too much. *Wessy McBennettface.* It was like getting a text from a dead person, and I'd been off-kilter the rest of the weekend.

Because what could he have possibly wanted?

Probably to thank me for trying to help him during the game.

That was what I told myself, but the part of me that thought things like *what if it was something else?* was still frazzled, days later. I took a deep breath and met his eyes.

God—the way he was watching me made butterflies go wild in my stomach, because he looked at me like he knew me better than anyone else in the world, like he was seeing my every thought and remembering our every moment.

His gaze not only saw through me, but it wrapped itself around me like a pair of strong arms.

His gaze was more than familiar.

His gaze was home.

His gaze was backyard bonfires and late-night phone calls and cross-country road trips that led to hotel rooms with soft sheets and cool, heavy comforters.

"Sad Songs in a Hotel Room" started in my head as I clenched my fists.

He had no right to look at me that way anymore.

"So," I continued, hitting the syllable a little loudly as I forced myself to keep going, to look away from something that he'd destroyed a long time ago. I chose to look at my fingernails when I said, "I guess text me your availability, and I'll let you know when and where."

"Is your boyfriend going to be there?"

"Who, Clark?" I asked, looking up, then wanted to kick myself because *who else would he be referring to, dumbass?*

"Do you have other boyfriends at the moment, Buxbaum?" His eyes were a little squinty, like he was amused by my obvious discomfort. "A harem of giant blond cameramen?"

"Funny," I muttered under my breath, rolling my eyes.

"I was surprised he was your errand boy on Saturday." He was watching me that way again when he said, "Really interesting relationship dynamic, by the way, having him pass notes to your ex."

"It isn't. At all," I said, instantly regretting the defensiveness in my voice because the Wes Bennett of my childhood lived for that reaction. I tucked my hair behind my ears and said, "I mean, I don't even think he considers you my ex because he knows it was just a few forgettable months when I was a teenager."

"Did you know that you always swallow after you tell a lie, Libby?" He tilted his head and his mouth slid into a slow, wide smirk that was such a throwback that I felt it in my toes. "You say the untruth, then immediately swallow and push your hair behind your ears. It's the same tell you had when you were eight years old."

I rolled my eyes again, forcing myself not to mess with my hair. I wanted to say something biting, something that would hurt him, but I still needed his help. So I just said, "Okay."

Which was so unfair; I hated that.

I also hated that he was seeing my cheeks get red.

"Okay." His smile went away, but the light was still in his eyes when he said, "And yes—I'll text you my schedule."

"Thank you," I said, unsure how to behave when he was giving me what I wanted while also kind of being an asshole. "I really appreciate this."

"No problem," he said, his eyes meeting mine. "As long as it's you, not Lilith."

"So we have a deal?" I asked, needing confirmation.

"Yes, ma'am," he said, his dirty half smile returning. "Did you want to shake on it? Or . . . something else?"

My cheeks caught fire and my mouth kind of fell open for a second, momentarily incapacitated and unable to come up with a single word of response.

Which made him say, oh so quietly, "There she is."

"What? Who?"

"Little Liz."

Before I could respond, he turned and started jogging up the steps, but not before I saw his grin.

It wasn't fair, the way he still managed to get the last word. It was irritating as hell, and it annoyed me the entire trek back to Morgan. I didn't see the green trees or yellow flowers as I marched across campus, because in my brain, I kept seeing his dickish smirk and hearing his deep voice saying *there she is—Little Liz*.

But the irritation dissolved the minute I stepped into Lilith's office and gave her the news.

"That's wonderful!" she said, looking like perfection in her white button-down, man's necktie, black cigarette pants, and perfectly tailored pink wool blazer. She was standing in front of her brainstorming glass dry-erase board, scrawling illegible notes that only she could read when she added, "I don't care who asks the questions as long as I get to write them and edit the film. Thank you, Liz."

"You're welcome," I said, relieved Wes's condition wasn't a dealbreaker for Lilith.

"I've already drafted the interview, so I'll just send you the questions. I've got a direction in mind," she said, pushing up her black glasses, "so even though some of the inquiries might seem irrelevant, you'll have to trust me that they're leading somewhere."

"Okay," I said, nodding, entirely confident she knew what she was doing.

"I also find it interesting that young Mr. Bennett requires you exclusively," she said with a grin. "But I'm not saying a word."

"Oh, no, it's not like that," I sputtered. "He just—"

"Liz, I know. It's fine," she said, turning to give me her full attention while her smile was almost a laugh. "It doesn't matter. I want his story, and you're getting him to give it. Relax."

"But I just want to make sure you know that—"

"I do, I promise." She held up a hand and said, "So when is this happening?"

"He's going let me know later today what time he's available."

"Okay." She went back to her board, scribbling something impossible to read. Lilith was back on her outline and in her own head when she said, "You can use my office for the interview, and I'll clear out whenever it's set."

"Perfect," I said, and for the first time since my conversation with Wes, it hit me, the fact that I was going to be doing another interview. I'd been so busy scrambling to get him to agree, then scrambling to get Lilith okay with his terms, that I hadn't had a chance for it to sink in.

I was going to have to sit down with Wes.

That thought hung over me the rest of the day, totally filling me with dread as I went to class and the library. Because asking him random baseball questions was no big deal, but I was worried about *his* questions.

Was he going to ask me about the note? About Clark? I just didn't want to deal with the *everything* that accompanied a conversation with Wes Bennett.

At ten thirty that night, when I was exhausted and exiting the library, my phone buzzed.

I took it out and my heart stuttered—again—at the sight of that stupid contact name.

WESSY MCBENNETTFACE.

I needed to change that immediately.

I clicked into "edit profile" and changed the contact name to WES.

Wes: I have time tomorrow morning after lifting. Does that work for you?

I'd make it work. I replied: **Yes. Do you know where the Morgan Center is? We can do the interview in MC491.**

Wes: Sounds good.

I texted: **Great. See you then.**

My phone buzzed again.

Wes: WAIT WAIT WAIT.

I looked at the message. God, what was he doing? I rolled my eyes and replied: **What?**

Wes: What are you doing this very second?

I replied: **Besides regretting that you have my number?**

Wes: Yes. Besides that.

I don't know why I answered, but I texted: **Just walking out of the library.**

Wes: Oof—late night on campus. Which library?

I stared at the phone, unsure how to proceed. I could ignore him, but since I had to meet him for an interview in the morning, that seemed stupid.

But I didn't want to text with him either.

We weren't friends.

I replied: **Powell.**

I'd gone there specifically because I was afraid of running into Wes if I went to the music library.

Wes: No shit? AJ's at Powell right now. I'm literally sitting on a bench outside of Royce, waiting for him.

Powell and Royce were directly across from each other. The two buildings literally faced each other, so Wes was in the vicinity.

I speed-walked toward the steps, wanting to get out quickly before I ran into him.

I texted: **You didn't have anything to study tonight?**

Wes: I did, but I studied at the music library. Just got done.

Ha—I knew it! I *knew* he was going to be at the music library. I started down the steps, proud of my mind-reading abilities as I texted: **Cool. See you tomorrow, Wes.**

Wes: Good night, Buxbaum. Also—Liz?

I texted: **Yeah?**

Wes: The speed at which you're descending those steps is terrifying. Slow down before you trip.

I cough-squeaked a noise as I read his words—gaaah, he was watching me from somewhere in the dark—and forced myself not to look over my shoulder as I replied: **Good night, creeper.**

CHAPTER NINETEEN

"I'm scared of walking out of this room and never feeling the rest of my whole life the way I feel when I'm with you."
—*Dirty Dancing*

Wes

"I don't know what you're so nervous about."

"I don't either, to be honest." I probably looked like I was talking to myself as I jogged down the hill, talking to Sarah on the phone as she jogged with me from Stanford. Running together had become a thing with us over the past couple of years, so even though we were at different schools, we still ran together a few times a week.

She said, "I think it's probably because aside from Dr. Allison, you've never really talked about the specifics of that era with anyone but me."

"*That's* true," I said. Not even Noah had known what things were really like, and I'd talked to him all the time back then. And Michael found out eventually, but even he didn't know everything. I squinted into the bright sunrise and said, "I guess I just feel . . . *unprepared* to talk about it."

"But maybe look at it this way," she said. "It felt good to discuss in therapy, right?"

I went right at the bottom of the hill. "It did, but this isn't private, and oh, yeah—*Liz* will be the one asking the questions."

"Because you requested that, dipshit," she said, and I knew if she were here, she'd be giving me her patented you're-an-idiot look. "But for real, there's nothing to be afraid of. They want to know how you came back to baseball, so you just tell them about how it happened."

"But Mom—"

"Mom is fine," she interrupted. "Mom has overshared her side of this to anyone who'll listen. Mom tells strangers at the grocery store about how it all shook out. Mom would be disappointed if you failed to mention her issues, and you know I'm right."

She *was* right.

Our mom entered therapy as a broken woman and came out . . . well, *less* broken and filled with the unstoppable urge to tell everyone she met about her experiences.

Even the experiences that didn't paint her in the best light.

"Just treat this as free therapy, stop overthinking, and talk to Liz like you're telling *her* the story. Do it and be done."

Do it and be done.

That was a good way to think of it—I was going to do it and be done.

"Speaking of Mother Dearest, has she confirmed that she's picking us up from the airport?"

"Yeah, she finally got back to me yesterday," I said.

The house had finally sold, so Sarah and I were going home next week to help my mom with the closing. Neither of us were looking forward to it, but we couldn't expect her to do everything herself.

I also kind of wanted to say goodbye to the house.

Even as I absolutely *didn't* want to say goodbye to the house.

I went back to my dorm and showered, and by the time I was walking into Acosta for the team lift, my hesitancy about the interview was gone. Or minimized, at least. I was going to do it and be done, check that box, and then hopefully never be asked about it again.

After jumping on the force plate and going through dynamic warm-ups on the turf, I headed back to the weight-lifting racks.

"Where's your boyfriend, Lizzie?" I heard Eli say as I turned the corner.

And I froze in my tracks when I saw her, even though Liz filming workouts shouldn't have been a surprise.

There was Eli, doing medicine ball two-way dribbles against the wall while Liz filmed him.

"He has a name," she said, her attention on her work. "And he wanted to get film of the strong guys today. So that's why I'm on you."

"Hey—why so mean?" he asked, smiling.

"You called me 'Lizzie,' so you're asking for it, aren't you?"

Neither of them noticed me, so I took a second to drink her in.

She was wearing jeans and a black T-shirt, but the Docs she had on and the black bow in the back of her curls made it more than just a T-shirt and jeans.

They made it Liz, even without the flowers and pastels.

I watched her record him, and there was something about seeing her work that fascinated me. She obviously knew what she was doing, but it was also obvious that she was enjoying herself. Her body—and her camera—were in constant motion while she filmed, and her focus reminded me of the way she focused on music when she was working on a playlist.

The rest of the world existed, but she was uninterested in anything other than what she was working on.

God, I love that about her.

"Good to see you made it home okay last night, Buxbaum," I said, needing to see those green eyes on me.

As expected, she whipped around like I'd startled her.

But just as quickly as she'd looked shocked, she covered it up. Liz swallowed and said, "Of course I did. I trust you had no problems getting back to your dorm?"

"I love when you worry about me, Libby," I said, eating up that frustrated fast-blink, *hell yes*.

She rolled her eyes, raised her chin, and I wanted to drop to my knees.

"I just need you alive for the interview this morning." She tilted her head and said, "After that, feel free to fall off a cliff."

Eli started laughing, and so did I. Liz's mouth softened, like she wanted to smile with us but wouldn't allow herself the luxury, and I was taking that as a win.

"*Now* you seem like exes," Eli said. "Also. Liz. Am I allowed to call you 'Libby'?"

"Not if you want me to answer," she said, borrowing the line from *Pretty Woman*. Her lips lost any idea of a smile, and she said, "I hate that nickname."

"Oh, you do not," I said quietly, teasingly, wishing I could step closer and lower my face to the spot on the side of her neck that always smelled ridiculously good. *"Lib."*

I walked away because there were some dead lifts with my name on them, but the casual run-in with Liz had me anticipating our meeting. Not the interview itself, but because Liz and I in a room together, even if there was a camera and a boyfriend, was still better than not being with her.

And I was starting to suspect she didn't like Clark *that* much.

I mean, they seemed happy enough when I saw them together, but I'd spent a lifetime watching her crush on guys. Wide eyes, pink cheeks, knowing smiles—those were her symptoms. I'd witnessed them time and again, hating them at the very same time they charmed the hell out of me.

No one wore lovesick like my Libby.

Maybe it was wishful thinking, but I'd never seen her look at Clark that way.

I showered after lifting, putting on a decent shirt and jeans instead of my usual shorts/T-shirt combo. I didn't know what was expected of me, clothing-wise, but I didn't want to disappoint Liz, so I was erring on the side of caution.

The sun was bright when I exited the building and walked toward Morgan, and for the first time, I wondered what my dad would think of this. I'd avoided thinking about him lately because

I didn't want to regress on the field, but I couldn't help it now, as I prepared to talk on camera about his death.

Part of me thought he wouldn't like anyone knowing anything about our life, but I also knew he'd relish any opportunity for my game to be under the spotlight.

Hell, if he were here, he probably would've already called Lilith to see why they weren't doing a bigger piece on my pitching. He'd say something like *Why would you waste time talking to every mediocre player—some of them won't ever see the field—when you can showcase a future star?* I kind of wanted to laugh at the realization and call Sarah, because it was 1,000 percent what he would've done.

That realization actually made me feel better about the whole thing.

When I got to Morgan, I went straight to MC491, even though I was a little early. I raised my hand to knock on the office door, which was cracked, but then I stopped myself when I saw Liz sitting behind the desk.

My breath kind of got trapped in my lungs for a second, to be honest.

Because I'd never met this version of her before.

She'd changed since lifting, switching out the casual T-shirt for a black blazer, a crisp white shirt, and a tangled mass of pearly necklaces wrapped around her neck. Her eyes were lined, her lips red, and her hair was all pulled back into a tortoiseshell clip.

She looked like a force, like she could head a boardroom without a single nerve, and I was hungry to know this person.

"Hey," I said, my voice cracking like I was a middle schooler talking to his crush for the very first time.

She looked up, and the power of those eyes almost dropped me.

God, I love her.

"Hey." She turned her Retrograde Red lips into a polite smile. "You're early."

"Is that okay?" I asked.

Her eyebrows went up. "Did Wes Bennett just ask permission? I feel like I should check your forehead for a fever or something."

"I feel like you should do that too." I pushed open the door and walked into the office, pulled to be closer to her. Needing less space between us. "Where do you want me?"

"We're going to do the interview over there," she said, pointing to a small conference table to the right of the desk. "But Clark isn't even here yet."

"So we're off on the right foot, then," I teased, smelling her perfume and feeling like a bloodhound who'd been given the scent. I had it, and now it was all I could focus on. "Which chair?"

She got up and came around the desk, and *sweet holy foxhunt God save me*, she was wearing tall black pumps. I was intimidated by Liz as she said, "The one with the picture behind it."

"Okay," I said, pulling out the chair and sitting.

Until now, I'd never given any thought to the two years between us, educationally speaking. But as I watched her move effortlessly around expensive film equipment in stilettos, she very much seemed like a junior who knew a hell of a lot more than this nervous freshman.

And those heels. I couldn't stop looking at them. She moved like she'd been born to wear them, looking a million light-years away from the Little Liz who'd wobbled around in toy princess shoes.

"Please don't be pissed at me for saying this, Liz," I said quietly, very aware that this was her world. "But I'm kind of intimidated by how cool you are now."

CHAPTER TWENTY

"I love you very much. Probably more than anybody could love another person."
—*50 First Dates*

Liz

"You are?"

I was impressed by how unaffected I sounded as I managed a two-word response. I think I totally pulled off *mildly amused*, but the truth was that I was kind of having an internal freak-out.

Because over the past couple of years, every time I imagined running into Wes, I just wanted him to think I was cool.

Confident, successful and waaay over *us*.

Too cool for him.

Hell, if I was being honest, Little Liz had worked her ass off her entire *life* in hopes of that jackass next door thinking she was cool.

So it was really jarring to hear him say the actual words.

"I am," he said, his eyes sweeping over me. I felt them everywhere as his mouth slid into a boyish grin. "I tried on two different shirts for today, for fuck's sake."

Oh God. I lowered my eyes to the empty chair across from him, pulling it out and sitting down. My face was hot as I gave him a nonchalant "That's funny."

"Those cheeks," he murmured, his voice deep and quiet.

"Hey, kids!" Clark breezed into the office, dropping his stuff next to Lilith's desk. "Am I late?"

"No," I said, my voice a little scratchy. "Wes was early."

"Attaboy," Clark said, nodding and grinning before walking over and dropping a peck on the top of my head.

Gah.

I risked a glance at Wes, expecting a mocking smirk, but his self-deprecating grin had been replaced by a clenching jaw and hard eyes.

Why does he look like that?

"Did Lil finally send the questions?" Clark asked as he checked the stationary camera I'd already set up on the tripod, the one that would record the entire interview.

"She did, and don't call her that," I said, my stomach filled with the butterflies that had been tearing me apart since I'd opened her email. Her questions were fine, but the thought of asking them—to Wes—was stressing me out.

Somehow I hadn't walked through just how awkward it was going to be to ask him about the worst time of his life. I read her questions and wanted to throw up, so I parlayed that tension into finding the most professional outfit I had in my closet.

I was going to focus on my job, on getting Lilith the footage she'd be proud to put in her film, and try to pretend I'd never heard this story before.

My hands were literally shaking as I grabbed the questions I'd just pulled off the printer before he appeared. "And just a reminder, Wes—these are Lilith's questions. I'm just the one asking for her."

"Got it," he said, his face tense as he sat across from me.

He was wearing a black pullover and jeans, and for some reason they looked really good on him. Not to me personally, but as someone conducting an interview, I recognized that my subject presented well on camera.

Ahem.

"And ignore me, dude," Clark said, looking down at his camera. "I'm just going to be moving around the room to get varied shots. Pretend I don't exist."

"I'm trying," Wes said quietly, "but it isn't easy."

He was looking at me as he said it, and I wasn't sure why it felt like something was hovering between us.

"Okay," I said abruptly, inhaling through my nose and looking down at Lilith's notes. "Are we ready?"

Clark hit record on both cameras. "Ready."

I cleared my throat and said, "Start off by telling me some of the things that made you fall in love with baseball as a kid."

His eyebrows furrowed together, like he didn't understand the question, and for a second I wondered if I'd asked it wrong somehow.

God, I don't want to screw this up. I was so worried Lilith was going to watch the interview and regret sending me. My eyes were frozen on Wes, my brain begging him to give more than a two-word answer.

"Uh . . . it was easy for me, I guess," he said, seeming relieved that the first question wasn't more difficult. He looked into the stationary camera, not at me, when he said, "Hitting the ball was fun, catching the ball was fun, and it felt like I'd always been doing it. I'd go out and swing the bat at my Little League games, not really even trying that hard, and the people in the stands would go crazy because I crushed the ball every time I was up. But it just happened for me, you know? I fell in love because I was doing what everyone else was doing—having fun trying to hit the ball—but for me, it was as natural as breathing."

Thank you for giving a good answer, I thought, relief spilling through me as I nodded. I could still remember the way he'd run around the neighborhood like he owned it, always laughing. It seemed like life had come easily for him back then.

"So how did those specific things push you to get where you were?" I continued, looking down at the paper as I read Lilith's question. "Coming out of high school with nearly every school in the country taking their shot at you?"

I could still remember the first time I learned he was that good. We were in the Secret Area, before we ever dated, and he offhandedly mentioned that he wasn't sure which school's offer he was going to take.

Was that the night we smoked Swishers together?

He made a noise in the back of his throat, like a sarcastic laugh, and said, "It was all my dad. He pushed me to not just be satisfied with what came easy, but to chase what was hard."

"And what was hard?" I asked, mostly because Lilith had mentioned multiple times that I should follow his responses and not just stick to her questions.

"Pitching," he said without a second of consideration. "He pushed me to pitch, pushed me to learn more pitches, pushed me to throw more pitches, pushed me to attend every pitching clinic on our side of the country—he was the driving force that led to it all."

If I hadn't known his dad, this would've seemed like a sweet father/son sports story. But I remembered how hard his dad had pushed, and I knew how much that pressure had weighed down on Wes when he started at UCLA.

"So it must've been huge when you got the offer to come here," I said. "To play for one of the best baseball schools in the country."

"We were pretty pumped, especially after I tore out my shoulder." He nodded and started talking about his senior season, but I got temporarily distracted by his mouth. By his entire face, actually. It was an interesting situation to be sitting across from your ex and allowed to stare at the details of them.

Wes had changed, but it was impossible to put my finger on a specific thing.

He'd just become the man version of the boy that he'd been. It was like everything had been photoshopped to be slightly bigger, slightly harder.

"So we were definitely thrilled with the offer," he finished, his eyes still on the stationary camera.

"I bet." I looked back down at Lilith's questions and wanted to do just about anything other than ask the next one. I was trying my hardest to listen to his story like he was a stranger who I knew nothing about, but the next question—and his answer—was going to ruin that.

There was no way it couldn't.

I kept my eyes on the paper, my pulse pounding in my ears as I asked, "When you initially got to UCLA the first time, walk me through some of the feelings early on—especially those first few days."

As the words left my mouth, my brain played an unwelcome montage of our road trip out to California. The world had been ours as we'd laughed through the mountains and kissed through the desert, and neither one of us would've ever guessed how close we were to the end.

Wes made that noise again, the one that sounded like I was asking him about something ridiculous. He looked down at his hands and said, "I mean, it was everything an eighteen-year-old baseball player dreams about. I was at this big-time campus and everyone was treating me like I was the man. It was exciting and it felt like I was on top of the world with a shiny new life. It was literal perfection, every single piece of it."

It was, I thought, remembering the day we moved Wes into his dorm. There were baseball players all over the place, laughing and trash-talking, and I don't think either of us stopped smiling the entire afternoon. We walked to In-N-Out for lunch and lost our minds over how cool LA was, over the surreal amazingness that we were both there, together.

It *was* literal perfection.

For two weeks.

"I mean, there was baseball hell week, and I kept getting lost on campus," he said with a little smirk, and it felt like I couldn't breathe as I remembered teasing him about his terrible sense of direction.

It kind of felt like yesterday.

"But I was head over heels in love with everything in my life."

He was looking into the stationary camera, but I couldn't stop staring at the brown eyes that I'd been head over heels in love with.

Clark cleared his throat—*thank God*—pulling me out of my own head. I went back to the questions, but my stomach dropped when I read the next one.

"Th-then you got the news of your father's passing," I said, my voice barely there because my mouth didn't want to form the words. "How did you find out initially?"

Pain crossed his face like a storm. His jaw clenched, his nostrils flared, and his Adam's apple moved around a thick swallow. I wanted to tell him not to answer, that he didn't have to answer, but this was only the third or fourth question; I couldn't.

I needed to pull this off for Lilith.

"My mother called," he said, his voice a little raspy. "We were working on pickoff plays at Jackie, the day before our exhibition game, when Coach Ross came out to tell me I had an emergency call."

I couldn't look away from his face, even though I knew the story.

"And she told me he was gone." He shrugged, looking out the window like the scene was playing out on Bruin Walk. His voice was hollow, matter-of-fact, and I felt like he'd forgotten about Clark, the camera, and me.

"Just like that. 'Wes, your dad is gone.' I actually asked her where he went, like an idiot, because I couldn't comprehend her meaning. I mean, I'd just talked to him that morning."

I didn't know this part. My side of the recollection was of him walking into my dorm room when he was supposed to be at practice. Of me saying *What are you doing here?* and of him saying *My dad died* and then breaking down a little.

Honestly, I wasn't sure I'd ever even known exactly how he found out.

"Next question."

"What?" I said, blinking fast, unaware that I'd drifted away.

"What is the next question?" Wes repeated, his face a tight mask, his eyes still *not* on me.

"Oh. Yeah. Sorry." I inhaled through my nose and looked down at the sheet, hating myself for asking him to do this. "Um, what was it like to process that news at that time?"

"Come *on*," he mumbled, exhaling and sitting back in the chair. I didn't know what to say, and I didn't think he was going to give me an answer (and I wouldn't blame him for passing), but then he said, "Um, it was terrible, but processing the news that he was gone—while I was still in LA—was, uh, incorrect, I guess you could say. I processed it in a kid-loses-his-father way, devastated that he was gone, but the gravity of my situation hadn't hit me yet. It didn't occur to me at all that I would go home for his funeral and never sleep in my dorm room again, y'know?"

I didn't want to do this anymore. I knew the story—I was there, beside him, for this part of the story—but I didn't think either one of us should revisit it together. I opened my mouth to comment, because these film packs were supposed to be moderately conversational, but I couldn't force myself to speak.

Or even move on to the next question.

It felt like a lie, like we were acting out the most depressing play in the world, because I knew the answers before I asked them.

"I—I don't think I can do this," I heard myself say, and I struggled for any rational explanation that would make sense to Clark or Lilith. Wes was looking at me in confusion, and I felt Clark's eyes on me as I stood and managed to come up with, "I think someone who didn't know your family and your dad is probably better at—"

"I've got it," Clark interrupted, lowering his camera and coming over to my side. "Why don't you take off, Liz, and I'll finish? We can connect afterward."

I glanced at Wes and had no idea what he was thinking, or what Clark was doing. I only knew that I couldn't do this. I managed to say, "Um, okay . . . ?"

"Yeah, just go," Clark said, smiling as if this was normal. "And the three of us can coordinate the rest later."

"Um, okay. Thanks." I turned and walked over to the door, and as I pulled it open, Clark asked the next question as if there hadn't been the world's biggest hiccup.

"What made you understand that it wasn't the right time to be playing? How did you decide to pack up and leave?"

I didn't know if Wes would answer him at first, but when I looked back over my shoulder, he swallowed and looked at Clark. For the first time since the interview began, he was speaking to someone when he said, "When my mom left and wouldn't come home."

CHAPTER TWENTY-ONE

"No matter what happens to us, every day
with you is the best day of my life."
—*The Notebook*

Wes

Clark lowered himself to the empty chair and set down his camera. "Where did she go?"

For a half second I thought he was talking about Liz, but then I realized he meant my mother.

I looked at his face, and God help me, I wanted to keep going. It didn't make sense, but maybe Sarah was right. Maybe it *had* been too long since I talked about it, or maybe enough time had passed where it was becoming a story instead of something that cut me open and made me bleed.

Even weirder than that was the fact that I was glad Liz was gone. Something about telling *her* the story felt wrong, probably because she'd been there. I'd seen it on her face as I answered, the second she started remembering, and I didn't want her to have to sit across from me and be reminded of a time that brought her pain.

"Wait—getting ahead of things," Clark said, and as much as I wanted to hate the dude, he was just so nice that I couldn't. And I hated *that*. "Why don't you talk about what happened when you got home."

I let out my breath and closed my eyes for a second, remembering.

What happened when I got home.

"Obviously everyone was grieving, but it didn't take very long for me to realize that my mom wasn't handling the loss very well. That she needed help."

Understatement of the century. She couldn't stop crying, couldn't eat, couldn't drive, couldn't work—my mother was a mess.

"But you were eighteen," Clark said. "What could you do?"

"Everything that needed to be done, I guess." I shrugged and said, "She tried, but she was the one who found him, and she just never got over that, I think."

"Is that part of why you left school?" Clark asked, obviously no longer reading prepared questions. "Because your mom couldn't take care of things?"

How was I supposed to answer that?

My mom tried to find a way to cope, but for her, that meant not being in the house where he died. Which was understandable, but Sarah was still in high school and needed a place to live. A guardian. She wanted my mom to come home, but my mother couldn't bring herself to leave her sister's house.

I just said, "She did her best, and I stuck around to help."

The reality had been slightly more nightmarish. No life insurance, coupled with my mom not being healthy enough to go back to work, left me no choice but to work two jobs to keep the house out of foreclosure.

Thank God for the therapy that eventually brought her back to us.

Clark asked, "So at what point did you realize you were done with school?"

"I'm not sure, to be honest."

That was a lie. I remembered the *exact* moment.

Liz came home for the funeral—all my friends had—and the night before they were heading back to school, everyone was meeting up at Liz's to hang out. I was getting ready to stop over when my mom called and asked when I was going back.

I was a little surprised that she was calling, as opposed to just coming over since she was going to *have* to come back soon, but that surprise turned into total disbelief when she asked me who was going to take Sarah to school and make her dinner after I left.

Because my mother had no plans to come home.

She'd started crying, telling me she couldn't handle being in the house where she found my dad and that she couldn't handle *looking* at my sister without remembering that day. I tried everything I could think of to get through to her and make her listen—*Sarah needs you!*—but I finally gave up when the conversation stopped and the only thing I could hear over the phone was the sound of her sobs.

I didn't go to Liz's that night. I sat in the kitchen, drinking my dad's beers and tearing apart the desk, looking at bills and bank statements and trying to figure out how I was going to cover for my mom while she was out.

Because we didn't have some big extended family who would jump in and save us. My aunt Claire was my mom's only sibling, and she was already struggling to make ends meet as a single mom with a deadbeat ex.

And my mom didn't get along with her parents, so the fact that they didn't come to the funeral showed just how helpful they might be. And my dad's parents died before I was born.

So as badly as I wanted to return to my life and go back to LA, how could I?

When I waved goodbye to Liz at the airport the next morning, I could barely manage a fake smile as the oppressive weight of everything lowered its every crushing pound on top of me.

"Okay." Clark looked down at the paper and read, "How did the coaching staff respond when you told them you were quitting school?"

"Uh, they were cool," I said, realizing I'd been so mentally done with baseball at the time that I barely remembered their reactions. "They said they understood that I needed to do what was best for my family."

"Did they try to change your mind or tell you that you could come back?"

"No," I said, remembering a lot of incoming calls that I'd intentionally ignored. "But I made it very clear that I was done with baseball."

Clark looked surprised at that. "You didn't see a path back because of your responsibilities?"

"I didn't *want* a path back," I corrected, scratching my chin. "I never wanted to touch a baseball again after my dad died."

"Tell me about that," he said, and I knew that question wasn't on his paper.

I swallowed and just said, "He was always the center of my baseball world, so I couldn't imagine playing without him."

"Okay." Clark cleared his throat and read the next question. "Did you keep in contact with your UCLA friends after you went back?"

"I did for probably a month," I said, remembering feeling so goddamn alone, like I was on this deserted island that no one else knew existed. "But our lives were so different that after a while, I just couldn't. They were experiencing new things like parties and dorm life, while I was experiencing new things like enrolling in health insurance plans and trying to understand an escrow statement. They were studying so they wouldn't fail their exams, and I was learning how to rewire the thermostat on our furnace because we couldn't afford an HVAC repairman."

I remembered trying so hard, when Liz called, to make it sound like life was normal for me back home because I didn't want her to feel guilty for not being there.

"So what changed last year?" Clark asked. "What made you start throwing again?"

Finally, we'd reached the part of the story that I liked.

"A mean-as-hell friend. One of my buddies swung by the house to say hi, and he found me shit-faced and home alone."

"You were drinking a lot?" he asked, and I wondered if I should've kept that to myself.

Although—*screw it*—it was the truth. Until Michael stepped in, pounding beers while listening to Noah Kahan on repeat was my go-to.

I said, "I got hammered whenever I could, as long as Sarah was in bed, because underage drinking is illegal, you know, and I wouldn't want to be a bad role model."

Clark smiled. "Of course."

"I was a mess, to be honest," I admitted. "So Michael screamed at me and pushed me into a wall. Asked me what the hell I was doing with my life."

"Did you hit him?" Clark asked, grinning.

"No," I said, shaking my head. "I broke down and cried like a baby."

"No," Clark said empathetically.

"Oh yes," I said, smiling at the memory. "You can ask Michael—I was very pathetic. But instead of feeling bad for me, he shoved my drunk ass in his car and drove me to the baseball field. Flipped on the lights and tried to force me to play catch with him."

"*Forced* you?"

"Well, at first he *asked*, but when I refused to even put on the glove, the dick just started throwing baseballs at me."

"Seriously?" Clark started laughing.

"For real. Hard as hell. He pummeled me with baseballs until I had to put on the glove and protect myself because those baseballs fucking hurt. And once I had the glove on, he physically hauled me out to the mound—dragged me, literally—and forced me to throw a pitch."

"And did it feel good?" Clark asked.

"No," I said, letting out a big exhale. "I threw up all over the mound and kind of wanted to die. But he made me give him ten pitches before he'd take me home, and by the time I was done, I realized that pitching made me feel something I hadn't felt in a long time."

"What's that?" Clark asked.

"Control. Since my dad died, I'd had zero control of anything in my life. But that ball in my hand was under my power, and it felt good."

"Is this when you started trying?" he asked. "When did the switch *officially* flip?"

"When my mom got better and my genius sister started getting full-ride offers to great schools, Michael convinced me to reach out to my UCLA coaches."

"And . . . ?"

"And I made some calls and sent some emails. They were nice and sent a few responses back, but when I mentioned the possibility of throwing for them or getting a tryout, they ghosted me. I couldn't reach anyone anymore, which I absolutely understood. A pitcher who takes two years off? That's an absurd gamble. I would've done the same thing."

"So what'd you do? How'd you get them to finally respond to you?" Clark asked.

"I started texting every staff member—all of them—every single day, sending them time-stamped videos of my pitching practice," I confessed, grinning at the memory. "I even emailed the AD every damn day. My high school coach let me use the gun, so I just spam-texted them all videos of me throwing hundred-mile-an-hour fastballs that were right in the zone."

Clark was laughing when he asked, "So did they fly you in for a tryout after all the spamming?"

"Oh, no," I said. "They told me that if I was ever going to be in LA, to reach out and they'd let me throw for them."

I'd never say it on camera, but Ross was the only one who'd been honest with me. He'd called me one afternoon, and said in that minimalist cowboy way of his, "I like you, kid, so I'm going to tell you what you need to hear. It's been too long, and you need to move on. Knock this crap off before you ruin your life wishing."

Clark asked, "So you flew there, right?"

"I couldn't afford to fly; are you kidding me?" I laughed at that, able to laugh now at how impulsive I'd been. "No, I left that night and drove my shitty car straight to campus, with Sarah sleeping in the back seat when she wasn't taking turns driving."

"How long of a drive is that?"

"Twenty-two hours."

"Woooow," Clark replied, his voice loud. "Were they happy to see you?"

"Between you and me," I said, "I think they were pissing themselves. Like, *oh no*, he actually came."

Clark threw his head back and started cackling. He half yelled, "And how was the tryout?"

"Better than I could have ever hoped for."

Two coaches, begrudgingly letting me throw even though it was obvious they weren't considering me. Lots of hushed conversation and awkward tension.

Ross shaking his head when he saw me.

An obnoxious little sister, loudly cheering me on from the empty stands.

A slight anxiety attack as I took the mound and got ready to throw the first pitch.

And then—*perfection*.

Strike after strike after strike.

More coaches watching, one with the gun.

Ross grinning.

More strikes, faster pitches. Ridiculous changeups. Badass breaking balls.

It'd been better than the movies, I swear to God.

When we finished the interview, Clark hugged me—"bring it in, man"—and it pissed me off.

Because it made me feel like an asshole.

I mean, it was an asshole move to be in love with someone else's girlfriend, right? Especially when he was kind of starting to feel like a friend. Like how the hell had he done that, become something similar to a friend?

I didn't want to like the guy, dammit, because it was unfair for me to feel guilty for wanting her.

She was mine first.

As soon as I left the office, I checked my phone and saw a message from my sister.

Sarah: So?? How'd it go?

I quickly fired off: **Shockingly well. I spilled everything and don't regret it yet.**

Sarah: Proud of you, kid.

I replied: **Gee thanks, Ma.**

Sarah: So how did Liz react?

I wasn't sure how to explain it, so I just texted: **Late to class—I'll call later.**

That was actually *not* a lie, so I found an e-scooter and hauled ass toward Kaplan, because we had a test that day that I couldn't miss.

But as I flew across campus, I was kind of a shitshow of feelings.

And not the ones I'd expected.

I felt like I could cry—literally—because I'd just talked through the entire nightmare and hadn't wanted to rage. I also wanted to cry with relief because I *hadn't* felt like crying. Talking about it hadn't gutted me, which felt like a win.

I finally had closure, it seemed.

But it was the idea of that—having closure—that made me emo as hell.

CHAPTER TWENTY-TWO

"You were my new dream."
—*Tangled*

Liz

I was pacing around the production office when I heard the door open.

"That is *quite* the story," Clark said, walking over to his desk and dropping his gear.

"Finally," I said, so happy to see him. I'd blown off my class to wait for him, and it'd been killing me. I'd been pacing like a caged animal, wondering if he was asking Lilith's questions properly, if Wes was answering him, and if Lilith was going to kill me for my unprofessionalism. "Oh my God, tell me everything that happened. And I'm so sorry for falling apart."

"Don't apologize—I get it now," he said, taking the scrunchie off his wrist and pulling his hair up. "The entire time I walked down here I've been thinking about how poor little freshman Lizard must've been so sad."

"Wait—did he mention me?" I asked, scared of the answer.

"Oh, no, he was very careful about that." Clark crossed his arms and said, "He never even mentioned he had a girlfriend when his dad died."

"Oh. Good," I said, relieved. "Now tell me everything he said."

"I don't have time," he said, glancing down at his watch. "I'm late as it is, but you're going to die when you hear the story. Just pull the card and watch it yourself."

"Okay. Thank you so much, by the way," I said, standing to hug him. "I really appreciate you saving my ass."

"What are boyfriends for?" he teased, hugging me back. "I think Lilith is going to love what your boy gave us."

"He's not *my* boy," I said defensively, irritated that he'd say that.

"The way you're focusing on that and not what I said about Lilith speaks volumes." Clark stepped away from me and grabbed his backpack from under his cubicle. "Text me what you think."

"I'll probably show it to Lilith and *then* text you," I said, dreading the fact that I was going to have to show her what an absolute unprofessional I was. She was going to have video proof that I'd lied when I said I could be professional with Wes.

"Cool, cool," he said, and then he was gone.

I took a deep breath, for some reason ridiculously nervous to watch the interview. I'd purposely avoided filling in the blanks via internet research once I knew I'd be interviewing Wes, so I still didn't know the logistics of how he came back. I was dying to find out, but for some reason, the thought of watching him tell the story filled me with dread.

I sighed and loaded the drive, knowing with absolute certainty that I was going to hate what I saw.

But it wasn't just bad—it was *awful*.

The worst thing I'd ever seen.

Because it couldn't have been more than thirty minutes of content, with only a few questions I hadn't seen on Lilith's list, but so many of his answers seemed wrong. *Weren't they?* They couldn't be right, because I'd been there at the time and had known nothing about the things he was saying.

In my recollection, he found out his dad died, and after the funeral he decided to take the semester off because he missed his dad too much to play baseball. It'd gutted him, realizing that he literally couldn't touch a ball without feeling physically ill, but I told him it was fine.

Because it was.

I didn't care if he ever played baseball again.

He took a job at Hy-Vee so he'd be able to afford school second semester (in Omaha), and I used to talk to him every night when he got off work.

So where, in that, did these things he said to Clark fit in?

Had his mother had a breakdown and Wes had to take care of his family? And if the answer to that was yes, why hadn't he told me? And my heart was in my throat when he answered the question about his friends back at UCLA, because I couldn't help but wonder.

Was he talking about me?

It felt like he was.

Had it really been like that for him?

I'd loved texting and FaceTiming every day, and I thought he had too. We used to joke that there was something kind of fun about it, even while it sucked, and we laughed that when he got back to school the next fall, we'd probably miss little things about it.

Like the way he always took a screenshot of our FaceTime calls before we hung up.

I'd felt bad for him that he wasn't in school and had to work, but in my wildest dreams, I hadn't imagined that he was the one taking care of his family.

Escrow statements and rewiring the thermostat?

He hadn't been able to trust me—was that it? He'd felt like he couldn't tell me that his world had collapsed? I remembered him celebrating my tiny school victories via FaceTime, seeming excited when I shared little anecdotes from my music classes; was that a factor? Had I made him embarrassed? Had I been too obtuse?

Should I have known?

When the video stopped, I took it out and went up to Lilith's office. Clark was right—she was going to love Wes's interview. His story about begging for a tryout, then driving cross-country all night with his sister? Even *I* loved that part because wow—what a gamble.

What a perfect ending.

It also made me miss Sarah, who I hadn't thought of in ages.

Lilith's door was closed when I got to her office, and I was nervous to knock. There was no doubt she'd love the interview, but that didn't mean she wasn't going to lose total respect for me, given the fact that I'd choked.

I took a deep breath and knocked, feeling like a naughty child when she said, "Come in," and I nervously opened the door. "Do you have a sec?"

"Of course—come in. What's up?"

I took another deep breath and started talking as I entered. "We finished Wes Bennett's interview, and I wanted you to take a look. Now, I—"

"Ooh, gimme," she said, standing and reaching for the drive in my hand. "Thank you so much for making it a priority."

"Yeah, um, here's the thing," I said, handing it her, unsure how to even explain what happened. "I started the interview, but we didn't get very far before I stepped out and Clark stepped in with the questions."

She looked at me over the top of her glasses. "Was he out of line?"

"No," I corrected, "nothing like that. He was helping me."

"Okay, well, let's watch it. No worries."

It took Lilith no time to have the interview loaded up and playing on her wall monitor.

She steepled her fingers under her chin and watched without a word, her face unreadable. I squirmed in my chair when it got to the part where I stood up and sounded like an unprofessional teenager with my whole *I can't do this* thing, but Lilith's expression didn't change.

And *this* time, I watched Wes watching me freak out, which made my stomach flip. A wrinkle formed between his eyebrows, and he looked up at me from his conference room chair with a million questions in his eyes, almost as if he was asking how it was that *I* couldn't do it when he was the one who'd lived it.

Yeah, fair.

Lilith sat perfectly still until the interview ended.

My armpits were sweaty, and I knew my cheeks were beet red.

"Wow," she finally said, looking across the desk at me. "I already knew the general story, but I am still blown away. Great interview."

"Thanks," I said, waiting for the rest.

"And I have thoughts about Clark's unexpected on-screen appearance."

Aaand here it is.

"Obviously you were struggling, so your intuition—with Clark—was spot-on. It gets so much better when they're talking." She was nodding while she said, "I'm not sure if Wes opens up better with a guy, or maybe it has to do with the fact that the two of you dated, but it's like a night-and-day difference. Don't you think?"

"Yes, I do," I agreed, relief flooding me that she wasn't mad.

"Okay, great," Lilith said, grabbing a pen and writing something in her planner. "I have a million ideas now that are bouncing through my brain, so I need to organize them before they disappear. However, before you go, I wanted to tell you that I watched the Reel you sent over, and I love it. Post it."

"Already?" My voice was a little too high-pitched, but Lilith's glowing endorsement was too fantastic for my voice to remain at normal human decibel range.

"It's perfection—don't change a thing."

"Thank you," I said, beaming like a kid who'd just given her art project to Mommy.

Lilith's praise had me buzzing as I scrambled to make it to my next class on time. *It's perfection—don't change a thing.* I was at a near-run toward Schoenberg Hall when I remembered that I told Clark I'd text him.

I pulled out my phone without slowing, but when I unlocked it, I had an unread text.

From Wes.

I stumbled to a stop, making people go around me as I tapped the message. I was frozen in place, because why would he be texting me?

Wes: You okay?

I blinked and definitely wasn't okay. Not *now*.

Because why would he send me a message like that? I glanced at the time of the text, and he'd obviously sent it sometime after I left him in Clark's interviewing hands.

I had a meltdown and left, which made him send me a text.

Asking if I was okay.

I knew I should probably respond with something like *I'm good, but how are YOU?* or maybe *I am—thanks for checking!*, because he was being nice.

Thoughtful.

But as I kept rereading those two words, hearing them in his voice, I hated all the feelings they elicited.

I didn't *have* feelings about him anymore, dammit.

I put the phone away and went to class, irritated that I was irritated after Lilith had been happy with my Reel. I should've been skipping across campus, but as I took my seat in the lecture hall and rifled for a pencil, I realized that Wes's thoughtfulness had really ruined my mood.

So that night, when I was sitting on the couch, eating beef Top Ramen straight from the pot in front of *Gilmore Girls*, I wanted to scream when Clark dared to plop down beside me and say, "How would you feel about me being friends with your ex?"

I slurped up the noodles while glaring at him. "What does that even mean? Has he offered you a spot in his posse or something?"

He sighed patiently, staring directly at the curly noodles disappearing into my mouth while Kirk performed "The Journey of Man" on the TV. "It just means I really like the guy and don't want you to be pissed that I do."

"Yeah, well, he's a really likeable guy." Had anyone ever not liked Wes? I wasn't a child, and I couldn't tell Clark who he could be friends with, but it annoyed me at that particular moment. "So are a lot of people. I mean, do whatever you want, as long as I'm still number one."

"Don't pout; of course you are," he said, putting his feet up on the coffee table. "But hear me out about something. You should maybe forgive him for breaking your heart. It was a long time ago, and he was going through a lot at the time."

"*What?*" I kind of yelled it. "Are you serious right now?"

"I just, like, sense he wants to be your friend."

"Oh, so you're *high* right now," I corrected, insulted by the way he was butting his nose into a past he knew nothing about.

"For the love of God, Liz, I just felt it this morning, okay? Like, I could see it in his eyes when he looked at you."

"Yeah, well, those eyes *cheated* on me, so no." I gritted my teeth, steeling myself against the anger that was supposed to be gone by now, and said, "I have no ill will regarding Wes, and I wish him the best, but I'm content to stay very far away from him, thank you."

"He *cheated*?" Now Clark was the one kind of yelling, his eyes huge in his face. "He cheated on you? I didn't know that."

"Yeah, well, it's not my favorite thing to discuss."

"I can't *believe* it," he said, shaking his head slowly as if I'd just told him Wes was an actual vampire.

"Right?"

"It's just so hard to believe," he said, looking shocked. "He just doesn't seem the type."

"Trust me, I know," I replied, really wanting him to shut up about it.

"Are you *sure*?" he asked, his eyes narrowing. "I mean, it's just *impossible* to believe—"

"Oh my God, I don't want to talk about this, okay?" I dropped the silver pot on the coffee table and stood. "Be his friend, I don't care, but please just stop talking about him."

I went into my room and slammed the door, so frustrated that I wanted to throw something. After a long day of shutting out unwelcome emotions regarding Wes, I'd just wanted to come home and escape. To watch comfort TV and think about nothing.

Instead, I was treated to my best friend asking me if I was *sure* Wes had cheated on me.

Was I sure?

What kind of question was that?

Wes Bennett had looked me in the eye, on New Year's Day, and told me that he had.

CHAPTER TWENTY-THREE

"I can't figure out the mathematics of this—
I just know I love you."
—*The Holiday*

Wes

"Knock, knock."

I stood at Ross's office door, clueless as to why he'd asked me to see him after practice. I'd thrown well and had been on top of my shit during PFPs, so unless he wanted to kiss my ass for being awesome (which Ross did not normally do), something was probably wrong.

"Bennett." He was sitting behind his desk, looking annoyed. "Come in."

I stepped inside, and when I did, I noticed the blonde.

She was probably in her early thirties, LA beautiful, wearing smart-girl glasses and shiny black high heels that you could see your reflection in. She was sitting in one of the chairs by his desk, smiling like she knew me, while Ross glared like he didn't want to know her.

Interesting.

"What's up?"

"This is Lilith Grossman," he said, looking pissed about it. "She's a film—"

"We've met, though not in person," she interrupted, standing and coming over, holding out her hand. "You've been kind enough *not* to tell me to go to hell when I sensed you've wanted to."

"Nice to meet you," I said, shaking her hand and giving in to a laugh because I liked her honesty. "And you're welcome . . . ?"

That made her laugh, and she said, "I'd like to talk to you for a second—"

"She'd like to *pitch* something to you, is what she means," Ross said.

She gave a little shrug. "He's actually not wrong for once. Do you have five minutes?"

Before the interview the other day, I would've said no. I would've treated her exactly the way Ross was treating her. But it hadn't been too bad, and she'd sent a thank-you email afterward that was really sweet. Apparently she'd lost her dad when she was in high school, so she said a lot of things hit really close to home.

Add that to the fact that Liz worshipped her and Ross seemed to hate her, and she was definitely the most interesting person in the building.

"Sure," I said, following her over to the chairs.

"Before she pressures you," Ross said, "feel free to say no. I fully support your no on this."

"Thank you for that, Ross," she said with a smile.

"Anytime, *Lil*," he drawled, and I was dying to know what was up with those two.

"Y'know, if you want to go throw some balls or guzzle protein powder, I can let you know when we're done with your office," she said, and her smile was deadly this time. "No need for you to stick around."

"It's okay. I'm happy to do it," he said.

"Okay. Wes." She turned her chair toward mine and scooted a little closer. "You gave such a fantastic interview the other day, giving us a peek into your inspirational journey back to UCLA. I was blown away by the picture you painted of your life back home, juxtaposed against your college baseball life here. I can almost picture it. So when I heard from Clark that you're going home to help your mom close everything out, I had an idea."

"Buckle up, Bennett," Ross growled.

She rolled her eyes. "Now, I promise you I'm not trying to capitalize or throw a camera on your tragedy, but as a filmmaker, I know that getting some shots of the house that you grew up in—*and the high school field where you pitched a no-hitter*—could really add to the human side of your story. You repeating what you already told us, while walking through your empty house, would add such a lovely detail to the story."

My stomach sank as I listened, not necessarily because of what she was trying to sell, but because she reminded me that it was almost time for me to walk through the house for the very last time.

"Now," she continued, holding up a hand like she was expecting my immediate refusal. "I absolutely understand if you don't want us there. Frankly, I'm expecting you to say no. But I would be remiss if I didn't throw it out there, just on the off chance that you don't mind having Liz get a little film while you're in town."

Liz.

"You want to send Liz?" I asked. "To Omaha?"

She nodded, and I wondered what that would look like.

Because even though I couldn't imagine having her—and probably Clark—following me around while we moved out the last of my mom's stuff, the idea of Liz being nearby while I said goodbye felt right somehow, or at least the *thought* of it did.

"Uh, can I think about it and get back to you?" I asked, wanting to talk to Sarah and figure out why I wasn't totally opposed to the idea.

Because I should be, right?

"Of course," Lilith said, and I didn't miss the way she looked directly at Ross with a smug smile. "Just let me know as soon as possible so I can book flights if it's a deal."

"Sounds good."

I left the building a little weirded out by the fact that I felt calm. It was surreal that this was happening, that Liz and Co. would be joining me in Omaha, but I felt pretty okay about it. Although to be fair, I was a Liz junkie, always looking for my next fix, and this scenario assured me that one would be coming soon.

I forced myself to go straight to the library because I had a paper to write, and I didn't trust myself at home anymore. Lately, every time I went back to my dorm room, I ended up hooping with the guys instead of studying. It was great living right next to basketball courts, but not so great for my studying.

I slid into a spot at a table, flipping on the table lamp before pulling out my computer. I put on my headphones and got to work, but two things were messing with my concentration.

The first was the guy at the table across from me, who appeared to be attempting to completely gnaw off his fingernails. I didn't know why he'd caught my eye, but I couldn't stop checking every few minutes to see if he was still doing it.

Read a paragraph, then look over—*yep, still chewing*.

Write some sentences, then check to see—*yep, still chewing*.

Focus, Bennett.

But the other thing was Liz. *Of course.* She was all over my brain, stuck in multiple scenarios and places, and I couldn't shake her. I was either thinking about the way she'd looked ready to cry during our interview, the way she'd run down the steps outside the library (in the dark) to avoid me the other night, or the idea of having her with me in my dad's house.

By the time I got back to my dorm, I'd decided to give Lilith the green light. And when I talked to Sarah about it, she was all in. I suspected it was still her trying to get Liz and me together, but she also made a lot of sense. *Since you've already given them the interview, what's the big deal about letting them get a couple pictures at the house?*

I punched in the code and opened the front door.

"Hey, we're getting pizza." Wade and AJ were each in front of their gaming setups, on opposite sides of the living room, playing *The Show*. Wade said, "Order it, bitch."

"What if I don't want pizza?" I did, I mean who didn't want pizza, but my suitemates all had way more discretionary income than I did. Their parents loaded their debit cards with all kinds of fun-money, whereas I was holding tight to the money I'd worked my ass off to put into savings.

When it was gone, I was out.

"It's free," AJ said. "Brooks complained last time that he found a long hair in his cheese, so they gave him a coupon. It's on the mini fridge."

"You want to order from a place that has hairy pizza?" I asked Wade.

"I think it might've been mine, but I wasn't sure."

"You're an idiot," AJ said, laughing.

"I know," Wade agreed. "Which is why I'm willing to give them another chance."

"Big of you," I said, dropping my backpack on the couch and grabbing the coupon from the front of the mini fridge. *Free XL one-topper.* "Pepperoni?"

"Nah—just cheese," Wade said. "Their pepperoni tastes like fungus."

"Because you know what fungus tastes like," AJ muttered.

"Are you sure we should order from a place with hair and fungus problems?" I laughed, pulling out my phone because it was free. *Of course* we were going to order it.

Their attention was on the game until the pizza arrived, but as soon as the box was open, they were at the table and back to being aware of their surroundings.

"Why'd you have to stay after practice?" Wade asked, grabbing three pieces and dropping them onto a paper towel.

I didn't really know what to say, so I just told the truth. "They want to send someone with a camera to Omaha this weekend to get pictures of my house and my high school field."

"What the fuck?" Wade asked, looking offended. "How come no one wants to go to my hometown with a camera? I'm a better player than you, and I'm *not* from NebraskaHoma."

"You are *not* better," AJ said, shoving pizza into his mouth.

"Bullshit." Wade made a face and said, "Well, I'm *as* good, at least."

Wade was funny because he was obnoxious and cocky, only he wasn't. He was all douchey attitude, and I would've hated him if that was truly who he was. But he was, in fact, a really decent guy who thought it was hilarious to behave like a jackass.

"Regardless of the fact that I'm better than you, it's only because during my interview I talked about having to go home when my dad died, and then come back. So it's just because they like the story—it has nothing to do with my game."

The entire team knew my story, but no one had ever spoken about it; not with me. Everyone just pretended I was a freshman, the same as every other freshman, and I preferred it that way. I kind of suspected that one of the coaches made some sort of an announcement when I committed, because it was odd that no one brought it up, but I'd also never asked.

"Who are they sending?" AJ asked, getting up to grab a beer from the fridge. He had zero issues drinking during the week, but I liked to avoid hangovers when I had homework to do. "Is it gonna be Liz?"

"I think so; I'm not sure."

"*Of course* it's gonna be Liz." Wade ripped off his crust, then rolled it into a ball. "She's from there, so she'll know all the spots. I wonder if she'll bring Waters."

"I still can't believe they're a thing," AJ said, looking at me and shaking his head. "He's a cool dude and I like him, but they seem more like brother and sister than a couple."

"Yeah, that is weird." Wade took a bite out of his crust ball like it was an apple. "Like, they're always together, but they have always been *always together*."

"You sound smart," I muttered.

"Fuck right off—you know what I mean," he said. "They don't act any differently than they've ever acted together. Last year she told me he's her 'platonic soulmate,' so now he's more? Like, when he puts his arm around her, it looks no different than my dad putting his arm around my sister."

"Can we not talk about this? I don't give a shit about their relationship," I said, sounding harsher than I'd meant to.

"Oh, it sounds to me like you really do." Wade reached over and pulled off another crust and started rolling. "And I get it."

"Same." AJ nodded. "Like, she's cute, but that's not the thing. It's the way she's so damn chill, right? Dating someone that cool about everything would make everyone else seem like . . . too much."

I took a bite of pizza, blown away that that was how they saw her. As a super chill cool girl.

And they weren't wrong. That was exactly who she was now, but it was wild because she'd been chill about *nothing* back in the day.

I'd fucking loved it, how quickly she got riled up.

I'd loved it, yet my new obsession was the confident content producer with the quiet one-liners.

I was dying to get to know her better.

"I have to think that after dating Liz, you would forever care about her relationships." Wade took a bite of his crust ball and said, "How the hell do you get over someone like her?"

Yeah, that was a loaded question. I grabbed a Gatorade out of the fridge and absolutely knew the answer.

You don't was the answer.

You don't get over her.

CHAPTER TWENTY-FOUR

"She gave me a pen. I gave her my heart,
and she gave me a pen."
—*Say Anything*

Liz

"Hey, guys."

I looked up from my screen and there was Lilith, standing beside our cubicles with a big smile on her face.

"Hey," I said, surprised to see her.

"Hey, Lil," Clark said, and I quickly shot a glance at her to see if she was going to kill him for that.

She looked like she hadn't even noticed.

"I am here to ask a favor, and I'm a little nervous." She looked anything but nervous in her black leather jacket, jeans, and Mary Janes with three-inch heels.

"We are your humble servants," Clark said. "Ask away."

She crossed her arms over her chest and said, "Want to go to Omaha tomorrow?"

"What?" I looked from Lilith to Clark, wondering if I'd heard her right. "Omaha?"

"Consider me already packing," Clark said.

"I mean, of *course* I'm down," I said, trying to keep up with Clark's enthusiasm, "but why? I mean, Omaha isn't usually anywhere that people go."

I would love a free trip home, especially when I knew Wes wouldn't be next door, but why on earth would Lilith want to send us there? It had to do with him, though, right? That was the only thing that made sense, maybe . . . ?

"Here's the thing," she said. "Wes Bennett is headed home because his mother sold their house and he's helping move everything out. I would like for us to get footage of the house and his high school field to accompany your interview."

"Oh." I tried keeping my face calm when every part of me was flinching at the thought.

I mean, I wasn't even sure what I was freaking out about more. The fact that Lilith wanted me to go back home and follow Wes to all the old places I'd avoided for years, or the fact that the Bennetts weren't going to be living next door anymore.

"Are we sure about this?" Clark asked, running his hand over his chin as he looked at Lilith like he was unhappy. "I imagine this isn't going to be easy for him, so it feels a little ghoulish for us to show up with cameras. No offense, of course."

Good point, Clark.

Listen to him, Lilith.

"None taken," she said, nodding. "He said it's fine."

"He did?" Clark asked.

"He *did*?" I said at the same time.

"Yes," she repeated, looking amused by our matching reactions. "I fully expected a no, but he said okay."

I stared at her, shocked.

"I'd like to see if his sister or mother will consider an interview," she said. "I know it's obviously a tricky issue, but it's been a couple years, so they might be ready to talk."

"I'm sure Sarah will," Clark said, nodding. "From what Bennett told me, they're close and she's kind of a smart-ass. The mom, though—I'm not so sure about her."

The mom. It was beyond weird that we were discussing Mrs. Bennett from next door.

"Yeah, me either," Lilith said. "But we might as well try. Listen, the closing is Friday afternoon, so I was thinking if we fly out tomorrow after classes, we can all get a good night's sleep and then walk through the house with Wes first thing the following morning. Before the closing. Hopefully afterward, Wes will let us get some footage around town and at the ball fields."

"I don't have any classes on Fridays, so that's perfect," Clark said.

Was it me, or was he being a kiss-up? I'd apologized for snapping at him the other night, and he'd apologized for trying to get me to forgive Wes, but his *Wes love* still rubbed me the wrong way.

"What about you, Liz? Do you think you can make it work?" Lilith put her hands in her pockets and said, "We only go if you go."

"I mean, my parents would love it," I said as I tried to mentally work through what the weekend would entail. "And I'm sure I can talk to my teachers about missing my classes."

"But what about you?" she asked, looking concerned. "I want to make sure you're comfortable with this. If you're not, we scrap it."

I could tell by her face that she was genuinely asking, and I felt a rush of gratitude that she was willing to abandon this idea if I wasn't okay with it. That tiny bit of understanding was probably what allowed me to take a step away from my own feelings to recognize that if Wes was willing, the imagery would definitely add to his story.

"I think it's a great idea."

After that, we went into brainstorming mode, talking through the content she hoped for. It would be a nice supplement to see the inside of the house he grew up in and juxtapose it with locking the door for the very last time.

God.

It'd also be gorgeous to get some early-morning sunlight shots of Emerson Field, the place where he'd become a superstar pitcher.

Is this really happening?

It was surreal that the project we were talking through and the plans we were making would send us to Teal Street and my old high school. I loved that place, but I'd purposely taken summer classes and suggested family holiday getaways with my parents because I wasn't sure how to handle being there, next door to *him*.

I'd never *intended* to stay away for nearly two years, but I always just kind of found something *else* to do every time there was a break.

But now I was going home.

To his house.

With him.

Is this really happening?

Apparently it was, because twenty-four hours later, I was disembarking from a plane at the Omaha airport.

"This is the airport?" Clark said, looking around the small terminal like he couldn't believe his eyes. "Where are the stores? Where is the Starbucks?"

"You can get a mini Godfather's Pizza over there," I said, heading for the baggage-claim area while pointing to the right. It felt good being there, walking into a place I'd known my entire life and where I knew exactly which direction I was going. "And there's a Scooter's right under that sign."

"What in God's name is a Scooter's?" Clark looked disgusted as he walked beside me, dragging his carry-on behind him.

"It's coffee," I said, surprised he didn't know. Was that only a Midwestern thing? I loved Scooter's.

"Just say 'okay,' Clark," Lilith said, smiling. "I'm sure we can find decent coffee by the hotel. Wait—they do have decent coffee here, right, Liz?"

"*Of course* we have decent coffee," I said defensively, walking toward the hall that led to the baggage-claim area. "I think Omaha has close to a million people—it's not in the prairie, for God's sake."

"I'll be the judge of that," Clark said.

I was walking faster as I led them through the terminal, so

excited to see my parents. "I texted my dad when we landed, so he should be waiting."

My dad and Helena (my stepmom) freaked out when I called last night. As much as they'd been happy to come to California to visit me during breaks, apparently me coming home was much better. Helena screamed through the phone when I shared the news, and my dad sounded suspiciously like someone who was weepy.

I couldn't *wait* to see them.

But when we came down the escalator and there they were, standing beside the baggage-claim carousel, I was hit with all the emotion. No matter how fast I blinked, I couldn't keep in the tears. Something about being here and seeing them felt different.

I was coming home after what felt like a very long time away.

I tried keeping it together, but when I stepped off the escalator and my dad jogged over and wrapped me in a hug, I was done. The smell of him, the laundry detergent on his shirt and the lotion he used for his dry skin and the cologne from the eighties that he still thought smelled good even though it was crazy-strong, took me back to every loving hug from my childhood.

"It's about damn time," Helena said, smiling at us with tears in her eyes. "You little shit."

That made me laugh—even as I cried, and I pulled away from my dad to get my emotions in check. I introduced everyone, and Lilith and Clark both seemed (rightly so) to fall in love with my parents instantly.

"If you're too tired and just want to go to your hotel, we understand," Helena said as we pulled away from the airport. "But we'd love to have you guys over to the house for dinner. It's warm for October, so we picked up some T-bones to throw on the grill."

"*This* is warm?" Clark laughed, shaking his head. He was a California boy through and through, and his reaction to forty-eight degrees with a stiff north wind was akin to someone being set loose, naked, in Antarctica.

"Fall is my favorite time to grill," my dad said, smiling at us in the rearview mirror. "I'd loan you a sweater, Clark, but I think it'll be a crop top."

"That sounds lovely," Lilith said, looking charmed by my nerdy dad. "The steak dinner, that is—not the crop top."

The four of them chatted nonstop on the way home, but I couldn't keep myself from just staring out the window. I felt hungry to see it all, to lay my eyes upon every single place I hadn't seen in nearly two years. I was smiling like it was my first time in a car as the freeway took us past Charles Schwab Field, the downtown skyline, Dinker's Hamburgers, the Denny's on Eighty-Fourth where Joss and I used to get pancakes on Friday nights, and the Sapp Brothers coffeepot sign that I thought was a rocket until I was ten years old.

And the leaves—I hadn't realized how much I'd missed the colors.

The cottonwoods were bright yellow, the sugar maples that perfect shade of pinkish-orange, and the oaks were currently doing all the hues in that continuously-changing-until-the-last-leaf-falls way they had about them.

Damn, it's good to be back.

I avoided looking at the house next door when we got home,

even though I knew I was going to have to go inside it tomorrow, because I just wanted to relax and enjoy being home with my dad and Helena before everything else happened.

"Hand me your bag, sweetie," my dad said, and as I walked up the steps with him on my left, and Helena on my right, I wanted to soak up every second of this homecoming.

I regretted not doing it sooner.

Clark kept my dad company out on the deck while he grilled, and I stayed inside with Lilith and Helena and showered poor Mr. Fitzpervert with attention that he absolutely did not want.

Helena bought Fitz a blue-and-yellow bow tie for our visit, which reminded me of just how perfect of a stepmom she actually was, and as I sat between my dad and Lilith at dinner, I realized that my face was getting tired from all the happy smiling.

"This pasta salad is amazing," Clark said, wolfing down bite after bite like he was racing someone. He was chewing when he said, "I think I'm in love with you now, Helena."

"Actually, it's Bert Langenfarker you're in love with," she corrected, picking up her wineglass. "He's the guy at the deli who makes the sides."

"Is he single?" he asked, not even pausing in his food inhalation.

"He is not," Helena replied with a grin. "But I heard his wife's Facebook profile says 'it's complicated,' so there's a chance."

"Plot twist," Lilith said before finishing her glass of rosé.

"Hell yes," Clark said, nodding while still chewing a giant mouthful of food. "I'll take complicated if it means ingesting this twirly goodness every night."

Helena and Clark were two peas in a pod, like a his-and-her comedy team that kept the rest of us laughing the entire time. Lilith just kind of took it all in, seeming completely comfortable hanging out at my house in her stockinged feet, and it felt like a perfect night.

So I was a little disappointed when it was time for Clark and Lilith to go back to the hotel. Apparently he wanted to swim, and she still needed to put in some time on the treadmill, so they said their goodbyes, we made a plan to meet at nine the next morning, and then they drove off in the minivan my dad was letting them borrow while in town.

"I love them," Helena said, closing the door behind Lilith and Clark. "It makes me so happy you have good people around you out there."

"Right?" I said, leaning down to scoop up Fitz. He made a *mreow* noise, like he was unhappy, but I knew he'd been waiting for me. "They're the best."

We went into the kitchen and cleaned up with the TV on, so we were moving at half speed, really into the old episode of *Monk* that we'd seen multiple times. It felt like the old days, when Helena used to get takeout and the three of us would sit hunched over our food, at the center island, watching mindless reruns, and the entire evening had somehow made me homesick while I was home (nonsensical much?).

Which *of course* made me want to go see my mom.

"I think I'm going to go for a quick run," I said, wiping down the counter as my dad started the dishwasher. "I know it's dark, but I've got my pepper spray and I know the route by heart."

"Keep the music quiet, then," he said with an eyebrow raise, "so you're aware of your surroundings."

"I know," I said. "I will."

And for once, I actually ran with no music.

Usually I hated that, but I didn't want to miss out on the sounds of my neighborhood. I hadn't realized how much I'd missed them, or even that they were a thing at all, but I was all warm fuzzies as my ears drank in the cacophony of suburban instruments.

The random leaf blower, the *Thursday Night Football* game playing in the garage of the old guy down the street, the barking of a big dog in an unseen backyard; it was the soundtrack of my wonder years, the comforting white noise that'd lulled me to sleep on countless warm nights.

And when I got to my mom's headstone, where bright yellow mums were in their full autumnal glory (yes, I used my phone light to check on them in the dark), I wondered how I'd ever stayed away for so long.

CHAPTER TWENTY-FIVE

"Because the first time that I saw these hands,
I couldn't imagine not being able to hold them."
—*Definitely, Maybe*

Wes

I wish I believed in ghosts.

I sat there, on the one remaining chair in the Secret Area, wishing I could feel my dad's presence. It was the last time I'd ever be out there in the dark by the fire, the last night I'd ever see the inside of that house, and I knew if I were in a movie, I'd find his old steel-toed boots and somehow know he was proud of me.

That he forgave me for what I'd done.

But nah—it was just me and the quiet as I said my goodbyes.

The Secret Area had been taken over by thistles and milkweed—and moles apparently, I thought as I looked down at the dug-up dirt beside the overgrown bush. It felt like some sort of depressing analogy for my former life as I pressed the soil back down with my shoe.

But I chose not to overthink it as I chucked a few more sticks into the fire.

It was childish, my plan to spend the night in the house, but I couldn't resist. I was a sentimental dipshit who wanted one final sleep in my childhood bedroom before someone else lived there. Noah offered to come over because he was that kind of friend, but I preferred to be alone. If it was Sarah, I would've said yes because she'd been a part of this Teal Street life, but anyone else would just feel like an intrusion.

And my mom had zero interest.

Finding my dad in the living room had destroyed the house for both of them.

I opened Spotify and scrolled for something that my dad would've liked, but nothing sentimental enough to make me cry.

I was already on the edge.

Bingo. Foo Fighters, the guy's guilty pleasure. I clicked on "The Deepest Blues Are Black" and wondered when the hell it'd gotten so cold. I'd only left a few weeks ago, but this breeze was packed with autumn's chill.

Which seemed appropriate.

Saying goodbye to a lifetime of memories was an activity *meant* to be wrapped in bone-chilling cold, right? My fingers were freezing when I left my house keys with my dad an hour ago. The new owners were rekeying the place, so they only needed one set of copies to get them in tomorrow, and it felt wrong to just toss the keys I'd had since I was seven or eight years old, so I gave them to Stu.

I felt like the key chain would've made him happy.

You know, as happy as a dead man can be.

It was asinine, the way I felt when I visited his grave. It'd become a habit that was somehow comforting, even though it was like the polar opposite of how Liz had once explained her daily visits to her mother's grave.

When Liz used to visit her mom, she would sit down beside the headstone and talk to her mother like she was talking to her best friend. She told her what was going on in her life, and I remember Liz saying it made her feel like her mom was still involved in her world, even though she was gone.

My trips to the cemetery were a little different.

I pretty much just sat down on the grass beside the STUART HAROLD BENNETT headstone and stared into space, thinking things and assuming somehow the ghost of ol' Stu could drill into my thoughts. I knew it was absurd, but I also knew that I always felt a little better when I left.

I'd spent so many panicked hours there at the beginning, right after his massive heart attack rocked our world, desperately seeking guidance from the grave because his headstone was the only place I could turn. There was no one else to tell me how to make enough money to pay the mortgage, what I was supposed to do when my mom wouldn't come home, or how the hell to install a new starter so I didn't have to take my car to a garage that we couldn't afford, so I left it at Stu's feet.

Sometimes, like earlier tonight, I just found a Cubs game on my phone and put it on speaker. I didn't necessarily believe in the romanticized notion of dead relatives hanging out with us, but I also knew there was something about listening to a game there that made me feel closer to my dad.

But whenever I allowed myself to feel closer, to let all the memories rush in, the voice in my head whispered the reminder that always made me want to run and hide.

You're responsible.

Because I was. It was just a fact.

I leaned my head back and remembered that phone call like it was yesterday. It'd been two days before the exhibition game, my *first* freshman year, and I'd told him, "I don't think you should come."

"Save it, Wesley," he'd said dismissively. "Your mom and I are leaving in a few hours. The car's gassed up and everything."

I remember taking a deep breath and powering through the words, forcing myself to do it. I didn't want to hear him lose his shit, but I needed it for my mental health. I'd said, "Please don't come. It's just an exhibition game, Dad—I don't want you to spend the money for a game that doesn't count."

"A game that doesn't count?" he'd come back with, sounding agitated. "Do you know who you sound like right now? Like a pitcher who's gonna blow it in the exhibition game. This game counts the *most* because it's your first time on the mound in college."

I'd been so stressed at the time, so nervous I was going to let everyone down, that I kind of snapped.

"Do you think I don't know that?" He wasn't even there yet, and he was making me more stressed about a game that I was already out-of-my-mind stressed about, and it'd been too much. "I'm just saying you guys don't need to drive twenty hours for it."

"If I don't make the drive, kid," he'd insisted, "who's going to make sure you're ready? Not your coaches. They've got you doing yoga and writing in goddamn journals instead of throwing the baseball."

"Dad—"

"And not you. No, you'll be playing grab-ass with the redhead instead of focusing—"

"I don't want you to come," I'd blurted, yelling over the phone even though I'd *never* yelled at him. "Okay? I'm already stressed about this game, so the last thing I need is you in my head. Just stay home for this one. *Please.*"

"Listen, kid, you've got to channel that psychological nonsense and stop being a pussy. Do you think—"

"Just stay away, okay, Dad?"

I rubbed the back of my neck and stared into the fire, still able to hear the argument like it'd just happened. I'd sounded exactly like him when I shouted, "You're the worst part of baseball for me, and I dread seeing your face in the stands—is that what you want me to say? Because it's the truth. I don't want you there."

It was dead quiet after I said that, and my heart had been pounding out of my chest. He was going to go apeshit on me for talking to him like that.

But . . . he didn't.

He didn't say *anything*. I could hear the TV in the background, so I knew he was still there, but he didn't say a word.

And then the call was disconnected.

"Screw this." I stood and poured water on the fire, my gut roiling as sweat beaded on my forehead in the cold breeze.

I didn't drink anymore, not really, but tonight was an emergency.

CHAPTER TWENTY-SIX

"I'm the exception. . . ."
"You are *my* exception."
—*He's Just Not That Into You*

Liz

"I promise I'll come back sooner this time."

I sat beside the mums, wiping away my tears. The tears that wouldn't stop.

I'd never meant to stay away for so long.

After I'd come home for Christmas my freshman year and everything terrible happened with Wes, I had jumped at the chance to go on spring break with my roommate a few months later. The thought of seeing Wes had been unbearable, and thankfully my parents had been cool with the trip.

Then I decided to take summer classes.

Then, last year, I found a Vrbo in Colorado where my parents and I spent Christmas break.

And then I begged them to let me go on spring break with Leo and Campbell.

Rinse and repeat with summer classes.

My goal had never been to stay gone forever, but the anxiety I'd felt at the thought of returning home led me to desperately grab on to any method of avoidance, every single time.

I'd been surprisingly okay with not being able to visit my mom's grave. I'd grown up, it seemed, because I was now able to talk to my mom (pretty much every day) without being in close proximity to her headstone.

So it didn't make sense that the moment I touched the letters of her name tonight, engraved in the cold marble, I fell apart.

I was a mess.

I'd been sitting on the ground, on top of a pile of leaves, sobbing my eyes out as I told my mother every tiny thing that'd happened to me since I'd left for college two years ago.

It was mostly good stuff, the happy accounting of the nice things in my life, but telling her about it was making me miss her so much that it was painful.

What is wrong with me?

On top of that, the thought of leaving her again felt just as awful as it had the first time.

Perhaps I was never going to get over it. Never be past it.

I climbed to my feet and dusted off my leggings. It was really dark now, and I needed to get home. I walked up the road, the road I'd sprinted so many times over the years, and it seemed like a lifetime ago. Who was that girl who'd jogged to the cemetery on a daily basis? I couldn't remember.

Ironically, the last time I'd been here, I hadn't even visited my mother's grave.

It'd been for Mr. Bennett's funeral.

What a terrible day.

It hadn't been cold, for Nebraska, but it'd rained hard the entire day.

I'd been with Wes in the big funeral car, holding his hand, while his mother sobbed uncontrollably and his sister looked like a lost little bird, staring into space the entire day. He'd been stoic, *very un-Wes-like*, while he behaved as the head of the family, ushering his mom to her seat under the makeshift awning, answering the pastor's questions, watching his father's casket be lowered into the ground.

"No," I muttered under my breath, walking faster as the autumn breeze picked up and blew my hair in front of my face. The last thing I needed to be doing was thinking about Wes or how awful that day had been, so it didn't make any sense that I was walking toward Mr. Bennett's grave.

But I just had to see it.

It was illogical, but I felt the need to visit him while I was there, to at the very least say hello. I knew I was nuts when it came to cemeteries, but I didn't like the thought of no one visiting him, even if he had been a bit of a jerk 75 percent of the time.

I went straight to the cottonwood tree it was under, the biggest tree in the cemetery and my absolute favorite. Its leaves were probably bright yellow by now, but it was impossible to tell in the darkness. I ducked underneath its lowest branch and knelt at the grave marker I could barely see.

STUART HAROLD BENNETT

I burrowed my chin into the collar of the jacket as the name *Wesley Harold Bennett* whispered through my ears, and before I could process that, I saw the baseballs.

I got out my phone again and turned on the flashlight, because maybe I was seeing things.

Only . . . *nope*; they were baseballs.

At the base of the headstone, there were no fewer than fifteen baseballs, each one burrowed into the mud and dirt just enough so they stayed put. I set a finger on one of them, wondering if Wes had left them while knowing it had to have been him.

I leaned down to dust a few leaves off the top of the marble when I saw a key ring on the ground, the metal glinting in the light of the flashlight. I picked it up, and it was a Bruins Baseball key chain with a few keys on it.

They had to be Wes's keys, right?

I picked them up and put them in my pocket; he was probably freaking out, trying to find them, especially when the closing was tomorrow. As soon as I got back to the house, I'd figure out how to get them to him. I could text him, but maybe I'd give them to Clark to give to him instead.

I didn't want to be thinking about Wes right now, even as I knelt at his father's grave.

I looked down at the baseballs, blinking back more tears—*what the hell is wrong with me tonight?*—as I said, "Hey, Mr. Bennett. Sorry I've never come to see you."

I pictured his face, handsome like Wes's but not as kind, and I just started rambling.

About how well Wes pitched at the exhibition game.

It was what he'd want to hear if he was alive, so I assumed his preferences hadn't changed. I told him how hard his son had thrown, and I told him how no one had been able to hit off him.

I even said he really "threw 'em the gas," Mr. Bennett's favorite expression.

By the time I was finished talking to ghosts at the cemetery, I was frozen.

I ran home, took a long, hot shower, and after hanging out with my dad and Helena for an hour, I finally went up to bed.

But before I could sleep, I needed to tell Wes about his keys.

I think I found your keys.

Nope. I backspaced, not wanting him to know I'd visited his dad's grave.

I typed: **Your keys were on the ground at the cemetery.**

Gaaah—backspaced again. Why was I overthinking this? I just needed to tell him I found his keys—no big deal. I texted: **I found some keys that I think might be yours. I'll drop them in your mailbox.**

Send.

Finally.

I'd been randomly looking out the window since I got back from my run—*yep, the silver car I saw him get out of earlier is still there*—but there weren't any lights on inside his house. It looked vacant and asleep, so maybe he'd left the car there or something.

My phone started ringing in my hand, startling me.

God.

I looked down, and Wes was calling me.

Whyyyyyyy?

I took a deep breath, then raised the phone to my ear. "Hello?"

"Keys?" Wes's voice sounded weird, like it was too close to the phone or something. "What keys?"

"Um, there are a couple keys on a Bruins Baseball key chain," I said, mildly confused by his tone. "I just assumed they were yours."

"Did my dad give them to you?" he asked, sounding wildly confused. "How the hell did you get them?"

His dad? "What? No, I found them on the ground."

"The ground," he said, dragging out the words. "The ground where? The cemetery? Are you back?"

Only it sounded a little like "shemetery." "Yes. Are you drunk?"

"Little bit," he replied, his words slower than his usual fast-paced rate of snappy sarcasm. "But that doesn't change the fact that, like, did you visit my dad's grave? Or did one of those dickhead squirrels run off with the keys? They used to take the stuff I left all the goddamn time, little dickheads."

Definitely drunk.

"I was walking by his grave," I lied, dumbstruck by his intoxication. "And happened to see them lying there."

"I left him the keys because it was his house, y'know?" he said, kind of mumbling. "He should have them."

I didn't know what to say because I was having trouble processing all this. "Is Michael there with you?"

"No one is with me," he said, sounding distracted. "I couldn't have anyone over for the last night at the Bennett house—are you kidding? He'd hate that."

His *dad*?

"Maybe you shouldn't be alone, Wes," I said, looking out the window but only seeing darkness from his house. Why was he alone? Why was he alone and *drunk*? Was he sitting on the floor in the dark, all by himself, with a bottle of booze? I wasn't sure why, but I felt like I should call someone. It seemed dangerous for him to be drunk and by himself in an empty house.

My throat was tight when I suggested, "Can you call someone?"

"No, 'cause I'm gonna sleep now, Lib," he said, and his subconscious use of my old nickname made that throat tension even worse. "I'm so tired."

I'm so tired. Something about that statement was worrisome, and I wondered if I should try to find Sarah's number.

"Okay," I said, not knowing what to say. I knew he had to be hurting, but I wasn't the person to be helping him anymore, right? I swallowed and said, "Well, good night, Wes."

"I miss our 'good nights,'" he mumbled—to himself, it seemed—and then the call ended.

I sat there with the phone in my hand, frozen in place, not sure what to do. My stomach hurt as I pictured him drunk and alone in an empty house, but he wasn't mine to worry about anymore. He was just my old neighbor, a guy I'd dated for a few months, and our lives had moved on, right?

It wasn't my business if he was sad.

But as I turned out my light and went to bed, I couldn't stop thinking about him. I kept picturing his dark eyes full of tears at the funeral.

And his slurred voice when he said, *Did my dad give them to you*?

I tossed and turned, Wes on my mind when I was awake *and* when I was asleep. Then my worries switched to the alcohol and his aloneness. How much had he consumed? What if he'd been drinking straight from a bottle all night?

At two fifteen, I reached for my phone. Texted: **Are you okay?**

Twenty minutes later, he still hadn't responded.

"Dammit."

I sat up and flipped on my lamp, realizing I had no choice.

Just knock on the door, make sure he's alive, say goodbye.

I knocked on the front door of his house, nervous, because it was the middle of the night, and I was prowling around outside. *This is stupid.* There were still no lights on inside. Zero. Black space in every window. Not a single light to be seen, yet Wes's car was still in the driveway. Part of me wanted to just run back home, but I had to make sure he was okay.

I looked behind me, toward the street, but it was quiet except for the chilly fall breeze and the sounds of the dry leaves blowing in the wind. Very creepy.

I knocked again.

And then I heard it.

Foo Fighters. Coming from inside his house.

The deeper the blues, the more I see black

Loud.

"Wes?" I knocked harder, a little irritated. I wasn't sure if he was even inside, but I wanted to be finished with the standing-alone-in-the-dark-outside portion of the evening. Especially since my dad and Helena were sound asleep. If I disappeared, no one would even know I'd left the house until morning.

After another ten seconds, I said, "Screw it." I stuck the key that was obviously a house key into the lock, turned the doorknob, and pushed in the door. "Wes? It's Liz."

I stepped inside, letting the screen door close behind me. I quietly shut the front door and wondered what the hell I was even doing.

The music sounded like it was coming from the living room, so I went up the five steps that led from the entryway to the main level. I walked slowly, because it was so incredibly dark in there. Suddenly this seemed like the worst idea I'd ever had. "Wes?"

I looked to my left, and it was a little easier to see. The front curtains were wide open, so the bright moon and streetlights illuminated the very empty living room. Not a picture, not a piece of furniture, not a single familiar item remained from the Bennetts' former home.

I could see the glow of the tiny red light on the Bluetooth speaker that was playing the Foo Fighters, but no one was in that room.

Dammit. I hit the wall switch and the recessed light above the fireplace turned on, confirming the room's emptiness.

I started down the hallway, walking in the direction of the bedrooms, my heart pounding in my chest.

I didn't know what I was doing, but it seemed very stupid.

"Wes?" I said quietly, not wanting to scare him.

I walked past his room and Sarah's room, which were both dark and quiet.

Then I heard a sound coming from his parents' room at the end of the hall, like someone was talking.

Thank God. I'd pictured him unconscious in a puddle of his own vomit.

"Not," I heard him mumble, but then he made a weird noise.

Like a whimper. Like a moan.

Oh my God, is he with someone?

I turned on the hall light, my heart pounding in my chest as I crept closer to the bedroom.

"Wes?" I whispered, and when I reached the bedroom doorway, I could see him lying shirtless on the floor of the empty room. There was a sweatshirt under his head, and he was facing the other direction, but he was agitated in his sleep.

He was thrashing, his head moving as he made a sound that sounded a *lot* like a sob.

Oh my God, is he crying?

In his sleep?

"Wes," I said a little louder, wanting to wake him up but not scare him.

"Help me," he muttered, his sleeping voice infused with panic. "Do something!"

"Wake up, Wes," I said, feeling panicked as I dropped to my knees beside him and touched his arm. I didn't want to scare him, but he *needed* to wake up. *"Wes."*

"I'm so sorry, so sorry," he mumbled, and my heart broke for him as his voice cracked.

"Wes!" I lightly slapped at his cheeks, my heart in my throat as desperation to wake him from the nightmare clawed at me. I didn't know what was going on in his subconscious, but I knew he needed to escape it. "Wake up!"

Suddenly, he sucked in a huge gasp of air, sounding like someone who'd just come up from being held under water. His eyes flew open, and he looked completely disoriented.

"Help me," he gasped, sitting up, turning his head to look down the hall. "We have to do CPR."

"Wes," I said, setting my hands on his shoulders, trying to calm him while he woke up, empathy burning in my chest for the raw anguish I could see on his face. "It's okay. You were dreaming."

"No, though," he said, his voice panicked, his eyes glistening with tears in the darkness. "He's by his chair and needs us—"

"It was a dream," I interrupted, wanting so badly to get him back from whatever terrible place *had* him. "Wes. Shhhh, it's okay."

"It's not okay; it's my fault." His chest was rising and falling, like he was breathing too much and couldn't catch his breath. He shrugged off my hands and climbed to his feet. "I have to go help my dad."

Oh my God oh my God oh my God, I thought, having no idea how to help him. *Should I shout the truth, that his dad is dead?* That didn't seem like a great idea, but he needed to snap out of this, right?

What am I supposed to do here?

"Your dad is gone," I said in a voice so quiet, it was almost a whisper. I looked up at him, a little scared but not even sure of what, and hated having to say, "Wes. He's gone."

"No," he said, shaking his head as the light from the hallway showed me the tears on his cheeks. He turned and stumbled toward the living room, saying, "I have to fix him."

"Wes!" *Dear God, how drunk was he?*

And I desperately wanted this to be drunkenness, because if it wasn't, what was this pain? I grieved my mother every day, but this was very different. I stood and went after him, and when I got to the living room, he was staring at the spot in the corner where his dad's recliner used to sit.

Just staring into space as the Foo Fighters screamed against the walls.

Shaking like the thunder

I blinked back tears as he fell to his knees, like the reality of the moment was just too much for him to take while standing.

"Wes." I knelt beside him and put my hand on his back, desperately needing to find a way to help, to somehow lessen whatever this pain was. Even if this was a drunken stupor, I'd never seen him—or anyone—hurt quite this much.

He looked at me through lost, tear-filled eyes, and he shook his head. "I can't fix it."

"I know." I pushed back the hair on his sweaty forehead and had trouble seeing him through *my* tears. "But it's okay."

"It's not okay," he said, and I *felt* the anguish in his unsteady voice. I could smell the alcohol on his breath, but I suspected this had very little to do with that fact. "It's my fault."

"Just calm down," I said quietly, because his chest was rising and falling too fast, like he couldn't catch his breath.

"No, you don't get it," he said, shaking his head, and yeah—he was *definitely* breathing too hard.

As someone who'd dealt with her own panic attacks, I recognized the familiar.

"Wes Bennett, look at me. *Now.*"

CHAPTER TWENTY-SEVEN

"I propose we not make plans. I propose we give this thing a chance and let it work out how it works out. So what do you say—do you wanna not make plans with me?"

—*Leap Year*

Wes

I couldn't breathe again. My heart was racing, and my breath was coming too fast as it all screamed back at me. This happened sometimes after the nightmares, but this was the first time it was happening in front of somebody else.

Fucking awesome.

"*Wes.*" Liz's face was suddenly all I could see as she moved closer. "Eyes on me."

I nodded and tried to catch my breath.

"Deep breath through your nose," she said, setting her hands on my chest. "Come on."

Her eyes became my whole world. I inhaled, feeling her fingertips on my skin, and she nodded. "Good. Now listen to me."

She moved her hands to my jaw, grabbing my cheeks and pulling my face closer to hers. It was dark, but I saw the shimmer of tears as she spoke loud and slow. "It wasn't your fault."

I stared into her eyes, desperate to believe her. Wanting so badly to just let her words manipulate reality and make it all go away.

Her fingers flexed on my skin, squeezing like she was demanding my attention. "I don't know how you could think that, but it isn't true."

"But I said—"

"Wes." She set her forehead on mine, her tone soothing as her gentle fingers warmed my skin. Her voice was sweet and breathy, a melatonin cloud, as she insisted, "You need to forgive yourself for whatever this is, okay?"

I felt a little lightheaded as I closed my eyes.

I'd never forgive myself.

I opened my eyes and lingered, reveling in Liz's hands on my face, her forehead on mine. She was right there, with me, my Libby.

I raised my hands and pushed back her hair, sliding all ten fingers into the soft, thick curls that always smelled like freesia. She was watching me with damp eyes, her lips sweet and soft, and the magnitude of my longing was like a punch to the solar plexus.

"Lib," I whispered, lowering my head and kissing away a tear. I could feel her long, jagged inhalation as I tilted her head with my hands, as I went back for the tear on her other cheek.

My hands were shaking as I slid them lower, so my palms were on her warm throat, my fingers buried underneath the back of her hair. She didn't move, didn't speak; we were in slow-motion quicksand, and the only thing I knew was that we were about to kiss. Liz's eyes dipped down to my mouth, and I was done fighting it.

Need flamed up like sizzling oil on a dancing flame.

Her fingertips tightened on my jaw as I lowered my mouth to hers.

But just as our lips touched, I remembered.

She had a boyfriend.

Why does she have to have a boyfriend?

I wanted to ignore it so damn badly, to put it out of my head and slide into the only thing I'd ever needed. I wanted to forget that everyone and everything existed except for my mouth and Liz Buxbaum.

Especially when those green eyes slid shut.

Every molecule in my body buzzed, and every cell came alive as I felt the softness of her sigh and the offering of her mouth.

My entire existence roared to attention and wanted so damn badly.

Dear *Lord*, it hurt to want that much.

My heart was pounding in my chest as I forced myself not to be an asshole.

"Thank you, Lib," I whispered against her lips, selfishly dragging my teeth over her bottom lip for a split second before pulling back. I couldn't kiss her, not now, but I was too starved for a bite not to steal a sample.

Her eyes fluttered open, and the expectation in her gaze was torture, so much that I had to close my eyes for a second if I was going to be strong enough to resist being a prick.

One, two, three.

I dropped a barely there peck on her lips, a soft brush that was more of a breath than a kiss, and it didn't make sense the way it brought the tightness back to my throat and made something in my chest pinch so hard it burned.

It wasn't even a kiss.

"Of course," she whispered, a tiny wrinkle in her forehead as she looked up at me, and *dammit* I could still feel the fullness of her lower lip between my teeth. Missing her was normal, like my default nowadays, but the way I felt—as I pushed the hair away from her face and stared into her eyes—was like missing her, but to the nth degree.

"I don't deserve you, what you did for me," I said, my fingers sliding through her silky curls. "After everything."

"I didn't do anyth—"

"Yes, you did," I said, watching my hands as they slipped through her hair.

"I woke you from a bad dream," she said in a near-whisper, closing her eyes and leaning into my touch, offering up her hair to my hands. "That's all."

"Lib," I said. "It was a lot more than that."

"Was it?" She opened her eyes, and a thousand butterflies went wild in my stomach, because the way she was looking at me was . . . God.

It was just, *God*, all I could ever want in the world.

But it disappeared in an instant because I saw her remember.

I *watched* as she recalled my sins.

She jerked away from me and sat up straight, clearing her throat and tucking her hair behind her ears. "Um."

All the soft vulnerability left her face, replaced by a raised chin and a hard swallow. I flexed my fingers, still feeling the tangle of her hair's softness wrapped around them, and I sat up straighter too. "I'm sorry about the whole nightmare freak-out, by the way."

"Don't apologize," she said, shaking her head but *not* looking at me. "I'm the one who let myself in."

I'd been so disoriented that I hadn't even registered the logistics of her presence. My eyes swept over her, and I only just now realized she was wearing pink flannel pajama pants, like she'd been roused from her bed. "Yeah, uh, why *did* you do that? I mean, I'm glad you did because you dragged me out of a whopper of a nightmare, but did you need something?"

"Well," she said, shrugging like she was embarrassed. "I guess I just wanted to make sure you weren't succumbing to alcohol poisoning, since you were drinking alone."

So she thinks I'm pathetic.

"Ah," I said, nodding. "Pictured me drowning in my own vomit, did you?"

"Exactly," she agreed, also nodding.

Fuck, fuck, fuck. I am a pathetic, drunk loser.

Perfect.

"Well, thanks for checking on me." I gritted my teeth, mortified that she'd witnessed my shitshow. "It was very thoughtful."

"Of course," she said, climbing to her feet. "Are you going to be okay now?"

"I'm a little disappointed by how sober I've become," I said, trying hard to sound casual. "But yes."

"Okay, well then, I'm going to take off," she said, nodding her head and keeping her eyes away from mine.

I moved to stand, to walk her out, but she held up a hand and said, "No need. I'll see you tomorrow."

I watched from my spot on the floor as she left, taking those stairs as quickly as she possibly could, and I felt it in my gut when the front door slammed behind her.

"What the *hell*?" I said, the words echoing off the walls of the empty living room. If it wasn't for the faint scent of her perfume and the way I could still feel her bottom lip between my teeth, I might think it'd just been a dream.

But *hell no*, it wasn't a dream.

I climbed to my feet and went over to the window, the one with the perfect view of the Buxbaum house. It was dark over there, as if everyone was sound asleep, but I knew *she* wasn't.

She was probably toeing off her shoes in the dark entryway and petting Fitz, second-guessing her impulsive move to check on me.

I wonder if she's thinking about that almost-kiss.

She *had* to be, I thought, because that *almost-kiss* between us felt like so much more than so many *full-on* kisses between other people.

I'd barely been awake, but I could've been in a coma and it wouldn't have mattered. I didn't need to be conscious to know that Liz's mouth was underneath mine, a breath away, and her eyes were on my lips, like she'd *wanted* me to kiss her.

Want. What a ridiculous word.

Because the *want* that I felt when she'd lifted her lips to me like an offering was so much greater than four pathetic letters. I mean, people wanted things like coffee and new cars, right? How could the same word be used for what I felt when she looked at my mouth?

It couldn't.

The English language had yet to create a word that could capture my level of frenzied, desperate need.

The feel of her full lower lip between my teeth was like . . . like holding a freshly grilled steak up to the mouth of a starving man. *Okay, shitty analogy*, but I swear to God that every one of my fingers clenched, every muscle in my body trembled, and every instinct in my being reared up and wanted to feast.

God, the way I want everything with her.

Liz's bedroom light flipped on as I looked out the window, and I imagined her climbing into bed and pulling up the covers.

Good night, Lib.

I sighed, regretting my decision to be a decent human, because I *was* a starving man when it came to her.

Which made me an idiot for not filling up when I had the chance, right?

I sat there, lost in want and regret, until I finally saw her room go dark.

Then I drove myself crazy in a multitude of ways.

I paced the main level of the house, continuing to torture myself by replaying the almost-kiss and the way she'd looked at me in that moment. *Dear God, the way she'd looked at me.*

I did push-ups as I revisited my half-sober recollection of my freak-out (over and over again), and then I lay on the kitchen floor as I tried figuring out what *exactly* I'd told her about my guilt regarding my father.

Because the alcohol and exhaustion were really messing with my recall.

I was pretty sure I'd only *alluded* to my culpability, falling short of actually confessing the details. Which—thank *God*, because if she'd looked at me like I was a pathetic loser for my drunk freak-out, I could only imagine how she would've looked at me if she discovered I'd been a monster to my dad, on top of everything else.

I wasn't sure how I was going to get her to forget about the mess I'd been, but I'd find a way just as soon as we were back in LA.

I *had* to, because I was going to die from this *want* if I didn't get her back soon.

I was happy to see the sun come up a few hours later, and after showering and packing up all my stuff, so the place was ready for the new owners, I texted Sarah.

What time are you coming over?

Sarah: Mom and I are on the way.

That wasn't what I expected. I looked out the window at the place next door and texted: **She wants to come to the house?**

Because even though therapy had helped my mom get okay enough to return home for my sister's sake, she'd always *hated* the house after my dad died.

Sarah: She wants to take PICTURES of the house.

That made me smile in spite of everything else, because I'd really come to appreciate my weird new mom.

It was bizarre, how much she'd changed.

She was just *Mom* for my first eighteen years, the woman who made dinner, put Band-Aids on my scrapes, and kissed me good night after the sun went down.

But when my dad died, she disappeared.

She became this unreachable person, a shell of the mother I'd grown up with. If she wasn't crying, she pretty much wasn't doing anything at all. Part of me had hated her at the time—even though I felt like a jerk for thinking that—because her PTSD had forced *me* to take on a role I'd never wanted.

But now she was like an entirely different version of herself.

She was funny, self-deprecating about her issues, and the woman who'd once been relatively private was now the most open book anyone had ever met. It was annoying a lot of the time, to be honest, the way she'd tell anyone *anything*, but I'd take it, because she was alive again.

Hearing her laugh again was something I'd never grow tired of.

Although I was really second-guessing that sentiment an hour later, because as Lilith, Clark, and Liz did their thing, hauling equipment around the house while randomly asking me baseball questions (that didn't involve my dad's death, thank *God*), my mom kept filling them in on information no one needed to know.

"So this is where it started, huh?" Clark asked, throwing the baseball to me while Lilith filmed.

"Wow, Clark, such hard-hitting questions," Sarah quipped

from where she was sitting on the railing of the deck, watching.

Yeah, she is definitely Team Wes and being a little brat, I thought as I squeezed the ball in my glove.

"Listen, Tiny Bennett, when I want your feedback, I will ask for it," he said, grinning like he'd been waiting all morning for her to mess with him.

We were playing catch in the backyard, and it was totally cheesy, but I was always more comfortable when the ball was in my hand, so I was okay with it. I threw him the ball, and as he caught it he asked, "Is this where your dad taught you to throw a baseball?"

"Another one," Sarah muttered.

"I guess it is," I replied, very aware of Liz as she recorded us with a smaller camera. "We used to spend hours back here when I was in Little League."

"Did your sister shag balls to help?" Clark asked, throwing. "Or just deliver smart-ass comments like some kind of stock side character from a Disney show?"

"Wow," Sarah yelled, laughing. "Did you just call me a Disney character?"

"All Zuri, no Jessie," he said, which was a reference I didn't even get.

But apparently my sister did, because she pointed at him and said, "Zuri was a little badass, so thank you."

He glanced over at her, shaking his head. "Can you zip it so I can ask a few questions?"

"I'll zip it," she said. "But I'm not sure you *can* actually ask any decent questions."

"Sarah isn't good at quiet," my mom said. "Her fourth-grade teacher moved her desk into the hallway because she wouldn't shut up."

"So on-brand for our Zuri," Clark said, grinning. Then he asked me, "So Liz was next door when you were playing catch back here with your dad? That's so funny to me."

"Those two used to hate each other," my mom said, sounding happy as she leaned against the fence and explained, "Liz was this quiet little thing who was easily ruffled, and Wessy's favorite thing in the world was to ruffle anyone and everyone."

I glanced at Liz, who met my gaze for a second before quickly looking down at her camera. She'd pretty much pretended I didn't exist since they showed up on my doorstep, keeping her eyes on everything *but* me. Tension hung between us, the color of her cheeks telling me she remembered every little thing that had transpired mere hours before, and I couldn't stop staring at her lips.

So close.

"She used to get *so* irritated when errant throws interrupted her playtime," I said calmly, like I wasn't totally struggling to focus on conversation while being hyperaware of Liz's every movement.

"No, I got irritated when my obnoxious neighbor jumped the fence and harassed me." She was filming, her attention on the camera, but her tiny smile was *mine* when she added, "He might seem nice now, but Bennett was a menace."

Fucking yes, tease me, Buxbaum.

"Okay, so I think I've got everything I wanted from the house," Lilith said to Liz, lowering her camera. "The living room, Wes's bedroom, and the backyard where he learned to play catch. Can you think of anything else we should get here?"

It was obvious Lilith valued Liz's opinion, and I could tell by the brightness in her eyes that it made Liz happy.

"Um, I think we're good," she said, lowering the camera.

"Excellent." Lilith looked satisfied with that and went back inside, with Sarah and my mom following, so I seized the moment before it was gone.

"Can I talk to you for a quick second, Liz?" I blurted, not exactly sure what I was going to say, to be honest, but needing to clear the air. "It's about someone we went to high school with."

Her eyebrows furrowed together. "Who?"

Who? "Uh." I glanced toward Clark, who didn't seem to be listening, and said, "Dean Forester."

Yeah, that only made those eyebrows scrunch together even harder. "Dean Forester?"

I don't know if Clark heard or not, but he walked over to the patio and started packing up his equipment, his back to us.

"Okay, uh, it's maybe not about Dean," I said, stepping a little closer to her and lowering my voice.

"You don't say," she murmured, giving me a *duh* look.

"I just want to apologize for last night. I drank too much and was a mess," I said quietly, rubbing the spot over my right eye where a headache was raging. "You were really cool when you didn't have to be."

"It's fine." Her eyes traveled all over my face. She swallowed. Bit down on her bottom lip before saying, "I'm glad you weren't alone."

My eyes got stuck on her mouth as my brain delivered instant replay, bringing back the hot slide of that full lip between my teeth for review.

So close.

That was apparently my dismissal, and she turned her attention to her camera.

God, she's so pretty.

I knew she had to be exhausted after taking care of me in the middle of the night, but those green eyes were clear, her cheeks pink under a few escaped tendrils from her ponytail as she started breaking down her equipment. She was wearing a fisherman's sweater with a brown skirt, and the thick socks she wore with her Docs did amazing things for her legs.

Holy *crap* those legs.

"Dude."

"Huh?" I looked at Clark, and he was watching me watch Liz. *Shit.*

I could tell by the expression on his face that he'd seen it. That he knew I was leering at his girlfriend. He didn't look mad, though. His eyes were a little narrowed, like he was processing, but he seemed relaxed when he said, "Thanks again for being cool about us being here."

I am such an asshole.

"Yeah," I said, focusing on not following Liz with my eyes. "Of course."

"So we're going to let you go to the closing, and you're still cool with meeting at Emerson Field in a couple hours?"

"For sure," I said, feeling guilty for thinking about his girlfriend 24.95 hours a day.

"Great," he said, his face being swallowed by his huge grin. "Thanks, man."

Everyone left then—my mom and Sarah were meeting me at the bank—and the second I shut the door behind them, the finality of everything reared its ugly head. I wandered through the rooms of the house, my footsteps loud on hollow laminate flooring as a million memories from my childhood flooded my brain.

It was a strange mash-up, the combination of childhood nostalgia and traumatic grief.

I could close my eyes and smell my mom's spaghetti sauce, the one that used to cook for six hours on the Sunday stove, but I could also still look at that same stove and remember the night I set off the smoke alarms attempting to make pork chops for Sarah a few days after coming home for the funeral.

I straightened and grabbed my backpack from the counter. There was no reason for me to stay any longer. Sarah was right. The bad memories were too bad and only managed to stain what remained of the good. I needed to drive away from Teal Street and never look back.

But as I unlocked the rental car, I did.

I looked back at the house one final time, only this time, I remembered the note Liz left on the porch for me, after prom. I could still picture it, after all these days, and I could still feel the hope that had settled into my body when I realized she'd been waiting for *me* in the Secret Area.

That she'd made that CD for *me*.

Thank God that memory isn't stained, I thought, and then I got in the car and drove away from my childhood.

But not before taking a moment to pull into The Spot one final time.

CHAPTER TWENTY-EIGHT

"I would have stayed for two thousand."
"I would have paid four."
—*Pretty Woman*

Liz

"Okay, here's the plan." Sarah put her hands on her hips as we exited Emerson Field and announced, "Clark is going to ride with me and Mom, Wes is going to ride with Michael, and Liz is going to take Lilith and the equipment back to the hotel and then meet us at Nicola's."

Michael had shown up at Emerson while we filmed, which thrilled Lilith because it gave her more interview content to play with as he and Wes reminisced, and by the time we were done, Michael had organized an impromptu dinner meet-up with some of Wes's friends (the ones who'd stayed local for college).

I was over-the-moon excited to see everyone, because it'd been *way* too long.

"So fricking bossy," Clark said, looking at Wes's sister like he'd never met anyone like her.

Which was fair for sure.

"So fricking *boss*, you mean," she said, then laughed when he groaned at how lame it was. "Go dump your gear in the van before we leave without you."

"Oh, we won't leave," Wes's mom said. "She's just being a snot."

"She's good at that, isn't she?"

"She was born that way."

"Why are you assigning car pools, exactly?" Wes said, but I didn't look at him because I couldn't.

Meeting his eyes was *beyond* difficult after last night.

I can still feel him kissing away my tears.

I'd lost my mind, swept up in the moment of trying to help an old friend, and I'd almost kissed him.

It was fine, because it was simply the product of exhaustion and emotion, but I didn't want to look in his eyes and see that he thought it was more.

That he'd *seen* how much I'd wanted—*in that vulnerable moment*—for him to kiss me.

"Because she's clearly a leader," Lilith said, smiling as she looked down at her phone.

"She's clearly *something*," Clark replied. "But I'm too hungry to debate. Let's go."

Clark, Lilith, and I were walking across the parking lot, and the second Lilith answered a call, Clark said to me, "He's not over you."

"What?" My head whipped around to gawk at him, and then I glanced to see if Lilith was listening.

She wasn't, thank God.

"Who?" I asked, even though I knew damn well what he was saying.

"You know damn well who," he said quietly, his gaze spearing me with total accusation as we approached the minivan. "I know what you told me, but it's obvious there's unresolved stuff between you two. The dude looks at you like he knows he's going blind in an hour and he's trying to memorize every detail of your face."

My stomach flipped, and I remembered the way he'd looked at me on the floor of his living room.

No. I wasn't going to revisit it. It was all about grief and had nothing to do with other emotions. *Nothing.* I calmly said, "He does not."

"He *does*, and it makes me feel like trash."

I darted a glance at Lilith, who was nodding her head and looking in the other direction as she listened to the caller.

"There are thick undertones when you two are together," he insisted, looking a little mad at me. His barely visible blond eyebrows were furrowed when he said, "And I don't like the way our dating lie makes me feel."

"How does it make you feel?" I asked, hitting the button on the remote that opened the back of the minivan.

He glanced over his shoulder, like he was making sure no one else was close enough to hear.

"Like I'm hurting Bennett," he said. Then he pointed at me and said, "And don't be flip about how sentimental I am. I think he's into you, which means our lie is probably causing him pain."

"But we haven't even fake-dated very much, not really," I said defensively, because it was totally true. "I doubt he even remembers I said that."

"Oh, he remembers," he insisted, and it appeared Lilith was ending her call. Clark looked guilt-stricken when he muttered, "I can see it in his eyes when he talks to me."

"Hey. Gigantor." Sarah pulled up with her mom, honking the horn. "Cut the chatter and get in."

"Oh, look—it's my ride," he said to us, his mouth curving into a big smile as he dumped his equipment in the back of the van. "Have a good time in your room, Lil, and Liz—I'll see you at the meatballs."

I was torn between wanting to roll my eyes and laugh out loud when he climbed into the back of the car and Sarah took off. His door was barely closed before she stomped on the gas, and he let out a howl.

"That's obviously the fun car," Lilith said, loading her equipment in the back and closing the door.

"Right?"

Lilith and I talked about the footage we'd grabbed the entire way to her hotel, and it was obvious she was excited about the content. I was too—everyone had been incredibly generous. But as excited as I was, it felt like a relief to drop her off and to *not* think about it anymore.

Because I wanted to focus on seeing old friends and enjoying my last night at home before going back.

Wes would be there too, but I wasn't going to let the night be about him.

After I dropped her off, I parked at a meter spot in the Old Market and walked to the Italian restaurant.

I heard Noah's loud voice before I even got to the corner.

He was yelling something about Louisville football, *of course*.

It was impossible not to smile as I strolled down Jackson Street, the crisp autumn evening providing the perfect backdrop for a long overdue reunion. Nicola's had an amazing outdoor dining area, with strings of lights illuminating the corner patio, and when I got close to Thirteenth Street, there they were.

Gathered around the biggest table out there were my old friends, and it was like a snapshot of the before. My brain grabbed the chorus of "Old Days" and wrapped it around the moment.

Wes was leaning back in his chair, laughing with Noah about something Gigi (the restaurant owner's daughter) was saying to them, and I was happy to see they were still close. Noah was the biggest smart-ass I'd ever met, the kind of person who would debate virtually *anything* until he was proclaimed the winner, and I'd missed his sarcastic grin.

No matter how *I* felt about Wes, I was glad he still had Noah in his corner.

Michael (my former crush) was holding out his phone while Joss (my high school bestie) stood behind him and watched over his shoulder, and Wes's cousin Charlie was drawing something on a napkin that was making his girlfriend Bailey full-on belly laugh.

I miss the us from the old days . . .

"Lizard!" Clark was sitting at a smaller table with Sarah, and he raised his hand so I'd see him.

His booming voice made everyone look in my direction.

"Holy shit, you finally came home!" Joss yelled when she saw me, then ran over and threw her arms around me. I was overwhelmed by how much I'd missed my friend, and we were both a little teary when we finally pulled apart. She wiped her eyes and said, "I hate LA for stealing you from us. Come sit by me."

I followed her to the table. "But now you have more time to devote to Noah."

"Yeah, thanks for that, Buxbaum," he muttered, but his eyes were all over Joss. They were one of those couples whose love language was sarcastic roasting, I swear to God.

"Why are you over *there*?" I said to Sarah and Clark, even though they were so close they were basically within touching range.

"Because I didn't want to sit with my brother's stupid friends, so I borrowed your boy toy for company."

Clark was looking at her face as she spoke, and . . . he looked a little interested.

Interesting.

"Cool." I sat down between Joss and Michael, and I could feel Wes watching. I didn't look in his direction, but I knew.

"This is the best Italian in the city," I said to Clark, trying my hardest to act unaffected when I knew that absurdly long-lashed brown eyes were on me. "So choose your dinner carefully."

"I always choose my dinner carefully," he replied, looking at the menu.

I felt awkward for the first five minutes when I ran through all the what-are-you-up-to questions with my former friends, but then it was like we'd never been apart. I mean, it was different being with them when I wasn't *with* Wes (I connected with most of them because of him), but time and good food had a way of mellowing everything.

Dinner was great. Even though Clark turned on his camera and recorded the casual hangout, it felt like a comfortable old cardigan, warm and soothing and something I'd needed for a long time.

Clark asked a few interview questions while he inhaled portobello ravioli, but they were so braided into the friendly meal that we barely noticed them. Even when he mentioned Mr. Bennett's passing, it felt like old friends recalling their memories, as opposed to a formal interview.

"Remember how he never got my name right?" Noah said, grinning at Wes as he shoved a meatball into his mouth. "The man called me 'Isaac' for half my life."

"Well, they were both biblical names," Wes said, laughing. "Almost the same. Can you blame the man?"

"Yes," Noah loudly insisted. "Because we became friends in the *third* grade. I'm pretty sure Stu was just messing with me."

"Oh, for sure he was," Wes agreed. Then he added, "He thought you were a smart-ass little shit."

Which made Joss say, "He wasn't wrong about that, Isaac."

Everything was perfect until the lemon cake.

Which, for the record, was always perfect.

But I'd just shoveled a huge bite of delicious cake into my mouth when Clark asked Joss and Noah, "So did you guys check on Wes a lot after he quit school, since your college is so close?"

They went to UNL, which was an hour away.

"*I* did," Noah said. "But Joss was so pissed at him about New Year's that she wouldn't even let me say his name."

Oh God. The cake turned to cement in my mouth as I heard them talking like it was in slow motion.

"It's true," Joss said, throwing me a wink. "He was *dead* to me."

Shut up, shut up, shut up, I thought, wanting to disappear.

Wanting everyone to stop talking.

I felt queasy as panic shot through me—as I dreaded every possible word that was about to be spoken. We were having a fabulous time—why the hell did we have to go back to this?

Why the hell did it always go back to this?

Wes was on the other side of the table, and my cheeks burned at the thought of looking at him. I reached for my water because I didn't know what else to do.

"What happened on New Year's?" Clark asked, sounding amused, like he expected a funny story.

"Everyone slept late, the end," Sarah said, and I *did* look at her. We exchanged a knowing gaze, each remembering that morning, and I felt a little lightheaded.

And queasi*er*.

"Oh, come *on*," Clark said, his instincts just as bad as ever. "I need to hear this story."

"Nothing happened," Wes said, a warning in his voice. "I got drunk and acted like a jackass."

"Is that what we're calling cheating now?" Joss said, and it was clear that she still hadn't forgiven him either. "That seems like—"

"Joss!" I interrupted—*shut up shut up shut up*—desperate for a subject change. "Let's not. Let's just—"

"Pretend he's not the reason you've stayed away for years?"

"Oh my *God*," I bit out, my heart racing as I refused to look at Clark. Or Wes. I felt embarrassed and angry, all at the same time. But I put on a fake smile and said, "I think we should really be talking about the way Michael checked in on Wes and kicked his ass into shape."

"What?" Michael looked at Wes and said, "How does she know about that?"

I did look at Wes, then, and he was watching me closely, like he was trying to read my mind. His eyes stayed on my face as he said to Michael, "I told everyone the way you threw baseballs at me and made me vomit on the mound."

I looked down, because the intensity in that direct gaze was too much.

"For real?" Michael said, cracking up. "I thought it was our secret."

The moment *kind of* passed as Michael shared his side of the story, but Wes got quiet after that.

And so did Clark, who kept looking at me like he was thinking hard.

And he stayed that way, silently introspective, as we closed out our tab and left the restaurant.

He looked downright pensive when we started walking.

"Where did you park?" I asked Joss as we headed down Jackson Street.

"At the pay lot by Upstream," she said. "Walk with us, and we can get ice cream on the way."

"Ooh." I turned to Clark, on my other side, and said, "Ted and Wally's is on the way."

"I'm always down for ice cream," he said, but he was still looking at me in a very weird way, like he was thinking . . . processing . . . conspiring. I didn't know what to make of it, because Clark was usually the easiest person on the planet to read, but maybe I was just overthinking because I was exhausted.

We started walking toward the ice-cream shop as a group, and as everyone talked and laughed, I wished I wasn't leaving so soon.

Even after the awkward moment, I wanted to stay.

"Are you coming?" Charlie said to Bailey, who was walking behind him.

"These shoes are uncomfortable," she whined, pointing to her adorable chunky boots that laced all the way up the back. "They aren't broken in yet."

"So cute, though," Sarah said. "What size are they?"

"You're not borrowing them, because you're in California," Bailey said, in a way that made it clear Sarah had overborrowed from Bailey in the past. "Also they'll destroy your feet."

"Come on, Glasses," Charlie said, stopping and looking at Bailey over his shoulder. "You know I'm always willing to volunteer for piggybacking duty. Get on."

She smiled and in a second, was sprinting and jumping on his back.

"You *liar*," he said as she wrapped herself around him. "If you can run up on me like that, you little shit, you can probably walk."

"But why would I walk when I can bury my cold nose in your warm collar?"

I looked away from them, because something about the way they were together felt familiar.

"We need to talk, Liz," Clark said as we approached the ice-cream shop.

"What?"

He grabbed my elbow, stopping me, pulling me away from Joss and the rest of the group. He gave me a wink before he loudly said, "I can't do this anymore."

"Do what?" I said, having no idea what he was talking about.

"This," he said, sounding frustrated. "Us. It just isn't working."

"Us?" I said, and then I wondered.

Is he fake–breaking up with me?

"Clark," I bit out, looking toward my friends, who'd stopped by the door and appeared to be watching us. "Can we talk about this in the car?"

"No," he said, driving his hands into his hair and dramatically exclaiming, "because I can't take another minute of this. I can't, Lizard."

Dear God, he *was*.

But why? Why would he be doing this without talking to me first, and in front of my friends?

"Of, um, what?" I said, unsure if I was supposed to play along or what I should do. I'd never had a fake boyfriend dump me before, so this was new territory.

"Of feeling *nothing* from you," he said, putting his hands over his heart. "You looked at your *pizza* with more emotion than you look at me."

"Dude, chill," I heard Noah say, sounding annoyed.

"Oh my God," Sarah said, and I could see her covering her face in my peripheral vision.

And just like that I was irritated. *Why* wouldn't he talk to me first? My face was on fire, and I said the only thing I could think of. "I had the penne ragu with meatballs."

Charlie snorted.

"When was the last time you felt anything at all, Liz?" Clark asked melodramatically, and his eyes were twinkling. It was Clark Clarking, fully committed, and I wasn't sure whether to laugh or throat punch him.

I grabbed his tree-trunk arm and tried moving him. "Can we at least go around the corner and discuss this, where we aren't on a busy street?"

"No," he said with flourish, throwing my hand from his arm like a tantruming toddler. "I'm done—"

"Whoa," Wes said, stepping toward Clark. His face was normal, but his voice was tense when he said, "No need to manhandle her, Waters."

"He's not," I said, watching him watch Clark, wondering what he was thinking while looking so intense.

"Yeah, I'm not," Clark repeated. "I'm just ending things while we're still friends."

"Oh, is that what you're doing?" I said drily.

"Dude, ever heard of privacy?" Charlie muttered.

"Joss, um, will you order me a chocolate malt?" I said, needing to end this spectacle. "We'll be inside in just a sec."

"Yes, I will." She understood and said to the group, "Let's go order, guys."

Everyone followed—*thank God*—and as soon as the door closed behind them, I whirled on him. "What the hell, Clark? Why wouldn't you tell me before you took it upon yourself to fake-dump me?"

"I'm sorry," he said, "but it just *happened*, Liz. I was already feeling guilty about Wes, you know that, and then I rode with his sister and mom to the restaurant, and after listening to them, I just couldn't do it anymore."

"Well, you could've given me a little warning—"

"Liz." He grabbed my upper arms and squeezed, looking more intense than Clark *ever* looked. He didn't really *do* intensity. "There are things you need to know. Things I am *positive* you're unaware of."

"About Wes?" I asked. He obviously thought this was important, but I was already on Wes-overload after last night. I couldn't *handle* more Wes information.

"Yes," he said. "Sarah said—"

"I don't care," I interrupted. "There is nothing I need to know—"

He cut me off by putting his hand over my mouth and giving me stern dad eyes. "Yes. There. Is. Can you please shut up for ten seconds so I can speak?"

I sighed and nodded.

"Do you trust me?"

I nodded again, and he dropped his hand and said, "So here's the thing. I started interviewing Sarah and her mom in the car, but decided to scrap it because the mom has verbal diarrhea and overshared a lot that I don't think Bennett would want in the doc."

"Okay . . . ?" I wondered what she'd shared, but I also knew I was better off not knowing.

"But, like, it was insane stuff. Stuff that you need to see." He unlocked his phone and held it out to me. "Watch it. It's only, like, four minutes long."

I am dying to, but I can't. "Clark, I don't want—"

"I'm going to go inside and smooth things over so your friends don't kill me," he said, setting his phone in my hands as he spoke over me yet again. "The company line will be that you and I have agreed we're better as friends, and all is well. You're on a phone call and will be in, in a couple minutes. Got it?"

I looked down at his phone and wondered what I was going to see. "Okay."

"The worst that can happen is that nothing changes," he said quietly, reaching out a big hand to grab my shoulder and start pushing me toward the bench on the side of the building. He gently pushed me to a sit and tousled my hair. "But I feel like it's important for you to see this."

I watched him walk away, and after he went inside the ice-cream shop, it felt *still* outside.

Like everything in the universe was on pause.

I stared at the phone in my hand and didn't know what to do. The best move would be to *not* watch it. Their words were for Clark, not me, so I had no business eavesdropping. I'd be doing the *right* thing by moving it into the trash file and forgetting what Clark told me.

I mean, what could Wes's mom possibly say that would be *that* important for me to see? I barely knew the guy anymore. Aside from a weak moment on a living room floor (that my brain would just *not* let go of), we were merely acquaintances now.

So why am I about to watch it?

My fingers were shaking as I took a deep breath and started the video.

Clark was in the front seat, and he was filming Wes's mom, who was in the back seat behind Sarah.

She was looking directly at the camera as Clark asked her, "What do *you* think makes Wes's story so special?"

From off camera, Sarah said, "He has a sister who's cool as hell."

"Oh, I haven't met her yet," Clark said under his breath, but the camera stayed trained on Wes's mom.

She crossed her arms, and said, "The fact that he survived everything that was thrown at him. Like, literally the fact that he's not in a gutter somewhere is a triumph, right?"

That made me want to smile, her flair for the dramatic.

"Like, everyone just thinks his dad died, so he came home to help out and managed to make it back to baseball. They think that's the story. But that's not the story, kid."

"Ma," Sarah said. "Maybe don't."

"What *is* the story, in your opinion?" Clark asked.

She tilted her head and narrowed her eyes, like she could see it playing out. "For starters, he felt like Stu's death was his fault, so from the get-go, he's had to deal with a lot of guilt."

I felt my breath catch, and my eyes were fixated on the screen, dying to know more because I'd seen firsthand that *something* haunted him. Some kind of heavy grief was eating away at him.

Clark sounded shocked when he asked, "Why would he think that?"

She gave her head a shake, like it was a sad story. "He called home, and they had an argument. Stu was bullheaded and pushy as hell when it came to baseball. So Wes got mad and said a lot of terrible things that he didn't mean, including telling Stu he didn't want him at his exhibition game, which we were already packed and ready to drive across the country for."

I watched, frozen, dreading the rest.

Because his dad died *before* the exhibition game.

"So Stu hung up on him, sat down to watch a ball game, and had a heart attack an hour later."

Oh my God. My hand covered my mouth, and I swallowed, blinking back tears as I tried to imagine how anyone would handle the guilt of that.

"Oh God," Clark said. "He thinks he killed his dad?"

"Yes, sir," she said, shaking her head with tears in her eyes. "And when he came home for the funeral, I was dealing with my own PTSD, though I didn't know it at the time. I'd completely checked out, but instead of going back to school, Wessy got two full-time jobs because I couldn't work. He paid the mortgage and the rest of the bills every month, while also making sure Sarah got to school every day and had what she needed."

Oh God, oh God, oh God. I stood and wiped at my cheeks, staring at the phone in the darkness. I started pacing around the Ted and Wally's parking lot as I realized Mrs. Bennett hadn't been melodramatic at all.

It *was* a triumph that he'd survived those hits.

"Enough, Mom," Sarah said, sounding angry.

Dear God, how can this be true? How did I not know?

Why didn't he tell me?

"Wes was the one who insisted I see a therapist, so he saved my life by being stubborn," she said, coughing out a laugh while wiping her eyes. "Like, what kind of a teenager does all of that? He gave up everything he'd ever dreamed of—school, baseball, dating—to take care of us."

"Don't use this, okay, Clark?"

Clark swung the camera over to Sarah, and she looked upset. Her brown eyes, so much like Wes's, were bright with unshed tears, and she shook her head. "I think it'd kill him for people to hear this."

"I won't," I heard Clark say. "I'll delete it all. But why wouldn't he want people to know how selfless he was?"

She shrugged. "If he thinks he's the one who caused it all, it probably doesn't feel like selflessness, does it?"

"You okay?" he asked Sarah, and then the video ended.

I stood there, staring down at the phone, its silent screen jarring after what I'd just watched. I looked around, at the dark downtown night, and it felt like everything had *changed*. People were still walking around, smells of delicious food swirling in the air, but it had become a different place.

It was now the setting for a heartbreaking plot twist.

How was it possible? My mind was racing through memories, comparing what I had with what I now knew. The silly, lighthearted Wes who'd FaceTimed me every night back then had been going through *that*?

And it was tough to decide what the worst part of the story was. Was it Wes thinking he was responsible for his dad's death, that his harsh words had *literally* killed his father, or Wes having the weight of the world resting on his eighteen-year-old shoulders?

"Liz."

I gasped and turned around in time to see the door to the ice-cream shop closing behind Wes. He zipped his jacket and walked toward me. I wiped at my cheeks, but it was no use as I saw him watching me like he could see the mascara tracks.

"Are you okay?" he asked, his eyebrows furrowed together. "Clark was an asshole to—"

"Why didn't you tell me, Wes?" I heard myself ask, my voice cracking.

"What?" He narrowed his eyes. "Tell you what?"

"Why didn't you tell me about everything you were dealing with after your dad died?" I asked, abandoning any hope of keeping it together. I couldn't hold back the tears as I imagined the way he must've felt, and I wanted *so badly* to be able to go back in time and know the truth so I could help him. "Why didn't you let me help you?"

His mouth opened like he was going to speak, but he didn't. He closed his mouth and squinted, like he was trying to figure out what he was supposed to say.

"We talked *every* day, Wes," I said, grieving for him two years too late. My voice was thick when I said, "And you never said a word about any of it. You told me you were working a lot to save money for school. Were you seriously working two jobs to pay all of your family's bills?"

"Someone had to do it; it wasn't a big deal," he said, looking uncomfortable.

"It wasn't a big deal?" I asked, my voice a high-pitched squeal. "God, why wouldn't you say something? I could've helped you."

"How?" he asked, shrugging like he was embarrassed. "How could you have helped? You were a teenager away at college—what could you have done?"

"I could've been there for you," I said, hiccupping out a sob that should've embarrassed me, but I was too emotional to care. "I could've supported you while you dealt with all of it. God, was I so self-centered, you couldn't tell me?"

I said it more to myself than to him, honestly.

"Was I so tied up in what I was doing at school that you felt like you couldn't say anything?"

"No," he insisted, stepping a little closer to me, shaking his head.

"That wasn't it at all. I was dealing with so much shit, spiraling and hating who I was every *fucking* day, and I didn't want to take you down with me."

"But you wouldn't have," I said, shaking my head as grief shook *me*. Grief for the boy he'd been and the people we'd been together. "You said it yourself, that I was away at college. You *couldn't* have taken me down."

"It was already happening, Liz," he snapped.

"What? No, it wasn't," I argued, irritated by whatever case he was trying to make. Because there was no reason he couldn't have told me. Maybe it was a guilty conscience, but I felt defensive, for some reason.

"Oh, really?" He raised his eyebrows and said, "Remember Jack Antonoff?"

"What?" I looked up at him like he was crazy because *what the hell* did that mean?

"You were invited to an industry event at Antonoff's house," he said, looking angry now. "Do you remember that?"

"Yeah. Sort of . . . ?" I *did* remember that I was invited but I couldn't remember why I hadn't gone.

Why wouldn't I have gone?

"You and your roommate Bushra were invited. She went, but you stayed home because you said you'd rather talk to me."

"Okay . . . ?" I said, unsure of the point he was making. I was also surprised I would've done that, to be honest.

He looked pissed that I didn't remember. His voice was a little louder when he said, "You had this incredible opportunity to do something that could help your career, but you chose to stay home and talk to your grocery-stocking boyfriend, in fucking Nebraska, on the phone, instead."

"So?" I said, unsure why we were kind of yelling at each other now.

Unsure, yet it was right. I was full of rage and sadness and angst about everything that'd ever happened with us, and it was boiling over as he spoke like freshman Liz had been a lovesick idiot.

"So I was already taking you down—don't you see?" His voice was loud with frustration when he said, "God, Liz, you blew off Jack fucking Antonoff for me!"

"Oh, come *on*, Wes—"

"Seriously," he said, cutting me off. His dark eyes were flashing when he added, "Who does that? Who has the chance to meet their idol but chooses to take a *nothing* phone call instead?"

"Are you *mad* at me for not going to Jack Antonoff's party?" I asked, confused by why *this* recollection from back then seemed to anger him.

"Yes!"

I looked up at raging Wes and had no idea what to say.

"Don't you see? That was *why*," he bit out in frustration, shaking his head back and forth while his eyes were hot. "That was when I knew I had to br—"

His mouth snapped shut. He stopped talking and scratched his eyebrow.

"Had to what?" I said, watching him censor himself.

"Nothing," he said, his Adam's apple moving around a big swallow. "I just—"

"No, Wes, what were you going to say?" My heart raced as I asked the question that I suddenly knew the answer to. "That was when you knew you had to . . . ?"

His jaw flexed and unflexed, his eyes on me, before he said, "That was when I knew I had to break up with you."

CHAPTER TWENTY-NINE

"Last night should've been the biggest night of my life, and it wasn't. It wasn't because you weren't there. So I just wanted to tell you, not to change your mind or keep you from going, but just so you know, that I know, that I do need you."

—*For Love of the Game*

Wes

"But." Her green eyes looked huge as she gazed up at me like I'd just hit her. "The Antonoff party was *right* after you moved home."

"Yeah," I said, not sure where this was going.

"So we didn't break up for weeks," she said, her eyebrows furrowing.

Because I wasn't strong enough to let you go, Lib.

I'd known it was the best thing for her, and I was determined to do it.

But every night, I was too weak.

As soon as I heard the sound of her incoming FaceTime, I'd tell myself *one more time* and get lost in Liz for one more conversation.

"Was that why you were so distant?" she asked. "You were trying to get rid of me?"

"I had to," I said, feeling weak from the recollection. "I *loved* you."

That flipped a switch. As soon as I said *I loved you*, her face went from sad and confused to straight-up angry.

"No, you were *cheating* on me," she said through gritted teeth. "Don't you *dare* act like you loved me, Wes."

"But I *did*," I yelled, because that was the only truth I'd ever known. "I *always* loved you."

"Shut up," she snapped, but her tears lessened the aggression as she shook her head and hiccupped out a little sob. I felt it in the center of my chest when she said, "I hate that you suffered, and I hate what you went through, but that doesn't erase what you did."

"I didn't, though," I said, ready to finally confess. "I didn't cheat on you, Lib."

She took a step back, putting her hands on top of her head and looking at me like I was out of my mind. Her eyes were huge when she said, "You can't lie about this now, Wes, because you were the one who *told* me that you did, remember?"

Yeah, how could I ever forget?

New Year's Day
Two Years Ago

I was lying in bed, hungover and depressed, when the doorbell started ringing.

The first time, it was a singular ring.

Since Sarah and I never answered the door unless we were expecting someone, we both ignored it.

And when it rang again, we responded in the same way.

But then, whoever was at the door lost their ever-loving mind and started lying on the bell, ringing that thing over and over and over again like a psycho.

"Go away," I muttered, covering my head with my pillow. Just being awake was bad enough; I definitely wasn't interested in engaging with another human.

But then I heard Sarah run down the stairs and open the door.

Idiot. It was probably those people who sold pest control door to door.

But in an instant, everything inside me roared awake and my heart started pounding *hard* in my chest, because I heard *her* voice. I heard Liz say, "I need to talk to your brother."

I wanted to scream *NO!*, to lock my door and hide under the bed, because there was no possible way I was strong enough to be alone with her and not beg her to love me forever.

"I think he's still asleep," Sarah said. I knew my sister liked Liz, so the odds weren't in my favor that she'd slam the door and throw the dead bolt.

"In his room?" Liz asked.

Please don't come up here please don't come up here. I looked around like a fool, trying to find some way to escape, but there was nothing.

Nothing but the sound of her footsteps on the stairs.

Coming down the hallway toward my bedroom.

I closed my eyes and pretended to be asleep, like a total coward, clueless as to what the hell I was supposed to do.

She knocked on my door—*please go away, Lib*—but then I heard her step into the room.

"Wes," she said, and my heart seized in my chest at the sound of her voice so close. "Wake up."

I opened my eyes and instantly regretted it. Because somehow she looked *more* wounded than she had last night, when I'd intentionally hurt her. Her cheeks were pink and her eyes were red, and I wanted to pull her down on the bed and kiss her until she forgave me.

Instead, I scratched my head and said, "Liz?"

I sat up, pretending I was half-awake and confused when all I really was, was a dick.

"Tell me about you and Ashley," she said, her voice cracking.

Dammit. As I'd been pouting on the deck at the party the night before, Ash laid a peck on me at midnight. There had been nothing to it—it was only because of New Year's, and I was surprised Liz had heard about it at all.

I wished I could make her feel better so fucking badly, but I shrugged and said, "It was New Year's Eve, Buxbaum."

"I'm not talking about last night," she snapped, looking like she wanted to hit me. Or bawl her eyes out. *I hated both.* She took in a breath and said, "People are saying that you and Ashley were 'hanging out' in October, when you and I were still together."

Of course not.

There is no one for me but you, Lib.

In October I was too busy missing you to notice other humans.

It obviously wasn't true—I worked with Ashley and that was it, but people in this town loved starting rumors.

I didn't know what to say as she watched me, gnawing on her

bottom lip. I wanted to reassure her more than I wanted to breathe, but maybe this idiotic rumor was exactly what I needed. I said, "Is that right?"

She nodded and asked, "Is it true?"

No, it's not true! God, Lib, do you really think I could ever do that?

I took a deep breath, staring into her eyes, and managed to sound bored when I said, "Does it really matter now?"

"*Yes*, it matters," she said, blinking back tears I wanted to kiss away. "Of *course* it matters. Did you cheat on me, Wes?"

I dragged a hand down my face, down the beard that belonged to an unfamiliar person, and I said, "I don't know—it's a blur, okay? I can't remember exactly when one thing ended and another began, y'know?"

My throat hurt. It was burning as I forced it to speak these ridiculous lies.

"Bullshit," she said, a hiccup in her voice. "Just admit it."

"Seriously?" I felt nauseous as she looked up at me, and I forced myself to groan like she was a total pain in the ass. "Okay, I guess I admit it."

I looked down, unable to look at her or anything because I was a half second from falling apart. I reached out and grabbed my phone from the nightstand, as if I was so uninterested in our conversation that I needed something to look at.

But she broke my heart when she said in the smallest voice, "Why?"

I did look at her then, because I realized at that moment, I'd probably never be that close to her again. I wanted to bawl as

I looked into her eyes and said, "Because she was here and you weren't."

"God, I hate you," she whispered before running out of the room, and I knew we'd never be okay again.

I took a deep breath and forced myself back to the present.

"But it's true," I said. "I only said I cheated to get you to move on."

Her face became impossible to read as she said, "Explain what the hell that could mean."

I took a deep breath and just dove in.

"When you showed up on New Year's Eve, I expected you to hate me for breaking up with you. I was positive you'd moved on. But then you smiled at me."

Her eyes narrowed, and I wasn't sure if she was glaring or listening intently.

"You smiled at me and even took the kiss bet. I realized, when you looked at me, that even though we weren't together, you still hadn't moved on."

She made a noise in the back of her throat, almost a growl, but I kept going.

"And you needed to because it was for the best. So I was an asshole at the party, on purpose, and when you accused me of cheating the next morning, I took the easy out."

"But everyone said you and Ashley had been—"

"We worked together after I moved back, and we commiserated a lot because we both had crappy home lives. So people saw us together and made assumptions." I stepped closer to Liz, needing her to believe me. "But we were always just friends, because there was never anyone else for me but you."

She growled again, then said, "So you broke up with me because you loved me so much, and then said you cheated on me because you needed me to move on but knew I wouldn't unless you did something terrible."

I knew something wasn't right in that, but I said, "Yes . . . ?"

"And this is the absolute truth?" she asked, her eyes everywhere on my face.

"Swear on my life," I said, feeling relieved because she looked like she believed me.

"Dear God, I cannot believe the ego." Liz shook her head, her eyes wide as she yelled, "How can you be so incredibly arrogant?"

"Arrogant?" I was truly confused. I was a lot of things, but arrogant wasn't one of them.

"*Yes!* Are you God? Are you my dad? How would it ever be your place to decide what's best for me without my input?"

"It wasn't like that—come on," I said, rubbing the side of my neck, wishing I could make her understand. "But I know you, Lib. I knew you'd stay with me no matter how big of a loser I became, and I couldn't let you do that."

"For starters, do you realize how insulting it is that you think I'm, like, so childish or lovesick or freaking *enamored* with you that I would just stay like a loyal retriever no matter what?" She was full-on yelling now, her eyes blazing. "You infantilized me by assuming you knew best. God save me from this ego."

"There was no ego involved," I argued, a little pissed because I might've screwed up, but my entire life was a pile of shit at the time. "For God's sake, Lib, you have no idea what it was like. Just put yourself in my shoes for five seconds."

"I don't know *how* to be in the shoes of God, Wes."

"And can you take a half second to recognize the fact that I never cheated on you? Can I at least get a reprieve for that?"

"No!"

"You guys?"

"What?" Liz and I yelled in unison.

I looked to my right, and Sarah was standing there, watching us with her eyebrows raised.

"We need to leave for the airport," she said sheepishly, holding the keys to my mom's car as she looked back and forth between the two of us.

"I need five more minutes," I said, not even *close* to finished.

"No—I'm done," Liz said, pushing her hair behind her ears. "Safe travels, Sarah."

She marched away from me and toward the ice-cream shop, her rage whipping like a breeze behind her. I stared as she went inside, and I could see through the windows as she walked up to Joss and started talking.

God, I love the way she talks with her hands when she's pissed.

"I'm really sorry."

"What?"

Sarah was looking at me like a worried parent, like she was afraid I was going to break down. "I feel like this is my fault."

"It's not your fault." I put my hands in my pockets and kept watching Liz through the window. "You didn't force me to lie."

"No, but I've been telling you for forever that you needed to be honest with Liz. Now you finally listened, and it backfired."

"How do you figure?" I watched as Joss shook her head and put her hands on her hips.

"Um, all the yelling . . . ?" Sarah replied, her voice full of sarcasm. "I hadn't imagined it would go off the rails quite like that."

"I actually think it's good." I looked back at my sister and felt relaxed all of a sudden. "The air has finally been cleared."

"Huh," she said, looking at me suspiciously. "I would *not* have pictured you responding this calmly."

"Well, you don't know everything, do you, Stanford?" I teased, then looked up at the sky. It was a clear night, so clear that I could see a few stars in spite of the downtown lights, and it felt like *something*.

"Rewrite the Stars" started playing in my head as I thought about the fact that Sarah was right—it *didn't* make sense that I wasn't more upset right now.

But two things had just come into my head, realizations as clear as those tiny stars in the night sky, and they were making me really fucking happy.

The first—Liz was single now. She was finally available, and she didn't seem to be all that broken-up about losing Clark.

All she'd screamed about was me.

Us.

And that was the second thing—her rage. Liz was livid, angrier than I'd ever seen her, and that was . . . well, kind of fantastic.

Because it meant she hadn't moved on.

She wasn't over us at all.

Something that felt a hell of a lot like hope was buzzing through me as I looked up at those stars and pictured her face when she'd yelled, *I don't know* how *to be in the shoes of God, Wes!*

Because instead of the measured looks I'd gotten used to from her, where it felt like her feelings were locked up tight, she'd looked at me with flushed cheeks and flashing green eyes, as if she was engulfed in the white-hot flames of her blazing anger.

Toward *me*.

There really *was* a fine line between love and hate, and Libby's rage fueled me to burn that line to the ground.

What if we rewrite the stars
Say you were made to be mine . . .

CHAPTER THIRTY

"I can't see anything I don't like about you."
—*Eternal Sunshine of the Spotless Mind*

Liz

I drank my malt and hung out with my friends after that, but it wasn't the same. I felt emotionally drained and didn't know what to do with all the thoughts that were going on in my head. I could tell everyone wanted to know what'd just happened, but I didn't want to talk about it.

I mean, how could I talk about it when *I* couldn't even make sense of it?

When I took Clark back to his hotel, he tried mentioning the video but I wouldn't let him. Which was ironic in that when I tried going to sleep, that video was on repeat in my head. I lay there in my childhood bedroom, the same room where I experienced so many emotions regarding Wes over the years, and I heard his words over and over again.

I didn't cheat on you, Lib.

I don't know why, but sometime around midnight, I was compelled to go sit in the Secret Area with my wouldn't-be-silenced thoughts. I knew it didn't belong to the Bennetts anymore, but I also knew the new people hadn't moved in yet, so I wasn't going to get arrested for being back there.

I quietly slipped out the patio door and ran through the backyard, the way I'd done so many times to meet Wes the summer after my senior year, and I climbed over the fence.

But I wasn't ready for what I saw.

Oh my God. "Overgrown" didn't even begin to describe it. It was impossible to believe it was the same place, to be honest. It was like it'd reverted to its former self, the wild place that lent itself to epic games of hide-and-seek. It was so overgrown that it took me a minute to even *find* where the firepit was.

Where the space used to be an oasis, it was now just a crooked firepit with a lawn chair sitting beside it. The fountain, the flowers—they were long forgotten. I wasn't sure if they'd been removed or just swallowed by nature. I reached down and grabbed an empty bottle of Corona off the ground, wondering if that was what Wes had been drinking last night.

God, was that really only last night? The universe had shifted since then.

There was a big piece of wood in the firepit, and I pulled the matches and lighter fluid I'd snagged from the kitchen out of my pocket. I lit a tiny fire, for some reason needing the ceremonial feeling of ritual as I soaked in the dark night.

Because I was feeling melancholy, I scrolled through Spotify until I found the OG playlist, the one from senior year. I hadn't let myself get in my feels about Wes in a long time, but there was no avoiding it that night. I turned on Adele and leaned my head back, looking up at the sky.

The night was clear, the stars were bright, and I was utterly lost.

"Hey, kiddo."

I looked up and my dad was climbing over the fence in his stupid banana pajama pants and LUKE'S DINER T-shirt. I don't know why, but seeing him and hearing his voice made my eyes get a little misty.

"Tell me what happened," he said, coming over and dropping to the ground beside me. "We could tell when you got home that you were upset, but we decided to leave you alone."

"What changed?" I asked, amused by the wonderful way my dad was always the same.

"When I heard you sneak out the back door, I figured you needed to talk to someone. I thought I'd volunteer as tribute. So what happened with Wes?"

"How do you know this is about Wes?" I asked, sniffling.

He just said, "It's always about Wes, honey."

"I don't even know where to start," I said, shaking my head.

"Just start at the beginning," he said, leaning back on his arms. "I don't have any plans."

"Okay," I said, and I just took off. I told him *everything*, then rambled to him about the way it was impossible for me to reconcile my feelings. I'd had two massive revelations that night, and each brought out opposing feelings.

Every time I thought about poor Wes and what he'd gone

through, my heart was broken for him. I was so sad for everything he'd lost and equally sad that he hadn't been able to tell me. I felt like somehow I failed him, that obviously there was some reason he hadn't been able to open up to me.

"But as soon as I think that, I get so frustrated over what we lost because we didn't *have* to lose it, right? It's probably unfair to be mad at him for doing something he considered selfless, that he thought he was doing for *me*, but it was just such a waste. It didn't have to end. Instead of trusting *me*, he made the executive decision that I couldn't be trusted, and he walked away."

And the lie about Ashley pissed me off. I didn't feel guilty about being mad at him for that. Because it just felt so childish, so *arrogant*, that he thought I would never get over him unless I thought he cheated.

"So did he apologize?" my dad asked, lifting his hands to warm them by the fire.

"No," I said. "Or, he might've said it during the fight, but it wasn't an apology-apology."

Had he? I really didn't think so.

"Did you tell him you were going to get back to him about this or something?" he asked.

"No, I yelled at him and left."

That made him smile a little, but he said, "So then who cares? Who cares about your conflicted feelings? It's okay for them to not make sense, and it's okay to be sad about him and pissed off at him, all at the same time."

He grabbed a stick and tossed it into the firepit. "It's fine to have no idea what you think about any of it—don't you see? You can say 'I don't know how I feel about him' and then just let it go. If you don't have to get back to him with an answer on something, like, he's not asking you out or proposing marriage, just be confused. You don't have to figure this one out."

"Oh my God, are you right?" I asked, shocked that his words were somehow making a lot of sense.

"I have my moments," he teased.

Could I really just shrug and *not* come to a conclusion on my Wes Bennett feelings?

My dad hung out with me for a few more minutes after that, but then I think he sensed I needed to be alone, and he went inside.

Which left me to stare into the fire and picture Wes's face when he'd said, *There was never anyone else for me but you*.

Cue "Anyone Else" by Joshua Bassett.

He'd looked so . . . old-school Wes.

The Wes of before, the Wes who'd been my everything.

I was still in shock that he hadn't stopped loving me and he hadn't cheated on me.

I just . . . I couldn't believe it.

I knew—now—what he'd been going through at the time, so technically I understood his motivations. And if I were watching this plot in a Netflix movie, I'd probably be yelling at my TV, *He did it because he loved you!*

But it wasn't a Netflix movie, and I just couldn't get past the fact that he'd completely shut down. Not once during our endless text conversations and daily multiple calls did he mention his concerns.

He told me about work and his sister and his dog, and he told me he loved me, but he'd never said he was worried about *anything*. At all. I'd thought everything was perfectly fine until he dumped me out of the blue. *It's just not meant to be for us anymore.*

But even then, as I bawled my eyes out, I hadn't been mad.

He'd lost his dad and his entire world had changed—*of course* our relationship wasn't his priority. I'd been devastated, yes, and surprised by how cold he'd sounded, but in my heart, I'd known it wasn't permanent.

Eventually, we'd find our way back to each other again.

I'd been certain of it.

Silly little love lover.

And then I learned he'd been cheating on me with Ashley. I'd hated him for that for so long that it felt like it was part of me now. *My name's Liz, I have red hair, and I hate Wes Bennett.*

So now I was supposed to not only be done with hating him, but accept the fact that he'd treated me that way to save me from myself? On paper it sounded possible, but I wasn't sure that it was.

Because it hurt my feelings, if I was being honest, that he hadn't been able to talk to me. That he'd been going through hell on the down-low. Had he faked our every exchange after he went home, then? When we were laughing together on FaceTime and talking about how we couldn't wait until I came home for Christmas, was it all an act on his part? Like a put-on-a-brave-face-so-the-kids-won't-know type of situation?

It also stung that he obviously saw me as someone who'd just abandon all her goals and aspirations in the name of love. I'd always assumed he saw me as strong, as someone with a little drive, but apparently he saw me as a wide-eyed, lovesick girl who'd blindly follow him around for the rest of my life unless I was stopped.

And man, had he stopped me.

I was still driving myself crazy with this emotional loop when I finally went to sleep, but I felt better about everything in the morning, thank *God.*

My dad's simple statement changed my entire outlook, because he was right.

I didn't *have* to understand my feelings about Wes.

Technically, they didn't even matter.

We weren't dating, we weren't really even friends, so it was okay to be conflicted. There was no one waiting for me to pass down my final decision, to render my judgment on Wes Bennett's sins. It was okay for me to ache for what he went through, and it was okay for me to want to punch him for giving up on us.

Really, my dad was right.

Nobody cares.

Helena went on a Krispy Kreme run while I showered, so I got to wolf down a couple of donuts before we left for the airport. We picked up Clark and Lilith on the way, and when I hugged my dad goodbye in the departure drop-off lane, he solidified my okayness by repeating his sentiment but in a different font.

"Remember—you don't have to overanalyze the past. Just live your now life."

"I love you," I said, squeezing him while wishing we could've stayed longer.

"Love you, too, kiddo," he said.

"You're coming home for Christmas, you little snot," Helena said with a smile (while she cried). "So don't even try to get out of it."

"I won't," I said, wrapping her in a hug while knowing I'd never want to stay away again.

Clark tried bringing up Wes on the plane, but he was cool when I told him I didn't want to talk about it. *All* my roommates seemed to respect my need for privacy on this after I got back, which was surprising when they were usually all over my business. I was able to spend the rest of the weekend getting caught up on my studies, and it was wonderful.

But on Sunday, as I sat at a table on the Kerckhoff patio, trying my damnedest to study for my copyright law exam, Wes was back on my mind. It was a gorgeous day, the trees giving me the perfect amount of shade as the patio buzzed with students, and I should've been having one of those top-ten-studying-on-campus kinds of days.

It was like a damn postcard for fall semester out there.

But I wasn't seeing any of it, not really, because Wes kept popping into my head.

There was never anyone else for me but you.

"I thought you were studying." Campbell sat down with a coffee and said, "It looks like you're just staring into space with your mouth wide open."

"What?" I blinked, slow on the uptake. "Oh, no. I was just thinking."

"Hey, has Wade asked you for my number yet?"

She was actually kind of interested in the mildly obnoxious first baseman, but she refused to engage until he took the time to get her number from me and actually call for a date. She said she didn't have time for *boys who only chase me at parties where they think they might score*, and so far, she was making the right call.

Because he never asked me about her when he was sober.

"Nope," I said. "I saw him at practice earlier, but he was busy. Sorry."

"It's fine," she said, taking out her laptop and acting like she didn't care, even though I knew she was disappointed. For someone who was beautiful and smart and ridiculously talented on a soccer field, she was shy when it came to guys. "I'm pretty sure he's an asshole, anyway."

My phone buzzed, and when I picked it up off the table, I couldn't believe my eyes.

It was Wes.

Wes: Hi.

I stared at the message, my brain misfiring and shooting screaming fireworks out my ears as I struggled to figure out what to even say. How did he expect me to respond to his stupid "hi" message?

I mean, what even was that? *Hi??* Like we were pals and he would just text me "hi" whenever he wanted to?

Hi????

Another buzz.

Wes: Obviously you don't know how to respond, and that's fine.

Wes: I just wanted to say hi because you're on my mind.

Wes: Have a great day. Also—I just listened to "You Could Start a Cult" by Lizzy and Niall, and if you haven't heard it, seems like a Buxbaum song.

And he dropped a link.

Damn him. How could he possibly know?

I gritted my teeth and texted: **A little too sweet for my tastes but thx.**

But because it was Wes, my message stopped nothing.

Wes: It's a gorgeous song, are you kidding me right now?

I replied: **I didn't say it isn't a good song, I said it's not for me.**

Wes: Liar.

I absolutely *was* lying. But it irked me, the way he acted like he knew what I liked when there was no way that he could.

Alexa, play "Hate That You Know Me" by Bleachers.

I texted: **I'm kind of busy right now. Did you need something . . . ?**

The phone buzzed almost immediately, and when I looked down, butterflies went wild in my stomach.

Wes: Oh, honey, you have no idea.

My head was about to explode as I read it, then read it again, wondering why it was so hot in there and then realizing I was outside.

Thankfully, I didn't have to respond.

Because he added: **But for now, I'll leave you alone. Later, Lib.**

CHAPTER THIRTY-ONE

"I was born to kiss you."
—*Only You*

Wes

"Stop laughing."

"I can't, though." Mickey popped up from his squat behind home plate and threw back the ten balls that'd been in the dirt beside him, shaking his head with a stupid grin on his face. "She's going to destroy you."

"No, she's not." Yeah, she probably was, but not for the reasons he thought. I caught each ball and dropped them on the mound by my feet, wiping my forehead with the back of my arm. It was already hot and humid, and it wasn't even nine o'clock yet. I'd convinced Mick to break into the high school field down the street with me, even though it was a Sunday, because I wanted to test myself.

And so far, so good.

"I have a full-scale offensive planned that is guaranteed to get me in the door," I informed him, so ready to go hard with this. "A brilliant, carefully crafted plan that is fail-proof."

He dropped back down and held out his glove. "Sounds stupid."

"*You* sound stupid." I flipped the ball, running my index finger along the seam before taking a deep breath.

"Seriously, you're gonna try too hard."

"The thing is, I know Liz because we grew up together," I said before winding up and letting loose with a fastball. "I know what she likes and how she thinks, because I've known her since kindergarten. And I know that if I go big on the romantic gestures, it's only a matter of time before she goes out with me."

"Dude," he said, dropping the ball he'd caught and holding out his glove to catch another. "She must've changed since you knew her, because no way would Buxxie like that romantic bullshit."

I threw hard, relishing the smack of the ball hitting Mick's glove. And though he might have a point—obviously we'd both changed over the course of two years—I was confident her romantic side was still alive and kicking, just buried underneath the surface.

"No offense," I said as I grabbed another ball. "But I know what I'm doing."

"My apologies," he said, sounding anything but sorry. "So tell me about this brilliant plan, Einstein."

I threw a curveball, watching it drop over the plate. "For starters, I'm going to need to borrow your car tomorrow night."

"No way," he said as he caught it. "I'll drive you somewhere, but no one borrows Alice."

"Do I want to know why your car has an old-lady name?"

"Don't besmirch my ride, you dick." He pushed up his mask. "Where do you need to go?"

I started telling him my plan, the perfect romantic plan to sweep Liz off her feet, and he started laughing again. *Hard.* As in, so hard that he couldn't stay upright and ended up sitting on his ass, in the dirt, cracking up.

"You're an asshole," I said, even though I was laughing too.

"An asshole who can't wait to drive you to Liz's," he said, wiping his eyes. "This is going to be the most entertaining spectacle I've ever witnessed."

I flipped him off, unfazed, because I had confidence.

I didn't know much, but I knew Liz.

I knew if I was ever going to have a chance at getting her back, I needed to apologize and show her that I could still be the guy she fell in love with two years ago.

That I *was* the same guy.

And what better way to apologize to Elizabeth Buxbaum than with *hundreds* of flowers?

I mean, did I discover the following day that two hundred daisies were a hell of a lot more than I'd pictured? *Yes.* Did I look like an idiot, wheeling a cart overflowing with flowers down Gayley Avenue? *Also yes.*

But I didn't care because I knew it would work.

It wouldn't win her over, but it would work to soften her.

It *had* to work.

"How the hell do you think we're going to fit those in here?" Mick yelled, getting out and coming around to the back of his Mazda.

"Pop the trunk. We're going to jam them in," I said.

"Won't that crush 'em?"

"I only need the petals," I said, gesturing for him to open the trunk. "So it's fine for them to get smooshed."

"You've officially lost it," he laughed, reaching into the cart and grabbing an armful of daisies.

After getting the flowers crammed in the trunk, we had to stop at two different dollar stores for a crap-ton of candles (they didn't have enough at the first one). And by the time we got back to the dorms, he'd notified Wade, Eli, and AJ, who were all waiting in my room with cameras and mockery.

"Well, would you look at little Wessy," Wade yelled as I came inside and dropped a few bunches of flowers onto the table. "Is he the sweetest or what?"

"Screw you," I said, going back out to get more flowers.

"I can't believe this is for Buxxie," Eli said, shaking his head. "Where are you going to put all those things?"

"Bend over and I'll show you," I said, quoting Clark Griswold as I hauled in the rest of the daisies.

"It's like a promposal up in here," I heard Wade say to AJ. "I can't believe what I'm seeing."

I couldn't either, to be honest, but the joke was on them.

Because I didn't give a damn.

I was bringing everything I had and leaving it all on the field.

Or on the balcony, in this instance.

Once I'd unloaded all the daisies, I put on headphones and cranked the playlist Liz made for me after prom as I sat on the floor and started plucking petals. "Feel You Now" was suddenly like my crafting pump-up music, and it also served to tune out my friends, who were taking photos as I worked and calling me "sweetheart."

They promised not to post them until after I swept her off her feet, so it was fine.

By the time I was done, I had a few gallon-size baggies full of white petals, a few gallon-size baggies full of yellow petals, marker-stained fingers, and a stomach full of nerves.

So yeah—I was ready.

Once it was dark outside, I loaded everything—except the bouquet of hot-pink gerbera daisies—into my biggest backpack, and Mick drove me to Liz's apartment building. I knew exactly which balcony was theirs—I'd staked it out with Mick on the way to flowers—and I also knew it was an easy climb up to the second floor.

Thank God the fancy building had garden-level apartments because that meant the second floor wasn't so high that I was risking my life.

I was merely risking broken bones.

AJ had a class with Campbell, apparently, so he helped me out by texting: **I need a favor, no questions asked.** To which Campbell responded: **Tell me what I'm doing.** She'd agreed to make sure Liz's drapes would be closed while I worked, and then as soon as I finished, Liz would be sent out onto the balcony, wherein she would see my display.

Then she'd look down and see me, standing below with my *Love Actually* knock-off posters. My Sharpie words weren't necessarily rom-com-worthy sentiments, but I felt like they were us, and I wanted to make her soften more than I wanted to breathe.

Mick parked the car, so I strapped on the backpack and grabbed the bouquet.

"You sure about this, Bennett?" he asked, half smiling like he still couldn't believe I was doing it.

"Yes," I said. "You can take off. And thanks, by the way."

"And you don't want me to stay?" He eyeballed me like I was making a big mistake. "Just in case . . . uh, anything goes wrong?"

"Nah, I'm good," I said, hoping that was true. Hoping she'd let me in after the big moment so we could talk and I could apologize.

"Okay, then." He gave me a little smile and said, "Good luck, man."

I watched him pull away, and then it hit me, that it was a little nerve-wracking, actually doing it. The back of the building was dark and quiet, like everyone had already gone to bed, and I sincerely hoped I wouldn't die, get my ass kicked, or get mauled by an angry rottweiler.

Out of the corner of my eye I saw a guy on the garden floor of the other building, doing something outside his sunken patio. *Go to bed, dude.* He looked like he was watering plants, maybe? He seemed focused on his work, unaware of my presence, so hopefully he stayed on task and didn't notice the moron scaling the building next to his.

I looked up at Liz's balcony.

Oof.

It definitely looked higher when you were about to climb up to it.

I took a deep breath, said a little prayer, then got to work.

I walked over to the garden apartment that was below Liz's and stepped on the railing. My shoe made a noise, the ring of hollow wrought iron being kicked, and I quickly grabbed the gutter and stepped up onto the limestone that jutted out from the building's facade.

I definitely did not want to linger in front of someone's balcony after dark and get accused of being a Peeping Tom.

Or worse.

"What the?"

I glanced down when I heard those words, but I couldn't see anyone, so hopefully that was just the sound of someone talking inside their apartment with the window open. My heart started pounding as I climbed farther up the limestone, using the gutter for balance.

When I got close enough to kick a leg out onto Liz's balcony, I damn-near had a heart attack when I looked below.

Because I'd miscalculated.

I was definitely high enough to fall to my death.

Shit, shit, shit.

I threw my weight over and landed on her balcony, a little harder than I would've liked, but thankfully it had a concrete pad that absorbed the sound. Pulse pounding, I took off the backpack, unzipped it, and started getting busy.

I set out the candles, one by one, lining them up to form a heart and then a larger heart around it. Once I finished that, I opened the daisy petals and sprinkled the white inside the smaller heart, and the yellow inside the bigger heart.

I stood back to look and, dear *Lord*, it looked good.

Liz will love this, I thought as I took a quick photo and put my phone away.

The nerves were still there, but now they were joined by excitement.

It's going to work.

I pulled the big lighter from the backpack, leaned down, and started lighting the votives.

Which looked *amazing* in the darkness.

"What are you doin' up there?"

Fuuuuck. I glanced down, and the guy from garden level was looking up at me from below with a scowl on his face and something in his hand. *Is that a hose?* It was too dark to tell from where I was.

"Shhh," I said, holding up my hand.

"He's trying to start a fire!" the guy yelled, and I realized the lighter was in my hand, the orange tip flickering in the dark.

"No, I'm not!" I released the button on the lighter, trying to yell down at the guy while also being quiet. Something with a motor was humming now, so I felt like he couldn't hear me, but I also didn't want to alert Liz to my presence. "Christ, I'm—"

My words were stopped by his pressure washer.

His fucking pressure washer.

That was the humming motor.

The guy pointed up with his pressure washer and sprayed me, the deck, the candles—*fuuuuck*. It was nearly impossible for me to see as he exfoliated my fucking head, but that high-pressured water wiped out the flower petals and blew out the candles.

"Will you stop it?" I whisper-yelled, trying to see while getting my face waterboarded by a dipshit with a pressure hose. I stumbled, kicking over candles, trying to shield my eyes with my hand as I said, "I'm not trying to—"

"What's going on?" A woman appeared beside him, squinting up at the balcony while holding out her phone. "Is there another possum—"

"There's an arsonist!" he yelled.

Yeah, I was pretty sure I was having a heart attack as my entire body went numb.

Shit shit shit, this was not going the way I'd imagined. I'd imagined falling to my death but hadn't imagined getting fingered for arson.

I needed to get the hell out of there.

"House on Fire"—smart-ass mental playlist shit—screamed through my head as I threw my backpack over one shoulder, climbed over to the gutter, and turned sideways so I was partially hidden by the corner of the building.

It was no use, though, because they were staring at me—she was filming, for the love of God—as I navigated that gutter like I actually *was* a possum. The building had a security light that was serving as my spotlight, and I wasn't sure how this could get much worse.

But then my foot slipped.

My foot slipped, and I started falling.

Thankfully I landed in an overgrown bush, so I didn't die, but my ankle killed as I scrambled to my feet and started sprinting down the street, running away like the criminal I was. I didn't stop for at least three blocks, hop-running on a wrecked ankle, until I hit a busy intersection where I felt safe enough to call Mick to come pick me up.

By the time he got there, my ankle had swelled to an ugly size.

"Thanks for coming, man," I said, opening his passenger door.

"What the hell happened to you?" he asked, his eyes huge as he looked at my ankle, the scratches all over my legs from the bush's thorns, my wet clothes, and my soaked hair.

"You wouldn't believe it," I said, climbing inside and shutting the door.

"Did *Liz* do this to you?" he asked, turning down the radio.

"No," I said. "But I have a feeling she would've enjoyed the spectacle."

I was in a crap mood for the rest of the night after my plan imploded, but I realized as the guys mocked me incessantly for being a lovesick pussy that it was nice to fail with friends. After a couple of years of being alone while also being proverbially pressure-washed by life, it sucked a little less when you had friends to mock you for it.

The next morning, after I finished lifting (and getting chewed out by multiple coaches for screwing around and spraining my ankle) and was headed for the exit, I saw her.

I'd never be sure if she was my type—*have I always had a fondness for redheads with green eyes?*—or if she'd *created* my type.

She was the prototype.

There was only her.

She was walking toward the door, her eyes on her phone, and she almost ran into me.

And I totally would've let her. *Run me down, Lib.*

She sort of glanced up, muttering, "Excuse me," under her breath, but then her eyes snapped into focus on me.

"In a hurry, Lib?" I said, my hand lightly brushing over her arm to steady her so she didn't stumble.

"Yeah," she said, looking like she had a lot of thoughts running around in her head. She had a crinkle between her eyebrows, and I wondered what she knew about my epic fail last night.

Did she know anything at all, or had she not even opened her blinds since I'd taken a dive off the building? I didn't know, but I didn't *want* to.

"See you later, then," I said, walking toward the door.

The entire exchange had lasted three seconds—four, max—so why did I feel so alive, like the world was spinning faster now that we'd had contact?

"Wes. Wait."

Any other time, the sound of Liz calling me back would've made me ecstatic.

But I just knew this couldn't be good.

"Yeah?" I said casually, as if last night hadn't happened.

How does she have such perfect lips?

She looked down at my wrapped ankle. "What happened to your ankle?"

"What do you mean?" I asked.

That's brilliant, you dipshit.

"It's wrapped," she said, her green eyes full of calling-me-out as she looked up at me. Had she gotten shorter or had I grown? It was a ludicrous thought, but the way we fit was second nature to me, like memory foam, and her head was tilted back a fraction more than it used to be. "Did you injure yourself?"

Hell yes, I'd injured myself, but what was I supposed to say?

What does she know?

"I fell," I said lamely, shrugging like it was a common occurrence for me to just fucking fall on the regular.

"Yeah?" she said, narrowing her eyes. "It seems like there's a lot of that going around. Last night, the weirdest thing happened at my apartment."

Here it comes. "Really?"

"Yeah," she said, rubbing her lips together as she looked up at me. "So our crazy neighbor came to the door and said there was someone on our balcony trying to start a fire."

Fuck, fuck, fuck. "No shit?"

She tilted her head, her eyes still accusing me. "No shit. There was no one out there, and this guy is kind of known as bonkers anyway, right?"

There was no way she didn't know. "Right."

I mean, was there a chance she was just telling me about it and had no idea it was me?

No way could I be that lucky.

"But then Bonkers's wife says she has video."

Nonononononononoooooo.

"Really."

She bit down on her lip, and I swear to God it looked like she wanted to smile when she said, "*Really.* It's a video of some guy falling off the gutter."

She knew, I knew she knew, yet I still said, "Weird."

Her lips turned up into a tiny grin and she shook her head. "What's even weirder is that he looks young, like my age, and he's got a Bruins Baseball bag strapped to his back."

"That *is* weird." *Come on.* "Maybe he was trying to pull off some amazing romantic gesture."

"Maybe he was acting like an immature jackass," she said, the smile disappearing.

"I would think that *you* would appreciate the romantic angle," I said, breathing in the smell of her perfume as I realized this plan might be more challenging than I thought. "Little Liz loved that stuff."

"Little Liz has been gone a long time," she said, breaking my heart with those words as she cleared her throat and readjusted the bag on her shoulder. "I just hope that guy learned his lesson before someone gets hurt."

I stepped closer, so she filled the space between my body and the wall as I lowered my head so my mouth was closer to her ear. Acosta was loud as hell, and I needed her to hear me when I said, "Y'know, I don't think he gives a fuck, Lib, because everyone's already been hurt. He's got nothing to lose and everything he's always wanted to gain, so you should probably brace yourself."

She turned her head a fraction, so her eyes were on mine.

"Brace myself?" she asked, trying to sound bored. But the breathiness of her voice gave her away when she said, "For what, exactly?"

I looked into those green eyes and said, "The hard press."

CHAPTER THIRTY-TWO

"I'm glad he's single, because I'm gonna climb that like a tree."
—*Bridesmaids*

Liz

The hard press.

Why couldn't I stop thinking about what he'd said? About the *way* he'd said it?

You should probably brace yourself.

It'd been hours since he said it, and I was still blushing and butterflying like the moment had just passed.

"So. Liz," Wade said, grinning. "Anything interesting happen on your balcony last night?"

I lowered the camera. "You know about that?"

A bunch of the guys were hooping at the courts behind Hitch, so Clark and I were filming, although Clark was *waaay* on the other end. Mickey was dribbling the basketball, giving me a stupid smile, while Eli and Wade laughed knowingly from the lane, like they had the keys to the vault or something. I still didn't know the specifics of what exactly Wes had been doing out there, and I was dying to find out.

"Shut up, man," Mickey said. But he was still beaming when he said, "Just because he's not here doesn't mean we should—"

"It's not a secret, though," Wade interrupted, reaching in and stealing the ball. "He saw us taking pictures and only said to shut up until *after* he was done. He never asked us to be silent forever."

"True," Eli said.

"Will you please fill me in?" I snapped. "All I know is that he climbed onto the balcony and then fell off the building."

"Into a rosebush," Wade volunteered, looking like he was thoroughly enjoying the spilling of this tea as he drove the lane. "Like an idiot."

"Stop," Mickey said, putting up a hand but failing to get the block as Wade's shot went in. "He wasn't *trying* to be an idiot, Liz. He wants to ask you out, and he thought that climbing on your balcony and creating a whole romantic scene would help his chances."

"What kind of romantic scene?" I asked, still trying to process the fact that not only had Wes climbed up the side of my building—*idiot could've been killed*—but he'd told his friends he was going to do it. "Like, there was only water and broken glass out there when I saw it."

"Guys, let me," Eli said, grinning as he walked off the court, toward me, pulling out his phone. "These are photos of Wesley preparing to woo you."

Why was my heart racing? I leaned closer as he held out the phone, hoping I seemed chill as I looked at the display.

"This is him coming back from the flower shop," he said, using his finger to flip through multiple pictures of Wes carrying flowers—*God, they were daisies*—into his suite. He scrolled through pictures—it was a *lot* of daisies—and I swallowed hard.

What the hell, Bennett?

"Now these are my favorite," he said, "where he is working hard on his little cupidy art project."

I leaned even closer, my throat a little tight as I stared at a photo of Wes sitting on the floor of their suite, wearing headphones and bagging up flower petals. The lyric from that Abe Parker song—*I miss your stupid face*—whispered into me as Eli slid his finger across the screen, showing another dorm picture of Wes, this time writing on poster board with a Sharpie.

The only word he'd written at that point was TO.

What had he written?

What the hell had he written?

And what had he planned to do with the poster?

He'd been right—Little Liz would've loved this.

Thank God she was long gone.

Little Liz can't come to the phone right now. Why? Oh, 'cause she's dead.

"Okay, don't be an asshole, Strauss," Mick said. Then he walked over and said to me, "The finished product really *was* amazing, even though your neighbor destroyed it."

Now he pulled out *his* phone and held it out to me, and I was pretty sure I didn't look chill at all anymore.

Because Wes took a selfie on my balcony. It was my balcony in the picture, but it had been absolutely transformed with flowers and candles.

By Wes.

Into something the old me would've loved.

"Wow," I managed, blinking fast, feeling unsettled. "That's, uh . . . wow."

"So?" Wade waggled his eyebrows and grinned. "Are you gonna go out with him?"

"Like I'm going to discuss my personal life with you," I said, rolling my eyes as my insides rolled with turmoil. He'd climbed a building to set up flowers and candles for me. *Gaaaah, what the hell, Bennett?* I sounded very detached and turmoil-free when I quipped, "You can't even remember to ask me about Campbell when you're sober."

That made Eli laugh, but Mick wasn't going to be distracted. "Bennett's a good guy, though. You should give him a chance."

"Yeah, Buxxie," Wade agreed. "He risked his life to sweep you off your feet."

Wes chose that moment to appear, casually dribbling a basketball, which did nothing to help my insides.

Because he was wearing those glasses again, the prick.

Then he looked over, as if sensing our conversation, but instead of even registering the way his friends were grinning, his gaze landed on me, and he smiled. It was big and wildly intimate, the kind of smile that stole the breath from my body, and my face instantly burned.

"You should go ask him out," Mick said, sounding excited. "And totally blow his mind."

"I have work to do," I said, grabbing my camera and raising it to my eyes.

Partly because I had work to do, and partly because I was desperate to cover my face so no one could see how confused—and utterly lost—I felt all of a sudden.

"Hey, Buxxie," Wade yelled, "can I get Campbell's number before you leave?"

"What?" I lowered the camera and loved that Wade Brooks looked sincere for once in his life. "You seriously want it?"

"I'm suddenly inspired by romantic idiots," he said, grinning sheepishly. "What can I say?"

CHAPTER THIRTY-THREE

"You can't live a fairy tale."
—*Kate & Leopold*

Wes

"Let me see what the group chat thinks."

"What?" I rubbed my forehead and needed to ditch my sister. Normally, I looked forward to talking to her on the phone, but I had a paper to write. "What group chat?"

She usually only talked about her roommate, so it was nice to hear that she had other friends at college.

"The one I have with Noah, Adam, and Michael," she said casually.

"What?" I couldn't believe it, but at the same time it made perfect sense. "You guys have a group chat? Add me to the chat. Now."

"As if," she said, sounding amused by my discomfort. Which was totally on-brand for her. "The last thing I want is you on there, no offense."

"What do you guys talk about? Is it just about me?" I asked, irritated and amused at the same time.

"God, the ego," she said cheekily. "We rarely talk about you, actually. I just like your dumb friends."

"Y'know what? We're gonna have a five-way FaceTime group chat. Right now. Call me back when everyone's on," I demanded, standing to pace around the room. The rest of my suitemates weren't home, so it was nice and quiet.

"Oh God," she laughed, and she was still laughing when I disconnected the call.

Three minutes later, I was looking at the faces of my friends on my MacBook.

"Seriously, though, dumbest lines in a song ever," Noah was saying, looking disgusted. "'You know Dasher and Dancer and Prancer and Vixen, Comet and Cupid and Donner and Blitzen. But do you recall the most famous reindeer of all?' Like, if you know the rest of them, obviously you'd know 'the most famous' of all of them. Stupid freaking question, dude."

"It's un-American to slander Rudolph, you asshole," Adam said.

"Blasphemous, really," Michael agreed.

"Can you stop being stupid for five seconds?" Sarah asked them.

"Why do we have to?" Noah replied, obviously confused by the change of topic.

"Because Wes is wondering if he should push forward with his plan to romance Liz," Sarah said, smiling like I was a toddler who amused her with my nonsensical adorability. "Or if he should pump the brakes since the first attempt didn't work."

"Pump," Noah said without pause. "It's not gonna work."

"It is too," Sarah said defensively. "You don't know."

"Joss said Liz was super pissed about Wes's whole I-didn't-cheat confession," he argued. "There is no way she's going to find cheesy romance—from *him*—to be charming."

I said, "Well, I—"

"Yeah, but Liz is Liz," Adam interrupted knowingly, like he had it all figured out. "She loves that stuff, right?"

"Not anymore," Noah said. "According to Joss, she's, like, anti-romance now."

"Bullshit," I said, half to myself, because I refused to believe that.

"Regardless, he needs to try," my sister said. "What does he have to lose?"

My phone buzzed, and the last thing I expected to see was a text from Liz.

Liz: I have a question for you.

I have never texted as quickly as I texted: **Continue.**

"Who are you texting?" Sarah asked, forever nosy.

"Liz, so shut up," I muttered, staring at the conversation bubbles on my phone.

Liz: The last time we spoke (before yesterday in the weight room), we were yelling at each other. So why would you think it was a good idea to climb a balcony with flowers after that?

That . . . was not the question I'd expected her to ask.

"What is she saying?" Michael asked from my laptop screen.

"Yeah, Wes," Sarah said. "What'd she say?"

"She wants to know why I'd bring her flowers on the balcony when we were fighting a few days ago," I mumbled, trying to think of a good answer.

"Fair question," Noah said.

I texted: **Just because we were yelling doesn't mean my feelings have changed.**

"What'd you say?" Sarah prodded.

"None of your damn business," I snapped, wanting them to go away now. "Shhhh."

Liz: Feelings? That is RIDICULOUS. Is that what the poster was about too? "Feelings"?

Was she trying to find out what the posters said? It was probably my wishful thinking, but I texted like that was what she wanted.

Yes. There were multiple posters, actually. The first one said TO ME, YOU AREN'T PERFECT

Liz: Um . . . okay. Humbling.

I took it as a good sign that she was making a joke. I texted: **The second one said TO ME, YOU ARE EVERYTHING**

I didn't expect a quick response, because I imagined her squealing or kicking her feet or texting a friend. But she immediately texted: **THAT IS ASININE, WES. No offense, but you don't even know me. How could I be everything?**

"Why are you scowling?" Sarah asked. "What did she say?"

"Tell us," Adam said. "We're dying over here."

I reached over and disconnected the FaceTime call, and then I dialed Liz's number. I didn't expect her to answer, so I was surprised when I heard, "Hello?"

I stood and started walking around the room, pacing as I said, "I know you. Come on, Liz."

"No, you don't," she replied, very matter-of-factly. "We haven't had a real conversation in years. How could you think that we know each other at all?"

"Because we just do," I said, aware that it made zero sense, but also, it did make sense for us.

"Oh, really? Okay, then. What is my new favorite show to watch on the weekends?"

"What?" I cleared my throat and thought hard. "Um, that's a trick question because you still like to watch *Gilmore Girls* and Nora Ephron movies."

"Wrong, it's football," she said, sounding happy I'd gotten it wrong.

"Wait, what?"

"I love to watch football—college and the NFL. See? You know *nothing* about me now."

"Well, I *want* to know you," I said, sitting down on my bed and turning my body so I could lean back against the wall. I knew she was proving a point to me that I didn't want proven, but even in spite of that, it was nice to be talking to her on the phone again. "You should go out with me, and we can get to know each other all over again."

She immediately said, "No, thank you."

"What about as friends?" I said just as quickly, needing to keep her on the phone. "Can't we do that? It doesn't have to be a date-date; we can just eat food and catch up. I'd at least like to be your friend again. What are you doing Friday night?"

"I have plans," she said, striking me down. "Nick Stark's—"

"Ski Mask-erade?" Everyone was talking about the Halloween party where you wore a costume and a ski mask (the only rule was no exposed faces).

"I'm going too," I said, way too excitedly. It was impossible for me to be cool when Liz Buxbaum was involved, but especially when we were going to be in the same place. "We can hang out at the party."

"But you won't be able to find me," she said, a smile in her voice. "Because I'll be in a costume, with a ski mask over my head."

"Trust me, Lib," I said, picturing her lips. "In a crowd of a million ski masks, I'd still be able to find you."

"There is no way you'll know who I am. No way."

I wanted to wrap myself up in the warm breathlessness of her voice.

"Want to make a bet?" I asked, knowing I was going to win. "If I find you, you go on a date with me Saturday."

"What happened to just going for friendship?" she asked, sounding a little amused (though that could *also* just be my wishful thinking).

"If we're making a bet, I'm going bigger, Buxbaum," I said, feeling like an unbelievable opportunity was presenting itself. "You in?"

"No," she said, but I could tell she was smiling. I don't know how I knew, but I did.

"Oh, come on, are you seriously going to force me to make the noise?" I asked.

"The noise?"

"The *bokk-bokk* chicken noise because you're scared to take the bet. You know I know you too well and will find you," I teased, confident she wouldn't be able to resist the challenge. "And then you'll be forced to endure a delightful evening with the charming Wesley Harold Bennett as punishment for losing."

"Save your *bokk*ing—I'll take the bet." I wondered if she was in her room, ready for bed, or if she was studying somewhere. "But there have to be rules. You can't just walk up to someone and say 'Liz?' because then you can luck into winning."

"Fair." *I love her mind.* "How about we have a code word that I have to shout when I see you?"

"A code word," she repeated slowly, like she was really considering the idea. "I like it. How about you have to yell 'I am a huge jackass' when you see the person that you'll think is me but actually won't be?"

"I am happy to say that, you little shit," I agreed, leaning my head back against the wall and picturing her face. "But you will definitely be the person I'm saying it to."

"In your dreams, Bennett," she teased.

"Every damn night, Buxbaum," I replied, wanting to beg her to spend the rest of her life on the phone with me.

Her voice was soft and sleepy when she said, "I have to go study. See you Friday, even though you *won't* see me."

I love you.

"See you Friday, Lib," I said, terrified by the hope that was pumping through every one of my veins. "G'night."

After she hung up, I sat there with the phone in my hand for the longest time, just staring into space. Liz suddenly felt possible again, like something could actually *happen* with us, and that kind of possibility was the scariest thing in the world.

Eventually I got my head out of the clouds enough to write my paper, and I was in the middle of formatting the godforsaken *works cited* page—why did I struggle so much with those?—when my phone started ringing.

I picked it up and was *shocked* when I saw the name on the caller ID.

Helena Buxbaum.

Why would *she* be calling me? I'd only spoken to her on the phone once in my life, and that was a couple of years ago. It was right after Liz and I broke up, and I'd seen the 402 area code and took the call, assuming it was some kind of bill that needed to be paid.

It would forever go down as the coolest phone call I'd ever received.

Shut up and don't say a word. I hate you for hurting Liz, and the Wes Bennett that was her boyfriend is dead to me. However, I want to let Wes Bennett the neighbor kid know that we're always here next door, no matter what, if he should ever need anything that has nothing to do with our daughter. Okay, bye.

There were very few people in the world I respected as much as I respected Helena.

"Hello?" I answered, a little nervous.

"Oh—hey, Wes. Um, it's Helena Buxbaum. I can't believe you answered the phone," she said, sounding shocked. "I thought only old people answered incoming calls. I fully expected the voicemail."

"I saw it was you," I said. "So I *had* to pick up."

"Do you have two seconds? I don't want to interrupt a kegger or anything."

That made me smile and relax. "I've got all the time in the world, and I'm shockingly free of keggers at the moment. What's up?"

"Okay, so the lady who moved into your old house—Mrs. Eggers? Yeah, she seems like a type-A lunatic, by the way, but it appears she found some things in the house that the Bennetts left behind."

"What?" I'd personally checked every single surface of the place before leaving. "What did she find?"

"Homies."

I waited for more, but when she said nothing else, I asked, "I'm sorry, did you say *'homies'*?"

Helena laughed as she said, "Oh, I did. And she gave them to me, your *homies*. She found one taped up in the back of every single closet. May I text you a photo?"

"Yeah. Of course," I said, still clueless.

"Sending," she said, and when the text came through, I completely lost it.

I'd forgotten all about the homies.

The gas station down the hill used to have a gumball machine full of "homies," little plastic dudes you could buy for a quarter. Sarah bought them all the time when we were kids, because they were the only things she could afford, and it appeared that she'd saved them.

Saved them so she could tape one in the back of each closet when we moved out of the house.

I looked at the photo and shook my head, because there was a tiny note attached to each little guy that said HOMIE IS WATCHING YOU, EGGERS.

"Are you *kidding* me?" I said, giving in to a laugh as I looked at the picture. "I wondered why Sarah wanted to say goodbye to every bedroom in the house."

"Mrs. Eggers was a little freaked out until I told her that the Bennetts were clowns," she said. "Your sister is my freaking hero, I swear to God."

"Mine, too."

"So whenever either of you are back in town, feel free to swing by for the homies." Helena cleared her throat and said, "We'd love to see you."

"Same," I said. "Thanks for calling about the homies when I'm dead to you."

"No, you're Jesus, Wes," she said. "Back from the dead because apparently you *didn't* cheat on Liz."

"Right," I said, having no idea what exactly Helena knew about all that. "Good."

"So come by anytime," she said, and it sounded like she meant it. "By the way, I have the nicest memory of your dad, of the last time I talked to him. Would you like to hear it, or will it hurt?"

"I'd *love* to hear it," I said, leaning back in the desk chair.

"Okay, so I was having a bad day because Liz and I got in an argument, right? This was *right* after she went away to school. I took out the trash, and Stu was taking his out too. Now, I didn't really ever talk to your dad, aside from a 'hey, Stuart' whenever we saw each other in our respective driveways, but he looked at me and asked if I was okay."

"He *did*?" I was shocked to hear this, because the guy hadn't been particularly social.

At all.

"Yeah—weird, right? And I was in such a funk that I actually spilled to him about the way I thought Liz was ignoring my calls and that she asked me to give her some space. I rambled all over the place like the empty nester I suddenly was."

Yeah, I'm sure my dad *loved* the lady next door getting all emotional. Probably referred to her as *batshit crazy neighbor* after that.

"But instead of grunting at me, your dad gave me a hug."

Impossible. "You're kidding, right?"

"No! I couldn't believe it either. And I'll never forget what he said to me, Wes. He hugged me and said, 'Here's the thing about kids, lady.' And I honestly don't think he knew my name, by the way—I *was* 'lady.'"

I coughed out a laugh while my chest pinched a little. "All women were."

"But he goes, 'Here's the thing about kids, lady. They're stupid with words. They say shit all the time that they don't mean. They're wrong, or they're being emotional little shits—basically you have to understand that what they say isn't what they mean.'"

I tried swallowing, but my throat was too tight. "He said that?"

"He did," she said, sounding serious all of a sudden. "He basically mansplained to me that our kids love us even when they act like little assholes, and then he informed me they're going to grow out of it and take it all back once they stop being stupid."

I barked out another laugh, but my eyes were scratchy. "Good ol' Stu."

"I just thought, since your dad was intense a lot of the time, that you might enjoy hearing about him being kind and giving me probably the best parental advice I ever received."

"'Little assholes' is the best advice?" I teased, my voice a little choked by emotion. "Come on, Helena."

"Your dad knew, Wes," she said, her voice quiet. "He knew what his kids *really* felt, even when their words said otherwise."

I took in a deep, jagged breath, wondering if she might actually be right. "Thank you, Helena. You're really—"

"Incredible, I know," she interrupted, sounding like she, too, was a little choked up. "And you're welcome. Now let's get back to our keggers, shall we?"

"Yeah, we probably should," I agreed, clearing my throat.

"Take care, kid," she said. "And I'll see you at Christmas break."

"You will?" *She's probably forgetting we're no longer neighbors.*

"You want these homies, don't you?" she said, and something about her mothering was really getting to me. Especially when she added, "I'll be pissed if you don't come get them."

"Then I will make it a priority."

"Later, then, Wesley," she said.

"Later, then, Helena," I replied, staying on until the call dropped.

It was probably a random coincidence, but that night, for the first time in years, I had a long night of deep sleep without a nightmare to be found.

CHAPTER THIRTY-FOUR

"Look, I guarantee there'll be tough times. I guarantee that at some point, one or both of us is gonna want to get out of this thing. But I also guarantee that if I don't ask you to be mine, I'll regret it for the rest of my life, because I know, in my heart, you're the only one for me."

—*Runaway Bride*

Liz

"I can*not* wear this."

"Why not?" Campbell stood behind me, looking at my reflection in the mirror over my shoulder. "If you want to trick him, this is the way. He's going to be looking for a Liz-coded costume, so he will never even consider that this is you."

My stomach was full of nervous butterflies. It was all well and good what my dad said, about me not having to worry about my confusing Wes feelings, but it made things feel precarious when I was preparing to go to a party that could end with me having to go on a *date* with him tomorrow.

Did I want to?

Definitely not.

But his idiotic balcony attempt had left me shaken. I wasn't

Little Liz anymore, but I wasn't unaffected by the lengths he'd gone to either.

I looked at my reflection and wanted to cover myself with a cardigan. I was wearing Campbell's costume, which was a black latex Batgirl dress paired with thigh-high black boots. The dress was short and showed some cleavage, but the part that had me feeling like I looked obscene was how tight it was.

Skintight, shiny black, no room for secrets.

"Yeah, but it's so . . ." I trailed off, turning around and making sure it covered my ass.

"Watch yourself before I'm offended," Campbell said, crossing her arms. "You look hot, and your face will be covered. No one will know it's you unless you want them to."

I looked at my reflection again. *No one will know it's me.*

"Just enjoy it and have fun." She tilted her head. "Feel sorry for me, that I'm stuck wearing the cat costume."

"The costume from *Cats the Musical* is cute, though," I defended. "You'll look adorable."

"Yeah, adorable isn't hot, but I'll make it work." She grinned, which made me worry for her. She'd stayed up all night talking to Wade on the phone, and she was downright smitten. I liked how happy she was, but I was nervous she'd end up hurt.

Even with a good guy, things could change quickly, but with a cocky dude like Wade? It was worrisome.

She said, "I'm gonna go change, then let's do a shot before we go, okay?"

We did a couple of shots and Leo fed the raccoons before we

locked up and loaded into an Uber. Campbell was dressed as Bombalurina, Taylor's character in *Cats*; Clark was Thor; and Leo was Cupid (he'd sewn a confetti pocket into his toga-thing and was very excited to randomly toss love confetti at people).

"Okay, remember—if you need to talk to me, do it *quietly*," I said, my buzz making me excited about the challenge of not being discovered. "All Wes has to do is follow Thor around, and he'll find me in a second."

"Like I'm going to be hanging out near *you*," he said. "I have my own person I'm trying to find."

"What?" Campbell said, making the Uber driver look at us in the rearview mirror. "Who are you looking for?"

He just shrugged. "I haven't decided yet."

"What does *that* mean?" Leo asked.

"It means a world of interesting people are awaiting us at the party," Clark said in that very Clarky way of his, where it seemed like he was being ironic but he actually was not.

We rolled up our ski masks (decorated to match our costumes, of course) on the ride there, but when we pulled up in front of Nick's house, we lowered them over our faces.

"It's go time," Campbell said, opening the door.

We probably terrified the Uber driver as we climbed out with our faces covered, and when we got inside, the party was already wild.

Which wasn't a surprise.

Everyone loved the Ski Mask-erade, so it was packed. The house—a guesthouse in Bel Air—was brimming with people, all in ridiculously decorated ski masks, but even over the loud noise, I heard Wes's laugh right after we arrived.

I couldn't see him, but his laugh was unmistakable.

I could close my eyes and be so many places with that laugh. That laugh was the cohesive thread, the little recurring melody that showed up in so many scenes of my life, like Mia and Sebastian's theme in *La La Land*.

Always there, playing in the background.

My eyes searched the crowded living room, and it seemed like it should've taken me longer, but I found him in a quick minute.

Wes was Batman.

Talk about ironic.

He was wearing black baseball pants, a yellow belt, and a long-sleeved black Under Armour workout shirt that had a yellow bat—made of paper—taped across the front. He was laughing hard at whatever the horse beside him was saying, and I realized as I watched him that I probably would've found him even if he hadn't been laughing.

Because no one else moved like Wes.

I mean, of course there was the tallness, the long arms and legs that hinted at his identity, but it was more than that. The back-tilt of his head when he laughed, the prominent Adam's apple on that neck, just below where the mask ended, and the relaxed way he moved his body, like he could just as easily pop out silly boy-band choreography as he could bench-press a car.

It was like Wes was his own brand of human.

Also—it looked like he was wearing one of those padded-with-fake-muscles costumes, only it was his actual body.

"I need a drink," I said, pulling Campbell with me toward the keg as I wondered three things.

Would Wes be able to recognize me?

Did I want him to?

Was I actually going to go out with him if he did?

CHAPTER THIRTY-FIVE

"You love me. Real, or not real?"
—*The Hunger Games*

Wes

I have to find her.

I was listening to AJ, but my eyes were everywhere. I needed to find Liz and win the bet.

"So she's wearing a long robe, like she's a wizard or royalty or something. This chick isn't showing a bit of her body, like I'm not even sure it is a girl—could be a man or a tall child or a short yeti—but Mick looked at her and was like, 'I'll be right back.'"

"Yeah?" I said, turning my body to look at the people on the other side of the room.

"Yeah. He's been gone for, like, an hour." AJ shook his head and said, "So I'm not sure if he's getting action or getting murdered."

"I mean, who can really say, right?" I muttered.

"Are you even listening to me?" AJ asked, sounding annoyed behind his mask.

"No." I glanced toward the kitchen. "I'm trying to find Liz."

"Buxxie," he said, grinning and shaking his head. "I love this whole bet thing. You have to find her because I'll be bored when your adventure ends."

"So glad I can entertain you."

"What about that one?" he said, pointing toward the person in the cat costume.

It was a costume Liz would wear (she would know the name of the *Cats* cat for sure), but as I watched, I just knew it wasn't her. Not because I'd know the curves of her body in a lineup (come on, but I *would*) or anything like that, but because of her hands.

Is it weird to love someone's hands?

The cat had average hands, with long pink fingernails, but they weren't *Liz's* hands. I'd watched her play piano so many times, and I'd always been distracted by the sight of her long, graceful fingers, moving over the keys.

With perfectly clipped and almost-always polished fingernails, her hands were capable of so much.

I'm losing it when her hands make me want to write a haiku, right?

I searched like a man on a mission, but no one was her.

An hour later, I was starting to panic.

What if she wasn't there? Or what if she was, but I was failing?

I hadn't even considered the possibility of not winning.

I was stressing out when I went upstairs to look for Mick, and then I found her.

The hallway was full of people, and I was about to give up when

I caught a whiff of her perfume. I froze, looking around. There was a person dressed as a Pop-Tart—*not Liz*—someone wearing a latex Batgirl costume—*definitely* not Liz—a cupid whose hairy chest totally ruled out the Liz possibility, and Scooby-Doo—whose feet were way too big to belong to Buxbaum.

I was getting *very* impatient.

I was about to go downstairs when Batgirl turned sideways, talking to the cupid. It was too loud for me to hear her voice, but blue eyes—not green—were looking out from the ski mask.

Her lips, though.

I looked closer, and her slick, wet, shiny red lips were turned up in a smile that I knew better than my own reflection.

Those were Liz's lips.

Holy *balls*.

My eyes went back to the costume and I damn-near swallowed my tongue.

Those boots, those legs—dear *God*.

My gaze traveled up her body—taking its time over black latex that made me weak in the knees—and when it got to her ski mask, I couldn't believe what I saw.

She was wearing colored contacts—the little *shit*. I wanted to laugh my ass off at that blue-eyed huckster for being so devious, and I wanted to laugh manically and howl at the moon because, *praise Jesus*, I'd won.

I'd won, and I was going to have Batgirl all to myself for an evening in the very near future.

I moved through the crowded hallway, and when I was finally

behind her—she still hadn't seen me amongst all the people—I took a hit of her perfume before quietly saying into her ear, "I am a huge jackass."

I heard the gasp before her head came around and she stared up at me with big blue eyes.

That lipstick.

If her hands drive me to distraction, her mouth drives me to madness.

"I can't believe you found me," she said in a breathy voice, her eyes wide with shock.

The cupid leaned closer to Liz and said something into her ear, which took her eyes away from me as she listened.

Who the hell was this guy? He was smallish, but a little too shredded in my opinion.

And standing a little too close to Liz.

"I cry foul on the contacts, by the way," I said, unwilling to let a damn cupid steal her attention. "You little cheater."

"It's part of the costume," she replied, shrugging.

Which did things that made it difficult to be a gentleman. My eyes definitely wanted to roam, but I kept them trained on red lips and curled black lashes because I wasn't an asshole. "You're telling me that Batgirl has blue eyes, Buxbaum? That you know this to be a fact?"

"Everyone knows that," the cupid said, and I watched him grin at Liz through his stupid pink ski mask.

That's a very punchable mouth.

"So we should probably schedule our date," I said, lightly

grabbing her elbow, feeling a jolt as my fingertips slid over soft Lizzie skin.

"Now?" she said, irritation in her tone.

Which irritated *me* a little.

"Do it later," Cupid said, waving a hand like it was silliness that could wait, and *that* irritated me a lot.

Then he reached into his half dress and threw pink dust in my face.

"I wasn't talking to *you*," I said through gritted teeth, looking around for an escape. For somewhere—anywhere—where Liz and I weren't with the goddamn cupid.

Which was ironic, right? Weren't cupids supposed to be shooting arrows of love at us? This guy sucked at his job. I reached for the knob on the door beside us and it turned.

Yes.

"Here," I said, pushing open the end-of-the-hallway door. "Just give me two minutes."

She was blinking fast as I sort of *moved* her—gently—toward that door. *"Wes—"*

"She'll be right back," I said to the cupid, who tilted his head but didn't say a word.

That's right, Cupid—shut up.

We walked through the door, but as soon as it closed behind us, I couldn't find a wall switch. And it was *dark*.

"*Wes,*" she exclaimed, jerking out of my hands. "What the *hell*?"

"I just need a minute without Cupid butting in. Where are the lights?" I said under my breath, moving my hand over the surface of the wall.

"Oh, this is perfect," Liz muttered, and then her phone's flashlight lit up the darkness. She gasped, "Oh my God!"

"Oh my God, indeed," I agreed, freezing as my eyes took in all the creepiness of the rickety staircase in front of us, of the boxes of God-only-knows-what that were piled beside the steps.

"You shoved me into an attic?" she said in a whisper-scream, as if she thought someone was in there with us.

"I didn't know," I said, reaching for the doorknob. "This is spooky as hell."

"Understatement of the year," she agreed.

But the doorknob wouldn't turn. I applied pressure, but that thing wasn't budging.

At all.

"Okay, don't freak out, Buxbaum, but we're kind of maybe locked in."

"What?" Her hand covered mine and tried turning the doorknob, but it was very stuck. "Oh my God."

"It's okay," I said calmly, taking off my ski mask. "I'll text AJ, and he'll come let us out."

"I'll text Campbell, too," she said, pulling off her ski mask and swiping into messages.

We each sent a text, our screens bright in the creepy darkness, but I wasn't freaked out. I mean, the party was so loud that no one would hear us if we started knocking, but we had fully charged phones, and I was with Liz.

Even a terrifying dark attic seemed like a perfect place, all of a sudden.

There were butterflies going wild inside me as I stood next to her in the darkness. *She's so close.* It was the last thing I should've been thinking about, but my body was hyperaware of the smell of her and the way those tall black boots were close enough to touch.

My phone lit up when AJ responded: **I'm on my way.**

"So is Campbell," she said as her phone also lit up.

"I'm sorry I dragged you in here." I wasn't sorry to be locked in the dark with her—that was a total lie—but I was sorry if *she* was unhappy to be in the dark attic with me.

I expected a snappy comeback, but all she said was, "Why do college guys even have an attic that looks like this?"

She held out her phone, illuminating the cobweb-covered boxes and blurred shapes that were packed in the small area.

"Because they're serial killers, obviously," I said, but my eyes were stuck on the way her hair looked in the darkness, the perfection of her profile in the dim light of the phone.

"Obviously," she agreed, watching me watch her before quickly looking away.

There was a noise, like someone was messing with the doorknob, but I set my hand on it and it wasn't turning. At all.

"Powers?" I yelled, putting my mouth next to the door.

I could hear male voices, but there was too much noise for me to make out what they were saying.

My phone lit up. **AJ: There's a tiny problem.**

"Uh," I started to say, but then Liz said, "Campbell said the doorknob isn't budging. They're going to find Stark and see if he's got a key."

"A key?" I bent my knees and raised my phone so I could see the knob. "I don't see a lock on this side at all."

"This is freaking *great*," she said, sounding annoyed.

"I'm sure he's got a key," I said, trying to reassure her.

"You said yourself that it doesn't look like there's a lock," she snapped, her voice thick with frustration.

"Relax, Buxbaum, it's going to be okay," I said, wondering if this was about the closet or if it was about me. "Are you claustrophobic?"

"No," she bit out. "I just don't want to be here."

So it *was* about me.

"They're probably going to find our bloated, spider-bitten corpses when they finally get in," she said, and it reminded me so much of Little Liz that the disappointment took a back seat to amusement.

"Christ. That's a little dark."

"Well, something made all of these webs, right?"

"I choose not to think about it." I turned my head and said, "I wonder what it's like up the stairs."

"A graveyard of demented dolls and mannequins, I would guess."

I heard Liz's phone buzz, saw the screen light up, and she said, "It's Campbell."

I watched her as she read the message.

"Nononono," she whined, looking up at me. Her face was illuminated by the phone, that slick mouth all lit up, and something about it made my pulse speed up. "Look."

She held out the phone so I could read the message. Apparently Nick's landlord had a key, but the guy was thirty minutes away. Campbell and Leo were going to go get it, but we'd have to wait until they returned.

I knew I shouldn't be happy, especially when it was obvious Liz wasn't, but how could I not be? I'd just been given the gift of thirty uninterrupted minutes with Liz. I was going to make the most of this situation and try to nudge us past this place we were stuck in.

"I know exactly what we can do while we wait," I said.

Her expression was priceless, like she seriously thought I was suggesting we get after it in the creepy attic full of spiderwebs. I was half laughing when I said, "Get your mind out of the gutter, Buxbaum. I only meant that we can play twenty questions and get to know each other."

"I thought you already know me better than anyone," she said in a mocking voice.

"Well, then, now's my chance to prove it," I said, wondering if it were possible to hyperventilate on someone's perfume.

Because I could never quite stop myself from taking little sipping sniffs whenever I was near her.

"But let's see what's up the stairs first."

"Are you kidding me?" she said in a high-pitched voice. "No way am I going up those rickety steps."

"Oh, come on, Lib," I said, turning on my flashlight and stepping closer to the stairs. "Where's your sense of adventure?"

"That's what the next victim says in every horror movie."

She wasn't wrong, but as I put my foot on the bottom step, I saw it. "There's a window up here."

"So Chucky can push us to our deaths?" she quipped, sounding hesitant.

"Grab the back of my shirt," I said, "and follow me. I will slay any villains who come for you; I promise."

"Yeah, but what if you're the villain?"

"Luring you to the creepy attic after making sure there's no key to the door?" I asked, wanting to grunt in satisfaction when I felt her fingers grab on to the bottom of my shirt. "Then I'd say I'm really incredibly brilliant."

"Yeah, and I know you're not that," she teased, and it felt like a win. Teasing was one of the ways we'd always communicated, so it felt closer to "right" with us when she forgot herself and mocked me.

I started up the stairs, and she fisted the back of my shirt, following. I honestly hadn't expected her to do it, to touch me, so I was kind of in no hurry to get those stairs climbed.

And when we got to the top, it was surprisingly . . . empty.

"Where's all the stuff?" I shined the light around, and the big open attic was almost completely vacant of things, aside from a few random small boxes and a rocking chair. The antithesis of the area down the steps.

"The ghosts have to live up here," Liz said, her hands still on my lower back. "So they Marie Kondo'ed the space."

"Makes sense," I said, walking over to the window.

I tried sliding it open, and after a moment of sticking, it came free and, *hell yes*, I saw exactly what I'd been hoping for.

"Come on," I said, unwilling to turn around because I didn't want her to let go of my shirt. "This is perfect."

I stepped through the window opening and out onto the roof, which, thankfully, was the perfect kind of roof to sit on. It didn't have a crazy pitch, and there was a flat area just outside the window, as if the space was created especially for midnights under the stars.

"I'm not sure we should go on the roof," she said, following me through the window, and then I heard her breathe a startled "Oh."

I did look back at her then, and she smiled.

"Right?" I said, and she let go of my shirt. "Not too bad for being locked in an attic."

"Those Dollanganger kids would've loved this."

"Sit," I said, pointing to the flat spot just outside the window that had a wooden ledge instead of shingles. "And who the hell are the Dollanganger kids?"

"From *Flowers in the Attic* . . . ?" She looked at me like she thought that would make sense as she tucked her dress—*Good God that dress*—underneath her and sat down on the roof. "The book?"

"Never heard of it," I said, sitting down beside her.

"Probably for the best—it doesn't hold up well to analysis." She looked out at the night sky and said, "This is a little incredible."

"Wow," I said, resting my arms on my knees and looking down. Not only could we see stars, but we had a nice vantage point over the streets of the neighborhood. I hadn't planned to get locked in an attic with Liz, but this was a spectacular setup. "So question number one."

"I never agreed to twenty questions," she said. "For the record."

"Let the record show Miss Buxbaum is answering under duress. Question number one—what is your current favorite food, and why did you pretend Clark was your boyfriend?"

She looked surprised that I knew about the fake-dating thing (Clark, overcome with guilt, had confessed the first time I saw him in LA after the Omaha trip) but not upset. She shrugged and said, "I panicked when I saw you, and it just happened. And I've been all about the tacos lately. The street-taco scene in LA is ridiculous."

"Interesting," I said, thinking yet again how much she'd changed. "I haven't actually had a taco in LA yet."

She was looking out at the city when she asked, "What are you waiting for, Bennett?"

"For them to be free," I admitted. "On-campus food costs me nothing, so basically B-Plate and Rendezvous are my new favorite restaurants."

"Smart," she said, looking over at me, and I wondered what she was thinking. Somehow I knew her brain was drilling into that, into the reality of my financial situation. "So *my* question number one, asked under duress, is where the hell is Otis living these days?"

That made me laugh, because she'd always pretended to find my dog annoying while sneaking him table food through the backyard fence when I wasn't looking. "He is now the adopted son of one Michael Young."

"Shut up," she said with wide eyes, forgetting all about the way she didn't know how to act around me. "Really?"

I nodded and said, "Sarah and I couldn't bring him with us to school, and I was afraid he'd be ignored if he lived with my mom. So Michael is now his father, and we have FaceTime visitations once a week."

"No way," she said, smiling in spite of herself.

"You were absolutely right when Michael moved back and you thought he walked on water," I said, nudging her shoulder with mine. "He does, I swear to God."

"I'm glad I was right," she said, nudging back, and I knew she was acknowledging the way he'd helped me last year. "Question two, asked under duress, of course."

"It's *my* turn," I said, scowling at her while wanting to do a goddamn happy dance because she'd leaned her shoulder into mine.

And she wanted to ask *me* questions.

Please, God, don't let this be a dream.

"Don't care," she replied. "Question two. How did you recognize me? I must've forgotten some tiny detail and I need to know what it was."

Was there a way to answer that wasn't a verbal vomit of my obsession with her? *I was looking for your perfect fingernails* was psycho enough to require a restraining order.

Still, what was the point of lying? I didn't want to lie to her anymore.

"Your smell," I said, and *of course* my voice cracked like I was a lovesick teenager. "I smelled your perfume, and then I saw your mouth."

"My mouth?" she repeated, scoffing like it was a silly accident.

"Libby, I don't know if you know this, but I am obsessed with your mouth," I admitted, knowing I should back off, but I felt bold as she started fast-blinking. "I've never seen anything as beautiful as the way your lips slide into a smile, so that slick red lipstick served as, like, a matador's cape—"

"Please don't call yourself a bull," she interrupted.

"To this bull right here," I said, unable to look at anything but her mouth.

"God save me," she sighed, her voice light as a breath. "From a boy who refers to himself as a dangerous bovine."

"Dangerous bovine?" I looked into her eyes, so close, and didn't even know what we were talking about because her lips were so close to my lips. "You really know how to make a guy feel uncool."

She shrugged. "Any guy comparing himself to a raging bull *is* uncool."

"So mean." I shook my head, and my eyes were back on her mouth, on those slick lips. "I can't keep my eyes off of your mouth for real, though."

She swallowed but didn't say anything, and I wasn't sure if that was a good sign or a bad sign.

"Can I ask you a question?" I said, my gaze on hers as an invisible string pulled me closer.

"That's the game," she said, but it came out as almost a whisper.

"If you and I were just a random Batman and Batgirl at a Halloween party, with zero history, and we were locked in an attic and taking refuge on the roof," I managed, feeling like I was drugged as she watched me with interest in those eyes.

"Yeah?" she replied, and it *was* a whisper this time.

"And I did this," I said, lowering my head and sipping at her breath with my own. "Would you let me kiss you?"

"In that scenario," she said, her lips almost touching mine. "Probably yes."

My head exploded.

"That's not who we are, though," she whispered, her eyes heavy-lidded.

"But." I ran my knuckle over her cheekbone, my hand shaking as she watched me, as she didn't pull back. "What if we pretend?"

She swallowed and said nothing.

But she still didn't pull back.

It felt like we were both leaning toward each other, hovering, waiting for the decision to be made for us.

So I lowered my head and played the part of a random Batman. "C'mon, Batgirl."

"Um," she whispered, then slid her fingers through the sides of my hair, pulling my mouth to hers.

Time shifted, because everything went slow motion at first as I felt her hands on me, as my mouth met those slick lips. Every nerve ending in my body crackled, every hair stood on end, as the awareness of Liz overwhelmed my senses.

And then it detonated.

And sped out of control.

Suddenly my mouth was opening her mouth, my palms sliding up the smooth skin of her face as I held her in place. I felt weak when she angled her head and opened her lips underneath mine, her fingers flexing in my hair as her tongue slid inside my mouth. It was outrageously hot, the way she licked into me, and everything in my head exploded as she made a noise in her throat—impatience—that left all indecision behind.

I forgot everything—where we were, how to be chill—and devoured her mouth, desperately taking every kiss she was willing to feed me. Liz was in control, her teeth driving me wild while her busy tongue warmed me with its hunger, and it felt like my chest was too tight.

Am I having a heart attack?

She'd always kissed like some sort of a mythological sex goddess, demanding everything while delivering more, and—*holy shit praise the lord*—that hadn't changed a bit.

My heart was racing as one thought—*this is Liz this is Liz*—yelled through my mind. My hands found her waist and pulled her closer to me on that roof, wrapping around her and squeezing her body tighter against mine—*home home home home*—as I ate at her sweet mouth like it was a delicacy I'd begged for and knew I'd never get again. I wanted to hold her there and never let her go. I consumed her, dipping into everything I could get as I felt her arms snake around my shoulders, taking everything she was willing to give and pulling it deep inside me.

Her breathing was erratic, and I loved it, because it mirrored my own. I could hear noises from the street below, but I didn't care about anything other than Liz Buxbaum. A stadium full of priests watching wouldn't have stopped me at that moment.

Literally.

They wouldn't.

Feast your eyes on this, Fathers.

I opened my eyes, somehow needing confirmation that it was actually Liz and that she was actually back in my arms, and her bright eyes fluttered open at the same moment. Something was exchanged in the look—questions, maybe—but we didn't stop kissing. Our mouths turned slow and languid, tracing tongues and nipping teeth, and it was somehow even hotter than the wild, hungry kisses.

It felt like so many other times, stolen kisses in quiet moments—her dorm room, my dorm room, the beach at sunset—back before I lost my mind and lost her completely.

She blinked, blinked again, and a tiny crinkle formed between her eyebrows. I lifted my mouth and whispered against her lips. "You okay, Lib?"

CHAPTER THIRTY-SIX

"It isn't that I don't like you, Susan, because, after all, in moments of quiet, I'm strangely drawn toward you, but, well, there haven't been any quiet moments."
—*Bringing Up Baby*

Liz

Was I okay?

That depends.

On the one hand, I was hot and cold and feeling more alive than I'd felt in years. *Two* years, to be exact. But on the other hand, I felt queasy as I looked at him, because this felt like such a terrible idea. *That handsome face* was the one I'd pictured while I cried a thousand tears.

And even though he *hadn't* cheated, my brain couldn't change the fact that he was the avatar of my heartbreak.

God, was I seriously trying to do this again with him?

I was an idiot, right?

A big, huge, foolish idiot.

Who kind of just wanted to stay there and keep being an idiot.

I nodded, looking into his brown eyes and wondering how

to feel safe with this. He was watching me, his face impossible to read as his fingers stroked along my lower back, and I said, "I can't believe Otis lives with Michael now."

His eyebrows lowered a little, like he was confused by my words.

Or like he didn't like them.

He probably expected we'd talk after the kiss, because we definitely weren't a random Batman and Batgirl at a party, no matter how badly we wanted to pretend. Random superheroes didn't kiss like *that*. Everything about the kiss had felt like coming home, like a reunion, like some kind of agreement had been reached.

That kiss had been the heroine and hero, running toward each other while the music crescendoed.

That kiss had been Elizabeth Bennet telling Darcy that his hands were cold.

That kiss, God help me, had been the one that lets you know the characters are *finally* going to end up together.

But no agreement had been reached, and I wasn't ready to talk.

Because I had no idea how I felt or what I wanted.

"Yeah, and he loves it." Wes kept his hands on my lower back, holding me in place, and I could feel the press of all ten fingers. His dark eyes were intense, so directly *on* me that it seemed like he could see my every thought when he said, "So we just kissed, Lib."

I swallowed and looked out at the night below, mostly because I needed to avoid his gaze. Looking at Wes made me so confused. "We were pretending, remember?"

He made a noise in his throat. "Come on."

"What?" I said lightly, as if it was no big deal.

As if that kiss hadn't just scrambled my brain.

"Don't *what* me," he said, half smiling, but his voice was dead serious. "That wasn't pretend—"

"Liz?" Leo's voice came from inside the attic.

"Out here," I yelled, jumping away from Wes and awkwardly climbing to my feet. I stumbled in the stiletto boots, but Wes's hand was just *there,* steadying me, like that was where it belonged.

"You sure you're okay?" he asked quietly, watching me with an unreadable expression.

"I'm fine," I managed, looking into those dark eyes just before Leo popped his head through the window.

"You're free," he said, and Campbell was beside him, holding an *actual* flashlight. Their ski masks were a little jarring now, because I'd been a million miles away in a land where nothing existed except Wes Bennett and the stars.

"Thank you," I said, ducking to climb back inside. "For going to get the key."

"Of course, sweets," Leo said, helping me in. "Was it terrible?"

I sensed Wes climbing inside behind me, waiting for my answer. *No, it wasn't terrible at all.* That was what was so confusing; being with him was never terrible. I could be locked inside a creepy spider attic, forced to take refuge on a roof, yet somehow still have a great time.

And be kissed like *that*, like he was leaving for war and knew he'd never kiss again.

"No," I managed, realizing my hands were shaking. "I was with Batman, so it was okay."

"Hey, Wes," Campbell said, smiling at him and then giving me a *holy shit* look. "If you're really Batman, how come you couldn't break out of here?"

"Maybe I didn't want to," he said in that deep voice, and *dear God*, there was no way I could look at him.

Leo giggled, which made Wes say, "Who *are* you?"

And he said it in the same tone he'd use if he were asking Leo why he'd just soiled himself, like he was disgusted.

"I am Cupid, the god of love," Leo said dramatically, tossing a handful of confetti at Wes. "Let's go do shots, Batboy."

"*Man.* It's Bat*man*," Wes growled, which made Leo and Campbell burst into laughter.

We all exited the attic room, and the second we stepped into the hallway, we were back in loud chaos. The party was even more crowded than before, and after I followed Leo downstairs, embarrassed because I'd lost my ski mask so everyone could see that Latex Batgirl was Liz Buxbaum, I looked behind me and realized he was gone.

I scanned the packed party, but I couldn't see him anywhere, which immediately made me panic.

Was he avoiding me now? Was he mad?

I hated how insecure he made me feel after everything that'd happened, like things could shift at any given moment.

But then my phone buzzed.

Wes: Three things, Buxbaum

I'm more obsessed with your mouth now than ever before

AJ almost got in a fight so we're leaving before he does something stupid

I'll pick you up tomorrow at 7

CHAPTER THIRTY-SEVEN

"I will never stop trying. Because when you find the one, you never give up."
—*Crazy, Stupid, Love*

Wes

"Oh my God, would you look at our boy?"

I did a spin as I walked into the living room, grinning at AJ and Wade as they mocked my jacket and tie. I knew it was probably overkill for a date, but this wasn't just any date.

This was the date that had the power to change everything.

So, yes, I spent some extra time on my appearance.

"Is Mick in his room?" I asked, anxious to get going. He'd agreed to let me borrow Alice for the night (after much begging), so I was ready to get the keys and take off.

"Yeah," Wade said. "But I think he's on the phone."

I knocked on the door before pushing it open and saying, "Keys, please."

Mickey looked up from his computer. "You ready to go?"

"Hi, Wes," his mom said from the screen, smiling. He talked

to her every day, the little mama's boy, and I'd be lying if I said I wasn't a little jealous of how close they were. "How's your ankle?"

I glanced at Mick, who shrugged and said, "It's a funny story, and I had to tell her."

"It's better, Mrs. Solomon," I said. "Thank you."

"Nice suit." She gestured with her hands for me to do a spin. "Tonight's the big date?"

"Christ, did he tell you everything about my life?" I said, laughing in spite of my nervousness as I spun around.

"Of course I did, because she likes to know what my little pals are up to." Mick pulled his key ring out of his pocket and tossed it over. "Be gentle with Alice—she's fragile."

"I will. Thanks a lot, man."

"No problem."

"Good night, Mrs. Solomon," I said, waving to his mother on the FaceTime screen.

"Good night and good luck, Wesley."

As soon as I closed the door to his room and he started talking again, I put on my shoes. Of course, it was hard to tie them while flipping off AJ and Mick for taking photos like they were my parents and I was going to prom.

I was laughing my ass off as they yelled to me from the stairs, and it wasn't until I was in the car and driving toward Liz's place that I got insanely nervous. Not to be with her, because that was the easiest thing in the world to be.

No, I was nervous about how hopeful I was.

It was so close—*finally within reach*—that I was terrified it was going to disappear.

Which explained why I could barely speak when Liz opened the door and said, "Hi."

I couldn't think of a response, or any words at all, so I parroted Liz while my heart rate skyrocketed. "Hi."

She was standing there in her apartment doorway, looking like a goddess, and I was reduced to a caveman who just stared with his mouth hanging wide open. But she was wearing this frothy, gauzy black dress that exposed her bare shoulders and a lot of leg, leg that was supported by black high heels that had crisscross ties around her ankles.

Hella distracting, those.

"I feel like it's cliché to say this as I arrive for a date," I said, lost in the way her long curls framed her face, "but you are so stunning, it hurts, Buxbaum."

The arch of her eyebrows, the high flush on her cheeks, the clear gloss on her mouth; would I ever get tired of looking at her? Her face was the only thing my eyes ever wanted to see, I swear to God.

And she smelled incredible.

"Thanks," she said, her lips turning up into a tiny smile. "You look good in a suit, Bennett."

"Quit hitting on me—I just got here," I said, trying to calm my nerves.

But tonight felt important for us, like a gateway to the possibility of something. I had no margin for error, no wiggle room, so I was determined to make it count.

"Sorry I'm so aggressive," she teased. "My bad."

"You've got to ease into it," I said, loving her tiny smirk as she tilted her head and pretended to be annoyed by me. "Stick with me and I'll teach you how to have game."

"That's what I'm afraid of."

Neither of us spoke as we took the elevator downstairs, but I was impressed by my ability to appear relaxed in spite of the fact that my chest was tight and my heart rate was elevated to what was surely an unhealthy triple-digit readout.

So far, so good.

"Mickey let me borrow his car, and I vacuumed it out, but she's pretty rough," I said as we walked outside.

"Alice and I are old friends, so it's fine," she said, and I was still amazed that she was already friends with the teammates who were my new friends. "At least she's running."

"True," I agreed, and I was glad she seemed nervous. Hopefully it meant that she saw this night as important too. The good thing was that we both seemed nervous, yet it wasn't an awkwardness that was heavy on tension.

It was, like, typical first-date jitters.

But then I started the car and things got weird.

She was buckling her seat belt as I pulled away from the curb, and she was humming a little.

Three seconds later she asked, "Is this 'City of Stars'?"

I kept my eyes on the road, not wanting to seem too self-congratulatory as I said, "It *is*."

"Wow," she said, sounding confused as the song from *La La*

Land swirled around us in Mick's piece-of-crap car. Confused instead of charmed. "I haven't heard that in ages."

I'd intentionally turned it on because she used to love that movie, so I was shocked as hell when she hit the arrow to forward to the next song.

Oh-*kay*.

Unfortunately, my music was on shuffle, so the next song that came on was "Club Sandwich." Which meant that instead of romantic date music, Alice's interior was now being soiled with a punk/rap song about eating a sandwich in *the club*.

Great running song, but not so great for a date.

"What is *this*?" she asked, and when I glanced over, she looked like she was fighting back a smile.

Which made everything okay.

"'Club Sandwich,'" I replied around a laugh because it was *ridiculous* that my perfect-date song had been replaced by Joey Valence & Brae. "It's a great lifting song."

"I'm not sure I believe you," she teased, a smile *finally* curving her lips.

I'm in the club with my sandwich
Yo, call that a club sandwich . . .

"Yeah, I get that," I said. "But kudos to me for finding a song Liz Buxbaum doesn't know, right?"

"Sure," she said, deftly stealing the Bluetooth connection with her phone. "Here—palate cleanser."

I knew it from the first note, even though she probably assumed I didn't. I'd listened to a lot of LANY in the Secret Area when I was depressingly alone in Omaha, and "Cowboy in LA" had been one of my favorite ways to pick at the ironic scab that had *been* my new life.

"Where are you taking me, by the way?" she asked, her eyes out the window.

I thought I'd selected the *perfect* place, but her knee-jerk deletion of what I'd considered the perfect-date *song* had me second-guessing my decision. So I said, "It's a surprise."

When we moved to LA two years ago, we'd always said we were going to go on a date to the restaurant from *La La Land*. So my thinking, for tonight, had been *What better place to take her for dinner while her favorite song from the soundtrack played on the way?*

She didn't say anything when the restaurant came into sight, and I worried I'd gotten it wrong. I wanted to give her the perfect romantic night, a new beginning to the version 2.0 of our story, and I honestly thought I'd killed it.

I didn't know why it was wrong, but I could tell it wasn't right.

"Is that okay?" I asked.

"No, that's great," she said, pushing up a very fake smile. "I'm excited."

It wasn't, and I suspected *she* wasn't.

But why?

Did she hate *La La Land* now? God, she used to love that movie, even though it made her cry every time.

I hate not knowing her like I used to.

I was fascinated by the person she'd become, but tonight felt like one of those times when I needed to nail the correct answers. So I wasn't happy when, as I pulled up to the valet stand, the car made a weird noise. It sounded like a cough, then it sputtered, and then it turned off.

No, no, no, no.

"That's not good," I murmured, turning the key and giving it gas, but the car just whirred and wouldn't catch. "Come on, Alice."

Shit.

"Good evening, sir," the valet said, pulling my door open as the man looked at the car like it was going to be physically painful for him to have contact with it.

"Miss," I heard another fancy employee say from the other side of the car as he opened Liz's door.

"Hang on for a sec," I said, trying again to get it to start. "It just needs a minute."

Dammit, dammit, dammit.

Liz got out and stepped onto the curb, while I kept trying the same things to get the car to start, even though they weren't working. *Insane much?* I could feel the valet glaring at me from his spot beside the car.

"I don't know what the problem is," I said, repeatedly turning the key like an idiot.

"Sir, we need this car out of the valet lane," the valet—Gregor, according to his name tag—said.

Oh, no shit?

"I'm trying, buddy," I snapped, wanting him to disappear.

"We cannot have it stalled here." The valet looked over the top of the car and gestured to Liz, like she had the power to make it magically start again.

"Neither can we," she said, her voice loud. "We're doing our best here."

"Sir, you're going to have to push it out of the way," the guy said to me, pointing to a spot farther down the street. "Over there, and then you can have it towed."

I could sense the eyes of other customers on me, as well as Liz's, and I was mortified. She was probably so embarrassed to be seen with me.

With all this.

"Well, I'm going to need your help, then," I growled at Valet Dude, gritting my teeth and wanting to rage. "Can you at least get in the car and steer while I push?"

"That's against policy, I'm afraid," he said, looking very happy with that fact.

Yeah, you should be afraid, you dick.

"I will," Liz said, coming around the car. "But I have to say, you are very not helpful, Gregor."

I would've laughed at that, but I was too busy climbing out of the car and being up-close-and-personal with all the onlookers who were staring. I could see in my peripheral vision that my tie was wonky, and my face burned as I said to Liz, "I'll call Mickey, because you are *not* helping while dressed like that."

"Yes, I am," she said, rolling her eyes as if the thought of not helping was ludicrous.

"No, you're *not*," I repeated, rolling *my* eyes.

"Shut up and push, Bennett, while I steer," she said, putting her hands on my chest and giving me a little push out of the way. "And quit looking so grumpy."

God, I love her.

I looked down into her stubborn face and said, *"Fine."*

She climbed into the car and put it in neutral, and when I yelled "go," she steered while I pushed. It was a warm evening, so I was sweating my ass off when the car was finally parked and Liz got out.

"I am *so* sorry about this," I said, taking the keys and setting my hand on her lower back, guiding her toward the sidewalk in front of the restaurant.

"It doesn't matter." She shrugged and said, "It's not even your car."

I called a tow truck, and once it was arranged, I held out the keys to Gregor, that fuck. "We have a reservation inside, and the tow truck will be here in an hour for the car. Here are the keys."

Gregor looked at the keys like they were filthy. "I'm sorry, sir, but you'll have to stay with the car until the driver arrives."

"But we'll miss our reservation," I said calmly, refusing to let my anger get the best of me. "I already told the driver to get the keys from the valet."

"It's company policy—you have to stay with the car."

"Can we change our reservation?" Liz asked. "We'll be in as soon as the car is picked up."

"I'm sorry, miss, but we are booked this evening so we cannot make any changes."

"I'll leave the keys in the car, then," I said, wanting to lose it. Wanting to throw a temper tantrum because why the hell was this happening on the night where I was supposed to be pulling off the *perfect* date?

"Sir, you have to stay with your car until the tow arrives."

I looked at Liz, then said to Gregor, "What if I don't? It's not like this is the airport, where cars aren't allowed to be parked, for God's sake."

"We will have your car towed if it's left unattended, unfortunately, because this is private property."

"Well, that's perfect, isn't it, because it's already *being* towed," I said through clenched teeth, wanting to hurt Gregor the Shit. "We're going to go eat, Greg."

I grabbed Liz's hand and tried to lead her toward the restaurant, but she wasn't budging. She gave me a look and said, "Wes. It's Mick's car. It's Alice. We can't have it end up at some random impound lot."

I dragged a hand through my hair and felt the perfect date slipping away. "But we have a reservation."

"I'm not even hungry," she said, shrugging, then added in a very loud voice, "and I heard the food here *sucks*."

Marry me, Buxbaum.

She squeezed my hand and said, "Let's just wait for the tow truck to get Alice, and then we'll come up with a plan B."

I sighed and looked for disappointment in her green eyes, but I couldn't find it. "You sure?"

"I'm positive," she said, nodding. "Plan Bs are always more fun."

CHAPTER THIRTY-EIGHT

"My nightmares are usually about losing you.
I'm okay once I realize you're here."
—*Catching Fire*

Liz

"Is he looking?"

I glanced toward the valet, my abs seriously sore from laughing so hard. "Oh, yeah. He wants to kill us."

"Perfect." Wes grinned and climbed on top of the trunk beside me.

On top of the red-and-white plastic tablecloth that he'd draped over the trunk.

When I'd said the words "plan B" to Wes, he got that twinkle in his eye, and then it was on. Wes Bennett was supercharged in a way that only Wes became supercharged. He clicked into his DoorDash app, placed a few orders, and now, a mere twenty minutes later, we were having a trunktop candlelit dinner.

The tablecloth, candle, and battery-operated disco ball were from CVS, the food from McDonald's. We were sitting there, eating Big Macs on top of the trunk, while Mick's car stereo blared the song "Fuck You" by Lily Allen.

On repeat.

"Nice musical selection, Buxbaum," he said, lifting his burger to his mouth, and I realized I was having a very hard time looking away from him. It'd been that way since he'd picked me up. Because he'd always been an attractive person, but now he'd become something more.

Bigger, stronger, harder—he was almost too gorgeous to look at.

And the suit amped his gorgeousness to an impossible degree. I'd nearly inhaled my gum when he showed up at my door.

"The Lily Allen version felt somehow classier than CeeLo Green's," I said, glad it was too dark for him to notice my cheeks.

"And this is why you're the expert," he said, taking a bite. "Unmatched elegance."

I started laughing again, glad the car had broken down.

Because it felt safer with Wes when we were far removed from our past. Sitting here, eating on the trunk of a car in front of a famous Burbank restaurant, was, like, a different us. It felt like we were two UCLA students on a date, not two exes with a pile of historical baggage.

And I could somehow handle that.

It was almost like our past was too exhausting and confusing to my heart, like a complex algebra equation on a test where it seemed safer to skip it and just move on to the next question. Like, yes, it was an important problem, but how could I finish the exam when I didn't even know where to start with that question?

It was too overwhelming.

When I'd heard "City of Stars" on the way to the restaurant, I couldn't stop my brain from remembering the times we'd watched that movie together. Wes used to think it was adorable, the way it was impossible for me to *not* cry when Mia sees Sebastian at the club, and he used to make it his mission to "kiss the cry out of me."

So the fact that he got us a reservation at *the* club from the movie, the one we'd talked about visiting on a date during our *first* time together at UCLA? God, I'd struggled to keep my eyes from tearing up as he proudly told me his amazingly romantic plan.

Too overwhelming, reconciling all that.

But as I sat there with him on the trunk of the car, it felt different enough that I could relax a little. The part of me that was dying to be with Wes wanted to go that route, to just pretend the past didn't exist for a night.

It was nonsensical, but it kind of felt like a cheat code.

Like a skip-to-the-good-part card.

"So this internship with Lilith," he said, picking up his Coke. "How's that going? I Googled her, and she's, like, super legit, right?"

"Yeah," I said, grabbing a fry. "She's the real deal, and it's kind of amazing."

I went off then, because it was impossible not to fangirl over Lilith. I told him all about her work and the ideas she had for my career, and he asked all the right questions.

"So you get a job in music licensing, and you've got a nine-to-five with a salary and benefits. But while you do this, your entire job is working with—and helping out—all the people you want to work with as a supervisor? No way, that's genius."

"Right?" I said. "And she volunteers all this helpful stuff to me on a daily basis. It's insane how much I've already gotten out of the internship, and it's still new."

"Is the constant baseball driving you crazy, though?" He reached out and grabbed my pickle, then paused. "Wait—can I have?"

That made me laugh. "Yeah, I still hate them. Go ahead."

"Sweet," he said, tossing it into his mouth.

"And the baseball thing *is* driving me crazy, but only because it's hard to find time to study." I wiped my fingers on a napkin and said, "I actually really like producing sports content, believe it or not."

"I forgot to tell you, Lib, the 'Supermassive Black Hole' Reel was so good," he said, grabbing a few fries from his plate. "I think I watched it a hundred times."

"Only because it showcases your pitching, egomaniac," I teased, feeling something in the center of my chest turn to hot liquid when he laughed. His eyes were squinty, his dimples popping, and I wanted to stay there on the trunk of the car, laughing with him, forever.

"Okay you *did* make me look good," he said, nodding in agreement. "But the song choice, the camera angles, the way you paired my release with the *perfect* spot in the song—it was like a short film, swear to God."

"Thanks," I said, looking down because it was embarrassing how much I liked his praise. I needed to change the subject away from me, so I asked, "What about you? How do you handle all that math and science when your whole life is baseball?"

"Do you want the truth?" he said, giving me that little-boy half smile of his. "Or should I try to sound cool?"

"Truth only," I said, genuinely curious.

"The truth is that I probably love my math and science classes as much as I love baseball. Finding *time* is hard," he said. "But my classes challenge me in a fun way."

"God, you're *such* a nerd," I teased, shaking my head. "And you're still doing civil engineering?"

He nodded. "I was going to do architectural until I realized that would only have me designing things like HVAC and lighting, whereas I like to be a little more creative."

It was weird to think this when we were the same age, but I was so proud of him as he sat there telling me about his career goals. He wanted to go into *water* engineering, like designing dams and focusing on watershed management (I didn't even know what that meant), and he was so intent and purposeful that it was a little inspiring.

Wes Bennett had his shit together.

His phone lit up, and Wade's name popped up on the screen.

"Come *on*," he said, grinning as he looked at the message. "Look."

Wade: Text us a selfie. After much discourse, we no longer believe that Buxxie would go out with you.

"I should say no," I said, laughing at the thought. "And let your friends think you're a liar."

"But you won't," he said, leaning closer and holding out his phone. "Smile, Buxbaum."

He took the picture, and we both shared a stupid smile as we looked at it.

Because it was a great picture of two overdressed people eating fast food on the trunk of a car.

"He's going to give me so much crap about this fancy dinner," he said, sending the photo.

"Yeah, he is," I agreed. "How can he be so obnoxious yet still lovable?"

"It's his special gift."

After that, the conversation shifted to Wade and Campbell, which added to my enjoyment because they were friends that had nothing to do with our past. He told me that Wade really *did* like my roommate, to the point that he was too nervous to ask her out.

"Your tow truck," Gregor yelled from where he'd been stationed, shooting glares in our direction. "Is here."

"Thank you. To Gregor!" Wes said loudly, lifting his large McDonald's Coke.

"To Gregor," I repeated, tapping my cup against his.

The flashing yellow lights on the tow truck lit up the darkness, and I was honestly a little sad to see it.

Because I was having a great time.

CHAPTER THIRTY-NINE

"I'd say it was fate, but you probably
chose to be four minutes late."
—*Love at First Sight*

Wes

I don't want this night to end.

It had been a wildly imperfect date, but Liz didn't seem to mind. Even crammed in the front seat of the tow truck between me and the driver, she was grinning.

I need more time.

Which was why, when we pulled up to a red light beside the high school that was just up the street from campus, the one Mick and I hopped the fence at multiple times, I came up with a crazy idea.

"Can we get out here?" I asked the tow truck driver. "You can just set the car down anywhere in the Hitch parking lot."

The old guy looked at me like I was nuts. "You want to get out here?"

Liz, on the other hand, just narrowed her eyes and looked at me like she was waiting for the details.

"I need to grab my bag out of the back seat before you pull away," I told the driver. "Would you mind?"

He looked in the rearview mirror and shrugged. "There's no one behind me, so go for it."

I looked at Liz. "Are you up for more of this date night?"

She made me the happiest guy on the planet when she rolled her eyes, then said, "I don't have anything else going on."

I opened the door, and we got out of the truck, then ran back to the car to get my bag before he pulled away.

And once he did, we were suddenly surrounded by the silence of the residential neighborhood after dark.

"Wow, it's so quiet," she said, her voice nearly a whisper as we stood on the sidewalk. "So what's the plan?"

"I thought we'd take some BP." I'd noticed that Liz always seemed super engaged during batting practice. She was all over the place, taking a million shots and looking mesmerized, so why not hit some balls?

"The school is closed, dumbass," she said, her eyes narrowed as she looked at the dark, deserted baseball field.

"If I recall, you know how to climb a fence."

She made a noise that sounded like a cross between a laugh and a groan. "True, but I wasn't wearing four-inch wedges at the time."

"I'll throw you over," I volunteered.

"No, thank you," she said, making a face like I was ridiculous, but her mouth was sliding into a smile.

God, I love her.

"I will piggyback-climb you," I offered.

"That doesn't even make sense."

"Yes, it does," I said, walking close enough to the outfield fence to throw my bag over. "Get on my back, hold on tight, and I'll climb the fence for the both of us."

Her eyes got squinty, and she said, "I don't think that will work."

"I think it will, Libby—come on," I urged, bending my knees and smacking my ass. "Get on."

She gave a laugh and shook her head. "I think this sounds like a terrible idea."

"Untie those shoes, though," I said, looking at her feet. Those shoes made her legs look incredible, but they weren't made for climbing fences. "I don't want you breaking your ankle when we land."

"When we *land*?" she said, laughing harder. "So you're acknowledging we're going to fall."

"'Land' is a word that encompasses all landings, on foot or on ass," I clarified. "Take off your shoes, sunshine, and let's do this."

"You're such a bully," she teased.

I said, "You're such a chicken."

"Don't."

"Don't make me make the noise," I taunted, distracted by the twinkle in her eyes.

"Spare me your *bokk-bokk*s, Bennett," she said, kneeling down and untying her left shoe. "Also—how am I going to see the ball in the dark?"

"I have portable lights in my bag."

"Is that a normal baseball thing?" she asked, untying her right shoe. "To carry around lights."

"No, but I'm not a normal baseball player."

"That tracks." She stepped out of her shoes and held them in her hand. "Okay. What now?"

"Now," I said, grabbing her shoes and throwing them over the fence, "you climb on me like a good girl."

"I'm going to pretend you didn't just say that."

"Oh, I'm going to pretend you secretly loved it."

She started laughing again, and I bent down so she could jump on my back. "Just focus on holding on, and I'll get us over."

Heat rushed through me as she wrapped her arms around my neck and jumped, as my hands grabbed the back of those smooth legs.

"Are you good?" she asked, her breath warm on the side of my neck.

"Baby, I've never been better."

CHAPTER FORTY

"No matter what happens tomorrow or for the rest of my life, I'm happy now because I love you."
—*Groundhog Day*

Liz

"I'd like one in the strike zone this time, Bennett."

"I've been giving you meatballs, Buxbaum." Wes, who'd stripped down to his white undershirt and suit pants, made a face as he hollered at me from the pitcher's mound. "Come on."

"Meatballs that are high and outside," I hollered back, dissolving into giggles when he moved like he was going to hurl the ball at me.

We'd been playing for at least an hour, and I was fairly certain neither of us were ever going to quit. He'd given me his white dress shirt so I could wear it over my dress to avoid a wardrobe malfunction, and his jacket was lying on the grass in the dark outfield, right on top of my shoes.

We were a disheveled mess, with only home plate and the pitcher's mound illuminated, and it was wonderful.

I'd been with Wes for hours and had completely managed to forget about the past. To stop overthinking everything. Tonight had just been *fun*.

"Get ready," he yelled, giving me intense eye contact.

"Oh, I was born ready," I said, digging my bare feet into the dirt around home plate.

Wes threw the ball, totally giving me a baby pitch, but I nailed this one. The aluminum bat clinked, music to my ears, and I screamed and took off for first base.

(Since it was only the two of us, we had imaginary rules in place. The runner had to keep running until the outfielder caught the ball or was six feet away from a ball on the ground. Only then were you allowed to stop at a base.)

Wes caught it but dropped the ball—obviously on purpose—and I kept running until he had control as per our rules.

"You don't seriously think you can make it home, do you?" I heard him yell when I didn't stop at third, sounding like he was sprinting toward me.

I just screamed, "Gaaaaaaah!" and ran as fast as I could toward home plate.

I felt him bearing down on me, and then I felt him tag me with the ball.

"Noooooooooo!" I yelled.

But his arm came around my waist to hold me steady, so he wouldn't knock me over.

And then he lifted me off the ground, wrapping both his arms around my waist.

"Bennett," I squealed, cackling. "Put me down!"

"Not until you take back the 'high and outside' comment," he said, his voice deep and growly in my ear.

"I won't," I said, breathing heavy from the sprint. "You know I won't."

"Well, then," he said, setting my feet on the ground and somehow managing to spin me so I was facing him, without letting me out of his arms. "Guess I'm going to have to teach you a lesson."

"Oh, big man," I said, my breath coming fast, but now it was because of the heat in his dark eyes as he looked at me. "Please teach m—"

His mouth cut me off.

One minute I was speaking, the next his lips were on mine, his tongue in my mouth, my whimper in his. *Dear God,* I thought as his arms pulled me closer, where I was pressed against every inch of him and my eyes closed automatically, *it feels good to be back in his arms.*

CHAPTER FORTY-ONE

"There I was, standing there in the church, and for the first time in my whole life I realized I totally and utterly loved one person. And it wasn't the person next to me in the veil. It's the person standing opposite me now . . . in the rain."
—*Four Weddings and a Funeral*

Wes

The minute my lips landed on hers, the teasing torture was left behind, and all that remained was want. I kissed her mouth the only way I knew how—obsessed, crazed, needy—and she returned the favor, delivering hot suction that drove me wild.

I squeezed her waist, not caring about anything but the way she kissed me back like she didn't want to ever stop. I could feel every inch of her body against me, and when her fingers slipped under the back of my T-shirt, I growled like an animal.

She made me feral for her.

I dropped the ball and pulled her tighter against me, my body pressing into hers from memory, like a key into the only lock that would ever fit. I cursed into her mouth when I felt her legs wrap around me, my knees literally weak from the intensity of my want.

I put my hands underneath her and started walking, away from home plate and toward the dugout, and the way she tightened her long, bare legs around me set me on fire. It got quieter as we entered the dugout, and I didn't stop walking until her back was against the wall in the darkness. Until I was pinning her body against it as we kissed like we were about to die and this was our last moment together.

I had missed her for what felt like my entire life.

And she was in my arms, kissing me.

Like she'd missed *me* for her entire life.

It gutted me, to be honest. Finally having her in my arms, meeting me kiss-for-kiss after we'd spent the past few hours together, felt terrifyingly perfect.

Like each and every wish I'd made upon a lifetime of stars was coming true, all at once.

This was *my* Liz, finally back in my arms.

"God, I love you," I said against her mouth, every part of me lost in what was finally found. I leaned into her, breathing in her perfume as her fingers gripped my shoulders. "I've missed you so much."

"Wes," she breathed, her eyes still closed as she whispered into me. "Don't."

"What?" I lifted my mouth, breathing heavy, looking down into sleepy green eyes that fluttered open like butterfly wings.

She gave her head a shake. "Don't say that."

"Don't say what?" I lowered my head and rubbed my nose against sweet freckles, flexing my fingers against the softness in my palms.

"That you love me," she said, blinking at me with a wrinkle between her eyebrows.

"Why not?"

"Because you can't," she said, shaking her head. "It's too soon."

"Too soon?" I wanted to laugh at that, because how in the hell could it be too soon? "Did you seriously just say that?"

"It's, like, our first date." She dropped her hands from my shoulders and rubbed her lips together, finding her feet and stepping back from me. "You can't love me already."

I felt the distance between us grow, inches that felt like miles, as my hands became empty. I watched her retreat as I said, "Well, I do."

"No, you *don't*," she said emphatically, passionately, almost as if we were arguing. She put a little smile on her face, like she was kidding, but it was forced.

"Please help me understand what's happening here, Lib," I said, a weight settling in my stomach as the thing I thought had returned to me backed farther away. "Because I've never *stopped* loving you."

She shook her head back and forth, tucking her hair behind her ears and biting down on her lower lip. She looked haunted—hunted—as she insisted, "No. Let's not talk about that. I don't want to talk about the past."

"I'm not . . ." *What the hell is happening?* I looked into her eyes and explained, "I'm not talking about the past, Liz; I'm talking about my feelings for you."

"Wes." She said it through gritted teeth, like she was trying to hold on to her patience or something. "I don't want us to do that.

Let's just go forward, okay? Let's just, like, pretend this is new. You're a freshman who took me out on a date tonight. A really great date. Can't we just be that for now?"

Pain—*was it pain?*—pinched in my chest as she said those words, because the whole time I thought we'd been coming back to each other, had she been trying to pretend I was someone else? To forget everything she'd ever known about me?

Is that what she has to do to be okay with me?

I swallowed and tried to come up with words, but the only one that came to me was, "No."

Her eyebrows furrowed together. "No?"

"We aren't that, Lib. You can't pretend that I'm some guy you just met—"

"Why not, if it means we're able to move on?" she interrupted, looking frustrated and almost desperate to convince me.

"Because you shouldn't have to mentally split a person in two in order to love them," I replied, a little too loudly with a voice that was cracked but *fuck*.

"Don't you get it? You either love me or you don't," I said, not wanting to face the truth of that statement. "Because I'm not the kid next door, or the asshole who broke your heart, or the goddamn freshman who took you out on a date tonight."

I took a deep breath and proceeded to tell her what she apparently never wanted to hear.

"I am just Wes fucking Bennett, Lib, the guy who can't remember a single day in his life when he didn't love you."

She watched me with wide eyes, frozen in place, probably thinking I was absolutely unhinged. I felt like I should add something, like *just kidding* or *that's totally fine*, but it wasn't fine.

"Do you know how many 12:13s I've watched pass without you? Tonight it'll be the seven hundred and twentieth," I said, the words burning my throat. "The last thing in the world I want is to say something that makes that number infinite, but I also can't let you erase our history. I don't want to remember the bad parts, but I refuse to forget the good."

I looked into the only eyes I'd ever loved and confessed, "Because our good moments were the crumbs that fed me for seven hundred and nineteen 12:13s when I was alone."

"God. Wes." She wiped her eyes and stepped closer. "When you told me the truth the other day, I was so mad at you for giving up on us, and for not talking to me before you made the decision to end us, that I couldn't think beyond those facts. I knew you'd been trying to do the right thing, but I also knew that my heart would never recover from the loss, right?"

That made my stomach hurt, the way it always had, when I thought about how much I'd hurt her.

"So my anger made me kind of blind, I guess, to your sacrifice. I was so mad that you did it, that I didn't take the time to think about what it must've been like, for you, to do it."

I wanted to touch her so badly, but I was too afraid of where this was going.

"And in my wildest dreams," she said, her voice thick, "I never would've imagined that while I was crying through so many 12:13s, you were too."

You have no idea, Lib.

"But here's my honest confession," she said, her eyes bright as she looked up at me. "I've loved you, and I've missed you, and I've hated you and regretted you, but I've never forgiven or forgotten you. So I just—"

"Excuse me." A bright flashlight shone directly into our faces as a deep voice said, "Do you two have permission to be here?"

My eyes adjusted to the garish brightness, and I could see a cop, staring at us from just outside the dugout.

A cop, with his cruiser lights flashing in the parking lot.

I looked at Liz as she stared into the light, her eyes enormous.

Oh, shit.

CHAPTER FORTY-TWO

"I'm always gonna love you."
—*La La Land*

Liz

Keep going.

It was seven o'clock, the sun was in my eyes, and I just wasn't feeling the run today.

But I was going to keep going.

Usually, running calmed my thoughts, but all it'd done so far was make me *more* stressed out as I replayed last night, over and over again, in my head.

It'd been perfect.

Then it wasn't.

And then the cop showed up.

Hooooow is that the way the night ended? I thought (in mental-screaming form) as I ran past the sculpture garden. One minute we'd been on fire in the dugout, the next we were fighting, and then we were being questioned by the officials for breaking and entering.

Officer Nerada had lectured us about sneaking onto the field, told us that he could charge us if he wanted to (but he didn't), and then he proceeded to drive Wes and me home like naughty children.

Since Hitch was closer than my place, he dropped Wes off first. And by the time I got out of the cruiser at my apartment, he'd already sent a text.

Wes: Can I come over and talk to you?

I stared at that message for the next twenty minutes, trying to figure out what I wanted my answer to be.

Which had driven Clark crazy because he was 100 percent Team Wes now. *Why not talk to him? You're going to leave him on read? You're a monster.*

Because if I was being honest, *yes*—I still had huge feelings for Wes. Maybe they'd never left, or maybe he'd successfully wooed them back, but last night, with him, had felt a lot like love.

And that was the problem.

Even though I had those feelings, I still wasn't sure I necessarily wanted to follow them. There was a very loud voice in my brain that kept telling me it was safer to just move on from Wes forever. It was good to know he'd never cheated and wasn't a jerk, but that didn't mean it was good for *me* to go back to him now.

So when he called—three times—after I ignored his text, I turned off my phone.

Clark disgustedly went to bed at that point.

But I needed to think.

Even though I knew it was an irrational thought, something had occurred to me last night while I sat on the sofa and binge-watched

Friends until around two. I knew Wes was sorry he'd hurt me, and obviously he'd been going through hell at the time and had done what he thought was best, but would he behave differently if something happened again?

If he threw out his shoulder or lost his scholarship and had to quit school, would we deal with it together, or would he walk away from me this time too? It was an unlikely scenario, but my cautious brain couldn't stop asking the question.

I was still pondering this idea while I finished my run, I was still pondering it while I showered, and I was still pondering it when I let myself into Morgan to upload some footage and check out equipment for the scrimmage that was later that day.

Would history repeat itself?

I really didn't want to see Wes until I figured out my own thoughts, so the timing of the scrimmage really sucked.

Because there was no way for me to get out of going without looking like a total coward.

When I got to my cubicle, I distracted myself by editing film until Clark showed up.

"So," Clark said, dropping his stuff onto his desk. "Did you talk to him?"

"No," I said, not looking up from my computer.

"You're a dick," he said grumpily, and I heard the tone of his laptop turning on. "At least respond."

"I can't, though," I said, dragging a hand through my hair. "He's going to want to talk, and I don't know how I feel, so I can't actually have that conversation."

"You can, too," he disagreed, his keyboard clicking. "I don't know what your problem is, Liz. As long as I've known you, you've always been levelheaded. Like, not dramatic at all. But for some reason, you're acting like an emotional teenager about this."

"No, I'm not," I argued, turning my chair and wheeling it back a foot so I could glare at him. "This isn't as simple as you want to make it."

"Yes, it is."

"No, it's not!"

"For God's sake, it is, too," he said, looking at me through ridiculous round fashion glasses that had blue Bruins all over them. "Bennett loves you, is sorry for hurting you, and wants another chance. If you have feelings for him, why wouldn't you give it a shot?"

I sighed. "It's not that easy."

"It is, but whatever." He stood and said, "I'm going to get a coffee, and don't even ask me to grab one for you because I won't."

"Clark."

"Totally serious." He turned and left the production office, leaving me alone in the quiet that I wanted nothing to do with as the door clicked shut behind him.

Wonderful.

I stood, knowing I should probably go talk to him, so when the door squeaked open a minute later, I said without turning around, "I knew you couldn't stay mad."

But then I heard the sound of a familiar throat clearing.

And I smelled him.

I took in a deep breath and wondered if my imagination was running wild.

"Lib." His voice was deep and scratchy, like he hadn't really used it yet, when Wes said from behind me, "Can we please talk?"

My heart was instantly racing as I turned around.

He was standing beside Clark's empty cubicle, a step away, looking down at me with a seriousness I almost never saw on that face. His glasses amplified the intensity somehow as his dark eyes watched me from behind the lenses. The tips of his hair looked damp, like he'd showered but the walk across campus hadn't completely dried the curly ends, and he was wearing gray sweatpants with a white Bruins hoodie.

He looked like he'd woken up, thrown on clothes, and rushed right over.

"Um, here's the thing," I said, feeling shaky as I met his gaze, clueless how to communicate all the things I'd been thinking since last night. The sight of him made all my reservations impossible to remember. So I just said, "I'd rather not."

His jaw flexed and his eyebrows furrowed together. "You'd rather *not*?"

I nodded and tucked my hair behind my ears. Nodded again. "Yeah, um, I think I just need some time to think. Alone."

CHAPTER FORTY-THREE

"I felt so peaceful . . . and safe . . . because I knew that no matter what happened, from that day on, nothing can ever be that bad . . . because I had you."

—*17 Again*

Wes

Time alone to think?

"Why, though?" I asked, stepping closer. "I mean, we've had two *years* of thinking alone. Don't you think it might be nice to think about this *together*?"

She rubbed her forehead with two fingers, looking somewhere just past me, like she'd rather do anything than meet my gaze. Her voice was quiet when she said, "I just, I don't know, I just *can't* right now."

"I don't want to pressure you," I said, trying my best to sound calm when I was freaking out. I'd been freaking out since the minute the cop showed up last night and Liz stopped responding to me, because it was impossible to accept that we'd come this close and now we were going backward again. I touched her chin, watching my finger settle on the delicate dimple, desperate for her to stay with me and talk. "But I think we *should*, Lib—I think we need to so we can finally move forward. So much time and circumstance has happened, but when we're together, just the two of us, everything is the same, right? I *know* you feel it too, so let's talk through the bullshit so we can finally be *there*, at *that*."

"But I don't know if I want to be at *that*," she said, gnawing on her lower lip and blinking fast.

It felt like somebody cracked me across the chest with a board. I might've flinched as I searched her face for the lie. "You don't know if you want to?"

Her voice was even quieter when she angled her face so I was no longer touching her and said, "I mean, it's all just happening really fast. A month ago, I thought you were living on the other side of the country and—"

"And none of that *matters*, Lib," I interrupted, taking a deep breath, so frustrated I wanted to bang my head against a wall. I'd walked away because I thought it was best for her, and then when I finally made it back, I'd committed myself to being patient. To going slow, making her my friend first, taking whatever I could get until she eventually came back to me.

But patient wasn't working.

At *all*.

I cleared my throat and tried again. "We can reexamine everything that's happened, and we can debate whether or not we really know each other anymore and if we can get past the past, but if we're being honest, when you and I are alone in the same room, we are the same *together*. I am the same, *for* you and *with* you, as I always have been."

She was looking up at me, listening with her eyebrows scrunched together like I'd completely lost it.

"You're looking at me like I'm nuts, honey, and you're right. I am. I am out of my *mind* when it comes to you," I said, shrugging because it was a fact. "When I'm near you, the way I feel steals the breath from my body. It's like I breathe *for* you, like I exist to exist *alongside* of you. I know those feelings are probably too big and too scary and put way too much pressure on you, and I'm sorry for that. Truly. But it's the way I feel. The way I've always felt."

I needed to change her face, to find the perfect words to clear away the doubt in her eyes, but all my mind was giving me was *I love you*, which I knew she didn't want to hear, and random lovesick lines from songs.

How can I convince her?

I dragged my desperate hands through my hair and barked out a laugh, even though nothing was funny. My voice cracked when I said, "And you've screwed me up, Lib, because now I'm thinking in lyrics instead of original thoughts. I'm looking at you and trying to find the words to convince you to be with me, and do you know what comes into my head? *You showed me colors you know I can't see with anyone else.* They aren't *my* words, I don't even know what song or album they're from, for God's sake, but it's exactly how I feel. And *you taught me a secret language I can't speak with anyone else*—like, I can't remember who wrote that, but I feel it down to the marrow in my bones. Being with you has changed the threads of my existence, I swear to God, so now being with*out* you makes everything quieter, dimmer, and duller. So. Much. Smaller. And I fucking *hate* it."

She opened her mouth to speak, but I couldn't bear to have her cut me off with closure, so I cut her off first.

"You can take time alone to think, Lib, and you can put space between us and decide I'm not worth the risk," I said, lowering my forehead to hers for the briefest of seconds before stepping back. "There's nothing I can do to stop you from that. But just know that no matter what you decide, and no matter what happens, I will feel this way about you for the rest of my life."

"I got you one even though—" Clark walked into the office with two coffees in his hands, nearly mowing me down. "Oh. Hey, Wes."

I looked into her eyes, ignoring Clark, my chest burning as I said, "There will never be anyone else for me. Hard stop. So go have your think and do what you need to do. But Lizzie—*we* are worth the risk. We always will be."

I'm not sure how I forced myself to step away from her, but I did. I pushed past Clark and left the production office without looking back, mostly because I wasn't sure I could handle whatever came next.

The rest of the morning was a blur. I went through the motions with the guys, getting breakfast and riding over to Jackie and putting on my uniform, but I felt numb. Like the world was spinning around me but I was frozen in place. Because I was losing her—*if*

I ever came remotely close to having her at all—and it felt like there was nothing I could do to change that fact.

I stood in front of my locker before the scrimmage, trying my hardest to shut down the noise in my brain and focus on baseball.

But on top of everything else, my dad's voice was back in my head.

If you're thinking about the redhead on game day, Wesley, you're gonna screw up. Guaranteed.

Wonderful. *That's very helpful—thank you, Dad.*

But I couldn't stop. Liz was on my mind as we took the field, and she stayed there during warm-ups. My ability to tune out the world was failing because all I could think about was *her* and *us* and if we were finished before we ever had a chance to get started.

I glanced toward the stands as I played catch with Mick, and almost as if my brain had conjured her up, there she was.

Instead of being on the field or working just outside the dugout, Liz was sitting behind home plate, a few rows back, with a long-lensed camera in her lap.

And she was watching me.

Our eyes met—*please, Libby*—and I tried reading her face. I searched for any sign that might give me hope. The tilt of her head, the curve of her lips, the squint of her eyes; I sifted through it all but came away with nothing.

And then she lowered her eyes to the camera, as if she didn't want me to see her at all.

"What the heck, Bennett?"

I looked away from her, only to see Mick with his hand raised like he was waiting to throw me the ball. He shook his head and grinned like I was hilarious. "Maybe pay attention, you lovesick piece of shit."

"Shut up and throw," I muttered, embarrassed now on top of everything else.

Wesley, you're gonna screw up. Guaranteed.

CHAPTER FORTY-FOUR

"I feel like I've known you my whole life and
did I mention I'm in love with you?"
—*Descendants 3*

Liz

I want to go home.

I watched Wes go back to playing catch, and my stomach was so full of nerves that I was pretty sure I could vomit on command. Because the way he'd looked at me from the field, after everything he'd *said* to me in the office, was just too overwhelming.

"Perfect day," the guy behind me said, and he wasn't wrong. It was sunny and warm, without a cloud in the sky, and since it was the last scrimmage before fall ball ended, the place was packed.

I didn't care, though, because I couldn't think about anything but the pitcher.

I will feel this way about you for the rest of my life.

Dear God, who said things like that?

Clark had been extraordinarily nice to me on the way over, mostly because I'd burst into tears after Wes left the office, but that somehow made it worse. I needed to forget everything and work, so when we got to the field and Lilith was waiting for us, I was relieved. She was in producer mode, all geared-up, and immediately asked for a favor.

"What's up?" I'd asked, reaching into the pocket of my bag to pull out my sunglasses.

"Do you think you can sit in the stands and get some shots of the fans?" She turned and pointed her arm in the direction of home plate. "And I want some stills *from* the stands, like a fan's-eye view of the game. Can you do that?"

Could I do that? Could I put myself in a position to *not* have to engage with Wes—or the entire team?

She couldn't have asked for a more wonderful favor that day.

"Of course," I'd said, nodding. "Tell me everything you need."

Instead of being near the dugout, she wanted me with the crowd. So I wandered around before the game, taking photos of fans as they bought concessions and basically looked like walking advertisements for UCLA baseball.

It was escapism from the stress of figuring out what to do about Wes, thank God.

The only problem was that once he took the field for warm-ups, he was my focal point. If I looked straight ahead, there he was.

The center point of my sight line.

And it was impossible for me to tear my eyes away.

I'd always been obsessed with the way he looked when he was playing baseball, but that afternoon, after everything he'd just said to me, I couldn't stop looking at him.

I exist to exist alongside of you.

But then he saw me.

I gasped and looked away, but not before meeting stormy brown eyes that felt like they could read my very soul.

The game started, and I sat in my seat behind home plate about eight rows back, capturing the action from the center of the stands. My peripheral vision was always aware of where the tall pitcher in the number 32 jersey was, but I refused to focus on him.

Until he took the mound.

It was a laid-back scrimmage where everyone played, and apparently the fourth inning was his. I watched as he came out, and the sight of his intense face brought back memories of him kissing me against the dugout wall.

Of him knowing exactly how many 12:13s we'd been apart.

Seven hundred and nineteen.

Of him saying, *I exist to exist alongside of you.*

His eyes found mine through the long lens, and he swallowed and clenched that hard jaw. I felt like I couldn't breathe. I had no idea what that look was—*anger? sadness?*—but I felt it in my belly as we watched each other.

And then it was gone because he was throwing the ball.

The first pitch was a fastball that the hitter didn't even swing at.

Damn, he was good.

He caught the ball when Mick threw it back, gave it a flip, trailed his fingers over the seam before bringing it in for the next windup. He took a deep breath, kicked his front leg, and threw what looked like a slider. (I still wasn't good at identifying pitches.)

The batter got a piece of that one, sending a line drive into the infield.

Only it came straight back at Wes.

The ball hit him in the center of his chest before it bounced onto the field. The first baseman ran over and grabbed it, sprinting back to base to get the out, and it happened so fast that it almost seemed like it didn't bother Wes.

But then he put his hand on his chest and grimaced, took a few steps like he was going to walk it off, and collapsed onto the grass.

"Wes!"

I leapt to my feet, my heart in my throat as I watched him roll onto his side. A collective gasp went up from the stands as coaches ran over—and players—but it was hard to see as they crowded around him.

And he was facing the other way.

Move! I wanted to scream to every single person who was blocking my view. I couldn't see Wes, and I needed to know if his eyes were open.

Are his eyes open??

"Is he conscious?" I yelled to no one and everyone, staring at his legs, looking for any sign of movement.

But . . . there wasn't any. His long legs—white baseball pants and tall blue socks—were still.

As he *lay on the ground*.

Please, God, let him be okay. Please, please, please, please.

Fear clutched at my chest, and I stood on my tiptoes, trying to see, but I couldn't see *any*thing because everyone in front of me was on their feet.

"Excuse me," I said loudly, grabbing my stuff. "I need out!"

I pushed past the people in my row, blinded by tears as I scrambled to get free. I bumped off of everyone with my arms full of gear, rushing to get closer to Wes. *He has to be okay. Please, please be okay.* When I finally reached the end of the row, I ran down the steps to get closer to the field, watching from behind the net as Coach Ross crouched beside him, saying something I couldn't hear.

Please sit up, Wes.

God, please, sit up.

The seconds ticked by like hours as the only boy I'd ever loved lay on his side in the middle of the baseball field.

I wanted to tell him.

I wanted to shout the words I should've already said *so* badly as I gripped the net and waited to see any sign that he was going to be fine. I needed to see his face, to see his smile, because my brain was only showing me the unhappy look we'd exchanged a few minutes ago.

There will never be anyone for me but you, Wes, so you need to be okay.

"Liz."

I looked to my right and Clark was jogging toward me, and when he reached my side, he wrapped his huge arms around me. "He's gonna be okay, Lizard."

"Is he?" I said, crying into his shirt before quickly pulling away to go back to watching the field. "Because he still hasn't moved."

"At least he's awake, though," Clark said. "That's the—"

"He *is*?" I put my hand over my heart, scared to believe him. "Are you sure?"

"Positive," he said, nodding. "I think they're being super careful with him in case he's got broken ribs or something."

Broken ribs.

Just as Clark said that, Wes slowly sat up.

"Oh, thank *God*," I whispered, wiping at the tears that were obstructing my view. Relief flooded me as Ross and another coach helped Wes to his feet, but his face didn't look right. He looked out of it, and he looked like he was in pain as the coaches helped him off the field.

I stood there in shock for a few minutes, as the fans clapped for him and the scrimmage started up again, but then I couldn't wait anymore.

I needed to get to him.

"Come on," I said, pointing in Wes's direction. "He's not okay."

"Liz!"

Lilith grabbed my sleeve—I hadn't even registered she was standing next to me.

"Listen," she said, leaning closer and lowering her voice, looking around to make sure no one else could hear. "They're taking Wes by ambulance to Ronald Reagan. Ross thinks he's okay, but they want to get some X-rays and stuff to rule out broken ribs or a punctured lung."

"Is that a possibility?" I asked, feeling a little lightheaded. *By ambulance.*

Punctured lung.

I heard sirens in the distance and felt nauseous.

Dear God, please let him be okay.

"He throws ninety-mile-an-hour pitches, so it's definitely possible," she said, reaching out to take the camera from my hands. "Clark, I need you to drive Liz to the hospital. Can you do that for me?"

"Of course." He looked down at me and smiled softly.

Lilith was giving me such a motherly stare that the tears were instantly back. I swallowed and said, "Thank you."

Clark and I started jogging toward the car, but just before I opened the door, I heard Lilith yell, "Go get him, Buxbaum."

When Clark finally pulled up in front of the ER entrance, I threw open the door and ran inside.

"I'm gonna go park," he yelled out the window. "I'll find you when I get inside."

But when I went in, the woman at the desk wouldn't tell me anything and wouldn't let me go through the locked doors that led to Wes because I wasn't family.

Even when I begged.

With tears and whining.

So I had no choice but to wait.

"Once he's stabilized and the doctor has seen him, *then* I can call the nurse and see if someone can take you back." The lady looked at me like I was the most annoying person on the planet. "For now, just take a seat."

"I can't sit," I said to myself, stepping away from the desk.

There was a waiting room full of chairs, but I couldn't just plop down in between strangers and sit still like everything was fine. *Nothing is fine.* I looked around, searching for a place to pace without driving the other waitees nuts, but then I heard, "Liz?"

I turned around, and Coach Ross was walking toward me.

I didn't know the guy, and we'd never spoken, so it was a little jarring hearing him say my name. He had a reputation for being . . . well, *hot*, but I saw nothing but the crease between his eyebrows and the serious expression on his face.

"How is he?" I asked, running to meet him. "Is he okay?"

He looked past me, at the other people in the waiting room, before saying, "Why don't you come back with me?"

My stomach clenched when he said that, because he said it like he didn't want to have to tell me bad news in front of strangers. He put his hand on my lower back and led me through the locked doors—which the desk lady unlocked for *him* with a smile—and I wanted to scream.

As soon as we cleared the doors, he gestured toward a tiny waiting room. "Lilith called and told me you were on the way, so I thought you might prefer waiting back here."

"We can't go see him?" I asked, craning my neck to see down the hallway of exam rooms, not wanting to go into some empty little room where Wes *wasn't*.

"They gave him some pain meds, so he's resting while they wait on the blood-work results."

"*Blood* work?" I pushed back my hair. "Why would they need to do blood work?"

He smiled at me, like he thought I was funny, and said, "Jesus, will you relax? He's going to be fine."

"He is?" I stared at him and couldn't tell if he was messing with me or not. "Really?"

"He's got some bruised ribs and doesn't particularly enjoy taking deep breaths right now, but he's okay," Ross said, smirking like he'd been amused by Wes's discomfort. "The blood work is just to make sure his heart is functioning properly, but everything looks good on the X-rays and CT scan. They're just going to keep him overnight for observation."

"Oh, thank God," I said, feeling so relieved I was actually lightheaded. I blinked fast, not wanting to bawl anymore, and needed to sit even though there was no way in hell I was going to sit. "I have to see him. I promise not to wake him up or anything, but I really cannot wai—"

"Room eight," he interrupted, tilting his head and looking at me like I was downright pathetic. "At the end of the hall."

CHAPTER FORTY-FIVE

"The truth is I gave my heart away a long time ago, my whole heart, and I never really got it back."
—*Sweet Home Alabama*

Wes

I clenched my jaw and closed my eyes, trying my damnedest to function without breathing, because every time I took a breath, it felt like I was being kicked in the chest. The nurse gave me something for the pain before leaving to get my transfer paperwork going, but so far it wasn't doing a thing.

And I needed to use the facilities.

Now, I knew if I hit the call button for help as per my nurse's instructions, not only would that lady be holding my hand for the hallway stroll, but she'd also be joining me in the men's room for the entire urinal visit. Yes, it was her job, but I just wasn't in the mood for that kind of *up-close-and-personal*.

So I gritted my teeth and sat up, swinging my legs over the side of the bed.

Fuuuuuuuuuuuuuck.

I literally saw stars as the pain in my chest burned, and I put my hand on the spot in an attempt to absorb the pressure when I kept going, forcing my body into a standing position.

"Oh, holy *shit*," I bit out, leaning down and putting *both* hands over the spot as pain stabbed at me like a hot knife. I was still shocked the hit hadn't shattered each and every one of my ribs, because it felt like that ball had been shot out of a cannon.

For a solid thirty seconds after I'd fallen down, I was terrified I was going into cardiac arrest because it'd been *that* hard to breathe. Thank God Ross had been there to talk me through it.

I was careful to be quiet as I slipped out of my room (hunched over and shuffling like a one-hundred-year-old man) and ducked into the restroom just across the hall. Everything hurt when I stood, but it was worse when I leaned down to wash my hands.

And then I thought about Liz, which made my heart ache, in addition to my chest.

Does she know? Does she care?

It was totally emo for me to think of *that* at this moment, but I couldn't help it. It seemed I was destined to spend the rest of my life thinking about the girl who wasn't sure if she wanted to think about me at all.

So when I came out and crossed the hall, I couldn't quite believe my ears.

It was her.

"—so just keep resting while I talk, okay?"

What the fuck? I thought as I heard her voice. *Am I dead?*

Because that sure as hell sounded like Libby.

I stepped into the doorway of my room, narrowed my eyes to a squint, and *holy balls, yes*, that was definitely Liz's hair. Either I was dead and heaven was a hospital room, or she was standing there, talking to the privacy curtain that was pulled closed around my bed.

"I can't wait another second to say this, Wes, so if you're asleep, I'll just repeat it all after you wake up."

She thinks I'm in there. I knew I should tell her I wasn't, that I was wide awake and listening to her every word, but I didn't want to interrupt.

I put a hand on the doorframe for support, suddenly able to ignore the pain in my chest.

"Last night, after we got picked up by the cop, I *thought* I was conflicted over my feelings. This morning, too, I thought I was confused about everything. But I was such an idiot, Wes," she said, and her voice was thick, like she was emotional. "Because when I saw you get hit and you were lying on the field—"

Her voice cracked and she stopped, like she was trying to keep it together, which made me struggle to keep *my* shit together because *fuck*. Liz was here, in my hospital room, and it sure sounded like she hadn't enjoyed me taking a line drive to the chest. That was a pretty low bar, I had to admit, but I held my breath and waited for more.

She's here.

"When I saw you get hit, I realized there isn't anything confusing about it at all. I love you. *Of course* I love you; you're Wes. You are the only boy I've *ever* loved in my entire life. I think I've loved you—without stopping—since you set me on the trunk of my car after prom and kissed me at 12:13."

I felt like I couldn't breathe, but this time it had nothing to do with baseballs slamming into my ribs. I put my fist over my mouth to keep myself from speaking as I listened to her say what I'd daydreamed about her saying for nearly two years.

Hell, what I'd daydreamed about her saying for forever.

You are the only boy I've ever *loved in my entire life.*

It was killing me not to be able to see her face, but I was terrified that a word from me would make her—and this moment—disappear.

And I'd do anything to keep this moment from disappearing.

"So I don't want to waste any more time trying to *figure things out* with us because they're already figured out, right?" She took in a shaky breath and said, "There will never be anyone else for me—hard stop—so let's get on with us. I want *us* to start immediately. Like, zero-to-sixty, let's get to the good part where we're back in a continuous text conversation about something stupid like raccoon memes."

I opened my mouth to respond, because I desperately needed to look into those emerald eyes while her perfect mouth spoke those perfect words, but then I took a deep breath—*shit shit shit that hurts*—making it impossible to speak.

I put my hands over my ribs and clenched my teeth to keep from making a noise. But how could my chest hurt so much when my heart was finally fucking healed?

"And it's incredibly ironic, by the way, that you used the lyrics from 'Illicit Affairs' on me because I actually banished that song from my life, Wes. I *did*. I deleted it after we broke up because two specific lines—the very two that you quoted—were so painfully perfect for us that they broke *me* every time I heard them."

I tried swallowing, but my throat was too tight.

Of course I randomly quoted to her a pair of lyrics that she'd already associated with us.

The universe was in on it, the mastermind, *I swear to God*.

"Because I never stopped loving you, either," she said, and I needed to cut her off and force her to repeat that sentence. *A hundred times*, and then a thousand more.

I never stopped loving you.

She made a little laugh sound in the back of her throat and said, "Although technically, for the record, it probably started the day you fixed my bloody nose with your shirt, not prom night, but we can figure that out later."

That was it; I couldn't stay silent another second.

Liz was here, Liz was mine, and one second more was one second too many.

My pulse was hammering, pounding in my ears as I said, "That's total bullshit and you know it."

CHAPTER FORTY-SIX

"No measure of time with you will be long enough.
But, let's start with forever."
—*Breaking Dawn: Part 1*

Liz

"Oh my God!"

I gasped and turned around, covering my heart with my hands, and there was Wes.

Instead of lying on the bed behind the curtain, he was standing *behind* me in the doorway of the exam room. His hair was a mess, he was clutching his ribs with his left hand, and Wes Bennett was wearing a baby-blue hospital gown with bright yellow grippy socks on his feet.

I didn't want to cry again, but seeing him upright, looking so beautifully ridiculous, made me feel like bawling all over again.

Thank you, God.

I pointed to the curtain and stupidly said, "I thought you were in there."

He slid the door closed behind him, his mouth a hard line as he looked at me and said, "I went down the hall, and when I came back to my room, there you were."

His face was impossible to read. He didn't look *mad*, but he didn't look happy, either. Which was scary because I'd just bared my soul to him. My heart was pounding, my hands were shaking, and my face was on fire as I wondered what he was thinking. I said, "So you heard, um, what I—"

"I heard everything," he said, his jaw flexing. "And I call bullshit."

"What?" I'd been so desperate to tell him I loved him that I hadn't considered he might not believe me. "Which part are you calling bullshit?"

"Well, come here first," he said, his voice kind of growly. "Because I'm going to die if I don't touch you soon."

I crossed the room in a second, basically running to him on shaky legs as hot brown eyes burned me with their attention. *God, I love him.* When I stopped in front of him, tilting my head back to look up at him, butterflies went wild in my stomach.

"The dates are total BS, Buxbaum," he said, putting his big hands on my waist and turning us, maneuvering me so my back was suddenly pressed against the closed door. "It wasn't prom *or* the Mrs. Potato Head night."

"No?" I said, my heart going soft as those dark eyes went playful. Every bit of worry melted away as he looked down at me like he wanted to laugh.

"Oh, hell no." He grinned, his mouth in that wide, unapologetic smile that felt like home. His voice was low and rumbly, *so* intimate, as he said, "You fell for me in third grade, the day you punched me in the face. Admit it."

"The day you told everyone at recess that I had unicorns on my underpants?" I set my palms on his chest, careful to stay above where he'd been hit, and said, "Hardly. I hated you that day."

"I awoke the *passion* in you that day," he teased, wrapping his long fingers around my wrists. "The thin line between love and hate."

"Is that what that was?" I asked, my smile melting away as he gave me a scorching look.

"That's what it's always been," he said, and then he lowered his mouth.

Dear God, I thought, my knees weak as his lips sipped at mine, his eyes open. Teasing nips, tracing licks—Wes Bennett had been born knowing what he was doing, I swear to God. I watched him, my entire body shaking as his mouth played, and then my eyes wouldn't stay open any longer.

"Bloom" by Aidan Bissett started playing in my head.

All of the roads led me to you

I flexed my fingers against his chest, and as if that was his signal or something, everything instantly changed. He made a noise, angled his head, and went deep with the kiss, his hungry mouth ferocious. He pinned my hands against the door beside my head as the attack intensified. I raised my face and gave him all of my mouth, rearing up to welcome the onslaught as he leaned into me, sandwiching my body between the hardness of his and the door at my back.

He lifted his head and looked down at me, his dark eyes flashing with intensity. "Say it again."

I swallowed as his hands pressed mine into the door. I looked into his eyes and said, "I love you."

"Again," he growled, his voice quiet, his eyes dark. He leaned his weight more heavily onto his palms and his body, into me, his throat moving around a swallow as he watched me.

"I love you, Wes Bennett," I confessed, wondering how I'd ever thought it was possible to deny this. "I can't remember a time in my life when I didn't love you."

His jaw flexed and unflexed, and then he said—so quietly, "God, please let this be real."

"It's real," I said, pressing a kiss to his chin. "And I'm so sorry. For every moment you had to deal with things alone. I'm sorry I wasn't there for you."

"I'm the one who's sorry, Lib," he said, a streak of red on his cheeks as he clenched and unclenched his jaw. His voice barely above a whisper as he rubbed his nose over my cheek. "For every tear you cried because of me."

I blinked fast and breathed in the closeness of him, trying not to cry *any* more tears. "It wasn't you, I don't think, or me. I think it was just *life* that made us cry."

"Dammit," he said through gritted teeth, closing his eyes and releasing my hands.

"What?" I asked, my eyes searching his face. "What's wrong?"

"I just," he bit out, giving his head a shake. "Need a second."

And just like that, it hit me. My eyes traveled over him, and I saw the sweat on his forehead, the way every muscle in his face was clenched, and the way his left hand was gripping his chest.

"Wes!" I put my hands on his cheeks. "Oh my gosh—are you in pain?"

"You have no idea, Lib," he said on an exhale, his words a near-groan. "Just give me, like, two minutes and I'll be ready—"

"Two minutes?" Was he serious? "You need to rest—are you kidding?"

"No," he whined, biting out the syllable like it was physically painful to speak. "This is our moment, dammit."

I wanted to laugh, but I forced it down to a smile as I took his arm and carefully led him toward the bed while his breath hissed through his teeth and he pressed both hands against his ribs. I said, "I don't want *our moment* to be one where you're whimpering in pain, Bennett."

"I'm not whimpering," he whimpered.

"Did it hurt this much when you were in bed?" I asked.

"No," he said tightly, like he was trying not to breathe. "It's better when I lay flat."

"But you've stayed on your feet this entire time to kiss me." How could I ever love anyone but this stupid, selfless, amazing boy? I pointed and said, "Get in bed."

"I don't want to," he said, taking one hand off his injury to tug on my hair before immediately bringing it back to hold over his ribs. "I'm scared if I stop touching you, you'll disappear."

"I won't," I said, pulling back the curtain and moving the blanket out of the way. "I *can't*. Because you're the only one who knows our secret language, remember?"

"How could I forget?" he said quietly, looking down at me in a way that made me want to cry again.

So I said, "Well, I mean, you forgot that song was from *Folklore*, so . . ."

"So you're really gonna give me shit when I just almost died?" he said around a laugh, which made him grunt "sonofabitch" before getting back on the bed.

"I don't think you almost died," I said under my breath, ecstatic to be *us* again. I reached down to touch his hair as I fell into a lovesick smile. "Now lie down."

It took a few minutes of nonstop cursing from Wes for him to finally be lying flat, and I dragged a chair over to the side of the bed so I could hold his hand.

I'm kind of scared to stop touching him, too.

As if reading my mind, he said, "Promise this is real?"

I nodded, so happy that it felt a little painful. "I promise. If we were in a movie, the first notes of the closing song would be starting this very minute."

"Oh, yeah?" he asked, smiling as he squeezed my hand. "What song would it be, Buxbaum?"

"'One and Only' by Adele," I said without missing a beat.

It was so perfect for the scene. The two main characters, finally coming together in ER room number eight—that song was made for this moment.

You'll never know if you never try
To forget your past and simply be mine

"Good choice," he said, his eyes squinting around a smile. "Hey, Siri, play 'One and Only' by Adele."

I wasn't sure how his phone heard that, but from somewhere on the other side of the room, I heard the first few notes begin to play.

"Impressive."

"I am, aren't I?" He released my hand, grinning the Wes grin that warmed me from the inside as he lifted his palm to my jaw and cradled my face. "So what would the big closing line be, in our movie?"

It was hard to think of words when he was looking at me like that, when his thumb was stroking over my skin. "Uh—"

"Maybe something about how you've always wanted to be Elizabeth Bennet, and I'm the only guy who can give you that?" he asked, tugging on my hair.

"Ooh, that's good," I said, my soul happy as I watched him wrap my hair around his fist. "But technically there *are* other Mr. Bennetts in the world."

"Not for you," he said, tugging a little harder. "I'm your one and only."

"That's a little heavy-handed, don't you think?" I teased.

"But perfect, right?"

I looked at that face, at those dark, laughing eyes, and said, "The *most* perfect."

EPILOGUE

OMAHA—SIX(ISH) MONTHS LATER

COLLEGE WORLD SERIES CHAMPIONSHIP GAME

"You're perfect. You, and the ball, and the diamond, you're this perfectly beautiful thing. You can win or lose the game, all by yourself. You don't need me."

—*For Love of the Game*

Wes

"All right, Bennett—go pick up Benevento."

I gave a nod, took a deep breath, and left the bullpen.

Second inning with the bases loaded.

Not exactly how I'd anticipated entering the final game of the series, but when did anything ever go as planned? Benevento was usually money, but today his pitches were all over the place, and we'd gone from being up 2–0 to being down 3–2 with the bases loaded.

Zero outs.

LSU's bats were on fire, and the packed-out stadium was loud and electric. I headed for the mound as Bennie headed for the dugout, and I tried shutting everything out as I heard the beginning of "Power" start to play and the stadium got even louder.

I'd become a master at quieting the world during a game; it was my superpower. My dad always thought he was responsible for my fastball and my cutter, but the truth was that his legacy was my focus. He'd crammed *baseball first* down my throat for so many years that as long as I was able to shut *his* voice down, everything else went silent when I stepped up to pitch.

But this week was testing me.

Because the media—ESPN, KETV, Fox Sports—had a hard-on for my story. Not only was I the hometown kid, returning to Omaha to pitch in the CWS championship, but I was the hometown kid who'd dropped out of school two years ago to support my family after my dad died.

They were eating it up.

Which was fine. I got it—it was a great story.

But there was a twinge of pressure on my shoulders that usually wasn't there, a what-if-I-disappoint-them doubt in my head that usually didn't exist.

Because everyone I'd ever known was at the game.

My high school friends, my calc teacher, Mrs. Scarapelli from down the street (who'd been wearing a T-shirt with my face on it throughout the entire tournament), my mom, my cousins, my friends from Hy-Vee, Liz's parents, my Little League coaches—it was everyone from my past.

In addition to the Bruins fans, my teammates' families, and oh, yeah—MLB reps.

The place was full of my heart and my dreams.

I inhaled through my nose, trying to memorize the moment as Kanye's voice growled out the words, *"No one man should have all that power."* I wanted to capture every detail, even as I tried my best to act like it was just another game.

I stepped onto the mound, looking toward the LSU dugout as I went through my mental checklist, envisioning the way I was going to sit those batters, one by one. It'd been a long season—I pictured the ROAD TO OMAHA wall back at Jackie—and we were there to finish the job.

We were there to win.

But I couldn't deny myself a quick look—a one-second distraction—when I heard it.

Liz's whistle.

And yes—I *could* tell hers apart from a stadium of thousands.

She created it specifically so I would. She was so proud of the fact that she'd learned to whistle (loud as hell) around her fingers, and to make sure I could differentiate hers from everyone else's, she did five quick whistles, right in a row.

It was silly and smart and effective, just like Liz.

I glanced toward first base and immediately saw her, four rows back; the seat she'd been in for the entire series. But today she looked different.

They were the same sunglasses, and the same blue ribbon was tied around her curls, but she was wearing a UCLA jersey. That alone was remarkable, because she was firmly rooted in the opinion that wearing a jersey when you weren't a player was stupid, but holy shit—her jersey had my number on it.

It looked authentic, with a 32 sewn just underneath the cursive UCLA that stretched across her chest, and then—God help me—she did a quick spin, as if she knew I was looking and could see exactly what I was thinking.

BENNETT was stitched across her shoulders, the last *T* resting right around the spot where her tattoo (still) was.

Elizabeth Fucking Bennett, ladies and gentlemen.

Buxbaum.

Ahem. Elizabeth Fucking Buxbaum.

I flipped the ball, running my index finger along the seam before taking a deep breath.

And as I got set to throw, I heard my dad's voice.

For the first time in months.

Only this time he wasn't yelling.

This time, instead of shouting *throw 'em the gas* or something critical, he repeated the words Liz had sent to the dugout during the first exhibition game, so many months ago. His voice was calm, almost reassuring, when I heard him say, *Just pitch, Bennett. You've got this, kid.*

And I did.

EXT. CHARLES SCHWAB FIELD—DAY

The first notes of "Dreamland" begin playing.

As we see Wes throw the pitch and hear the roar of the crowd, the camera follows a green leaf in the outfield as it lifts up and floats away from Charles Schwab Field.

The leaf cartwheels through the summer sky, dancing over and past the downtown Omaha skyline, dipping down to briefly land on the Stella's neon sign before lifting again.

We continue blowing through the blue sky on the leaf until we reach Oak Lawn Cemetery and move down to street level. The leaf lands beside a cardinal that's sitting on top of a headstone before lifting yet again, this time tumbling over Teal Street.

The leaf slowly dances down toward the ground, fluttering between two houses before finally settling underneath the windshield wiper of Liz's car, which is parked on the street between the two houses.

FADE OUT

The Soundtrack of Wes and Liz
Version 2.0

1. TROUBLE'S COMING || Royal Blood
2. EVER SINCE NEW YORK || Harry Styles
3. CONGRATS || LANY
4. HEAVEN ANGEL || THE DRIVER ERA, Ross Lynch, Rocky
5. USE ME || Blake Rose
6. DISASTER || Conan Gray
7. AUGUST || Taylor Swift
8. EVERYWHERE || Niall Horan
9. PINK + WHITE || Frank Ocean
10. SUPERMASSIVE BLACK HOLE || Muse
11. CHANEL NO. 5 || VOILÀ
12. SAD SONGS IN A HOTEL ROOM || Joshua Bassett
13. EVERYWHERE, EVERYTHING || Noah Kahan, Gracie Abrams
14. THE DEEPEST BLUES ARE BLACK || Foo Fighters
15. OLD DAYS || New Rules
16. REWRITE THE STARS || Jess and Gabriel
17. ANYONE ELSE || Joshua Bassett
18. FEEL YOU NOW || THE DRIVER ERA
19. HOUSE ON FIRE || Hembree
20. STUPID FACE || Abe Parker
21. YOU COULD START A CULT || Niall Horan, Lizzy McAlpine

22. HATE THAT YOU KNOW ME || Bleachers

23. CITY OF STARS – From *La La Land* Soundtrack || Ryan Gosling, Emma Stone

24. CLUB SANDWICH || Joey Valence & Brae

25. COWBOY IN LA || LANY

26. FUCK YOU || Lily Allen

27. SECOND NATURE || Joseph Tilley

28. ILLICIT AFFAIRS || Taylor Swift

29. MASTERMIND || Taylor Swift

30. BLOOM || Aidan Bissett

31. ONE AND ONLY || Adele

32. DREAMLAND || Alexis Ffrench, James Morgan, Royal Liverpool Philharmonic Orchestra

https://open.spotify.com/playlist/3VbNtTH3dn3bvofSp4YMzC

ACKNOWLEDGMENTS

First and foremost, thank you, God, for giving me so much more than I could ever deserve.

Thank you, Kim Lionetti, my incredible agent, for driving the bus on this delightful ride that I never want to get off of. Did I just call you my bus driver? Yes. Is it a terrible analogy? Also yes. But you get the gist, right? Your route is my favorite, and I hope you pick me up and take me to my destination forever—gaaaaaaah it's a terrible theme and I must stop. YOU'RE SO MUCH MORE THAN MY BUS DRIVER and I love you. (Also your daughter, Samantha, is the coolest.)

Nicole Ellul, you are a dream editor. You make my stories SO MUCH better, and I'm sorry I made you write edit letters for three entirely different versions of this book. You were patient enough to wait for the right one—to say without saying that the first two versions were trash—and I'm so lucky to have you.

Thank you to *everyone* at Simon & Schuster. The incredible Simon Pulse team—and my OG YA editor, Jessi Smith—gave me a chance with *Better Than the Movies*, and it's been a dream come true ever since. Special thanks to Sarah Creech for designing my gorgeous covers, Liz Casal for being truly the best artist and creating rom-com masterpieces, Emily Ritter and Amy Lavigne for being social media goddesses, Anna Elling for being so incredibly on top of everything, and Amanda Brenner, Sara Berko, Cassandra Fernandez, Kendra Levin, and Justin Chanda.

I had a lot of help with the UCLA part of this book from people who were remarkably generous with their time and knowledge. Because of these folks, I am now a Bruin fan for life.

Thank you, Jack O'Connor, for letting me drop into your DMs and pepper you with questions about UCLA baseball. Your willingness to answer the stupidest of questions (and I had so very many) was so greatly appreciated. You have no idea how much your insight helped with this book (also, anything I got wrong is my fault, not Jack's).

Thank you, Michelle Chen, for giving me SO much assistance. When I asked a question about the dorms, you walked The Hill and sent me a video. When I asked about dining halls, you sent me links to the menus. You were a freaking rock star who made me feel like I was in Westwood, and I'm so incredibly grateful. I already thought you were amazing, but now you've taken it to the next level. #hero

Thank you, Lauren Mueller, you wonderful legacy Bruin, for offering so much information I didn't even know I needed. Fat Sal's, fours up, the logistics of getting from campus to the Rose Bowl via the Rooter Bus on game day—you are a human encyclopedia of all things UCLA, and I cannot thank you enough.

Thank you, Suzi Mellano, for inspiring the character of Lilith. I'm sure I got a lot wrong about how you do what you do, but I am in awe of your talent and want to be like you when I grow up (you know . . . if I were actually younger than you, were creatively gifted, and also knew how to use a camera).

This book was a journey to write, and I am beyond grateful to the dear friends (can I call them beta readers? I'm not actually sure what constitutes a beta reader) who stomached my early iterations. Lindsay Grossman and Misty Wilson, thank you for using nice words to basically say *THIS ISN'T IT*; Wes and Liz thank you. Abi Griffin and Daniza Jeanne, you enthusiastically read a lot of terrible material and never complained, and for that, you deserve a reward.

I will forever and ever be grateful to the wildly talented edit creators (that's probably not the right verbiage, but who cares?) on TikTok, Twitter, and Instagram. Every time I see an edit for one of my books or characters, I cry (seriously) because *holy shit*, you guys have taken these characters from my megadork imagination and made them real for me (and everyone) to see! It's like being introduced to someone who you met in your dream the night before, and I'll never be over it. Pure magic that I do not deserve and will never tire of.

And the . . . um . . . what do I call them—*bookfluencers*? That doesn't sound right, but thank you to the amazing people who use their platforms to READ BOOKS and TALK ABOUT BOOKS and entertain us with their love of books. That is just supreme entertainment right there, don't you think? Haley Pham and Steph Bohrer—you're like bookish serotonin, and I adore your content. And Larissa Cambusano, you always make me cackle—like a demented clown—while I add far too many books to my TBR. Also, FYI—I would SO be down for a reality show that's just you and Giant, doing life.

Random thanks to random people for bringing me random

joy: Taylor Swift; Gracie Abrams; Noah Kahan; my Berklete pals; my faves (taygracie's version); Emma; Diana; Sude; Eva; the other Emma; Colleen; my Omaha bestie, Jenn; Joyful Chaos Book Club (aka idiots who think that Tater Tots are good but whom I forgive because I adore them); the supremely talented @belltcvia; the supremely talented Annika @dunderperks; LizWesNation; Diana; Cleo; Allison Bitz; Chaitanya; Mylla; Becca; Anderson Raccoon Jones; Lori Anderjaska; Clio; Aliza; Tiffany Fliedner; Wes Bennett's entourage; Carla; Caryn; Alexis; Ally Bryan; Anna-Marie; Katie Prouty; Jill Kaarlela; Brittany Bunzey; Shaily; Steph Bolan; and Marisol Barrera.

Also thank you, Sara Echeagaray and Saylor Curda, for being my adorably cool LA friends.

This book was written in Omaha, St. Louis, Dallas, Kraków, Rio, Miami, Frankfurt, Denver, Charlotte, Los Angeles, and Fort Myers, so thank you to every airport and hotel that let me loiter in your spaces while playing with these little friends on my computer. Also thank you to every bookstore and festival that hosted me and let me make new friends in cool places. (The fact that I have friends in Poland and Brazil still boggles my little Midwestern mind.)

Also, to all the bookstores I've loved before (or, in this instance, a few of the amazing bookstores and festivals that've hosted me this year)—Barnes & Noble, Indigo, Monarch Books in Kansas City, the Bookworm in Omaha, the Novel Neighbor in St. Louis, Livraria da Travessa in Rio, Bienal do Livro, the International Book Fair in Kraków, the Madrid Book Fair, Fnac Paris, Gibert, La Mouette Rieuse, Dussmann, and Thalia Buchhandlung: I've felt so warm and welcomed everywhere I've visited, and you have all my thanks.

As always, thank you to my amazing family for being generally amazing.

Mom, thank you for ALL OF THIS. It may have taken me a long time to figure it out, but you gave me an obsessive love of reading that is at the core of this dream. You're strong and beautiful, hilarious and kind, and I'm so blessed to call you my mother.

Dad, I miss you every day and know that you—the real-life Clark Griswold—would appreciate all the travel stories.

And what can I say about my offspring? Cass, Ty, Matt, Joey, Kate—once again, you've done absolutely NOTHING to contribute to this book. That being said, I still love you. In fact, I think you're kind of the funniest, coolest humans that I know. Terrance and Jordyn, I commend you for putting up with all the Kirkle nonsense; I know that we're a LOT.

And finally—finally—KEVIN. {dreamy sigh} Thank you for supporting my daydreams, for always making sure I pack a carbon monoxide detector, and for making life so fun for Katie when I travel that she's sad to see me return. Saying that I love you (I LOOOOOOVE YOU) is far too *meh* for the way I feel about you. You are my favorite person in the entire world and my happiness IS you. You continually amaze me with your ability to be the very best version of a human while also being so hilarious that I usually laugh-cry at least once before you even leave for work in the morning. You are the Wes Bennett blueprint, and I'll never understand how I'm lucky enough to be loved by you.

Read on for a sneak peek into
Lynn Painter's *New York Times* bestselling
rom-com about a bet that goes horribly wrong—
or horribly right. . . .

THREE YEARS AGO

Bailey

The first time I met Charlie was at the airport in Fairbanks.

My dad had just said goodbye, so I was swallowing down heavy emotion as I left behind life as I knew it and prepared to fly to Nebraska, where my mother and I would now be living since my parents had officially separated. I lifted my chin and attempted to channel *maturity* as I traversed the airport with my rolling pink carry-on, but every blink of my eyes held back a weighted homesickness for the place and the memories I was leaving behind.

It was when I got stuck in a long line of people waiting to go through security, sandwiched between strangers and stressing over whether or not my braces were going to set off the metal detector, that we made contact.

The line started moving, but I couldn't take a step because the two people in front of me were kissing. Hard-core. As if their mouths were fused together and they were desperately trying to pull them apart by turning their heads from side to side.

Or else they were eating each other's faces off.

I cleared my throat.

Nothing.

I cleared my throat again.

Which made the guy open his eyes—I could only see one eye—and look directly at me. *While still kissing the girl.* As if that wasn't weird enough, he said *to me* while his lips were still attached to hers, *"Oh my God—what?"*

Which sounded like *omiguhdwhruut*.

And then The Eye closed and they were full-on kissing again.

"Excuse me," I said through gritted teeth, my emotional anxiety replaced by irritation, "but the line. The line is moving."

The Eye opened again and the dude glared at me. He lifted his mouth and said something to his girlfriend that prompted them to actually move forward. *Finally.* I heard his girlfriend chirp about how much she was going to miss him, and I could see by his profile that he was kind of half smiling and not saying anything as they stumbled forward, hand in hand.

But I couldn't get past the fact that they looked like they were my age.

What?

I was going into my freshman year. Of high school. People my age didn't make out in public; they couldn't even drive yet. People my age didn't have the audacity to totally *get after it* in the airport security line, where they could get in trouble.

So who *were* these obnoxious PDA renegades?

The girl stepped out of line and waved to the guy, probably relieved to finally be getting oxygen. After making it through security and reorganizing my things, I checked the time on my phone. I wanted to be right next to the door when the Jetway opened, so it was imperative that I get there as quickly as possible. I went around the face-eating jackass as he looked down at his phone, and I walked as fast as I could toward the departure gate.

It wasn't until I took a seat *right* next to the check-in counter, where I couldn't miss any pertinent announcements and would be guaranteed a spot at the very front of the line, that I was finally able to calm my nerves.

I scrolled through my phone, checked the airline's app for updates, then put on my headphones and cued up the freshly curated *Bailey's Airplane Playlist*. But as I sat back and watched the other travelers milling about the terminal, I couldn't help but wonder how many of *them* were being forced to go somewhere they didn't want to go and start a new life they had no interest in beginning.

If I were a betting person, I'd say zero.

I had to be the only person in that entire airport who was going on what was the polar opposite of a trip. I had a ticket to my own transplantation, and it sucked. I dwelled on this for the entirety of the hour wait, especially when Adorable Family of Four plopped down across from me, looking like poster children for the Disney resorts as they bounced around with palpable travel enthusiasm.

The sight of their familial bliss made me want to snuggle with the tiny scrap of blankie I still slept with (even though no one knew) and cry just a little.

So to say I was tightly wound by the time we lined up to board would be an understatement. I was first in line—*hell yes*—but buzzing with my *own* brand of palpable energy. My gurgling turmoil saw Adorable Family's enthusiasm and raised the pot by a hundred.

"Hey, you."

I looked to my left, and there was the face-eating jackass from security, smiling at me as if we were friends.

"I looked everywhere for you, babe."

I glanced behind me at the rest of the boarding line, because he couldn't possibly be talking to me. But when I turned back around, he was actually moving marginally closer, forcing me to take a step over so he could stand beside me. He nudged my shoulder with his and winked.

What in the actual hell? *Was he high?*

"What are you doing?" I whispered, clutching the strap of my carry-on bag as I tried scooting away from him while still maintaining my First in Line status. He was wearing a hoodie that said *Mr. Nothing*, with baggy shorts, and he didn't have a single thing in his hands. No carry-on, no book, no coat; what kind of person traveled like that?

He moved even closer, so his face was about an inch from mine, and said under his breath, "Relax, Glasses. I just don't want to wait in that line, so I'm making it look like we're together."

"But." I looked at him and wondered who Mr. Nothing actually was. He was obviously my age-ish and a generally attractive human. He had thick, dark, careless hair and a nice mouth. But his nerve was just too huge for a normal boy. "That's not fair."

He raised an eyebrow.

"Everyone else has to wait in line," I said, trying not to sound like a child screaming *It's not fair* while kind of wanting to throw elbows. "If you didn't want to wait, you should've gotten here earlier."

"Like you?" he asked, his tone thick with sarcasm.

I pushed up my glasses. "Yes, like me."

Why is this total stranger messing with me? Was this karma for daydreaming about Adorable Family being stranded at the airport? Karma was supposed to be a cat, dammit, not *this.*

He tilted his head to the side and looked at me. "I bet you used to be a hall monitor."

"Excuse me?" It was obvious he meant it in an insulting way, and I was torn between wanting to punch him in the face and wanting to sobbingly beg him to leave me alone. I glanced behind us again, and the man next in line was smirking, clearly eavesdropping. I turned back to Mr. Nothing and whispered, "Not that it's any of your business, but everyone had to take a turn at my school."

"Sure they did."

Sure they did? I made a noise, sort of a growl mixed with a groan, before fleetingly wondering if punching a fellow passenger was a federal offense.

"Are you . . . Do you not believe me?" I asked through gritted teeth. "About *hall* monitoring?"

He smirked. "It's not that I don't believe you; it's that we both know you would've signed up whether it was mandatory or not."

How would he know that? He wasn't wrong, but it pissed me off that he behaved as if he knew me, when our relationship spanned five awful minutes. I was squinting and my nose was scrunched up like something smelled bad, but it was physically impossible to unsquinch it. I managed to bite out, "Whatever."

He stopped talking but didn't move; he just stayed put, right where he was. We both stood there, side by side, staring in front of us in silence. *Why isn't he moving? He's not going to stay here, is he??* After another long minute of non-speak, I couldn't take it and very nearly shouted the words "Why are you still here?"

He seemed confused by my question. "What?"

I pointed my thumb over my shoulder, and he said, "Oh my God, you were serious about that? You're going to make me go to the back?"

I breathed in through my nose. "*I'm* not making you. It's the way things work."

"Oh, well, if it's the way things work . . ." He looked at me like I was an idiot.

The airline employee who'd been standing beside the door grabbed the speaker and began announcing our flight. I gave Mr. Nothing another pointed look, the patented *WTF are you doing* look, punctuated with bug eyes, which made him shake his head and step out of line.

He looked at the guy behind me and said, "It's the way things work; don't worry about it."

And even though I refused to turn around and watch him, I heard him mutter "It's the way things work" no less than five times as he made his way to the back of the line.

Whyyyyyy? Why was this smug, sarcastic jerk even part of my experience? *He's ruining flying for me,* I thought as I scanned my boarding pass and started down the Jetway, which was ironic when flying was the *only* thing I didn't hate about the day.

My first time flying alone was the one teensy-tiny thing that I'd been excited about, and Assbag Zero seemed determined to destroy that.

I didn't relax until we were boarded, my bag was stowed in the overhead compartment, I'd texted both my parents, and I was seated next to the window. People were still getting settled, but I'd made it. I'd been stressed all day, but now—ahhh. I closed my eyes and felt like I could finally exhale.

Until.

"What are the odds that we'd be seat neighbors?"

I opened my eyes, and there was Mr. Nothing, standing in the aisle, his mouth hard as he looked just as happy to see me as I was to see him.

Charlie

As if my day wasn't shitty enough, my seat was right next to Little Miss The-Line-Is-Moving.

Wonderful.

She gazed up at me with big eyes and blinked fast, like she was shocked to see me, but she looked like one of those uptight girls who was *always* shocked when life wasn't perfect. She crossed her arms over her chest and said, "One in a hundred and seventy-five, I would guess."

For some reason, she made me want to mockingly repeat her words in a high-pitched voice. *One in a hundred and seventy-five, I would guess.* I looked longingly at the rows behind ours, stretching toward the back of the plane, and wondered if anyone would be interested in swapping seats.

Also—*of course* that girl knew the number of seats in the plane.

The second I sat down, the phone in my hoodie pouch buzzed.

I knew it was my mom, and I also knew that if I didn't respond, she would keep sending messages.

I pulled it out and looked at the display.

Mom: Did you make it on time?

I leaned back a little in the cramped seat, way too fucking tall for flying.

I hated flying.

I replied: **Yes.**

I buckled my seat belt, but before I could even let out a sigh, my phone buzzed again. **Mom: Did your dad go in with you, or just drop you at the door?**

I reached into my pocket, needing a TUM already. After I popped two into my mouth, I ignored her question (because no good could come of the answer—*dropped me at the door because parking was too expensive*) and texted: **Nana Marie said to tell you hi.**

I knew that would stop the texts.

My mother and my grandmother had always been close, but as soon as my parents decided to divorce, that was history. Now my mom referred to her as "the old battle-axe," and Nana Marie called my mother "that woman."

Mature adults, right?

I rested my head on the back of the seat and tried to wrap my mind around the fact that summer was over. It seemed like *days* ago that I'd been pumped to fly to Alaska and spend the summer with my dad's family, but now here I was, leaving them (and Grace) behind, flying back to life with my mom and her new boyfriend.

I was too damn old to feel this fucking homesick, especially when the plane hadn't even taken off yet.

I felt a dull ache between my ribs as I pictured Grace, and I swear to God I could still smell the fruity mousse she used in her hair. My brain took off on an unwelcome montage that captured a summer full of Grace's laughter, and I gritted my teeth.

Fuck *me.*

I put the phone back in my pocket, even though all I wanted to do was get lost in one of our mindless exchanges.

But there was no point in texting Grace. Like, ever again. Because relationships failed on a daily basis when people lived in the same fucking house. Relationships were doomed to fail *period.*

So the mere notion of a long-distance one? Total joke.

The only good that could come from staying in contact with Grace was that I might finally be depressed enough to take up songwriting or flirt with drinking.

Walking away—no, flying away—was absolutely the way to go.

One of the flight attendants started on the safety checklist, and I glanced over at Hall Monitor. She was attractive, but the braces and poofy hair weren't doing her any favors. Her arms were still crossed, and she was listening so intently that I half expected her to pull out a binder and start taking notes.

Yeah, it was time to mess with her.

Messing with her in the boarding line had actually taken my mind off Grace for a few minutes, so perhaps it was karma that had assigned her uptight ass to the seat beside me. I'd been good all summer, so maybe karma knew I needed a distraction.

Maybe karma was a girl in glasses.

Bailey

"How much do you think she gets paid?"

"Shh." I tried tuning out Mr. Nothing so I could hear the flight attendant's emergency instructions.

"Oh, come on—you're not actually listening to this, are you?"

I refused to look at him. "Please be quiet."

"Everybody knows that if the shit goes down, we're dead." His voice was deep and rumbly as he murmured, "They go through these motions to give passengers a false sense of hope, but the reality is that if the plane crashes, our bodies are going to be splattered for miles."

"Good Lord." I did look at him then, because there was something seriously wrong with Mr. Nothing. "What is your problem?"

He shrugged. "I don't have a problem—I'm just a realist. I see things for what they really are. You, on the other hand—you probably believe this shit. You probably think that if the plane hits the ocean at Mach five, that inflatable seat is going to save your ass, right?"

I pushed my glasses up my nose and wished he'd stop talking about crashing. I wasn't scared, but it also didn't make a bit of sense to me how an object as heavy as a plane could stay in the sky. "It could."

He gave his head a slow shake, as if I were the world's biggest fool. "Oh my God, you are precious. You're like a sweet baby child who believes everything her mommy tells her."

"I am *not* precious!"

"Are too."

Why couldn't I have been seated beside a mature businessman or Visor Man in front of me, who was already asleep? Hell, the screaming baby squalling somewhere in the back would've been a better choice.

"No, I'm not," I said, irritated by how whiny I sounded but unable to stop myself. But this guy was really pissing me off. "And just because you say shocking things like *Oh, this plane could crash* doesn't make you edgy or any more of a realist than I am."

"Oh yeah?" He turned a little in his seat, so he was facing me, and he pointed to my carry-on. "I bet you put all of your liquids in a baggie before you hit security, right?"

"Um, that's actually the law," I said, unwilling to let the guy think he was hot shit, "so that doesn't mean a thing."

"It's not the law; it's just a stupid rule that isn't going to do dick to save us from a terrorist attack."

"So you don't follow the rule?"

"Nope."

Bullshit, I thought. No way did this guy—a minor, like me—disregard the laws of the skies. He was full of crap for sure. I humored him, though, and asked, "Then how do you transport your liquids?"

"However I want." He gave a half shrug and looked utterly relaxed as he lied, and I was jealous of his confidence. Even if the guy was a compulsive liar, I wished I were that comfortable in my skin. He said, "Sometimes I put a few in my carry-on if I have one, sometimes I pack the full-sized bottles in my checked bag, and today I even stuck a shampoo in my pocket just for fun."

"You did not," I said, unable to let that one go.

He pulled a trial-sized Suave from the pocket of his shorts. "Did too."

"No *way.*" To my horror, a laugh gurgled out of me. I raised my hand to my mouth, quick to cover any evidence that Mr. Nothing was the teensiest bit amusing. "Why do you do these things?"

Damn my curiosity.

"Because it feels good to know I'm besting them."

"Which *them* are you besting, exactly?" I asked, absolutely torn between amusement and annoyance. "The security people? The terrorists? The Man?"

"Yes."

I rolled my eyes and pulled my book out of my purse, desperately hoping he'd take the hint and do anything other than talk to me. It worked until takeoff, but once we were in the air, he turned toward me in his seat and said, "So."

I flipped my book over onto my lap. “We don’t have to talk, y’know.”

“But I can’t turn on my phone yet, so I’m bored.”

“You could sleep.”

“I’d rather talk.” He gave me a closed-mouth smile that confirmed he was *trying* to be irritating. “So how long have your parents been divorced?”

I almost gasped, but I caught myself. *How does he know they’re separating?*

And why did the finality of the word “divorced” still make my stomach hurt?

I looked down at the cut-up red heart on the cover of the book. “What makes you think my parents are divorced?”

“Come on, Glasses—it’s textbook,” he said, drumming his fingers on the armrest as he spoke. “The only kids who fly alone are custody kids. Fly to see the parent you don’t live with, fly back from a visit, fly to see the grandparents of the parent you no longer live with . . .”

I swallowed and rubbed my eyebrow, wanting to tell him to shut up because I didn’t like the picture he was painting. *Would* I become some sort of “custody kid,” racking up frequent-flier miles while getting to know flight attendants on a first-name basis? It’d never occurred to me that I’d have to do this whole sad solo flight more than once after everything was finalized.

God, I still wasn’t ready to talk about it, to use the d-word in regards to my parents.

Especially not with Mr. Nothing.